BRAVE IN SEASON

A NOVEL OF RACE, RAILROADS, AND BASEBALL

JON VOLKMER

MILFORD HOUSE

an imprint of Sunbury Press, Inc.
Mechanicsburg, PA USA

MILFORD HOUSE

an imprint of Sunbury Press, Inc.
Mechanicsburg, PA USA

For information about special discounts for bulk purchases, please contact Sunbury Press Orders Dept. at (855) 338-8359 or orders@sunburypress.com.

To request one of our authors for speaking engagements or book signings, please contact Sunbury Press Publicity Dept. at publicity@sunburypress.com.

FIRST MILFORD HOUSE PRESS EDITION: September 2023

Set in Adobe Garamond Pro | Interior design by Crystal Devine | Cover by Lawrence Knorr and Domenick Scudera | Edited by Diane Meyer and Lawrence Knorr.

Publisher's Cataloging-in-Publication Data
Names: Volkmer, Jon, author.
Title: Brave in season : a novel of race, railroads, and baseball.
Description: First trade paperback edition. | Mechanicsburg, PA : Milford House Press, 2023.
Summary: Set in 1950 in the rural Midwest, and inspired by real events, this gripping novel explores what happens when an African American railroad repair crew is dropped into a tiny, tight-knit farm community. Will frictions build to an all-too familiar American tragedy, or can tensions be overcome in that uniquely American way, on a baseball field?
Identifiers: ISBN : 979-8-88819-096-8 (paperback) | ISBN : 979-8-88819-097-5 (ePub).
Subjects: FICTION / African American & Black / Historical | FICTION / Historical / 20th Century / Post-World War II | FICTION / Sports | FICTION / Small Town & Rural.

For the Love of Books!

For those with the courage to keep trying

Into my heart an air that kills
From yon far country blows:
What are those blue remembered hills,
What spires, what farms are those?

—A. E. HOUSMAN

Tomorrow,
I'll sit at the table
When company comes.
Nobody'll dare
Say to me,
"Eat in the kitchen,"
Then.

Besides,
They'll see how beautiful I am
And be ashamed.

I, too, am America.

—LANGSTON HUGHES

1

THE DOUBLEMINT TEST

The boy looked upwards, into the most astonishing face he had ever seen. A face of outsized features—fleshy nose and huge brown eyes with veins slightly yellowed, and a crown of tightly curled black hair. The boy's hand raised to point at the face, which smiled, and a big hand pointed back at him. For long seconds no one moved. The boy's mother yanked him to her side with unusual vigor, and the boy wanted to cry. But wonder overcame hurt, and he continued to stare, open-mouthed.

The man had come in the door of Marchon Mercantile and paused by the mail window, next to the wall of darkly gleaming brass mailboxes, each with its own combination knob. Except for the boy, the patrons avoided looking. Farmers scrutinized dry goods and cleaning products. But they noticed him, all right. A colored man, right there in Julian. Well-dressed, too, with his blue shirt buttoned up to his neck.

It was late May after a wet March. The corn was planted, and the terraced hills were alive with slender stalks as tall as toy soldiers, as tall as the trophies in the window of Marchon Mercantile. Winning more trophies, that was the normal thing to be talking about now, when the season was as young as the corn, and as green with promise. Just last night, the boys had gone up to Nebraska City and demolished the best team in the county. So it brought a sense of general relief when Jack Scarborough bounded in, barely glancing at the stranger as he shouted joyously, "Game over! Hornets rule the world!"

"Rule Otoe County anyway," said Dave, wiping his hands on his apron.

"Great game," hollered Nicholas Reilly, brandishing a new broom. "You showed those city boys."

"Hush, Uncle Nick," said Millie Littman, still clutching the boy to her skirts.

Jack got down on one knee in front of the boy. "We gave 'em a spanking, didn't we, Timmy? Cause we're the champions!" Jack ruffled his hair, and Timmy giggled.

"Season's just started," said Dave. "Let's take 'em one at a time."

Jack straightened up. "Now Davey . . ." he began, but thought better of chiding his brother's modesty. Jack was three years out of high school. Dave had done two tours in the Pacific, and owned a Bronze Star for valor. Tall and easy-going, Dave had come home just in time to buy the store from old man Marchon, who'd gone senile during the war. People kept telling him to hang his own name out front, but here it was 1950 already, and Dave still hadn't got around to it. Didn't seem much point, when everyone already knew him. And they did. As family man, as proprietor, as big-hitting first baseman.

Jack pulled a quarter from his pocket and flipped it through the air, calling out, "Change for two bits?" He saluted Dave's catch with a radio announcer's twangy, "And he's out at first!"

People laughed and Jack grinned. He wasn't the best player. He wasn't even second-best in his own family. Middle brother Ernie had been a genuine phenom before the war. Jack was what people called a "character." Stocky and cheerful as catchers are supposed to be, he kept his teammates loose, the home crowd happy, and the other team off balance with an endless stream of chatter.

Jack pulled open the top of the pop machine, slammed a dime in the slot, and yanked out a Dr Pepper. He drank half in one swig, and gave a satisfied belch. But his grin faltered. The colored man was still standing over by the mailboxes, and he was looking at him. Jack turned away from the man, and with dogged cheerfulness sang out, "Hey Davey, how about when you gave that boy a shoe-topper? I thought you broke his nose!"

"Got lucky on that one," Dave replied. "Looked like an error to me."

"Error, heck! Pee Wee Reese himself would have kicked that ball."

"Right," laughed Dave. "Or Jackie Robinson himself."

For a long moment, the only sound was the squeak of the swamp cooler hanging in the corner. Jack's arms dropped to his sides. It had been awkward enough trying to pretend things were normal, and Dave had to go and say that.

The stranger was a big man of middle years, with close-cropped hair showing a few flecks of gray. He'd been there for a couple of minutes now, and he apparently wasn't going away. Nobody knew quite what to do about him.

Having burst the bubble of invisibility, Dave called out, "Hiya there. What can I do for you?"

The man nodded toward post office boxes, and when he spoke, his voice was quiet. "I came to check if any mail come for me, by general delivery."

"Just a jiffy, and I'll have a look," Dave answered. "For that, I need to have my postmaster hat." He took off the white apron and laid it over the counter. Once inside the cubicle, he put on a battered green visor, to nervous chuckles from the farmers. He leaned forward and addressed the stranger through the small window with the vertical gold bars.

"Now, what name would I be looking for?"

"Wallace," said the man. "Jerome Wallace."

"Wallace, Jerome," Dave said, rifling through a small pile. "That be a normal letter size?"

"Normal, yes."

"Hmm." Dave looked up. "I am sorry."

The man showed no reaction. "One other question, if you don't mind."

"Shoot," said Dave.

"If I was to get it set up with the bosses," he said, "can you work it so my pay can be sent to an address in Omaha?"

"You don't want to send cash money through the mail, is that what you're saying?"

"That's it, yes."

Dave scratched his head. "I'm not rightly sure how that's done. I could maybe get it up, but I don't know . . ." He paused again. "You're with the gandy crew?"

Jerome nodded.

"And you're going to be in our town how long?"

Even the sacks of flour seemed to be holding their breath.

Jerome gave a small glance around. "Until the section is done," he said. "The foreman could give you a better sense how long we are going to be in your town." He slowed down on the last two words, creating an emphasis that some townsfolk would find amusing and others would call something else. In any case, everyone was suddenly checking merchandise again.

Dave Scarborough took his elbows off the counter. "I could maybe get it set up," he said again, soberly. "Best if I talk to the foreman. Did I hear right, that's Moose Burdock?"

"He goes by that."

Dave gave a can-do nod. "I'll bring it up when Moose comes in."

There was a pause. It seemed a long pause, while everyone waited for the colored man to leave. But the man took a step farther in, a board squeaking under his foot. "Now," said Jerome, "I might take a pack of that Doublemint Gum." He pointed in the direction of the cash register. "That is, if you don't mind to put your other hat back on."

Jack erupted in a nervous giggle. Nick Reilly wore a mischievous smile. The farmers' wives looked frightened. Did they serve Negroes at Marchon's? As far as anyone knew, this was the first one ever to come in the store. There was a collective intake of breath.

2

THE ROOKIE

The appearance of the colored man at Marchon Mercantile was, in fact, not entirely a surprise. The mess car and three faded yellow Pullman sleepers had been hauled in by a switch engine the night before and left on the side track. Those same coaches had been parked at Auburn, ten miles south, for the last four weeks. Before that they were in Falls City for a spell, and before that in Hiawatha, Kansas. Julian was the logical next stop on the main line to Omaha. Word had gotten around that the whole crew was colored. Not the foremen, of course. But still. People looked at each other, shrugged, and reckoned that must be the way the Mopac was doing things now. You just never knew. Since the war ended, change was in the air everywhere. And in Julian, change rolled in on the iron wheels of the Missouri Pacific Railroad.

Julian was a train stop before it was a town. Generations were born, grew up, and died, with the smell of cinders in their noses. In the 1940s folks started hearing a new word, Dieselization. The steam locomotives were being side-tracked into history. In their place came powerful, reliable diesels. The new engines were heavier, so dieselization also meant replacing the 90-pound rail with 115-pound rail all the way from Kansas City to Omaha. This was not a job for local crews. For this job the Missouri Pacific brought in a veteran system gang from the White River, Arkansas, division. The foreman was a white-haired man of thirty-five years' experience, Mr. H.H. "Moose" Burdock, of Cedar Falls, Iowa. For assistant foreman and time keeper, they tapped a roundhouse manager from Wichita, Ivan Tarp. The rest of the crew comprised a dozen men, plus a cook and a caller. Besides the cook, every one of them hailed from Conway County, Arkansas. Except for one.

Jerome Wallace had never wanted to be a gandy dancer. He was an Omaha bricklayer by trade, and a damn good one. Worked his way up from scrap boy to hod carrier to apprentice to journeyman. Laid the south side of the Timmons Building practically by himself, and that was tricky work, what with those cornices. He was doing all right, almost too good it felt like. Married to Lucy, finally. Jerome Junior, now four years old. Owned his own home on the north side. In one day it all unraveled. He did not start the fight, and he never intended to hurt the man. Lies were told to the police. An inflammatory headline in the *World Herald*.

The lynching of a Black man in Omaha was in living memory. In 1919 a frenzied mob hanged Will Brown in front of the Court House, riddled his hanging corpse with gunfire, cut him down and dragged the body through the streets, poured oil on the corpse and burned it, and dragged the charred remains around town some more. Every person of color in Omaha knew the story of Will Brown. And Jerome Wallace knew it was a good time for him to get out of town. He was supposed to be grateful that Lucy's brother, Malcolm, who worked for the Missouri Pacific, had managed to get him on a gandy crew at a decent wage.

It would only be until things cooled off in Omaha, but Jerome knew how things worked. He could spend years living in retired sleeper cars, ripping and replacing rails, swinging that spike maul until his arms ached. And all the time worried sick about Lucy, especially with the things Malcolm was saying.

As Jerome left the store and headed back to the Pullmans, he looked around, shaking his head. This was the smallest town yet. One-block main street with one general store and a one-pump gas station. The other storefronts were boarded up. He saw buckets and boxes through the few remaining windows. The street wasn't even paved. Number two white gravel, by the look of it, from the quarry up by Ashland.

It wouldn't be half so bad if he could get home on weekends. But the foreman had them working nearly every Saturday, and in six weeks on the job, he'd only been able to get home just once. That was contrary to what the union said when he signed on. He had tried to get the other men riled up over this, with no luck. They welcomed the extra hours. It wasn't like they could go clear to Arkansas anyway.

And so, week after week went by, with Lucy at home with JJ, and the troubles mounting. If she couldn't find someone to mind the boy, she might lose her job at the nursing home. They'd taken out a loan to fix the oil furnace just weeks before Jerome got sacked. The bills kept coming, and Jerome was having a devil of a time trying to get money home to Lucy.

Nowhere Nebraska. He unwrapped a stick of gum and put it in his mouth. He called it the Doublemint test. When he came to a new town, buying gum was how he took the temperature of the place, sort of like the flow table test for wet cement.

He got to where Main Street met the side track. Straight ahead was the train station, a small building with a shallow peaked roof and generous eaves. To his left, a rumbling sound came from the grain elevator complex, along with a scrim of smoke. Jerome sniffed the air. Not smoke. Dust. Dust from that wheat or corn or whatever they were moving around over there.

Jerome headed up the side track to where the crew-cars sat. A new flat-car had been delivered, stacked with railroad ties, and the oily odor of creosote hung heavy in the air. Damn, he hated that stuff. It made oil slicks on your clothes. It burned your skin, and the stink didn't come off in the shower. He was going to kill Malcolm. He remembered his last conversation with Malcolm, over a scratchy phone line from Auburn to Omaha. Malcolm's sing-songy voice: "You tell them it's right there in the union rules. You get two consecutive days off. Plus you're entitled to free rides home on the Eagle. If you want to come home, that is." And then the snicker, the implied nudge and wink, the attitude that infuriated Jerome.

As Jerome made the last stretch, Ice Cantrell hurried up to him, smiling a broad, gap-toothed smile. "Hey Omaha, what you get?"

"Didn't get nothing."

"You went up to that store for something. Let's see."

Jerome held up the pack of gum.

Ice walked alongside of Jerome, too close. "Don't tell me that's all. I told you we got rookie rules. When the new guy goes uptown, he brings back something for the old guys, something in a bottle. It's the a-rrangement."

Ice liked big words, and he had a habit of drawing out the syllables to the point he sounded like a stage Negro. Jerome had to guard himself from mocking him. In clipped tones, he said, "We settled this in Atchison. I'm too old for games. The only rules I follow come from God, Mr. Mopac and the BMWE."

Ice moved closer, and in a menacing whisper he said, "Don't see no Brotha-hood of the Maintenance of Way Em-ployees doing much for you out here, O-ma-ha."

"Get off me," Jerome said, shoving Ice back.

Ice stumbled. He faked a punch and smiled mirthlessly when Jerome flinched. "You a rookie. That means you have no notion what trouble looks like out here. Un-for-tunate accidents happen all the time. You think about that." Ice glared for a moment longer, capped it with a smile, and peeled off to go over where a couple of the boys were tossing a baseball.

Rookie, they called him. Jerome was ten years older than any of them, but he knew the score. Those boys had come up the hard way, position by position, nothing for free. This was system gang, the top of the heap. It was obvious from the first day Jerome knew nothing of gandy dancing. He was here because he knew somebody. And they were right. He knew Malcolm. And from the start, he put them all on edge, provoking the foreman with union this and union that.

The dislike was mutual. The Arkansas accents sounded ignorant to Jerome. Some of them, like Delran, seemed genuinely slow-minded. But it was more important to be strong than smart. The new rails were thirty-nine feet long and weighed 115 pounds per every three-foot. That was one thousand four hundred ninety-five pounds a rail. And Delran, Jerome had to admit, Delran held rail tongs like he was holding a fishing pole. And he moved so smooth, like he was dancing.

That's where the name came from. The caller, Charly T, gave Jerome that lesson the first day. On their way to the site, Charly fell in beside him, limping like he did. "Gandy dancers," Charly said with some eloquence, "taken from the male of the goose species, known as the gander. That bird has a fine mating dance it performs to attract the female of the species, known as the goose."

When Jerome actually saw them doing it, with Charly T singing the cadence and the men moving together like in some old-time movie, he was appalled. Did those southern boys think they were still on the plantation? No self-respect among the lot of them? Jerome swore that as long as he had this god-forsaken job he would never, ever, act in such a degrading fashion in front of fellow human beings.

On this point, Jerome had been wrong, dead wrong, and he got humbled fast. It took about twenty seconds lifting his first rail to realize the dance was anything but clowning. It was an absolute necessity if the men didn't want to drop one thousand four hundred and ninety-five pounds on themselves. Twelve men on a rail, three sets of tongs at each end of the 39-footer. That came out to a buck and quarter a man—as long as the weight was balanced. Either you got precision or you brought that rail down on you and everybody else, with mashed feet, broken legs and everything else. No matter what kind of grudge you had against another man, when the rail was moving you worked together. You did not even breathe out of time.

Charly T himself got that limp from a dropped rail. Turned himself into a caller to keep his job with the crew. Otherwise the company would have made him a watchman or crossing guard at half-pay, like they did with all the men they busted up working on the railroad.

So Jerome learned to dance almost as well as the next man, and to appreciate the coordination and the power in moving and setting rails. Cantrell was the one that made him wary. With the diamond-shaped scar on his cheek, and a constant defiant grin on his lips, "Ice" was no stranger to trouble, and Jerome wanted none of that.

Jerome saw Sam sitting five feet off the ground in the crooked branch of a tree, reclining with his nose in the pages of a small book. Strange kid. But Sammy had some brains in his head, even if he didn't have a clue what to do with them.

"Jerome," Sam called out. "What's rue?"

"I told him," Cook shouted, swinging down from the mess car. "I did."

Sam read slowly from the book. "With rue my heart is laden, for golden friends I had."

Delran started snickering and calling Sam a sissy. Sam was the youngest of the crew, and the only other rookie. Jerome was shocked that Sam was just sixteen. The kid was strong—you couldn't be otherwise in this job—but he was skinny. Sam was a boy who shot up to his man height, but was taking longer to fill out his man shape. There was something childlike in his face, too, a face as delicate and beautiful as a girl's.

"Rue," Jerome said slowly. He felt an almost paternal affection for Sam, but tried not to show it. The kid got picked on enough without being the Omaha troublemaker's friend.

"Cook says it's a sauce, but I can't feature that."

"It makes perfect sense," Cook said impatiently, waving a wooden spoon. "What's that other word, laden? It's like ladle." He demonstrated ladling. "When something is close to your heart that means you like it. The man approves of his sauce."

"I don't know . . ." Sam frowned.

"What's the next line, Sam?" Jerome asked.

Sam's eyes went to the book. "For many a, uh, many a rose-lipt maiden, and many a light-foot lad."

"That r-o-o?"

"R-u-e."

"No," cut in Cook. "I believe you'll find it's r-o-u-x. It's Cajun for sauce."

"But that's not what's here," Sam protested.

"That ain't my problem, now is it?" Cook said. "I know what I know."

Cook was from New Orleans, and never let anyone forget it. He had even more contempt for the Arkansas boys than Jerome did, and he didn't try to hide it.

"When I get back home," Jerome said, "I'll look that up for you."

"Thanks, Jerome." Sam hopped out of the tree and stopped to stare down the tracks at the elevator complex. "That place on fire or something?"

Jerome shaded his eyes from the late afternoon sun. "It's dust. We used to get something like that off the dry mix at the cement plant. Only here, it's from grain, most likely."

Sam's big eyes stared at him unblinking, his head nodding a little, like a boy to his daddy. If he and Lucy had got married when they should have, they might have a son this age. But there were money problems, and then came the war. Anyway, Sam had more on the ball than the rest of them, even if he was shy and peculiar, always carrying that little poetry book around.

"There's a whole mess of buildings," Sam said, pointing at the grain complex. "But that one tower stands up so high. Why is it so tall? They must do something important there. Look how it shines. How's it work, Jerome?"

"It's for storing grain, and shipping it out in rail cars. But don't you go snooping around there. It's not your business."

As Jerome turned away toward the bunk cars, Ice sidled up to him again with that grin. This was his ingratiating side, but the mission was the same, as he started wheedling for Jerome to go back to the store for beer. Jerome said no, and added, "Anyway, it looks like a dry town to me. Go ask them yourself."

"Naw, man, I told you how it is. Ice comes round, all they see is the scar. You're lighter. You're good at all that 'sir and ma'am' talk. You from around here."

"Not here."

"Omaha or whatever."

Jerome climbed into the bunk car. It was late afternoon hot, but he lingered anyway. He got out his pen and two sheets of lined paper from his locker. He sat on his bunk. He looked at the top sheet, where he'd already written "My Dearest Lucy," but had not continued. What was there to say? He sighed, and after a time he began to write.

"Another Saturday, and Burdock had us working again past two. I agree Mrs. Randolph is not the best for JJ. If your mom and you worked out your schedules, maybe you could hand off the boy between you. As to Mr. Prosser at the bank, if you can just explain. Let them know we have the money. I know Malcolm says I could get home if I want to but he's wrong. He thinks being here is some kind of holiday, and I'm gambling or what have you, but I promise it is not the case. Today I went to the store in town, but the man said he didn't know how to send money. I swear to you I am trying my utmost to get home to you by every means . . ."

As if to mock him, the train whistle shrilled close by. The Missouri River Eagle roared through every evening at this time. The closest station was Nebraska City, ten miles away, where it stopped at 4:20 on its way to a 5:40 arrival at Omaha. He knew the schedule by heart. He was supposed to be able to get on that train and deadhead to Omaha every Friday and come back to work Sunday. That was how it was supposed to work.

It was a bitter irony that the same train that was supposed to take him home was the reason he couldn't go. Every morning they had to stop what they were doing and get the track passable for the 9:15 Eagle to go through southbound, on its way to Kansas City. And every afternoon they had to knock off early to get the track in shape for the Eagle to come through northbound. They'd hold up the freight trains for the track work, even the Red Ball Express, and creep them through one after another on slow orders at night. But the passenger train had to be on time. All that down-time was the reason Burdock gave for making them work on Saturdays, union be damned.

Jerome crumbled the letter and threw it on the floor. He couldn't be saying that to Lucy about her brother, not in a letter anyway. Jerome had been deeply provoked with Malcolm, almost from the first day Malcolm told him about the job. The way he grinned and poked his elbow into Jerome, as if getting away from your family for drinking and carrying on was just about the best thing that could happen to a man. Lucy knew how Malcolm was. And she knew her husband better than to think of him that way. But still. A man shouldn't be saying things like that in front of a man's wife. If she heard it enough, she couldn't help but wonder if some of it was true, especially when they first said he'd be coming home every weekend. Then Malcolm had the nerve to turn around and act like Mr. Union Steward, telling Jerome to stand up for his rights and all that.

He picked up the letter, uncrumpled it, smoothed it across his knee, and looked over what he'd written. He should be writing to her every day. Every day. But this sounded whiny and weak, like he was making excuses. He would try again later.

3

A GIFT OF APPLES

The Littman Grain office was a two-room shack with a squared-off storefront hiding its peaked roof. It sat in front of the silos and bins just off Main Street, a block below Marchon Mercantile. The truck scale fronted the office like a wide concrete welcome mat. In the late afternoons, a farmer or local might drop by for beer from the old Frigidaire in the corner. Today's visitor was the Missouri Pacific station agent from the Julian depot that sat between the main line and the side rail next to the elevator complex.

"And then," Denton Henry was explaining, "Dave gets him the Doublemint, and Dave says he likes Juicy Fruit himself. Pretty soon they're talking Cubs and the Cardinals like old buddies. Dave even called him mister. Mister Wallace, I believe it was. Ain't that right, Timmy?"

"Yeah, he did."

"Something wrong with that?" asked Ron. The elevator man was in his usual spot, leaned back in the swivel chair, his feet on the pulled-out bottom drawer of the desk.

"I didn't say it was wrong," said Henry. "Just peculiar. For Julian I mean. That's what comes of being in the Navy. Probably Dave met some Black folks there."

"His hair was curly," Timmy put in, drawing laughter.

"Well, you got a close enough look," said Henry. "I thought he was gonna eat you for a second there."

A younger man breezed in and grabbed a beer from the fridge. He had red hair, sharp features, and a growing grin. "They're here, Ronnie," he chirped. "Right up our side track, four or five bunk cars. Time to lock up the wife and daughter."

"Lock up?" Timmy was alarmed.

"No, Timmy," said his father, and then, in a warning voice, "Frank."

"I'd lock up the tool shed, anyway," Frank said.

Denton Henry turned to the redhead. "They shouldn't be a problem. Working for the Missouri Pacific, that's about the best job a colored man can have. They don't want to lose that."

"I heard that too," said Ronnie.

"What I heard," said Frank, leaning on the windowsill, "is they like their liquor. And I'd still lock the shed."

"It ain't got a lock," Ron said, and the others laughed. He sipped his beer. He did plenty of business with Mopac, sending grain to market in boxcars. But this was something new. His family lived just across the street. "What about Moose Burdock?"

"At the motel in Neb City," said Henry.

"Moose knows better," Frank put in. "Mopac's not paying him to play nanny."

Henry gave Ron an eye roll, and got up to leave. Frank hung around, being Frank, joking about the gandy crews with words that Ron didn't like his son to hear.

"Come on, Timmy," Ron said, cutting Frank off. "Dinner time."

"Got any work for me tomorrow?" Frank polished off his beer in a big gulp, and tossed the empty in the trash can. He knew the rules. The beer was free, but the hours were strict. At six o'clock straight up, the host went home, and he didn't mind telling others that they should too. "Two beers is social," Ron liked to say, "three beers is a drunk."

Ron said, "Nothing tomorrow," and waited for Frank to tear out, pulling Timmy out of range of the gravel spinning up from his tires. As man and boy crossed the street, they heard the clanging of a hand bell.

Timmy looked around. "What's that?"

"I expect it's dinner time at the gandy camp." Ron nodded to himself. He liked things done proper, and this was the proper dinner hour.

Jerome roused himself at the bell's jangle, got out of his bunk and joined the others outside. When the weather was nice they got full plates from Cook at the door, and ate sitting around the clearing, in the shade of the big trees.

Tonight it was bread and stewed vegetables, and some kind of canned meat. Jerome figured they must have had about hundred tons of it left over from the war, pink stuff that wasn't quite ham and wasn't quite meat. After everyone had a plate, Cook came out of the mess car with a stock pot in his hand and a big grin on his face. He went straight to Sam, and put a big glop of gravy on top of his food. "There," he said. "You know what that is? It's your roux, kid. With roux your plate is ladled."

Dinner was livelier than usual with all the rue jokes, and Jerome had to admit the gravy made the pink meat taste better. The foreman and the time keeper took lodgings in Nebraska City, and the crew was left alone at night. As foremen went, Burdock wasn't the worst of them. At least that's what the guys said.

Jerome ate quietly, looking around at the circle of boys sitting on the ground and on upturned spike kegs. A campfire smoked in the middle of a ring of rocks. They didn't need it for warmth, but it gave them something to sit around at night. Except for Sam, the crew gave Jerome wide berth. Jerome knew it was because of the rumors that he had killed somebody. The rumors weren't true, but he let it stand.

Jerome figured himself the third oldest there, after Cook and Charly T, the caller. The others, except young Sam, were all in their twenties, and they all had at least two years' experience on the gandy crews. Big Larry had the most time, and he was gang leader out on the job. Little Larry was the shortest among them, but not a man to be messed with, being almost comically broad at the shoulders for his narrow waist. Big Larry and Little Larry were best of friends, always together. George seemed the smartest of the lot, but Jerome knew it might be just the wire-rim glasses. George was a baseball fanatic, always trying to find out scores. Jerome sometimes saw him reading the old *Saturday Evening Posts* in the mess car.

They finished dinner, and the boys on clean-up detail went sullenly into the mess car to do their job. The rest of them sat around the fire, telling stories and whiling the time away. Ice had a dice game going over by the tool car. Sam had his nose buried in his book.

Jerome was first to notice the strange procession coming toward them down the road. It took a minute for his mind to focus, but he'd seen two of them before. The woman was at the store today, along with her little boy. There was also a man and a blond girl with glasses. As they got closer, he saw that the girl and the dark-haired lady—unmistakably her mother—each had one handle of a bushel basket.

The visitors stopped ten feet from the loose circle of gandy dancers. The Larrys were to one side having a catch with a baseball and mitts. They stopped throwing and stared at the intruders. The women set the basket on the ground, and Jerome saw it was full of apples, big red ones. He had never met this man, but even so he knew he wasn't talking in his natural voice—the words were rushed and strained. The man was very nervous.

"Since we're neighbors now, we should act neighborly," the man started. "So here's some apples for you. Our name is Littman. I'm Ron, and I got the grain elevator over there. This's my wife, Mildred, my daughter, Carlin, and that's Tim. I wanted my family to know that . . ." he faltered. "My boy Timmy here has never seen, uh, railroad men before, and . . . I want him to know it's just normal folks, no cause to be afraid."

Timmy was caught off guard, and thought it unfair to be singled out as the one who would be afraid. With everyone looking at him, he broke into a silly dance, waving his arms around. Ice broke the silence with a big laugh, and everyone else followed suit, although Carlin squeaked out an embarrassed, "Tim!"

Jerome shot Ice a glare, warning him not to be in-so-lent. The boy, encouraged, repeated his dance, while the girl crossed her arms and rolled her eyes. Jerome looked at Cook, then at Charly T, waiting for one of them to say something. Finally, Jerome stepped forward. "We are obliged," he said. "Those are the finest apples I have seen, and that is the truth. It is nice to have neighborly neighbors here in . . ." He looked around for help.

"Julian," supplied the girl, adding in a bored voice, "Welcome to Julian."

Other gandies said thank you's, and after some awkward good-byes the family headed back down the road. Before anyone else could move, Delran darted to the basket, picked it up and sprinted away, laughing. Other boys gave chase while he danced and dodged, keeping the basket away from them with grace and speed.

Cook called out, "Could you wait one minute before you embarrass us?"

As the crew scampered around after the apples, Jerome turned to Cook. "What do you think that was about?"

"The gift of apples?" Cook shrugged. "Maybe he's scared we'll take his tools. Or maybe they're just being decent."

"I've known some decent white folk," Jerome responded. "But usually a basket of apples comes with a bucket of Bible. They never made so much as a praise-be."

"Catholics."

Jerome was irritated by that. "What do you mean, 'Catholics'?"

Cook turned to face him, with his large eyes with heavy lids, his ginger skin and hair. The eyes blinked slowly, indicating incredible patience. "Catholics talk Latin on Sundays, and English the rest of the week. It would be your Methodist or your Baptist who mixes apples and Bibles."

"And you know all about Catholics."

"I am a Catholic," Cook said, with a flourish.

Jerome laughed.

"Monsieur?" Cook said, touching his chest elaborately. "I am from New Orleans. Of course I am Catholic."

"If you say so," said Jerome. He called to Delran, "Hey, save one for me," and an apple came whipping at him so fast he was lucky to catch it. So now it was speedball, with Delran firing apples at every man.

Most times Jerome hated this job. But just now, in the temperate light of evening with a breeze rippling the cornfield, he allowed himself a smile. Just now, he was pleased by the flashes of red zipping through the sweet air, and the sound of men and boys laughing. As the family shambled down the unpaved street, Jerome saw the young one turn and look over his shoulder. Their eyes caught for just a moment, and Jerome was pleased to consider the boy might be thinking the smile was for him.

4

INCIDENT AT THE ARGO

Jerome Wallace was not mistaken in thinking Julian a dry town. This was fine with him. He did not drink himself, and had seen the mischief that drink could bring to others. Three days after the gift of apples came an offer of another kind. The gandies were finishing dinner, taking their tin plates back into the mess car, when they noticed the pick-up truck idling on the road.

It was a Dodge, black, and the driver, white, had pale red hair. And he was staring at them. At dinner that night, the boys were complaining that Cook hadn't made the apple pie he'd promised them. Ice even accused him of selling apples to buy fancy French liquor, never mind that the nearest such stuff was in St. Louis. But gradually conversation died out, and the gandies were staring back at the boy who was staring at them.

Jerome said to ignore him and he'd go away. But Ice, who seemed to make it a point to contradict whatever Jerome said, went over to talk to the boy. In a minute or two Ice came loping back, his eyes bright. "That boy's going to give us a ride to town. He knows where we can buy wine. Or beer, anything we want. Who's going with me?"

Delran got up out of habit. The Larrys came over from where they were whittling sticks.

"I don't like the look of him," said Jerome.

Ice shook his head sadly. "That is such a shame. And he got all dressed up just for you, Omaha." He turned to the others. "Me, I'm not sitting here doing nothing again."

"How much is he charging you?"

"Five dollars."

"That's a lot for . . ."

"Each."

Jerome exploded to his feet. "I'll tell that boy what he can do with his ride." He started toward the truck, but Big Larry stepped in his way. Jerome pleaded, "You won't pay that, will you, Big Larry? That's plain robbery."

"You my banker now, Wallace? Let me get my good shirt on."

Ice waved to the truck, calling out, "Just a minute."

Big Larry and Little Larry, Delran and George went into the bunk cars and came out moments later looking ready for church.

"We're going to town!" Ice said triumphantly. "Sam? You like to have fun?"

"Uh, yeah," said Sam.

"No," Jerome said. "He's just a kid."

"We're going to see Nebraska City. It'll have parks and churches and everything."

"Now, Sam . . ."

"You let Mister Samuel Washington decide for himself."

Sam gulped. "I believe I would like to see this town," he said, and scrambled into the bunk for his shoes.

The truck's horn sounded impatient blasts.

Jerome watched, disgusted, as the driver collected the money, and the boys climbed in the back of the truck. Thirty dollars. Flat out robbery. Ice went to the passenger side, but the driver waved him into the back with the others.

The pick-up skidded off with a jaunty spin of tires, stirring up a cloud of dust from the gravel road that enveloped the gandies and their nice shirts. "Damn backwoods boys," Jerome muttered.

Later, sitting by the fire, he endured gentle teasing from Cook and Charly T. "Those boys been doing this a few years now," said Cook. "They know how to navigate these towns and mostly stay out of trouble."

Jerome smiled at the way *navigate* was flavored by the drawl. He said, "I just worry about the kid."

Charly said, "And you never did anything stupid when you were seventeen?"

"He's sixteen."

Cook tossed a twig into the fire. Silence stretched among them.

"I don't have a good feeling about this," Jerome said at last.

"And you may be right, *mon frère*."

He was right. He knew he was right when the boys were gone all night. He was annoyed with himself that he hardly slept, waiting for the sound of their return. He wasn't their nanny. Usually the crew had breakfast at seven. The foreman and timekeeper showed up at 7:15, and roll call was at half past the hour. On this Wednesday morning the remaining crew members stood around looking at each other, wondering what kind of trouble the boys had gotten into.

At 8:45 a two-car procession arrived, with Burdock and Tarp each driving one. They got out grim-faced, followed by the six gandies, looking the worse for wear. George had a swollen eye, but must have taken off his glasses first, as they appeared intact. Delran had traces of dried blood on his lip. Sam looked okay, Jerome was relieved to see. Another white man wandered over to see what all the fuss was about. Jerome recognized him as a Mr. Denton Henry, the Missouri Pacific station agent for Julian.

Moose Burdock made a good show of it. He ordered everyone out front, and then lined up the offenders and yelled at them for a solid fifteen minutes. He cussed and swore, called them worthless and stupid, said if they didn't like their jobs there were plenty who would be glad to step in and take their place. He said one more stunt like this and they would be sacked. He said he wasn't goddamn kidding and if they didn't goddamn believe him they should just goddamn try him.

Jerome stared closely at Burdock while he blustered, all red faced and rough-sounding. The foreman had once been a powerful man, but now his stomach hung out over his belt and his hair was white. Sixty years old at least. Even a rookie like Jerome could figure out he didn't have much hand to play.

Moose himself knew this better than anyone. The Mopac would have all their seasoned men out on crews by now, and the last thing he wanted was to break in more rookies. These boys had mostly kept their noses clean, and they were a damn good team. Burdock spent most of the day in a fold-up chair smoking a cigar, reading the newspaper, fanning himself with his hat. When they finished a job, he'd lumber over to check the work with spot board and rail gauge, though with his experience he hardly needed either one. In this moment he needed to be the hard boss, and he obliged. He carried on a while longer, walking up and down the line-up, cussing like a drill sergeant. The delinquents hung their heads in poses of regret and remorse, but there was something theatrical about the whole thing.

Jerome watched with detachment, but his mood soured when he saw Ivan Tarp wearing a malicious little smile. The time keeper was lean and hatchet-faced. He cheated the crew out of every minute he could get, shaving fifteen here, half an hour there—as if he was personally responsible for keeping the Mopac solvent. Jerome had been looking for a time to talk to Burdock or even Tarp about how to get money home to Lucy. After this, neither of them would be doing any favors for any gandies.

Jerome took a closer look at the third man, Denton Henry. Not much to see, a bland, fair-haired white man of middle years. His face registered some shock at Burdock's language, and that was a good thing. Not a hardened man. Maybe Jerome could get some help from the station agent.

Finally the southbound Eagle rumbled through, so they could get to work. There was no breakfast for the offenders that morning. They barely had time to change into work clothes and get their lunch cans from Cook before heading up the line to the work site. On the long walk up the track, some of the story came out. It seemed the boy in the pick-up, whose name was Frank, thought they were just going to run in the store and buy their booze, and then he'd bring them straight back to Julian. Ice had other ideas, and demanded social time. Frank put them out at a run-down tavern called the Argo, across from the Burlington roundhouse.

Ice was doing the talking, as usual. "I swear to you," he said, addressing everyone, "I swear we stuck to ourselves, causing no one any harm. Ain't that right, Big Larry?"

"That's right."

"Ain't that right, Delran?"

"Yeah, Ice. That's right."

"When we talked to the white boys, it was all in fun. About baseball, that's all. It wasn't even me that started it. George got sick of hearing them boys talk. He told them the Kansas City Monarchs could beat any team in the majors, even after the best players got stolen."

"George said it to us," Big Larry corrected. "You was the one had to relay it on to the white boys."

"And then this one fat boy," Ice went on, "he said Negro players was just a stunt, and was dumb enough to bet five dollars that no team had two of them. George told them it was the New York Giants, with Hank Thomson and . . .George!"

"Monte Irvin," said George.

"Mon-te Ir-vin, yeah, that's right. And even the white bartender said he was right so the boy had to pay up. Things would have been fine if Frank came back when he said." Ice went on with his story. "Now four more white boys came in, and they let us alone and we let them alone, until they figured out we worked for Mr. Mopac. Turns out they were just off shift from across the street."

"They thought we's after their jobs," laughed Delran.

"Yeah," Ice said. "Now you tell me how a dig-ni-fied Mopac system man would ever want to be a yard dog for the CB&Q? I tried to explain to them, didn't I Del?"

"You did."

"And I said nothing against Chicago, or Burlington or *Quin*-cy, did I Del?"

"No, you didn't."

"Then one of them had to go and say something in-*sul*-ting about Jackie Robinson."

The Mopac boys and Burlington boys were then asked to take their differences outside, and things got ugly from there. They were outnumbered, but Ice swore they were winning when the cops arrived. "Another minute," he said, "and they would have run away."

"And come back with twenty more boys," said Jerome. But he was preoccupied by Sam.

Big Larry saw him staring. "He missed the whole thing. Off to church or something."

"Hey Jerome," said Sam. "There's a museum in that town for John Brown and people who were against slavery. Abolishmenters."

"Abolitionists," said Jerome.

"And they have this cave," Sam said eagerly, "where John Brown hid runaways before they lit out for Canada."

Jerome said, "Sam, where'd you spend the night?"

"In jail with the rest of us," said Big Larry.

It turned out that Sam had gotten back to the Argo just as the others were being herded into a police van. The cops weren't picky. They took him too.

5

SALLY'S BISCUITS

At the work site, Burdock stopped his cussing out, and went over the plan for the day. The section of track they put down yesterday with temporary spikes had to be aligned, tamped and made fast before they could pull plates and spikes and tip the next pair of old rails off to the side. Each man grabbed a lining pole, six feet long and thirty pounds heavy. The men needed no direction. They strung themselves out at three-tie intervals, and on Charly T's signal they jammed the poles into the gravel alongside the tie.

The men waited, bouncing on the balls of their feet. Charly T slapped his thigh, establishing the cadence. Then he sang, crooning in a heavy beat.

> You know Sally, hip-HO,
> I know Sally, hip-HO,
> Sally's basket
> Always full, HEAVE-OH.

> Men come round for, hip-HO,
> Sally's biscuits, hip-HO
> Sally's biscuits
> Got gravy too, HEAVE-OH.

The men made two short pushes and two quick hard ones, over and over. The rail did not appear to move. But it did. Burdock was fifty feet down the rail in front of them. He didn't need the sighting board; Burdock could eyeball the track straight. When it got close, he hollered to Charly, and Charly slowed the song down until the signal came that the track was perfect. Then they traded their lining poles for mallets and secured the rail with spikes.

Jerome smiled to himself, watching Charly T standing by the track patting his thigh. Charly was in his fifties, mostly gray in beard and hair. He was a quiet serious man who kept to himself. His personality changed when he took up the gandy song. He smiled and kept the men loose but focused. Charly T had a lot of songs, but most often he was singing about 'Sally.' Charly was a good Christian and never sang anything improper. But hints were there, just at the edge of his rhymes, and his calls made the boys grin devilishly as they worked. Today he gave them a sly variation.

Sally's got a, hip-HO,
Negro outfield, hip-HO,
Sally's outfield,
Up to bat, HEAVE-OH.

Likes a fastball, hip-HO,
Likes a curve, hip-HO,
Likes the spitball,
Best of all, HEAVE-OH.

Moose, seeing that Charly had things under control, settled into his chair and lit a cigar. Burdock had once been the hardest of foremen. From Chicago to Denver he was loved by the bosses in the offices, because he got the job done—done right and done fast, with no excuses. The gandy dancers hated and feared him. They would take any kind of assignment to avoid his crews, especially the dark-skinned men.

They had good reason. Moose was a racist. Not the kind that spouted nonsense on street corners. Not the kind whose hate was fueled by fear. Moose believed that colored people were, in some basic way, all alike, like dogs or horses. And to get them to do what you wanted, you just needed a simple three-step plan. One, you had be very clear exactly what you want from them. Two, you had to punish any infractions immediately and severely. And three, you never, ever, varied from steps one and two. Consistency was the key. Just follow those three steps and your Blacks will be the best damn gandies on the system. And his were.

If you called him a racist, which no one ever did, he would have knocked you down. Then he would have explained that he was not a man of prejudice. He would have reminded you that these men were just a few generations removed from slavery, where they had to be sly and sneaky to survive. It wasn't the fault of colored people that they had drawn the short straw—but it wasn't his fault either. His job was to get track laid down, and by gum he got it laid down. Three steps. Simple and brutal.

That was the Moose Burdock of the 1920s and '30s. Sometime during the war, though, he started to change. Some said it was just age—a man can't keep bare-knuckling into his fifties. The day came when he refused to force an exhausted crew to work another day with no time off. The desk jockeys grumbled that he handed out doctor visits like Christmas cards. Word went around that he'd gone soft, and Moose was demoted to lesser projects in favor of younger, harder foremen.

By 1950, the reversal was complete. A new generation of gandies took it as an article of faith that Old Moose Burdock was the best foreman to work for. Too bad he didn't get the plum jobs. Too bad he'd fallen into disfavor with the Missouri Pacific brass.

In disfavor, perhaps, but not disrespected. Everybody knew Kansas City—Omaha was going to be a beast of a job. It was the busiest stretch of single-track main line on the whole system. In other places, where the line was double-tracked, if you wanted to replace rail, you just shut down that track, and you could single-track on the other. But this line was only one track, and the Mopac couldn't afford to shut down the line. That meant the rail had to be replaced piecemeal, every day, while keeping the line open for two passenger Eagles, two Redball Express freights, and three or four slow freights. You didn't have to be Cornelius Vanderbilt to see it was a logistics nightmare, with high potential for delays and derailments. With such a tiny margin for error, they knew that they had to have their best man on the job. That's why, when it came right down to it, they called on H.H. Burdock.

Moose was forty yards down the track from where the boys were lining up the rail. With this crew, he hardly needed to check. Charly T called the cadences, and it did look like a dance, the way they moved together so perfect. Not that there was any truth to that nonsense about it being like ganders or geese or however that yarn went. *Gandy dance*. The Black folk could make a flowery story out of anything.

The gandies dropped the lining bars and picked up the spike mauls. Time to secure the rail. He had been sorely angry this morning, and he hoped those boys knew it. They should know it, the way he'd let them have it. Burdock smiled to himself. One hour earlier, he been telling the police chief in Nebraska City what fine upstanding Christian gentlemen they were. The bastard had wanted to keep them another night.

Briggs and Little Larry were setters. They rolled the 200-pound kegs of spikes up to the rail and got to work. Moose watched how fast they used the small maul to get the spikes seated in perfectly straight rows, like soldiers at attention. Then came the fun part, the spiking. Here's where the job sometimes became a fierce and dangerous competition. The foreman heard some whoops and hollers as they got started. The spikers worked in teams, two men on a spike, alternating strokes. Jerome and Sam, the rookies, didn't have the skills to play.

But when any of the other boys squared off, it was something to watch. Like now, with Bones and Sillman Jones. The two boys faced each other and hit a whirlwind of blows. The first spike took five seconds. The next one took less. The third one, the fourth one . . . a sudden CLANG and Bones danced away from the track with a scream while the crew burst into laughter. "Sillman cut his head out," someone yelled. Bones came back to the rail, and the two commenced again, banging in spike after spike, faster and faster.

"Cutting the head out" was when one man brought his maul around so fast that instead of hitting the spike itself, he hit the head of the other man's maul. When it happened, the spike had to be reset, and guy who got his head cut out took a vibration up the handle that would rattle his molars. Moose remembered how, when he came up as a spiker, a million years ago, teams used to compete against other teams to see which *pair* could claim to be the fastest. Cutting the head was a mistake, and you apologized to your partner.

Times were rougher now. Maybe the change was connected with the legend of John Henry, maybe it wasn't. In any case, it had evolved to a contest of speed between the two former teammates. The idea was to be faster than the other man, and every spike was a test. Now when a man got his head cut, he was the loser, and the others laughed at his pain. Dropping the maul was a sign of weakness, like a big league batter who yelped when he got drilled by a pitch.

Every crew had a pecking order, and on this one, Big Larry and Delran were at the top. Face-offs between them were awesome events. As Moose ambled up the rail, he noticed neither of them were in a mood to be defending their place, not after the night they'd had. After the Jones-Bones face-off, the boys settled down and the rest of the spiking was routine.

Almost routine. Ice misfired on a hit, and the spike went flying, just missing the head of Jerome Wallace.

"Watch what you're doing!" Jerome shouted.

"Accidents, Omaha," Ice hissed. "Gandying dan-ger-ous work. That's why we got rookie rules. To protect you."

"I make the rules around here," Moose said, interposing his bulk between them. "Wallace, you're pulling plates next section. Cantrell, tie crew."

"Tie crew?" Ice spat. "Not my turn to be getting that oily stink on me."

Moose barked orders to the rest of the crew, then went to his folding chair and sat down while the men went to work. Moose watched Jerome pull plates—he was slow at that too. The foreman knew some strings were pulled in Omaha to get Mr. Jerome Wallace this job, and he had not been happy about it. A forty-year-old malcontent with no experience—not what he wanted or needed on his crew.

That's how he'd been thinking when they started, anyway. In the weeks since then he'd come to recognize what was plain as day, that Wallace was a man as smart and capable as you were likely to meet. Wallace was a family man, and Moose liked how he looked out for the kid, Sam Washington. And about the brick works. Well, Moose had done some asking around, and he was fairly sure it was a frame-up that got Mr. Wallace chased out of that trade.

Mr. William "Ice" Cantrell, on the other hand, had a history. He wasn't the worst sort, but he was reckless, had a temper, and liked the hooch. Today wasn't the first time Moose had picked him up from the police.

And that was the thing about three-step plans. Over the years, and almost against his will, H.H. Burdock had been forced to conclude that colored people were not like dogs or horses, at least not any more than white people were. Every one's got his own way, some better, some worse, some just different.

The crew humped it pretty hard to get two more old rails turned off to the side and two shiny new ones temporarily in place. Good enough, at least, for a slow-order Eagle and the night freights. As he was heading toward his car at the end of the day, Moose heard the step of someone hurrying up behind him. Jerome Wallace had detached himself from the group heading back up the track to Julian.

"I know this isn't the best day to be asking favors," Jerome began.

"You got that right," said Moose. He kept walking, and Wallace kept pace beside him, saying he needed to get his pay to his wife in Omaha. He seemed to think Dave Scarborough down at the Julian store could help. Then he started in on some complicated scheme. Moose cut him off.

"Trust your money to a three-cent stamp, and the post office will probably get it there. Beyond that, I don't know what you're thinking."

"I am thinking," Jerome replied evenly, "that the Mopac sets up accounts with the stores in camp towns. So I thought . . ."

Moose let him rattle on a while longer. He'd been tough on Wallace from the start, when they got into it over Saturday work. The man missed his wife. It was a shame. But that's how it was on the job, and he couldn't start making special deals, especially for new guys.

"Fourth of July's just a few weeks away," Moose said, finally. "I reckon you'll be able to get home then. Your money will keep, long as you don't lose it at dice or cards."

"Just consider what I'm saying."

The foreman stopped walking, re-lit the dead cigar, and took a pull. He looked away across the field. "A seasoned spiker," he began, as if to himself, "he can send a spike any direction he wants at pretty much any speed he wants."

Jerome thought about that for a second. "You mean Ice was aiming for me."

"I mean, if he was aiming for you he would have hit you."

"What are you telling me?"

"Not telling you anything." Moose tapped cigar ash on the weeds. "But I am thinking that sometimes a man's pride isn't worth what it costs. A new man on a crew might consider going along with some rookie nonsense, if it makes things go smooth."

"I don't think I can do that, Mr. Burdock."

"In that case," said the foreman, "I'd watch my back."

6

DAVE NEVER LIKED THAT WORD

The second most impressive building in Julian, after Ron Littman's main silo, was the school. Red brick, symmetrical, two stories tall, it sat at the top end of Main Street, three blocks up from the train depot. The commercial block, with Marchon Mercantile, was flat, but the next two, residential, climbed at a good clip, so the school stood eye to eye with the grain elevator. The school playground was grassy and shaded by oak trees. The swings and slide shared the space with scattered wooden picnic tables, so outdoor gatherings were common in nice weather. The playground was bordered by the left field-fence of the ball field.

The field was laid out on a rectangular plot better shaped for the football games played there in the fall. Left field and left-center were long and deep. But the hay field running along the side of the property cut off right field, making the fence so close you could spit over it from home plate, or that's what everybody said. Short field notwithstanding, Julian was the perfect place for a game. White wooden bleachers sat along the baselines; front row spectators leaned their elbows on the tarpapered dugout roofs.

That Saturday afternoon was perfect for a country league game, warm and sunny. The sun sat high in a cloudless sky, and the June air still had a crispness to it; summer humidity had not yet settled in. The bleachers were jammed with people, and more stood along the outfields. Some of the Julian crowd came from the town, but most, like the players themselves, lived and worked on the surrounding farms.

Plattsmouth always brought a lot of fans. The town was way up in Cass County, closer to Omaha than to Julian, but the games had an extra edge, on account of the Buchalter brothers. The Buchalters were big boys with white hair sawed off in flat-tops. They used to live on a farm just east of Julian, and moved to Plattsmouth after their barn burned down some years ago. There was a rumor one of them started that fire out of evil intent to the twenty or thirty cats living there. Whether that was true or not, it was the kind of thing people said about bullies, and the Julian schoolyard was a more peaceful place after they moved away. When they came back, the games had the air of grudge matches, and their rivals, the Scarboroughs, always seemed to come out on top.

Nobody who was around Julian in the pre-war days would ever forget the 1938 Southeast Regional Championship basketball game. Dave Scarborough, a skinny, six-one center, had led Julian High to an upset over the top-seeded Plattsmouth Blue Devils, captained by Big Bobby Buchalter. Folks also remembered the 1940 Track and Field Championships in Lincoln. That meet saw Ernie Scarborough add a state record triple-jump to his pile of baseball accolades. Second place went to Bruce Buchalter. Jack Scarborough carried on the tradition, in his way. In his junior year he sat down Dwayne Buchalter at a five-school spelling bee.

Jack needled his rival every time Dwayne Buchalter came up to bat, but Dwayne was absent today, and Jack had to settle for working over the other two. Bobby, the oldest, was getting fatter every time Jack saw him. Jack was himself sensitive about weight, but this was the Buchalters. This was war. As Bobby rolled up to the plate, Jack started chattering, "Easy-out, easy-out, fat-man, fat-man, easy-out."

"Shut up, pudge," Bobby sneered, taking off his hat to wipe his forehead with his arm.

"When'd you lose your hair? Your head looks like a butternut squash."

"I'm gonna squash you in a minute."

The ball smacked into Jack's glove.

"Strike one," called Hank Benkleman.

"Strike-him-out, easy-out," Jack sang. "Pumpkin head, pumpkin head."

Bobby turned on the next pitch, and hit a towering blast to left. He smirked at Jack as he started his trot. But the wind was blowing in, and left field was a mile deep. The ball settled in to Roy Hurst's mitt just inside the fence, and the trot became a walk to the dugout.

"Nice swing, Bobby," Jack called after him.

Plattsmouth was always a tough game for the Hornets. Nobody was getting on base for either side today, and the game settled into an uneasy lethargy. The league played seven-inning games, and this one was still zip-zip in the fifth. The crowd was growing anxious. They wanted their boys to win, but there were also chores that needed doing on a Saturday, and nobody had time for extras innings.

Jack began pestering Hank Four Eyes, who crouched behind him. Hank's thick glasses and hog pens made him an easy target. Jack liked to say how, when the wind was right, you could smell his bad calls. Jack laid it on extra-thick because Hank was a prideful man. He carried himself with importance when he came in to Marchon Mercantile, as if he was county judge rather than a hog farmer. It's a good thing Chick Beadle was on top of his game, his windmill underhand zipping a ball with a velocity of a major league pitcher.

In point of fact, Hank Benkleman was a damn good umpire, as Jack would admit. He realized it every time they went on the road and had those hometown umps stealing calls against them so plain it would embarrass a burglar. Hank called it like he saw it, and he usually saw it right. Big game, big play at the plate, Jack would take his chances with Hank Benkleman. That didn't keep Jack from regularly reminding him to get those glasses checked.

"Missed that one," said Jack, standing to toss the ball back to Chick.

"Ball," Hank repeated. "Low and away."

"Not by much." Jack squatted for the next pitch. His brother Dave was standing a few feet off first, glove parked lazily on his hip. Ernie was in center field, and Jack laughed to see he was standing in the same pose as Dave, weight on one leg, glove on hip. Must be a Scarborough way of standing.

But that was about all Dave and Ernie had in common these days. This was one of Ernie's good days. He had the game's only extra-base hit. Even better, he didn't walk off from center field, get in his car and drive home. At least he hadn't yet. Jack remembered how Ernie was before the war—quiet, funny, and solid as a hickory axe handle. It was sad to see him now.

Dave, on the other hand, seemed unaffected by the war, a man of easy authority and genuine good humor. Folks came round to Marchon's as much to banter with him as to pick up mail or groceries. As for himself, he was Jack the joker, and he liked it when people laughed at his antics. Sometimes he chafed that people never took him seriously, and was sorry he'd been too young to serve in the war. But one look at Ernie on a bad day cured him of that.

The Plattsmouth batter grounded softly to Randle Bazin, the pint-sized shortstop from one of the original French homesteader families. Bazin gobbled it up and flipped it to Dave for the third out. Jack trotted to the dugout and settled himself on the bench. The bottom of the order was coming up. He was due up fourth, and the way the Plattsmouth kid was dealing, he probably shouldn't bother taking off his equipment. Chick, Randle, and Frank Abernathy were ahead of him. Jack didn't mind being third best hitter in his family, but it rankled him to be at the bottom of the order. He should be hitting ahead of Frank, at least. He got more hits than Frank, and he didn't strut around like he was Ralph Kiner when he did.

There Frank was, at the center of the bench, bragging about some episode yesterday with those railroad workers at the grain elevator. "So Ronnie," Frank was saying, "Ronnie says he's going to hire those Negroes to push the stuck boxcar, and I told him, hell, if he talked to the foreman he could probably get them for free, courtesy of Mopac. But he says it's got to be done right now, so he goes over there. Next thing you know he's coming back down the track with a pack of them like he owned a damn minstrel show." Frank thought that was funny, and laughed.

"Did they get the car moved?" asked Evan Carpenter, the preacher and substitute fielder.

"We did, all right, after I showed them how. Ronnie gave each one a dollar. He offered me twenty bucks, but I told him I'm just happy to help."

That last part, at least, was bull. Jack could see Ron hiring the gandies, but twenty dollars to Frank? To help move one boxcar? Never in a million years. As always when Jack thought about the Littmans, his mind went to Carlin. What was that word she liked? . . . *ludicrous.* Twenty bucks was ludicrous. Frank was ludicrous. Carlin herself was something else. She was a handful, that girl was. Good looking too—don't let those glasses fool you. She was seventeen now, and swore she was going to college. He was four years older, which made her a little kid when he was in school. Recently he'd started seeing things in a whole new light. Many grown-up couples were four years apart. It wasn't hardly anything at all. He scanned the bleachers for her yellow hair.

Chick struck out on a low ball, told Hank he'd better get that call, and came back to the bench. Randle Bazin took a few practice swings and headed for the plate.

"Abernathy," said Dave. "On deck."

Frank stood up, but he wasn't finished. "I suppose you all heard," he said, drawing out a pregnant pause, "I took some of them up to town earlier in the week, and they ended up in jail. Drinking and fighting. Goes to show what happens when you try to do a favor to coons." He laughed as if he'd said something funny.

"I never liked that word." It was Dave, seeming to speak more to himself than the others. "I guess it's no worse than calling somebody a rat or a skunk, but it sounds worse."

"Careful, Dave," Frank said. "You're starting to sound like Evan."

Dave went on. "I remember this time at Camp Rucker, in Alabama. We were sitting in the mess tent and a colored soldier comes in. He gets his tray and goes to a table by himself." Dave was not talking loud, but his team hung on every word.

"So a guy from our company, a good old boy from Georgia, he runs over there, and he grabs the colored soldier, and yanks him up, hollering, 'Who said you could eat here?' The soldier says he has orders to eat there; the colored mess wasn't built yet. The Georgia boy won't hear it. He starts in smacking the boy around, and yelling *coon* this and *coon* that, until finally he throws that soldier right out of the tent. And that poor soldier just took it."

Frank was grinning broadly from on deck, which annoyed Jack. Frank was missing the whole point of the story.

"I saw awful things in the Pacific," Dave said, "but I never saw such a show of plain meanness as at Rucker that time. To this day, I have regret I didn't go up to that Georgia boy and say, 'Maybe that's how you do things in Macon, but that's not how I was raised in Julian.'"

Jack blinked back the tear that sprang to his eye. Dave didn't have to say that. It was enough to say it wasn't right, what that Georgia boy did. A man is not supposed to admit his mistakes.

"Jack. On deck."

Frank was at the plate. Randle had worked a walk, and was dancing off first. Jack unsnapped his shin pads sullenly. Frank had missed the most important part of Dave's story. On top of that he flailed wildly at the first three pitches, just the thing to help out a pitcher having control problems. Jack shook his head, tried to concentrate on hitting. As he headed for the plate he spotted Carlin standing along the bleachers, and she gave him a little wave and a big smile. That made concentrating on hitting damn near impossible.

7

CARLIN BURNS A BUCHALTER

Carlin Littman had three heroes, Willa Cather, Marie Curie, and Sister Mary Michael. As such, she had not decided yet whether to be a renowned author, a Nobel Prize-winning scientist, or a missionary to the starving children of Africa. Sister Mary Michael said she should keep her options open, and she agreed.

She sat in the sunshiny bleachers at the Julian ball field between Ron and Millie, watching the game. The Hornets should be whipping Plattsmouth, but there was still no score.

"Maybe Chick can get a hit," said her mother.

"Why not," Carlin answered. "He's had to do everything else today."

"Ernie Scarborough almost had a homer."

"Almost only counts in horseshoes and hand grenades."

"Carlin! That's not nice."

"Oh, mom. It's what everybody says." Carlin was anxious to see them score. She loved this team, and it made her mad when Julian girls said she didn't, just because she went to school in Nebraska City.

Chick struck out on a bad call. The crowd hissed, and Chick had some choice words for Hank. Randle Bazin came up, and Frank Abernathy strolled to the on deck position. Typical Frank: he didn't even watch the game, his jaw going a mile a minute to the guys on the bench. Serve him right to take a foul ball on the noggin.

Frank had gone to St. Bernard's too. Just because you went to school in Neb City did not mean you weren't for Julian. If you wanted to go to Catholic school, that's where it was.

"Where is Timmy?" Millie asked, looking around.

"He was out in the hayfield." She shielded her eyes, staring out past the right field fence where the home runs landed.

"It's your job to watch him."

"Where is he going to go? Okay, fine. I'll go find him after Frank bats."

Randle spoiled several good pitches on the way to a walk, and the fans showed their appreciation. The crowd buzzed as Frank strutted to the plate. Frank. Looking at him made Carlin's mouth screw up sideways. When she was a sophomore and he was a senior she had a crush on him, and he took her to the Harvest Dance. She liked his swagger and his black pick-up truck. The night had not gone well. He bragged on himself a lot. And they got into an argument about the First Crusade. The next day she looked up everything, and she was right right right. Peter the Hermit, not Richard the Lionhearted. Frank was such a blowhard!

Frank struck out. Amid the disappointed crowd noises, Carlin suppressed a giggle. Frank had struck out with her, too. Who did he think he was getting all handsy like that when he didn't even know who launched the First Crusade?

"Carlin. Timmy?"

"Okay!" She excused herself as she stepped lightly down the bleachers, putting her hands on people's shoulders for balance as she went.

Jack Scarborough was up next. He looked in her direction, and she gave him a wave. She lingered along the first base line to watch him bat. Jack was her buddy. She hung out with him on weekends in Neb City.

Of course, she adored Dave Scarborough. He called her Skipper. She didn't know why; maybe because he was in the Navy. But when she came in to Marchon's to get the mail, it would be "Hello, Skipper! How's the day?" It made her mad that he could make her blush just from saying that.

And, of course, she was in love with Ernie. So gentle, so sad, brooding over some terrible thing that happened in the war. She could not guess what that must have been like, but in her imagination there were grass huts and a mysterious island woman who dressed in bright sarongs and who broke his heart when she was killed by a Japanese bomb.

Jack graduated three years ago, a year ahead of Frank. Jack wasn't Catholic, so he went to Julian School, right over there, which was kind of a joke. They taught the kids from all four years in the same room. She liked how Jack made her laugh. He had this way of being sarcastic, but mostly about himself, like about his weight, for example. He wasn't fat. He was stout. That was the right word for it. She and Jack usually ended up talking about words, for some reason. They both liked strange-sounding words, like anemone, and strange places words came from, like the saxophone being named for Adolphe Sax. Well, that one wasn't so strange.

Jack hit weakly to third and the inning was over. Carlin walked out past the right field fence. She saw a bunch of kids there, but not Timmy. As she circled on out past center field her mind stayed on the game. The Hornets had stranded the runner, but at least they'd turned over the line-up. PD Klyber, who worked at the hardware store in Talmage, hit lead-off, then Dave and Ernie Scarborough, back to back, would give them a chance.

"Tim," she called out. "Timmeeeeeeee." Carlin heaved a dramatic sigh. The headstrong one. The willful girl. She was so tired of it. And lately it seemed her father was grouching at her for everything. She was gone to town too much. She was spending too much time with boys. She was getting wild. She rolled her eyes. Her best friend was a nun, for goodness sake! She didn't think her father was really worried about boys. What bothered him was that she said she was going to college. She had a better ally in her mom, but she didn't want to put Millie in the middle. A foreboding flashed through her. When she said "college," dad and mom thought she meant Peru State Teacher's College, seven miles down the road. Or maybe, just maybe, Creighton University, in Omaha, because it was Jesuit. And she let them think that. Nobody knew she had bigger plans, plans as big as Chicago. Nobody but Sister Mary Michael, anyway.

Timmy was at the playground, on one of the swings. He leapt off and charged into her arms. Carlin and Tim spent a lot of time together in the summer, since she was his designated babysitter. At the advanced age of six, he objected to the term; he was no baby. If Carlin had not found him on the playground, she would have assumed he had gone home, or to one of the neighbors. There were about thirty houses in Julian, and everybody knew everybody else. It wasn't like bad things never happened. In the last twenty years there'd been a hunting accident, a kid run over by a combine, a drowning in a pond. But those things happened out in the woods, or on the farms. For kids, Julian was one big playground, a common back yard. Even the littlest ones felt perfectly entitled to wander anywhere, including up the railroad track to see what those extremely interesting gandies were up to.

Carlin was a honey blond in a family of brunettes, with those Littman slate blue eyes, and an expressive mouth. She was saved from the straitjacket of the beauty queen by her willful ways and her Clark Kent camouflage. Everyone but everyone knew the saying, "Men seldom make passes at girls who wear glasses," and they all thought it clever to say it to her.

She caught Timmy in her arms and swung him in a circle. "Ugh, you're too heavy," she said, putting him down. Looking at his furry brown head, she was reminded of the anomaly of her hair. All her life people made it a point to bring up Bethie Sue, a cousin who was blond, as if they had to prove she wasn't a bastard. Bastard. She'd known it was a bad word for years before she'd learned what it meant. When she did, she had a puzzled reaction. Why would it be bad to be called a word that just meant your parents weren't married? You didn't have a thing to do with that. She just had blond hair, that was all. Which was completely possible with recessive genes like with fruit flies with their eyes and Gregor Mendel, the scientist-priest, with his peas. She learned about Gregor Mendel from Sister Mary Michael. MM had college degrees in biology and French. She was the smartest person Carlin knew.

Carlin absentmindedly held Timmy by his upstretched hands, letting him lean this way and that while he kept his feet planted between hers. The crowd noise washed over them, indistinct. She was lost in thought.

St. Bernard's Academy occupied the bottom floor of the large house made of timber and river stone, in Nebraska City, two blocks from St. Mary's Church. The second and third floors were the convent of the Ursuline nuns. It was the nicest home Carlin had ever visited, not counting the mansion at Arbor Lodge State Park. Arbor Lodge had been the home of J. Sterling Morton, Nebraska City's most famous person. He was the founder of Arbor Day, and secretary of agriculture for Grover Cleveland.

Carlin knew things like this because she cared about people that got out and made something of themselves, like Willa Cather, Madame Curie, and Sister Mary Michael.

"Hey Blondie."

No one called her that. She looked up to find three boys smirking from the Hudson convertible idling next to the playground. She didn't have to see the license plate to know it would start with 20, the prefix for Plattsmouth. Where else would they be from? With Timmy in tow, she sauntered up to the car.

"You need directions?" she said. "You look lost."

They thought that was just hilarious. "If you're Blondie," said the crew-cut driver, "then I want to be Dagwood."

"You do look like something out of a comic strip."

"Come for a ride with us. We got the top down."

She laughed. "I see that. Might be better keeping it up, at least when you get off the highway." She ran her finger over the fender, leaving a clean streak. "Look, Timmy," she said, holding up her dirty finger. He laughed with her. The whole car—up to and including the hair of the boy in the back seat—had a conspicuous coating of white dust.

"You could sit up front, right in the middle. See, it's nice and clean here." The driver patted the spot next to him.

"Game's tied up," she said, nodding in the direction of the field. "Your Plattsmouth boys . . . wait, aren't you Dwayne Buchalter?"

The driver did a double-take. "I'll be a son of a buck. You're Carlin. Ronnie Littman's kid. You were working the scale last summer at harvest."

"My claim to fame."

"You filled out since then."

She ignored that. "Why were you trucking wheat all the way down here? Plattsmouth elevator kick you out?"

"Your daddy was paying two cents more a bushel, as I recall. But now I got a reason to come back."

"Not good enough to make the team this year?"

"Oh, I'm plenty good, but . . ." Dwayne held up his left arm above the car door, showing a cast on his wrist. It was covered with scribbles.

Carlin said, "What a shame," and started to steer Timmy away.

"Wait," said Dwayne. "C'mon. Let's run down to the Tasty Swirl in Auburn for an ice cream."

Timmy was all for that. "Ice cream!"

Dwayne grinned and nodded to him, but Carlin was made of sterner stuff. She pulled him away. "No, Tim. No ice cream."

He wasn't going down so easily. "Ice cream!"

Over her shoulder she said savagely, "Thanks a lot."

"He can come along."

"And choke to death in the dust? No thank you."

A big cheer rolled over them from the stands. All heads turned toward the field. The volume meant the home team had prevailed. In a few seconds people were streaming out of the bleachers.

"Looks like your boys lost," Carlin said. "Guess it's time to head back to Plattsmouth."

"Now that it's over, you should come and get some . . ."

"Stop! Do not say the i-c-e word again, I warn you!"

"Blondie . . ."

"Time for us to get home. And don't call me that."

"But sweetheart . . ."

"That either. I said we're going. Now scram!"

As the car rolled off, another word was thrown back at her. Timmy asked what it meant, and she said, "Pickles."

8

MRS. WIGGINS' GIFT

Sam Washington hated catfish. He liked to eat catfish just fine, the way his mother fried it with corn meal. It was the fish itself he could not stand, a thickly writhing muscle, twisty and slimy, with those hateful whiskers. When the other gandies discovered there were catfish in the creek, that was almost as good as a tavern. Cook was happy to fry them up, as long as they cleaned the fish themselves and didn't throw the guts near the camp.

But the catfish weren't the worst thing about fishing. It was the boredom. Those other boys could sit there with a hook in the water, their minds empty as a jar, for hours on end. Sam had an active mind. He liked to think about things. Complicated things, like poems, or railroads. Or the Underground Railroad! If Sam could do anything he wanted on this boring Sunday afternoon, he'd go back to Nebraska City, to that place called John Brown's Cave. The woman seemed surprised he had twenty-five cents for the entry, but after he paid, she got less hawk-eyed, leaving him alone to wander around. But he'd been too timid, in too much of a hurry. There was so much to see!

As he wandered aimlessly around the camp, he thought of asking Jerome. He wanted Jerome to see the place, and to be impressed with him for finding it. He found his quarry in the bunk car, flat on his back, eyes open, staring straight up.

"Hey, Jerome," he said.

"Hi Sam. What's up?" Jerome glanced his way, then went back to staring.

"Most everyone's gone fishing." He brightened up his voice, "Jerome, what if you and me got to Nebraska City somehow, to that museum of runaway slaves."

Jerome sighed. "If I could get to Nebraska City, don't you think I'd be on the train to Omaha?"

"Yeah, sure. Well, I'm just going for a walk then."

"Don't go snooping around that grain elevator."

"You're not my pa."

"That's right. So you go walk any damn place you want."

"I will at that."

Sam set his chin and hopped down the steps of the bunk car. He went up into the next one, fetched the poetry book from his locker, and took off down the road in the direction of the grain elevator.

Julian on Sunday was like a cemetery. The store was closed and the elevator quiet. It reminded him of Menifee, except, on a nice Sunday like this back home, there would be people out on porches. Going to church was one thing he never thought he'd miss, but now that it wasn't there, he did miss it. He missed a lot of things. His mother's cornbread, the rope swing in the yard, the racket of little brothers and sisters laughing and running around.

Sam felt righteous and remorseful at the same time. *Any damn place you want.* Jerome never cursed. It felt like a slap on his face. On purpose, Sam walked right past the grain elevator. There were a whole mess of buildings, most of them covered in that wavy metal that shined silver in the sun. The tallest ones had pipes coming out of the tops that led down to the shorter ones.

They had grain bins in Conway County, but he'd never been up close to one, and never paid them any mind. Today he paused extra-long in front of the office, and stared up at the tall tower behind it. He admired the way it soared fat and square into the sky to a place where the sides sloped in to a smaller part with a little peaked roof. Staring up made him dizzy. He sauntered on in the direction of the hog pens. They were down the road a ways, where the houses stopped and the town turned into country.

The fence came right up to the road. Sam leaned his arms on the rail, pretending to look at the pigs. From here, he could stare back at the grain elevator.

What had made him dizzy? It was like when you spun yourself around, but it was more than that. He remembered feeling something like that when he stared up at that tall church steeple in Conway. His grandma told him the feeling came from God's divine mystery. Divine mystery. That meant you couldn't figure it out.

The workings of the grain elevator may be mysterious, but everything had a purpose, one that somebody knew and had planned that way. Those pipes going across from one bin to another, they did something.

Sam looked down at the book in his hands. It occurred to him that the poems were like grain elevators. They were full of confusing things, but it wasn't a divine mystery. Poems and the grain elevators could be figured out. There was only one poem he knew completely. He said the first verse to himself:

> Loveliest of trees, the cherry now
> Is hung with bloom along the bough,
> And stands about the woodland ride,
> Wearing white for Eastertide.

The book had been a gift from his teacher. Kind-faced Mrs. Wiggins with her coppery skin and fringe of gray curls like a halo. In her English class just two months ago—it seemed like years—she wrote out the whole thing in looping script across the blackboard. She explained that the tree covered with blossoms is like the white dresses girls wear for Easter Sunday. He had pondered this. And then, on his way home from school, he saw them. The line of trees on the Morrilton Road, all covered in white blossoms. They looked like girls' dresses. Then he remembered, next week is Easter! The enormity of it nearly knocked him in the ditch. He knew all poetry was written by old white men a long time ago, and he marveled that one of them would know that in Menifee, Arkansas, girls wear white dresses for Easter and trees would heap up with white at the same time.

His mind migrated to other images of Menifee. The kettle used for making soap. The privy with the wasp nest in the roof. He remembered the day when his father said he had to talk to him about something important. They went out to the porch for privacy, and Sam was scared somebody had a terrible disease. But no. His father told him that Mister Mopac was hiring, and that he, being the oldest, was obliged to work to help his family. If anyone asked, he was to say he was eighteen. He was going to make more money than he ever dreamed of, but he was not to spend it on liquor and never to gamble. He had to bring the money home.

It all happened so fast. That very night the grandparents came over for a ham dinner like it was Christmas, and afterwards Mrs. Wiggins stopped by the house. With tears in her eyes, she pressed the small book in his hands, told him he was special, he had "a light that glowed from within," and squeezed his cheek.

In the morning the truck showed up, its back end full of rough-looking boys. Next thing he knew he was bumping across Arkansas and Missouri in the back of that truck, with a ragged carpetbag with his clothes, a battered baseball mitt, and two books, the other one being the Bible his mother gave him.

He was glad it was small and slim, because the Bible was heavy. He didn't open the book until one of those boring hours on the hard bench inside of that truck. It had a green cover, with the A SHROPSHIRE LAD in gold letters. He sounded it out, but had no idea what it meant. Below that it said A.E. HOUSMAN. Inside it was poems, and the second one was "Loveliest of trees," the one from English class! His first reaction was joy, his second, panic. If the other boys saw he was reading poetry, they might start in on him, and mess up the book or toss it out the back. He folded it shut, and moved it slyly down into his carpetbag. He didn't know if he was special, but he did know he was different, with a knack for drawing the attention of bullies ever since he first started school. The poems were his friends. He promised himself to learn every one and go tell Mrs. Wiggins when he was back home.

But the friends were not easy to know. He read them over and over, making small progress here and there. He read the one with rue, and then the one where someone got shot in the first line. Sam just had to figure out who. There was so much of the world to know, so many things that a person would never ever think of and made you wonder how somebody ever did.

"Looking for something, boy?"

Sam looked up, startled, to find a tall man on the road. He had thick glasses and bushy eyebrows.

"I was looking at the pigs."

"You wouldn't be thinking of taking one off to that camp of yours?"

Sam considered the size of the pigs, and doubted he could lift one. "No, sir. I was just reading." Sam held up the book.

"Good," said the man. "Learning to read is good. Just go find someone else's fence to lean on while you're doing it."

Sam walked quickly away, wondering if that man really thought he was going to jump in that mud pen, grab a pig, and wrestle it all the way back to camp. Somebody should write a book about the strange ways of white folks.

He came back by the elevator, and, since no one was around, he indulged himself to walk across the long slab of the scale. When he stomped, he felt the slab move, just a tiny bit. He stomped again, working more response out of the slab, a little vibration. Maybe if he flapped his arms and pushed off in this direction. Now that direction. He was getting the huge plate to waver. He could feel it through his shoes.

Sam froze. He was not alone.

9

THE LEG AND THE LIFT

Sam slowly lowered his arms, and turned to see the elevator man staring at him from the office door. His little boy burst out from behind the man, and began jumping and waving his arms in imitation of Sam.

Sam had a terrific urge to take off at a sprint and not look back. His mind raced, grasping for some explanation. "I came to see if you need help again!" he blurted.

"What?"

"Like before, when you had us move that rail car," he rushed on. "If you have need, is what I mean. I'm skinny but I'm strong."

"We try not to work on Sunday," the man said tersely, "if we can help it."

"Yes, sir," Sam said. "I do know about that. I read my Bible, yes sir." He tried smiling. A wide happy smile. "I'm going back to over there where I live."

Timmy said, "Why were you jumping?"

Sam looked from boy to father, forcing a laugh. "Oh, yeah, heh heh. Jerome said this was a scale, and I was just trying to see how . . ." Sam shook his head back and forth, trying to imitate the way the slab had moved.

Ron stared at him. "This scale won't tell what you weigh. Maybe Denton Henry over at the station, with the freight scale . . ."

"I just like to study things, learn how they work, that's all."

Ron stared at him, as if deciding something. Finally, he jerked his thumb over his shoulder and said, "Come around here."

Sam gulped and followed. Sam hadn't been whipped in a long time and not ever by anyone not named Mr. Washington. But if that's what it took for Jerome and Mr. Burdock never to find out about this episode, Sam was ready to pay that price.

Sam followed the man and boy to the main elevator building. The big opening went clear through to the other side. The man pointed to the wooden grate embedded in the concrete floor.

"The farmers," Ron said, "they truck in grain from the field. They dump it here."

"In the pit!" said Timmy.

"We call it the pit. Then we run it up the leg here to put it in bins." He was pointing to a square tin shaft running from floor to ceiling.

"You can't touch the leg," Timmy added. "It's bad."

"The leg?"

"We call it the leg, you know." Ron rapped his knuckles on the metal shaft. "This is the actual elevator inside the elevator, if you know what I mean."

Sam did not. Ron took a square cover off the front of the tin chimney. Inside there were wide shallow cups on a black rubber belt. Instinctively Sam reached out.

"No," Tim hollered, at the same time as his dad said, "Keep your hands back."

When they had all stepped back, Ron flipped a switch. An electric hum filled the air. As Sam stared, the cups began to climb up through the opening, at first slowly and then very fast, becoming a blur. It also got louder, and made a huge racket. Ron killed the switch. The noise abated. The cups slowed, and came to a stop.

"Dad!"

The daughter was standing in the opening. "I swear," she scolded, "you are going deaf working here. Mom says you have to come right now because Mr. Ferholtz wants to borrow the long ladder."

"It's behind the back shed, hanging on the . . ."

"Mom says you should come."

Ron turned to Sam. "You go on home now."

"But tell me what that thing is, where it goes."

"I just showed you, it's the leg. Now that's enough."

Sam couldn't help himself. "Yes sir. But just tell me where it goes."

Ron was already on his way. "Carlin, tell him where it goes. Then get home yourself, both of you."

"He's nice," Sam said politely.

She made a sarcastic noise, blowing air out of her cheeks. "Yeah, nice. What's that book?"

Carlin wore a blue dress with cornflowers. Her hair was tied back with a blue ribbon. She stood with her weight on one leg and her hand propped on her waist, a pose of impatience.

She made him nervous. "It's poems," Sam said.

"What poems?"

"Just poems." He tried to put the book in his pocket. "You were going to tell me where it goes, the, uh, the leg."

"It goes to the headhouse. Is it Robert Frost? He's my favorite, next to Shakespeare, of course."

"No."

"'Two roads diverged in a yellow wood,' you know that one?"

"No."

"Is that the only word you know?"

"No," he said firmly, and didn't understand why she laughed. Then he got it and laughed too. Shyly, he said, "Your dad was telling me how the grain went down in that hole, and then up the leg, but what happens next?"

"If I tell you, will you show me your book?"

Carlin explained that when grain was dumped in the pit, the grain ran down into those cups. They scooped it up and took it all the way to the top of the elevator, where it poured out through a spout, and you could make it go different places. The room up at the top, that was called the headhouse.

But didn't the leg run out of cups? No. She showed him another tin chimney—the down leg—a few feet behind the first one. Sam nodded in appreciation: it was a continuous loop.

"What's this thing?" Sam pointed to a small steel platform just above the floor, held in place on two sides between thick boards. A rope rose from a hole in the floor and disappeared into the darkness above.

"The man lift," Timmy said, eager to be a part of this game.

"What's it for?"

Carlin rolled her eyes, making it clear this was the most boring subject imaginable. "We call it the man lift because that over there is the truck lift. Where does the man lift go, Timmy?"

"To the dompa ding!" he said joyfully.

"The what?" said Sam.

"The dompa ding!"

"That's what dad calls the spout up top," Carlin explained. "Mostly when he's mad because it doesn't work right. I think it's German."

Sam didn't follow. He was mesmerized by the lift itself. He leaned over its steel platform and gazed upwards into the dark shaft. A dim light seeped down from the very top. It made him dizzy to think of going all the way up there, and at the same time it thrilled him. There were no sides on the platform. You could fall right off. But when you got up there, the view from the windows!

"Is the motor up top?"

"No, you pull yourself up, using the rope," Carlin said.

Sam whistled. He had climbed ropes a few times in his life, and it was not easy. And that was just to a roof beam. This was high as fifty roof beams. "Your dad must be mighty strong."

"It's counter-weighted," Carlin said. "You know, like window sashes." She pointed to a five-gallon bucket beside the lift. "When Frank goes up, he has to put that bucket of sand on with him, or he'd go up too fast, because he's so skinny. The counter-weight is heavier than he is. Here look."

Carlin was not without a flair for the dramatic. She skipped onto the platform. "This releases the brake," she said, her foot hovering above a steel pedal. "Now watch." She stepped on it and the platform made a sudden lunge upwards that threw her off balance and clanged loudly when it stopped just as fast. The platform was now six inches higher off the ground, and Carlin was giggling wildly.

Sam breathed. For the briefest of seconds, he thought she'd made a terrible mistake and was about to go hurtling up the shaft. And she would have, if not for the safety bolt, as she showed him. It was a railroad spike that went into a hole in the wood and caught the lift. You had to pull that out to let the lift go up.

"Here, help me put it back down. Well, come on, both of you."

Timmy jumped right on. Sam was hesitant.

"Come on," she said.

When they were all squeezed onto the little platform, Carlin put one hand on Tim's shoulder and one on Sam's arm to steady herself, and stepped on the pedal again. The platform eased back down to rest on the floor. She took her foot off the pedal and the brake clutched fast.

"Simple as that," she said, stepping off the lift and walking out to the sunshiny doorway. Sam was right behind her. Safety bolt or not, her actions seemed reckless to him.

Now it was his turn. The book. He took it out from his pocket, and turned to the poem with "rue" in it. He explained how Cook said it was sauce, but spelled a different way.

"It's French for street," she said confidently. "Rue means street." Carlin took the book and squinted at the page. She read out loud:

> With rue my heart is laden
> For golden friends I had
> For many a rose-lipt maiden
> And many a light-foot lad.

"See?" she said. "He went to visit friends, and they live in France, on a rue. But he also misses home. "In France, before the French revolution, there was this king. They called him the Sun King because he had so much gold. So when it says 'golden friends' that means it's French people. French girls wear red lipstick, so they're 'rose-lipped.'"

"So the guy in the poem, he was visiting French people, in France?"

"Yeah, but they're all dead now. That's in the second verse."

She paged through, stopping here and there to read. They were both staring into the pages, they didn't notice the black truck until it came skidding into the elevator. The red-head swung out of the cab like he was in a hurry.

"Hi Frank," Timmy called out.

"Hi squirt." But he didn't look at the boy, only at Sam. "The rail gang lives up thataway," he said, jerking his thumb.

"Frank!" Carlin scolded.

"Can I ask him what business he's got here?"

"Can I ask you what's yours?"

At that moment Ron returned, deep in conversation with another man. They stopped abruptly, their gazes traveling from Sam to Carlin to Frank, to Frank's truck, back to Sam.

"Hi Ronnie," Frank said, cheerily. "We were cleaning up at the farm, and we had a few bushels sitting around. So we tossed it in the truck here, thought we'd let you have it. About twenty-five bushels, I'd say. I went ahead and weighed it at the office." He held up a scale ticket.

Ron turned to the other man. "George, the ladder's hanging on the back side of that shed. Carlin can help you put it on your truck."

"Oh, I can get it myself," said the man. He seemed reluctant to leave, but with everyone staring at him, finally, with one last curious look at Sam, he turned to go get the ladder.

Frank opened the truck's tail gate, and grain cascaded through the floor, sending up a scrim of dust. The leg roared to life, and there was more dust, and noise. The next thing Sam knew the truck was tilting up into the air. The front wheels were on some kind of platform with cables going up to the ceiling. He'd had no idea what Carlin meant when she said "truck lift" earlier. Now he knew. This place got more amazing by the moment.

When the truck was empty and lowered, its back end closed up and all the machines turned off, Frank turned on Sam. "Why are you still here?"

Ron said to Frank, "Come in tomorrow and we'll settle up."

"I would," Frank said apologetically, "But pa asked me to pick up some things for him in Neb City with the money."

"It's Sunday," Ron said, annoyed. "Stores are closed. Go around to the office. Carlin, your mother needs help at home. Timmy, you too. And you"—to Sam—"you've gotten enough education for one day."

As he walked back toward the camp, Sam was grinning. That's what Mrs. Wiggins used to say to him. Afternoons after the other kids all left, and he was still hanging around asking questions. She'd say, "Go on, get out of here. You've had enough educating for today." *Rue* was a word for street. That was good to know. He'd tell Cook, but Cook wasn't likely to be impressed by what some girl had to say about French things.

Some of the boys were playing catch with some kind of hard green fruit that fell off the trees here. They'd lost the baseballs hitting them into the thorny bushes along the ravine. Jerome was sitting on a stump, writing a letter. When he looked up, his eyes were kindly. He said he hoped Sam had a nice walk, and didn't ask where. "And, you know, I would like to see that museum some time. I hear our next camp is Nebraska City. Maybe we can see it then." After they talked a little more, Sam asked if Jerome could spare a piece of paper and the use of a pencil. One that still had some eraser on it, if he had one.

Jerome handed him a sheet. "You going to write your own poem?"

"Naw," said Sam. "I could never write like that." He saw that Jerome had one of the old *Saturday Evening Posts* to write on, and he went and got one for himself. He set to work, not on a poem but on a sketch. Gradually the image took shape, and he was proud of it, even if it didn't look exactly right.

He showed it to Jerome. "See, the truck comes in here—that's supposed to be a truck—and the grain goes down here and the leg carries it all the way up here." He did not say how he knew this, and Jerome did not ask.

"What I can't figure out," Sam said, "is how they know how much of it they have?"

Jerome gave him a long look before answering. "They weigh it in the truck," Jerome said finally. "They weigh the truck with the grain in it before they dump it out. Then they weigh the truck again after they dump out the load."

Sam stared at him.

Jerome chuckled. "It's the same way with bricks. You ever get offered a job as a scale operator, you take it. That's a nice job."

"What happened that you had to leave the brick works, Jerome?"

"Nothing I want to talk about. Just a word of advice. Any dealings you have with a white man, make sure there's plenty of witnesses around, because if it's just your word against his . . ."

He didn't bother to finish the sentence.

Sam nodded soberly.

"Which is why," Jerome went on, getting to the point that had been hanging in the air, "I hate to see you going over there by yourself. Nothing good can come of that, Sam."

Sam nodded again, but he was thinking that something good already had come of it. He knew the French word for street, and he knew about the elevator inside the elevator. He didn't know what good either of those things did him, but he liked knowing them.

F I E L D   N O T E S

Site: Conway County, AR. Prefabricated home, pale green. Dining room adjacent
to large kitchen with double range and two refrigerators. Cauldrons of collards and
beans bubble on the stove. Tinfoil-covered trays of beef brisket, pork ribs, and mac
and cheese line the counters and tables.
Subject: Richard Oliphant, Regional Maintenance Supervisor, Union Pacific Railroad.

Oliphant—salt and pepper hair and beard, crinkled face. Lean and rangy, he
moves easily as he greets me at my rental car and leads me up the three steps to his
home. He introduces Janella, and directs me to a seat at the dining room table. He is
elaborately polite, with the look and manner of someone permanently bemused by
life.

Engulfed in sumptuous aromas, heavy with the meaty smell of barbeque. Thank
him for agreeing to see me, and repeat what I'd said on the phone. That I'm working
on this project about gandy dancers, that Bartles at UP head office in Omaha
recommended him as the best source. Bartles also thought he might know an old
man, who, if he was still alive, would be one of the last gandy dancers from the
pre-mechanized age.

He waits me out patiently, nodding to each point. "To clarify," he says. "I worked
in Missouri quite a bit, "but not Nebraska. I don't know about the Omaha-line
upgrade in particular, but I'll be happy to help you where I can."

But first I have to eat. Janella runs a catering business out of her kitchen, hence the
big pots and serious equipment. She must have a big event this day, because all the
food is piping hot and ready to go. I should be brief—small portions, eat quickly.

Janella has other ideas. "Eat more!" she commands. She has tight cornrows, an
Arkansas State T-shirt, and a no-nonsense manner. "Grown man like you can surely
eat more than that. You like cornbread? Put you some cornbread on there."

She hovers while I wolf down the impossibly great food. She fends off my
compliments, saying, "Surely you can do better than that. Here's some more ribs."

Oliphant, smiling, nods to her encouragements. Between bites, I ask him about the
work itself, the ballast, the ties, the spikes. He answers with easy familiarity, animated
and enthusiastic. From a high shelf, he brings down a fifty-year-old safety manual
with illustrations of the gandies standing shoulder to shoulder with their lining bars.
"See, that's how it was done. I don't know if you've seen the mechanized rail work.
The robots do the same things, but there's no art to it. The names of them machines that

replaced gandy dancers?—the tamper, the setter, the spiker—all those names come straight from the gandies. Stole the names outright. It's like they were trying to wipe out what those men did, as if it never happened."

"The machines don't have a song caller," I say, trying to keep up.

"What's even worse, in my mind," he continues, "is the very name 'gandy dancer.' You know that name is homespun, come up through the men themselves. But the railroads, they put it out that the name came from a Gandy Manufacturing in Chicago, the name stamped on all their tools. But there ain't no such name stamped on the tools because there is no Gandy Manufacturing Company, and never was." He stares at me with a big smile, but his eyes blaze. "You know what they say, 'Control the name, control the man.' That's why so many Black folks are walking around today named Williams and Johnson and Washington. Same principle."

"That's why I'm here. I want to give them their own names, present their stories, their work, as best I can. I've learned so much from you already. And I'm looking forward to meeting Mr. Wicks."

There is a long pause, during which I am encouraged to get some more beans and greens.

"You know," he says, at last. "There is some people out there who care about these things, and they would have a problem with you being here."

"A problem?"

"Well," he says, smiling. "There's some might say, you come down here, you talk to us, you take our stories, then you go back up north, and you write it all down, and you make all the money. And we're sitting here, not seeing any of the money, not getting credit for our stories."

"But there is no money!"

My outburst hangs in the air. I take a breath. "Sorry. What I mean is, what I'm trying to do, I want to give the gandies their due, celebrate their lives. I don't see money coming from this."

His tone remains gentle. "You said on the phone you're writing a book. Now, what I know of books is, books are information. And you know what they say, 'information is money.'"

"I'm not trying to swindle anyone. Really."

"You seem like a nice enough man," he goes on. "But you need to understand. There's a long history of that kind of thing down here. Long history."

"I'm researching a real story, Black people and white people, a coming together of two cultures, a ball game!"

"And you're sure it's your story to tell?"

I feel stymied. I want to explain, to justify. If I only tell one side, the white people's story, isn't that so much worse? A step backwards toward silence and marginalization of the past? But I hold my tongue. I'm not a blockhead. Theft. Appropriation. Those are real things. But I'm not like that. At least I thought I wasn't. My mind spins through a dozen responses. Finally, I shrug. "If not me, who, Mr. Oliphant? I'm trying to patch together a real story that's been buried for years and years. Black people and white people—both sides. Isn't that a good thing?"

"Depends on how you tell it," he says with a friendly nod.

"I'll tell it as best I can," I reply. "And, and, in the unlikely case that there is some money, I will donate to a good cause, like the United Negro College Fund." I cringe at that last bit. I sound like a pompous ass.

"That's fine, that's fine," he says, laughing. "You do that. But you could also think about, you know, priming the pump along the way." He rubs his thumb and forefinger together, and rises from his chair. "I guess we'd better get on over. Wicks is expecting us, and he doesn't have a phone."

10

OTHER LINGUISTIC LARCENIES

Sam Washington's curiosity about grain elevators may have been unusual, but it could hardly be called either misplaced or trivial. It was an invention that changed the course of the nation. Thomas Edison. The Wright brothers. In the parade of American inventors, it is shameful that Joseph Dart has languished in obscurity.

Inventions are new answers to old problems. This problem began as one of geography. In the first half of the 19th Century, it was apparent that the American heartland boasted some of the best farmland the world had ever seen. Cereal grains practically raised themselves, and in great abundance. The problem was getting all that product to market. The endless ridges of Appalachia separated the new farm country from the population centers.

The opening of the Erie Canal in 1825 was one answer. It provided a narrow but reliable siphon through which the goods of the West could be sucked through to the east. Inland Buffalo became the most important port in the country, but also a bottleneck, as every bit of freight had to be offloaded from the Great Lakes steam freighters and put onto the longboats that plied the canal. For grain, that meant canvas sacks. Filling, carrying, and weighing sacks was slow and tedious. There was also the lengthy business of tracking and labeling. The many varieties of grain came from a great number of farms, some more renowned than others. A baker named Bednik in Brooklyn has a contract with a farmer named Fenwick in Fort Wayne. The baker's label boasts, "Bednik's Baked Fresh with Fenwick's Flour!"

Such a system may be appropriate for French wine, where *terroir* is linked to label. But a hungry egalitarian nation had neither time nor appetite for such specialization.

Along came Joseph Dart, Buffalo merchant. In 1842, Dart created a system for moving grain by use of a set of small buckets attached to a continuous belt run by steam power. The first such devices were designed to be lowered into the holds of ships to extract grain in bulk. Dart soon discovered the advantages of gravity. If you used a version of the same device to elevate the grain into tall storage bins, voilà, it was ready at hand to be poured out into cart or boat or rail car.

Skeptics famously claimed there was no cheaper way to elevate grain than on the back of an Irishman. They also said the public would not stand for the grain of fifty farms to be mixed willy-nilly into a common pile. They were wrong on both counts. Mr. Dart's novelty device soon became Mr. Dart's ten elevators with a combined storage capacity of more than half a million bushels. And it turned out that capitalist America loved homogenization. It put the "general" in General Mills (formerly Minneapolis Milling). The common piles became commodities, suitable for standard contracts, trading and speculation at the Chicago Board of Trade, which opened its doors in 1848, just six years after Dart's invention.

Why, in our history classes, does Joseph Dart not stand alongside Eli Whitney and George Washington Carver? The answer can be traced to the 1853 World's Fair in New York City. It was there, at the famed Crystal Palace, that Elisha Otis stunned and amazed onlookers when he ordered the cutting—by axe!—of the only rope holding him on his platform high above the gallery floor. The platform lurched, falling scant inches before his new emergency safety system locked his elevator in place. It was a gaudy event, and it put the word "elevator" on everyone's lips, referring not to a grain handling system, but to a crate for carrying passengers safely up and down multi-storied buildings.

A mere ten years after it was adopted in the grain realm, "elevator" was wrested away by a people-moving device. It is surprising that the grain gizmos never found their own distinctive name. Borrowed terms—mill, plant, silo—never gained widespread currency and were, each in its own way, inaccurate. Thus, these monumental and quintessentially American expressions of vernacular architecture surrendered their name to tiny claustrophobic cages inside that other American icon, the skyscraper. Yet another example of the urban trumping the rural.

The first grain elevators were built of wood; fires were a frequent hazard. Designers moved on to brick, and then to concrete. The iconic American grain elevator, the so-called "Cathedral of the Plains," features long ranks of conjoined white silos whose smooth white sides are constituted of poured reinforced concrete.

However, some smaller grain elevators, rural ones especially, were still made of wood well into the 20th Century. By the time Ron Littman bought the land along the Missouri Pacific in Julian, concrete was the norm. It was also expensive, and Ron had carpentry skills. He chose wood. Building methods had become more sophisticated over the years, and in this, the final stage of their evolution, wooden elevators were sheathed in corrugated galvanized tin, a covering that was shiny and beautiful, and helped protect them from rot and fire.

The grain elevator that captivated Sam Washington's eye, the grain elevator crafted by hand with artisanal skill, was eminently worthy of admiration. It was the last of a dying breed, a clipper ship of grain elevators—tall, graceful, with clean lines and an exterior that glimmered silver in the sun. The main tower, fat and square, soared ninety feet into the air. Near the top, three of the four sides sloped steeply inward. The headhouse, with windows fore and aft and a peaked roof of its own, looked serenely out across town and farm.

Locals, being locals, did not notice such things. It was just Littman Grain to them. But to a sharp-eyed boy from another part of the country, a boy with a budding aesthetic sense and a keen urge to know how things worked, it appeared a marvel.

In the coming days, Sam did not heed Jerome's warnings. Or perhaps it was simply that he could not help himself. Evenings after the gandies hung up their tools, he often wandered down the track. On a couple occasions, when his timing was right, Ron tossed him a shovel and he helped to feed grain to a machine or clean up a spill. He got paid for it, too, and Sam was proud of that.

Coincidentally, while the first grain elevators were rising over the skyline of Buffalo in the 1840s, at the other end of New York state, men were playing a new game. It was something like cricket, but different. The game was about to be codified into something called "base-ball," which, in its early, pure incarnation, was fast-pitch, thrown underhand.

11

AN OVERSIZED WHITE BALL

"Did you hear the news?" Jack Scarborough bellowed, bursting into Marchon Mercantile. The screen door caromed behind him, bouncing against the frame.

"What news?" called Dave from behind the counter.

Jack paused dramatically, stealing a quick look around. He'd hoped for a big crowd. It was almost dinner hour, after all, a time when folks stopped by the store. Hank Four Eyes was there, along with his wife. The best sight was Carlin Littman, right next to the pop machine, wearing yellow shorts and bobby socks. Minding Timmy, as usual.

"Hi short stuff," he said cheerily to Timmy. "Hiya Skipper."

"Not you, too," Carlin said. "Bad enough he calls me that."

"What news?" Dave repeated.

Jack looked around, making sure all eyes were on him. "Lincoln Thomas Ford is coming to Julian. We're going to play on the Fourth of July!"

Dave let out a long whistle. Hank Benkleman actually smiled.

"Lincoln Thomas Ford," said Carlin. "Here?"

Jack savored the moment. "Lincoln Thomas Ford. Here."

It was one of those three-word names that was always said in triplicate, like William Jennings Bryan or Robert Louis Stevenson. And it was, arguably, a name more recognized in this state than the Scottish poet or Nebraska's three-time presidential candidate. Only in this case it did not refer to a single person but was, as the good grammarian Sister Mary Michael could point out, a triple appositive noun: Thomas being the surname of the owner of a car dealership, Ford the make of car sold there, and Lincoln the state capital and the home of Harold Thomas, his dealership, and his state champion fast-pitch team.

"Lincoln Thomas Ford," Dave said slowly. "Why would they come here?"

"Why wouldn't they come here?" Jack said, bristling. "We're undefeated, they're undefeated. It's city versus country on the Fourth of July—an All-American story. We'll get reporters here from Omaha or even Kansas City. LTF has fifty-car convoys that follow them to road games. We should have more bleachers."

Dave laughed. "We'd better get to work. That's less than three weeks."

Jack couldn't help it. His voice swelled with pride. "And when we beat those boys, then Julian, little tiny Julian, will be state champs, and no doubt about it. Won't that be something?"

"Can I get your autograph now?" Carlin asked.

Jack grinned and held out his hand, miming a pen and a flourish. "You want one too?" he said to Timmy, beaming.

"Technically," said Hank Four Eyes, "they'd still be champions, since the teams are in different leagues. Technically, this is an exhibition game."

"And you're a near-sighted pig farmer, technically," Jack said. "And we still let you ump the games. I can't wait to see the *Lincoln Star* and the *Omaha World-Herald* on July fifth."

"Lincoln Thomas Ford!" Timmy shouted.

"You got that right, buddy!" said Jack. But he was disappointed how quickly things became routine again. Dave took to wiping the glass countertops. Hank Benkleman went to poking around among the white-paper-wrapped meat in the freezer, asking Dave if there was any chuck roast.

Jack asked Carlin if she'd seen the games. A weak opening—he knew she had—but it was something to say. He nodded, and tried to keep smiling while she rattled off the feats of his brothers. She'd driven to Tecumseh with her parents, and had seen Ernie go two for three, pinning three ribbies on the Indians. And, of course, Dave had the big walk-off home run on Saturday.

"Did you see the top of that inning?" Jack asked. "The play at the plate?"

"I think I was off chasing Timmy," she said. "I even missed Dave's home run. There was some Plattsmouth boys wanting me to go riding—including Dwayne Buchalter. He broke his arm, if you're wondering where he was."

"That right?" said, Jack, feigning indifference. "So the Plattsmouth catcher, he flared it into right, with Bobby Buchalter on second. Ken Mills scooped it up, and Big Bobby, he comes barreling around third, not even thinking to hold there . . ." Jack saw Carlin's eyes wander, and he felt deflated. He gamely finished the story. Ken's frozen rope to the plate. Fat Bobby plowing into him like a bull. Tumbling ass over elbow, sure he'd dropped it. Coming up with the ball in his hand.

The beautiful blue eyes showed concern. "Were you hurt?"

"Three broken ribs is all." He fished a dime out of his pocket and fed it to his old friend, the pop machine. He pulled open the top, revealing the lines of bottles upright in rows. He grabbed a Dr Pepper by its cap and slid it to the compartment where he could pull it up and out.

He looked up and found her grinning at him. "What?"

"Why do you always get Dr Pepper?"

Jack shrugged, looking at the bottle. "I don't know. I guess I just like it better than RC or Coke."

Carlin gave him a knowing smile. "Nothing to do with this big Dr Pepper sign right on the front of the machine, huh?"

Jack looked at it and shrugged again, smiling stupidly. It had the face of a clock with the numbers ten, two and four on it.

"This clock has three hands," she said, pointing. "Why three?"

"Because it's a cartoon?"

"And why are the hands set at ten, two, and four o'clock?" She pointed each number in a showgirl way, bringing chuckles from Dave and Hank.

"Sic him, Skipper," Dave called out.

She blushed prettily and went on. "And what time is it right now?" She pantomimed looking at a watch, bending over and sticking out her behind in a Hollywood pose. "Why, what do you know, it's just coming up on four o'clock."

Two men were entering the store. One glanced over and looked away. The other, a younger man with a triangle scar on his cheek, held his stare on her and smiled.

The burble of laughter died instantly, and Carlin was mortified. She was posing ridiculously, pointing like a glamour girl. She straightened right up. But Carlin had moxie. She would act as if strangers came into the store all the time, rather than have everyone stand there staring at them, showing what a hick place this was.

"Ten, two, and four o'clock," she repeated, just a little self-consciously. "Think they might be saying you should have a Dr Pepper at those times? And maybe you're being persuaded to have one?"

The man with the scar spoke up. "It does make a man thirs-ty," he said, plainly looking at Carlin.

Timmy giggled loudly, anticipating the general reaction to the funny-talking man. Instead, there was scandalized silence. Jack had a small panic, wondering if Carlin had been insulted, and if so, what to do about it.

"Ma'am," the man went on, "if you ever were so-inclined to that kind of work, I believe you could make a lot of money for the Dr Pepper com-pa-ny. They should put you on the radio, and I believe that to be the truth."

He was still talking to her, but not so swank. He called her "Ma'am." But still. Jack looked to his brother, hoping he would take control of the situation.

Dave did just that, with three words. "Mr. Jerome Wallace."

Just the man's name. He was calling him out. Golly. Jack turned to see how the dark man would react. He reacted by being nudged to the side as the older man stepped in front of him.

"Mr. Manager," said Jerome, matching Dave's even tone.

And just like that the tension went away—or at least went underground.

Dave snapped his fingers. "I believe we have a letter with your name on it." He made quick strides to the post office cubicle.

"Thank you," Jerome said, taking the letter.

"My pleasure," said Dave.

Jerome turned to leave, but Ice was in no hurry. He strolled up one side of the store, and down the other, looking at everything, with the townspeople's heads on swivels following him. He nodded and smiled and said "Excuse me" as he came by each person, and came to a stop in front of Dave, who was back at the counter. "While I am favorably inclined toward Dr Pepper," he said, nodding in Carlin's direction, "I am wondering where the beer is stored, in case I am desirous of a more adult beverage."

"Sorry. Dry town."

Ice nodded. "I've heard that. But some places, they have an understanding, or an arrangement . . ." He casually pushed a five-dollar bill across the counter.

Dave raised his hands in a big search-me gesture and said, "I am sorry," with a smile on his face.

Ice wasn't done. From the notions wall he picked up a ball of twine, and a roll of electrical tape. Ice held them up together and said, "Baseballs."

"Baseballs," Dave repeated.

"That's right. Or a home-made fac-sim-o-lee. A trick I learned in . . . in a place I went to for a while. The trick is to wind them real tight."

Jerome said quietly, "We have real baseballs. Let's go."

"*Had* real baseballs," Ice said, performing for the crowd, "until Delran and Big Larry hit them into the ditch and lost them. Now them boys are playing with rocks rolled up in socks. And those green things that rip up your hand."

"Hedge apples," said Carlin. "Their real name is Osage Orange. But most people call them hedge apples."

"Thank you." Ice bowed his head to Carlin. "Hedge apples."

"Then they'll just lose these ones too," Jerome said. It was a stupid conversation to be having at all, and he especially did not want to be having it in front of these people.

"At least they'll have something." Ice was enjoying himself. He turned to Dave and added, "Delran is one of those boys who can hit a ball farther than he can chase after it, you know what I mean?"

"Maybe he could find it better if he was playing with one of these." A large white ball rolled slowly across the counter, stopping between the tape and twine.

Ice grinned and picked it up, fat as a grapefruit. "Oh," Ice said, considering it. "I've seen these. This is what girls play with."

That brought Jack crashing into the conversation. "If that's all you've seen, you haven't seen much," he said, getting red in the face. "And you've sure never seen the Julian Hornets. Fast-pitch is every bit the sport that overhand is, and everyone with any sense knows it. Or else why would the Chicago Cubs come all the way here to scout my brother? And if not for the war, Ernie would be playing for them right now."

"We're sorry for your loss," Jerome put in.

"Oh, he didn't get killed." Jack faltered, but regained his momentum. "He's our center fielder, as a matter of fact. And we've got maybe the best team in the whole state. We already beat Nebraska City, Auburn, Plattsmouth and Tecumseh—that's four county seats—and Lincoln Thomas Ford is coming here to play us on Fourth of July. Lincoln Thomas Ford."

"Never met the man," Ice said approvingly. "But now, if we were playing baseball . . ." He rolled the ball back across the glass to Dave.

"It is baseball." Hank Benkleman had been standing by the meat freezer the whole time, simmering. "It is baseball," Hank repeated. "It is, technically, fast-pitch underhand baseball with a regulation three point eight inch diameter ball, as opposed to a regulation three inch ball."

"Right," said Ice. "And they call that a . . ."

"Squeeze that ball," Hank commanded. "Does that feel one bit soft to you? Feels pretty hard, doesn't it?"

Dave rolled the ball back to Ice, who tossed it in the air and caught it in one hand.

"And when you go bowling," Jack chimed in, "and you bowl a sixteen-pound ball, and your friend there a twenty-pounder, it's still bowling, ain't it?"

"There is a game called slow-pitch," Hank went on, ignoring Jack's attempt to help. "That game—also played with a three point eight inch ball—is sometimes called 'softball,' not"—he poked the air for emphasis—"on account of the ball itself, but for how it is delivered to the plate."

Ice beamed at him. "I am en-light-ened." He rolled the ball back across the counter to Dave. "Back in Arkansas, we'd still call that a softball. If y'all ever want to learn baseball, give a holler down to the camp and we'll show you."

For a moment nobody said a thing. Hank Benkleman frowned furiously. Carlin was trying not to giggle. Only Dave seemed unaffected; in fact, he seemed to be enjoying himself. It was to him that Jerome spoke. "If you could just tote this up, we'll be on our way. I've got a letter to read."

"Sure thing." The seconds crawled by while the register chirped and pinged. Jerome took the paper sack and hustled Ice toward the door, saying thank you as he went.

"You are welcome." As they were leaving Dave added, "Good day, Mr. Wallace, and Mr. . . . ."

"Ice," said Ice, turning back and smiling. "They call me Ice."

"And Mr. Ice. Good luck with those baseballs. And if you lose them, you might want to try this." The fat white ball sailed across the store. Ice caught it, and smiled at it like it was a pumpkin waiting to be a pie. He was about to toss it back, but Dave held up his hands. "Keep it," he said. "Might come in handy."

Ice started an elaborate reply which he did not finish, for being yanked out the door by his sleeve.

12

FAIR AND SQUARE

Carlin burst into a fit of giggles, and couldn't stop. The others stared at her. "What?" she said, looking around, catching her breath. "Wasn't he hilarious? 'Holler down to the camp if y'all want to learn.' I love how he talks."

Jack said, "He acted kind of superior, if you ask me."

"Him?" She tucked her thumbs into her belt in a hillbilly stance and said, in malicious imitation, "'That's four county seats we put a whuppin' on.' They must think we are the biggest hicks . . ."

"Who cares what they think." Jack felt his face grow hot while Carlin and Dave laughed.

"Jack makes a good point," said Hank, coming forward. "A very good point."

"And what, exactly, is your point?" Dave asked, staring at him across the counter.

"You shouldn't have given him that ball."

Dave made a frown of concentration, trying to make sense of that.

"Those people," Hank went on. "You don't want to encourage them to steal."

"And here I thought I was encouraging them to try fast-pitch," Dave said. "Fancy that."

Hank put up his hands, as if holding a chest protector. "I have nothing against them. I just believe that if we all stick to our own race then everyone is better off. If you were to ask me, yes, I would say I disapprove of you being overly nice to them, Mr. Scarborough. It just gives them airs."

"That all?" Dave asked curtly, referring either to the conversation or the merchandise, or both.

"I'm only saying it gives them ideas, that's all," Hank insisted. "I think your brother is with me on this."

Jack's eyebrows shot up. Now he was on Benkleman's side—against Dave and Carlin? It wasn't the side of the street he ever wanted to walk.

"Hank," Dave said, his voice tight and formal. "I don't know what ideas you think I am giving them. If it's that they can come in here and expect to be treated like anybody else, then that's an idea I'm all right with."

"I just meant . . ."

"It's like this," Dave cut in. "If you think colored folks are beneath you, then you don't give them a square deal. That way is always liable to backfire. Like when we go to Auburn and Hauptman is umping, and he gives Chick a strike zone the size of a stamp. He may think he's helping his team, but what it really does is just make all of us fighting mad, and we go on to lick them anyway."

"Yeah," Jack added, trying to get back across the street. "Or like that game at Talmage . . ."

"How dare you!" Hank broke in, leaning over the counter towards Dave. "You know I call 'em like I see 'em, that I would never make a bad call to anyone's benefit!"

"That was kind of my point, Hank," Dave said.

Hank was on his high horse now. "The baseball diamond is sacred ground. You have two competing teams, fighting for advantage. If the umpire is not absolutely fair, the game is ruined!"

"And that's how it should be off the field, too."

"You know I never cheat, Dave Scarborough!"

Hank was shaking a fist in the air just like he did when someone argued a call. Next thing he'd be trying to throw Dave out of the game. Only here at Marchon's, Jack thought smugly, Dave was in charge and Hank Four Eyes was the one about to be tossed.

Dave controlled himself. "How about this, Hank. Let's say we did have a game with those boys from the Mopac crew. And let's say you were the ump. Do you call the game honest and fair?"

"There'd never be such a game."

"But let's say, just for fun, that there was one. Coloreds against whites. Do you call the game honest and fair?"

"Of course I do!"

"Fair and square. You never give us a break because you don't want them putting on airs? Getting ideas?"

"I call them all fair and square, no matter who's playing!"

Dave took a step back, smiling broadly. "Then I don't believe we have any disagreement after all. Thank you, Hank. You have restored my faith in human nature and the great state of Nebraska."

Hank sputtered, coughed, flapped his chin a bit. He barked to his wife to hurry up, though she was just standing there, and marched ahead of her out the door.

Jack watched Carlin stare at his brother in admiration. She said, "You sure turned that around on him."

Dave laughed. "Kill 'em with kindness, ain't that what they say, Skipper?"

Jack could only agree. "He wasn't expecting the knuckler, that's for sure."

Next to Hank Benkleman, the person most aggravated by the scene at the store was Jerome. As he walked out the door, he had nothing to say to the preening gandy with his new prize ball. And he had a letter, a precious letter from Lucy. So he held his tongue and just told Ice to go back to the camp, adding, trying his own malicious imitation, "Don't you go pro-vok-ing any locals along the way."

Mistaking mockery for homage, Ice grinned. "Look at that," he said, pointing to the Marchon's store window. On a scattering of straw, against the backdrop of a cardboard school house, stood a row of four trophies, with another one sitting in front of the others. It had a figure of Winged Victory on top. Ice leaned over and read out loud: "Julian Hornets, CHAMPION, 1949, Country League Southeast." On each side was a bat, arranged heads down in the shape of a V, with the labels turned to gaze up at the trophies. Just inside the bottom of the V sat a 3.8-inch diameter baseball. The bats and the ball were covered in autographs. Ice gave a low whistle and turned to Jerome. "I've put down rail in some backwater places, but this, this is the old-timey-est . . ."

Behind the trophies, in the center of the store, it looked like there was a heated exchange going on. Ice tried to see in, but Jerome shoved him down the walk, saying, "Go!"

"I'm going. Don't push me."

Jerome waited for Ice to go on ahead, and followed down the street. Ice clutched his paper bag in one hand and tossed the ball in the air and caught it with the other. At the corner, Ice turned right, towards camp. When Jerome got to the same spot, he paused, pulling the letter carefully from his pocket. He did not want distraction from anyone. He looked back up the street, but the know-it-all farmer and his wife were coming out the store. So he walked straight ahead, crossing the side track and continuing on to where the station sat next to the main line. It was a small peaked building with the word JULIAN in a neat rectangular sign. It seemed empty, but he did not try the door, walking instead around back, to where the raised wooden platform fronted the gleaming tracks.

He sat down, his back resting against the building, the late afternoon sun in his face. He shaded his eyes with his hand. On the other side of the tracks was a tree-rimmed ravine. Beyond that, the field of young corn climbed at a gradual rate up to where a farm sat with its house and barn and fences, seeming to peer across at the town.

He delayed taking up the letter a little longer. Once he was done reading it, he wouldn't have the letter to look forward to. The smell of manure drifted across the valley. The faint breeze rustled the corn leaves, making them shimmer. Something unsettling. A vibration. A sound. A sudden growing roar. Before his mind could process it, a whoosh of wind rustled his sleeves just as the blur of the passenger train filled his vision, roared its five cars past him, and was gone. The Eagle. He never got used to it. The fast trains on the line made his heart race. He shuddered and pushed away thoughts of how easily such a train could be the end of him. How his life depended on the savvy of the foreman to post slow orders and get the crew off the rails on time every single day. He would not tell Lucy this part, how easily death could happen. This led him to thinking that same Eagle, the one that roared by, will be in Omaha in a little more than an hour.

He sighed and pulled the letter from the front pocket of his shirt. He very carefully broke the seal and pulled the three pages out and flattened them on his lap, and commenced reading.

"What are you doing there, boy?"

Jerome looked up. The man held a leather mail pouch in his hands. Jerome stared at him unsmiling until the man looked away. Then he got slowly to his feet. He was a full head taller than the station agent. "Wallace. First name Jerome. If you want to call me something, either of those will do. Mr. Henry, is that right?"

"Well, hell. Okay then, Wallace." Denton took an iron rod with a hook on the end, and used it to lift the mail pouch and hang it on another rod that was planted in the gravel alongside the track. They stared as it swayed gently.

"Reading a letter from my wife."

"What?"

"You asked what I am doing here." Jerome held up the pages. "My wife. Omaha."

"Ah. Well, hell. That's a good thing there, letter from your wife." Denton looked around uncomfortably, and pursed his lips. "It's only that, um, this is, properly speaking, private property. Authorized personnel. I mean, to me it doesn't matter, but, strictly speaking . . ."

He trailed off, as if hoping Jerome would get the point. Jerome did get it, and he held the man in his gaze. He did not dislike this Denton Henry. The station agent was like so many of these country people who thought they were supposed to be racist, but wasn't very good at it, having so little experience with anybody to practice on.

"Private property..." Denton said again. There was something almost pleading in his tone. He motioned with his hand to indicate the right-of-way along the tracks.

"That right?" Jerome pretended surprise. "Whose property is this?"

"The Missouri Pacific Railroad Company."

"And you work for Mr. Mopac?"

"I am the station agent for Julian, yes."

Jerome nodded slowly. "You see all that shiny new rail there? I laid that rail last week. For my many sins, it seems that I am working for Mr. Mopac too."

Denton waved a scolding finger at him. "Well. Yes. But . . ."

"And I believe I have a right to inspect my work."

Denton took a step backward. He put a hand on the tall iron rod where the mail pouch hung. "Well, just so you don't mess with the U.S. Mail. That's a federal offense, Wallace."

"Passenger trains," Jerome said, "to Omaha. They never stop here, do they?"

"They don't even slow down," said Denton. "As you may have noticed."

"But freight trains do."

"Just the local, not the Red Ball."

"Has it ever been the case, Mr. Henry, where folks got rides on freight trains?"

The station agent laughed. "Like hobos, you mean? We had a lot of hobos riding the boxcars in the thirties. Don't see many nowadays. Now and then."

"I meant like Mopac employees dead-heading to Omaha lawful."

"Ha, ha, that's good. Where would they ride, in the caboose?"

Jerome shrugged. "Do they?"

"Naw, that's never done. Not that I ever heard of anyway."

"Thank you, Mr. Henry."

"Now, back before the Eagle, when the Sunflower was still running on these lines—that was the name of the passenger train when it was steam—the Sunflower stopped here. By golly, she sure did . . ."

Fifteen minutes later, Jerome was in a sour mood as he walked slowly back to camp. For a man that started out trying to run him off, Denton Henry turned out to be real sociable. Too sociable. Once he started in talking about the old days, there was no stopping him. About how Julian before the war was a flag stop. A flag stop, did he know what that was? Well, a flag stop meant they had a red flag at the station, and if they hung it out on a wire, then that meant they had a passenger, and the train would stop. If no red flag, the train just went right on through. Of course in those days Julian had a water tank, and sometimes they had to stop anyway for that. It was called the Sunflower on account of it came up from Kansas, which is the Sunflower State. When the Eagles came on line, they dropped all the flag stops. Now you had to drive to Auburn or Neb City. There's progress for you.

By the end of it, Jerome was sneaking peeks at Lucy's letter while the man talked, and the glimpses he saw were disturbing. Walking back to the camp, Jerome wondered how he could get hold of that red-headed kid with the black truck. Five dollars for a ride to Nebraska City from a wise guy no longer seemed ridiculous, if it got him to the train station and home.

FIELD NOTES

Site: Conway County, AR. Small frame house, one story, with concrete porch. A square of blue vinyl covers one window. Trees and bushes close in from three sides. Weeds grow around an engine block in the yard. Three kitchen chairs are positioned on the porch.

Subject: Sawyer Wicks, retired track maintenance worker

Mr. Wicks waits on the porch, holding onto the back of a chair. He is small and dapper in a bright blue cable knit sweater. In his eighties. His face has a series of dark jagged lines creasing one cheek, and the side of his neck.

"There he is," Oliphant sings out.

"Just like I said I would," says Wicks.

I do not know how these men normally interact, but I don't think it is like this. My presence makes the scene awkward. We take our places at the chairs on the porch, and I start by asking about his name.

"I go by Tip. Got that name in the army, after I tipped over a big truck." He laughs shortly. "I was in the Engineer Dump Truck Company. I built roads all over France, and in the South Pacific.

"Was it a segregated unit?"

"Not so segregated as when we got back home, that's for sure."

He got on with the Mopac after the war, and worked for them for more than forty years. He worked on what he calls an "extra gang," called in for derailments, floods, major upgrades and new lines. Lived in bunk cars at the job sites. "Eight men to a car, with coal heaters and coal stoves to make food on."

"So you had a cook?"

He laughs. "Nah, we had to cook it all ourselves."

"What was the job like?"

"It was a hard job." He pauses, remembering. "How hard it was depended a lot on the foreman. Some of them foremen, they was terrible." A little laugh. "A man get hurt pretty bad, and the foreman take him into the doctor, and they'd be in cahoots. The doctor say, 'This man ain't hurt too bad, just give him some lighter work a few days.' And you're back on the crew that same day with regular work."

"Did that happen to you?"

"Sure did, lot of times. The worst was the derailment in Monroe, LA. The tank cars were full of acid, and they was burning high and hot all night. But the railroad was in a big hurry to get the trains running again, so they had us in there with cranes unpiling the cars while they was still burning. And then, wham, a big explosion, heard twenty miles away. Bunch of people killed. I myself got all this." He turns his head, lifting his face to show the scars. "That was the one time I got to go to the doctor and stay awhile. Three skin grafts."

After more general talk, I work my way up to the question I came to Arkansas to ask. "Mr. Wicks. Did you ever work up north? Is there any chance your crew worked to replace rail on the Kansas City – Omaha main line in the early 1950s?"

The old man cocks his head, as if thinking, as if remembering.

I can't help adding, "I've got good information the crew was from around here, from Conway County."

The old man shakes his head. "I was never north of Joplin, myself. Can't feature a crew from here going way up there."

Trying not to show disappointment, I bring the interview to a close. We are almost at Oliphant's car when I stop, turn, run back to Wicks, yanking out my wallet as I go. There are some twenties, some ones. In an awkward half-handshake, I press them into his palm, saying, stupidly, "An honorarium. Thanks again."

As I trot back to the car, I get a thumbs-up from Richard Oliphant. As we're heading back to his place and for my rental car, I say I'd like to send him a check to thank him for his help.

Oliphant waves it off. "I'm just glad to be able to say it. To have you thinking about it when you write that book."

"I will. And Please tell Janella thanks again for that great food."

"She's gonna say you didn't eat hardly a thing."

13

OVER THE FERRIS WHEEL

Ice was the center of attention when Jerome walked back from the station. He was banging the new ball off the side of the bunk car, catching it and banging it again, still talking a blue streak, making fun of the white boys for playing such a sissy game with such a sissy ball. George and Delran and Big Larry were all laughing along.

Jerome was in no mood for Ice's flapping jaw. He'd made the folks at the store nervous, talking to their girl, making fun of their game. Only bad things could come of that. Jerome stood beside Ice, and when the ball came caromed of the car, he snared it.

"Hey! That's mine." Ice tried to twist his arm to get it back, and Jerome threw him to the ground with more violence than was necessary.

Ice popped back to his feet, a wild look in his eye. "You've been asking for this!" He grabbed the bat out of Delran's hands and came up swinging. Jerome stepped back, then bull-rushed in behind a second swing and grabbed Ice in a bear hug, pinning his arms to his sides. Ice tried to twist out, cursing and threatening, but Jerome held him fast.

Jerome spoke into his ear, "You ever heard of Ace Hill?"

Ice was caught off guard. He stopped squirming to spit back, "No, I ain't never heard of no Ace Hill."

"That just shows your damned ignorance." He threw Ice to the ground a second time, ripping the bat from his hands along the way.

"Ace is a legend, and you never even heard of him, you stupid Arkansan." Jerome held the bat in one hand and picked up the fat ball. "Ace Hill throws this thing like Satchel Paige throws a baseball. He can throw a strike from between his legs. He can throw one behind his back. He can strike you out from second base."

He had their attention now.

"Who'd this Ace Hill play for?" It came from George, the fact man.

"He's played for a lot of teams," Jerome said. "In 1944, when he was just fifteen years old, he pitched the first Negro team to a Nebraska state championship in fast-pitch, Armour Meat Packing. In 1946 he almost did it again, playing for Omaha Brick and Tile."

"Isn't that where you were?" George said.

"You said 'almost'?" Sam put in. "What happened?"

"In '47 and '48 they went on the road," Jerome continued. "Barnstorming. Ace played with Bob Rodgers, Tank Hamilton, Popeye Smith, those boys. Rodgers was the player-manager. He could hit the ball a mile. They were called the Sioux City Ghosts, on account they were run by a big guy out of Sioux City Iowa, named Fischer. Fatty Fischer, we called him. Fischer, he'd go ahead and set up the games, and these nine boys, nine colored boys, they would play seven nights a week, taking on teams in country towns. Often as not, they'd have to sleep in their cars because there was no place in town would take them. But at every game stands were full to bursting with people come out to see their home boys play the colored team in fast-pitch. Play and lose to the colored team, as it turned out."

George would not let it go. "Were you on that team?"

Jerome bounced the softball several times on the end of the bat. "This one time, it was the Fourth of July, and the Ghosts were playing in a town called Beatrice, not too far from here. There was a carnival set up just past the outfield fence, with rides and a midway and all that, including a Ferris Wheel. They got Ferris Wheels in Arkansas?"

"We got Ferris Wheels," said Big Larry.

"Ace Hill, he goes to the mound in the first inning, and this giant of a white boy comes up to bat. The boy is big as a house. So of course Bob Rodgers and Ace do some clowning about how big he is, pretending they're afraid of him and all that. It was part of the show. Every time the boy settled in with his bat, Rodgers, who was catching, sneaks up behind the boy, acting like he was going to pull his pants down, but he is too scared. The crowd was almost wetting themselves."

Jerome smiled to himself. "So then, the boy finally settles in, and Ace deals him a pitch. And damn if that boy didn't get a hold of it. Those carnival rides were out there past the fence, and we watched that ball go up and up. . . . And over the Ferris Wheel!"

"Over the Ferris Wheel?" said Delran.

"Clean over it. Everybody said they'd never seen a ball hit so far on the entire planet. So Ace and Rodgers played it up, and the crowd went wild. They almost stomped the bleachers to bits from laughing and clapping and all that."

Jerome paused, and looked at the rapt faces of the men circled around him. Cook, standing behind, gave him a wink.

"Three innings later," Jerome went on, "the big boy comes up to bat again. Ace had struck out every other one of them, and here was their Babe Ruth a second time. Instead of clowning with the boy, this time Rodgers sends the whole team to sit on the bench. All except Ace. Then Rodgers puts on his mask and gets behind the plate. The crowd, they thought this was real funny, and the big white boy, he was smiling. They thought Rodgers was conceding another home run, that there wasn't any point even to have fielders out there. So Ace went into his wind-up, and . . ." Jerome paused, smiling, looking around.

"What happened?" cried the boys. "What happened?"

"Struck him out on three pitches."

A cheer went up from the gandies. "Who won?" George asked.

"The Ghosts never lost when they played serious. And after two innings of horsing around, they always played serious." Jerome took a step back from the boys. He tossed the ball in the air and with a sudden savage swing sent it a mile in the air in the direction of the grain elevator. If there had been a Ferris Wheel on the gravel road, the ball would have gone over it.

"Hey, that's my ball!" shouted Ice.

"You'd better go get it then," said Jerome," handing him the bat and walking away.

F I E L D   N O T E S

Site: Omaha, NE. Neat brick bungalow. Living room with plush couch and matching easy chairs. Iced tea. Doilies on side tables. An alcove adjacent, walls covered with awards, commendations, and news clippings. A small forest of trophies sits on a desk. Subject: Clarence "Ace" Hill, fast-pitch softball legend.

Sitting on the couch, sipping iced tea, Hill holds hands with his wife. He is clean shaven, bald, not big, but powerfully built. She looks on proudly as he regales me with stories of the barnstorming days, the championships, and teammates, like the legendary Bob Rodgers. The stories roll from him, delightful, and he clearly delights in telling them, especially the one about the Ferris Wheel.

I am a rapt listener for nearly an hour. The towns, the travels, the games. I thank him and get ready to leave. I reach for my wallet, which I have remembered to stuff with bills. At the door, he reaches out a hand to shake, and I take it, my hand empty. I can't do it. It feels wrong. He is so kind and welcoming, his hospitality so genuine . . . a wad of bills, proffered at parting, would be an insult.

Or would it have been? Afterward, I will often wonder if I made the right call.

14

BRAVE IN SEASON

The central problem, as Sam saw it, was did the boy shoot himself, or did he shoot someone else? He liked the first line so much: "Shot? So quick, so clean an ending?" It seemed he was shooting someone who deserved it. But the second verse sounded like he killed himself:

> Oh you had forethought, you could reason,
> And saw your road and where it led,
> And early wise and brave in season
> Put the pistol to your head.

But why would he do that? Sam looked up from the branch he was sitting on, a fat limb coming out of the tree practically horizontal, the way he liked it.

He'd taken to coming down here evenings after dinner. Lately, since Jerome got them all fired up over Ace Hill, the guys weren't so keen on fishing. They got up a game every night, and they wanted him to play. The more people out in the field, the less likely they'd lose the softball on a big hit or a crazy foul ball. No one wanted to be the one who lost the new prize.

Delran was learning to pitch underhand. The motion came natural to him, and he had ferocious power from day one. The problem was that the ball was as likely to hit a train car or a tree as it was to come near the strike zone. Sam wasn't a baby, but he didn't like to be standing anywhere near home plate, not until Delran got better aim. Yesterday Del had plunked Big Larry so hard they got in a fight about it. Sam would just as soon make himself scarce.

He looked back at the poem, frowning in frustration. Then out over the creek. It wasn't much of a creek. Sam had come to like it, though. He'd never learned to swim, and was afraid of water. But this creek wasn't more than ten feet wide in most places, and hardly came up to your knees. It snaked around at the bottom of the ravine, with trees overarching from along both sides.

"Good view from up there?"

Sam yelped, windmilling his arms to regain balance, and looked around.

Carlin plucked the book off the ground. "London. Grant Richards Ltd. Publishers. 1915." She looked up. "I could get you a newer one. By a different writer, I mean. I never heard of this one. I asked Sister Mary Michael, though. She said he's Victorian."

Sam jumped out of the tree. "I'll just take it," he said, reaching out.

She wasn't finished with it. She pushed her glasses up on her head. "Can you read Roman numerals?"

"Yes, ma'am."

"Don't call me ma'am. I'm Carlin, remember?" She put out her hand. Not the one that held his book.

Sam felt strange shaking her hand. He had no idea what she was doing out there by the creek, and it made him very nervous.

"This is Timmy's favorite place to play," she said, as the boy came crashing through the underbrush. "Timmy, can you say hello to Sam?"

He must have been watching, because he marched forward and put out his hand to shake.

Carlin said, "I can read Roman numerals. We did that in sixth grade, I think." She opened the book. "I'm going to quiz you. What's XLIII?"

"Forty-three." He held out his hand for her to give it back.

"Just hold your horses a minute," she said. "I'm not going to steal your book. I have a whole shelf of better ones at home. I've got a book by Robert Frost, the greatest living poet. And by William Shakespeare, the greatest poet of all time."

Sam wasn't worried she would steal his book. He was worried she would ask him another Roman numeral. He'd almost said eighteen. Using only this book he had painstakingly taught himself the numbers, but the system got fuzzy after LXIII, because that was the last poem.

"Where's the one with rues in it?"

"Closer to the end." Sam translated in his head. "Fifty-four."

"Timmy," she called. "Stay out of the water. I don't want you all muddy today, you hear?"

The boy had scooted down the bank, and was squatting at the edge of the stream.

She turned back to the book. "'With rue my heart is laden, for golden friends I had.' Aren't you glad you know it's a street?"

"I was wondering about forty-four."

She sat down with her legs over the edge of the ravine. Sam, hunched over, explained the problems he was having about who shot who.

"You were up in a tree when we brought the apples," she said. "Is that something you do, sit in trees?"

Sam shrugged. "I don't know. I always liked to be in high places generally. There's a place in the Ozarks, this tower they put on a mountain. You can see four states."

"You been up there?"

"No," Sam admitted. "I saw it on the highway sign."

"High places," Carlin said. They turned to look at the top of the grain elevator soaring above the trees. "I bet you'd like the view from up there. I could ask dad to let you go up the man lift." In the same breath she called out, "What is it, a turtle?"

"Bullfrog," Timmy called back. "A big one. Come and see, Carly."

"Don't hurt it." To Sam, she rolled her eyes and said, "I could have worked at Hested's Five and Dime in Nebraska City this summer. They needed a girl for the soda counter, and I know Dorine, the manager. She said I'd make tons of money on tips. But mom said she needed me for . . ." She nodded in Tim's direction, and had another thought. "Hey Timmy. Say the poem. The one about the swing. Go on, say it."

A boy's monotone: "How do you like to go up in a swing, up in the air so blue."

"Keep going. 'I do think it's the pleasantest thing . . .'"

A pause. An annoyed whine, "Carrr-ly."

"'That ever a child can do.' He knows it. He's just shy."

She returned to the book in her hands. "I think he kills himself to keep from doing something awful," she pronounced. "Like he was a spy for the Germans or something, and he was about to give away some secret. And he kills himself to keep from giving it up. I saw a movie like that."

"It's about spies?"

She squinted at the page. "Whatever it was, it would 'wrong your brothers,' and he doesn't want to do that. Would you sit down? You look like you're going to jump me hovering like that."

Sam did not want to look like he was going to jump her. Carefully, he sat down. She held up the book for them both to see.

"So, in the end, he's dead, but he was brave. That is so sad!"

"Yeah," Sam said, "but he did the right thing. Different times make you have to do different things, like in summer pull weeds and in winter chop wood. You have to be brave in season."

She looked at him and smiled. "That was smart."

Sam looked away, grinning foolishly.

Carlin flipped to the cover. "What's A.E. stand for?"

"Alfred Edward."

"Huh. He must not like those names much. PD Klyber goes by PD because he can't stand 'Palmerton.' Are all of them sad?"

"Mostly they are," he said, "but there's one about drinking beer."

"Which one?"

And so they settled down again over the book, and together they went

to Ludlow fair,
And left my neck-tie God knows where,
And carried half-way home, or near,
Pints and quarts of Ludlow beer.

15

COOK HAD A PLAN

My Dearest Jerome,

I didn't think it would be so hard, having you away like this. I know I'm supposed to be your "Rock of Gibraltar" & I try to be strong, but sometimes I feel more like sand than rock. Nights after I put the boy to bed are the worst. I miss your arms around me & I have to cry. I'm not supposed to tell you this. But I don't have anyone to tell. I tried to talk to Vera, but she only listens to her Malcolm & she thinks you could get free passes to come home any time you want to. That foreman must be an evil man. Mr. Prosser says if we don't make a payment on the loan they're going to put a lien on our house. I don't even know if the furnace got fixed right. How can you tell in the summer? That would be funny except it's too scary to think about November upcoming. At least you'll be home then—won't you? JJ misses you a lot. I swear he's gotten so much bigger just since you left, and he's talking a blue streak. I'm sorry to be "Mrs. Gloom & Doom." I told myself I was not going to burden you like this, but it helps to write it out. I will go now & try to write later with better thoughts.

Much love & kisses from your own

Lucy

Jerome let the pages slip from his fingers, onto the floor of the bunk car. He had the money. He had to get it to Omaha. He had to see Lucy. He couldn't just walk away from this job, but it was becoming a question of how much job security he was willing to risk. He needed a plan.

Cook had a plan, and it was going beautifully. He saved out some of the apples. He baked the pie when the crew was out on the job, so no one would track the aroma to his mess car. And while it was still warm he carried it down to the house across from the grain silo.

Mrs. Littman said he didn't have to go through all that trouble. He said it was no trouble at all, and a pleasure, in fact. He told her he made it with a special secret ingredient, and he hoped her family liked it. He did not tell her his secret ingredient was rum, although, being Catholic, they would not mind.

Once in the door, pie accepted and sitting primly on the counter, having received its due compliments, it was then just a matter of letting it slip how much he hated to miss Mass on Sundays. Right on cue, the missus said she would talk to her husband about giving him a ride. He protested mildly, and was eventually persuaded to let her inquire.

Cook's motivation came from equal parts piety and snobbery. He took the Sunday obligation seriously, and found comfort in the familiar ritual. At the same time, it was important to him for the rail gang to realize he was not one of them. He was no Arkansas sharecropper, grandson of slaves. Unlike them, he traveled easily among the higher levels of society. He was Armond Lavalier, gentleman.

16

COMBUSTIBLE. VULNERABLE. EXPENDABLE

Like Sam Washington, Ernest Scarborough did not care much for water. But until the war he never had a problem with buckets. Buckets terrified him now. But a man couldn't say that. Couldn't say he was scared of a bucket. That would make him crazy. Ernie sat in the rocker chair in the upstairs bedroom of the farm house, humiliated. It wasn't too often he got to work with Jack, and even more rare that Dave could get away from the store.

Ernie lived alone on the Camp Creek farm. The Scarborough brothers had one sister, Lucine, who lived with her husband and their kids just up the hill. The four siblings got together some Sundays and most holidays, but Lucine came to Camp Creek every day. Since the war, she'd been Ernie's companion and caretaker. He ate most of his meals with her family.

Today his bull had trampled the fence, and he had livestock running off every which way, along the road and down by the creek, a big mess. Ernie took the dog and went after Sampson, who could be a danger to people who didn't know better. In the meantime, Lucine rang up Dave at the store, then called the home place. Their parents were out, but Jack was home. He and Dave were there inside of fifteen minutes. And also Evan Carpenter, whose wife must have overheard it on the party line. With five of them it only took an hour to get the animals contained and the fence repaired.

Lucine went back to her place. The brothers and Evan sat awhile on the porch, trading stories and laughing about the great Camp Creek Round-up, as they were already calling it. They all, except for the minister, had bottles of Falstaff. Dave and Jack went on to tell the story of the two gandies who came in to Marchon's, how one of them was making fun of fast pitch, how Dave gave a ball to them, and how Hank Four Eyes got bent out of shape after they left.

"We should play them a game," Jack said, laughing. "Just to make old Four Eyes live up to his word."

"That would be good," said Evan, nodding.

"I was just kidding," Jack said. "I didn't mean a real game. They didn't hardly know what a ball is. A game would be . . . ludicrous. We wouldn't want to embarrass 'em. Right, Dave?"

Dave shrugged. "I heard talk like that a few years ago when that barn-storming team came to Nebraska City. I believe it was the city boys who got embarrassed."

"Aw, no," Jack said. "I mean, it's not the same. They had Ace Hill and all. Those guys were professionals! This is just a bunch of Mopac spikers."

"Gandy dancers," said Dave. "It's a poetical name. I don't know, I think hitting spikes all day might be pretty good kind of batting practice." He trapped his bottle between his boots and mimed taking a swing at it.

Ernie laughed. He was glad his brothers had something exciting to talk about, and glad the minister was there too. He himself wasn't very good at small talk, never had been. Probably why he never got married. He did love the way his brothers could laugh. They'd always been better at that too. He gripped the wooden arms of the rocking chair and smiled a tight smile.

"I see them railroad men on Sundays," Evan said, "sitting around that camp with nothing to do. I should go down there, offer them a service."

Ernie was glad his brothers hadn't left him alone with the minister. Evan was a good man. A fine man. But he was so deadly earnest that it wore a man down. When he was just back from the war and beginning to have his spells, the minister would show up at the house very regular to talk with him or pray with him, whatever he needed. Ernie was of a secular disposition, as some folks are, and felt self-conscious about praying out loud. At his worst moments, what Ernie needed most was to be left alone.

"And I was bragging on you, Ernie," Jack had said, going back to the more lively topic. "When that fellow tried to make fast-pitch into a joke, I told him how the scout came all the way from Chicago. You were a hitting machine back then."

Ernie nodded, smiling. "I hardly remember that now. I guess I was."

"I remember it plain as day," Jack said. "I remember thinking I'd give my left arm to be able to hit a ball like that. Hell, I still would." He made a slicing movement with his hand, and they all laughed again.

Ernie was feeling pretty good. But the next minute, Jack jumped off the porch, saying, "Oh, before I forget. Dad's grinder is on the fritz again. He told me to get some ground corn while I'm out here. Just a few buckets." He reached into the back of his pick-up and came up with four of them rattling in his hands, four tin buckets.

The terror hit Ernie just that fast, and it was all he could do to mumble he was sorry and go in the house and head upstairs where he always went. They stayed a little while, and then he heard their trucks leaving. He knew Dave would stop by Lucine's to let her know, and she'd be over to look in on him in a while. It was another spell. It would pass. He felt weak and stupid. The war was long over. But he could do nothing else when the terror possessed him.

Ernie sat in the rocking chair where he always sat, trying to breathe, trying to push down the feeling that he was about to vomit. Seasickness, that's what it felt like. He turned his sight from the glinting field of early corn outside of his bedroom window, and he focused on the white-painted wrought iron bed frame. It curled around and then curled around again. He tried to stop thinking.

But Ernie couldn't stop thinking. Was he really that good before the war? He knew he had been, and sometimes even now there were games when the ball looked the size of a full moon, and he went four for four at the plate. But other days he was just average and some days he could not go out there at all. On those days center field felt too open and exposed, too much like the deck of a carrier. The terror hit him and he had to come back to this room with its ceiling slanted on one side, its rocking chair, its curly iron headboard.

His thoughts drifted back to before the war, to that time when he was twelve and Dave was fifteen and they were farming the bottomland, and Dave said he would swim the river on a bet. Ernie had thought it was a joke. Nobody swam in the Missouri, not since the Army Corps of Engineers had dredged it into a deep, fast-moving channel forty years ago.

He still didn't believe it when they all piled into pick-up trucks and drove half a mile down to the bank. It was summer, sure, but not a drought summer like the one before. The Big Muddy never looked so big or so muddy as it did that day. It swirled in brown eddies, moving so fast that if you threw a stick in you could not pick your way along the shore quickly enough to keep up with it. Eldon Strunk was there, egging him on, and so was Ed Schmitz. Eldon and Ed got into an argument about whether the tumbledown cabin on the other side was in Iowa or Missouri. The state line was somewhere over there. Dave gave them a big smile, stripped down to his shorts and said, "We'll find out when you pick me up over there. Cause I sure as hell ain't swimming back." And he dove right into the damn river.

This was Ernie's first taste of the terror. He tried not to show it. The older boys must know what they're doing. It would be all right. But it wasn't all right. Dave was moving downriver a lot faster than he was moving across it, and it looked like he wasn't making progress.

They lost sight of Dave, already far downstream. The boys scrambled into the truck and peeled out for the Brownville bridge seven miles south. The older boys tried to be jokey, but Ernie wasn't fooled. As he straddled the four-on-the-floor gearshift in between Ed and Eldon, he knew they were scared. What had Dave been thinking? Nobody swam the river. They crossed on the Brownville bridge, high and narrow, and the highway dropped down onto the table-flat bottomland. They took the first left off the highway, trying to get to the river bank. The Missouri meandered across a flat grid of fields, as regular as fence posts. The dead-end roads seemed surprised to be interrupted by a brace of cottonwoods, and a turn-around at the riverbank. As the pick-up zigzagged across the grid searching out the river, Ernie wondered what he was going to say to Ma. And what on earth would he say to little Jack?

After two hours without a sight of Dave, they skidded into Watson, Missouri, intent on getting more men to help search. Ed and Elton burst into the tavern, with Ernie on their heels. And there, sitting on a barstool, was shoeless Dave Scarborough, wearing a dirty cook's apron for propriety's sake, sipping on the fourth or fifth beer the locals had bought for him. Seeing them, Dave's first words were a mock-dignified, "Boys, I do believe this is not Iowa."

Ernie, fighting to hold back tears, had never been so in awe of his brother, and had never wanted so much to kill him.

It might seem strange that a boy who thought he'd watched his brother drown would end up in the United States Navy. But the truth was that by the time the war started the memory had receded into the haze of fraternal hagiography. Dave had joined the Navy before him. Ernie didn't think too much before following suit. He was operating on some vague notion that they would serve together. He pictured them walking side by side in their smart uniforms down the streets of some exotic port city, ready to try out whatever beer they brewed in that fine country.

He never expected to be on the shakedown cruise of the aircraft carrier U.S.S. Fairmount Bay. They gave him a certificate, said it was some kind of great honor to be what they called a plankholder, a member of the ship's first crew. He never pictured himself on what they called a Baby Flattop—and that was the nicest name they had for them—steaming across the Pacific toward Pearl Harbor and the Japanese.

He was assigned to the galley and the laundry. Day after day he tried to narrow his mind, keep it focused only on the piles of dirty uniforms, on opening the endless, oversized cans of navy beans. But he could never escape the confined feeling from the low bulkheads. The vibration underfoot was a constant reminder of the miles of water beneath him. Cold fear gripped his gut from the first moment he stepped onto the carrier, and it never left.

The more he learned about his boat, the more he hated it. Baby Flattop? Hell, there were three or four times as many people on the ship as lived in Julian, and it was bigger than the town too, if you unpiled all the decks and spread them out. The Fairy B's official designation was CVE 70, a Casablanca class escort carrier. Escort carrier. Officially, that meant not intended as a main strike force, but to accompany a convoy or task force, its planes at the ready for submarine hunting. But the black humor of sailors got the word around quickly. Escort class was Navy-speak for defenseless. Rushed into production, they had hulls as thin as those of merchant ships—nothing like the four-inch thick armor of the Essex class. They were floating tin cans, ducks on a pond, Kaiser coffins. Target practice for Zeroes.

Ernie was gripped by seasickness and wracked by fear. It was all he could do to maintain the sour, stoic face that everybody made fun of and that earned him the nickname "Nebraska." He smiled grimly, and said nothing, but sailors can smell fear.

"Hey, Nebraska, you know what CVE stands for?"

No.

"Combustible. Vulnerable. Expendable."

"Hey, Nebraska, what are the two types of boats?"

". . ."

"Submarines and targets."

Majuro had been taken a couple months earlier, and the Marshalls were generally quiet by the time the Fairmount Bay got there. She sent out some anti-sub patrols for a few days and returned to Pearl. Saipan was another story. Rumor said Saipan was dug in deep with Japs, and there was going to be a lot of naval and aerial bombardment to soften it up. The Japanese Imperial Navy must not have gotten that memo, as they lashed out at the task force with terrible fury, filling the sky with Zeroes. When the bomb exploded in the aft hanger deck, Ernie was thrown hard against the galley wall. It took him some moments, after struggling to his feet, to realize that he'd lost his hearing.

What happened next was a slow-motion nightmare, strangely unreal and garishly lucid. The smoke-filled corridors, the screams that they were taking on water, the tense word that the main pumps had failed. The fire brigade. Ernie ran around, trying to do what officers told him, all sounds distorted and gong-like in his head.

The ship was listing to port and settling heavy in the stern. Ernie was sure it was sinking. Someone ordered him above decks, near the head of a long line of men snaking down into the bowels of the ship. He didn't understand at first. What was going on? Then the first bucket came to him, and he automatically handed it on to the next man. What? What? They were going to bail out an aircraft carrier with buckets? The horror. The futility. Like trying to empty a grain elevator with thimbles. Bucket after bucket came to him, through him, and he could see the yeoman at the rail, emptying them. Only the thing was, there was nothing to empty. Each bucket had to come so far, down corridors and up ladders, that by the time they got to Ernie there was little more than a dribble.

Even here, the gallows humor of the seamen could not be suppressed. They joked up and down the line about the pints and quarts of seawater they were returning to the sea. An ensign ahead of him, Shackleton, put his cigarette into one as it went by, saying, "It ought to be good for something."

The Zero came in low and straight over the water. Before anyone could react, the machine gun fire was spraying everywhere and ricocheting off everything. For Ernie, standing half inside the hatch, three-quarters deaf, it was a gruesome sight, played out in slow motion. Bodies jumping like dolls when the bullets hit. Shackleton staring dumbly at his arm, still holding a bucket, falling slowly away from the rest of him. Others tumbled forward, their uniforms blossoming with dark splotches. And buckets bouncing. Buckets bouncing everywhere.

Numb and in shock, Ernie helped where he could, staunching wounds, carrying bodies. In the midst of it a small sick part of him envied the dead. They got out fast, at least. He faced a slow death by drowning. The ship was going down.

Only it didn't. The men of the Fairmount Bay somehow got the fires under control, and somehow got the flooding confined. The boat limped back to Pearl with fourteen dead, including Ensign Shackleton, and dozens wounded.

Ernie was not listed among the wounded, although he should have been. He did not get treatment at Pearl except for the Navy doc who hollered to him that he'd probably get most of his hearing back. They patched up the carrier in record time. When she steamed back to theater, Seaman First Class Ernest Scarborough was on board. He was different now, however. He had that look some men get, and the voice that hardly goes above a whisper. Ernie had shell-shock, and he had it bad. With it came shame and humiliation. The rest of the crew had come through the same horrors he had. They still made jokes about dying; they still wanted to get back out there and splash some Zeroes. Other men served bravely. Why was he a coward? Every day was spent in paralyzing fear, and every night was filled with flying limbs and dancing buckets.

The Fairmount Bay got a presidential citation, and Ernie Scarborough returned to Julian a hero. He went back to farming, and it was some time before people knew that things were not right with him. Nebraskans did not go looking for problems in a man. But one Sunday in church he started crying. He regularly got the shakes so bad he had to stop whatever he was doing, whether it was raking hay or playing center field. People blamed the war, not Ernie. Many said he should visit the VA hospital in Omaha. He never did, mainly because of his former fame. It was bad enough around Julian; he couldn't stand the thought of strangers saying, "Are you Ernie Scarborough the ballplayer?"

The one secret he kept was that the sight or sound of a bucket would bring it on every time. Regular old buckets. That part felt too shameful to admit to anyone, even Lucine. When an episode did come on, it was all Ernie could do to make it to the bedroom and sit and stare at the white painted curls in the steel frame of the bed.

17

THE OLD COUNTRY

America has always had an uneasy relationship with the French, starting with their aqueous language. German, on the other hand, is guttural but largely intelligible, a burly uncle to English. Bread is *Brot*. Beer, *Bier. Guten Morgen. Guten Abend.* Two world wars and Hollywood war movies added certain cruel words to the American idiom. *Achtung. Sieg Heil. Verboten.* Despite its half century of insanity, Germany retained strong ties in the new world, where grandchildren of immigrants embraced amnesia and hearkened back to the beer steins and cuckoo clocks of dear old Deutschland.

For the Littmans, dear old Deutschland was Schweidnitz, Lower Silesia. Ron's father, Alfred, had been six years old when his father, Anton, came to America in 1871, for reasons that can be answered generally or specifically.

Generally: religion, war, liberty.

Specifically: Catholicism, The War of Austrian Succession, and the policy of impressment practiced by the victorious Prussians.

A saber-wound convinced Anton Littman to give up his minor bureaucrat's position and walk his wife and four children to the gates of Breslau, beginning a long journey that ended at a homestead in southeastern Nebraska. They brought with them no wood-carved saint or Meissen plate. The saber had sliced the sentimentality from Anton's bones.

The language adapted better than its speakers. Life could be cruel on the prairie, but there was nothing quite like German for the harsh realities of the farm. I speak to my friend in English, the old saying goes. I speak French to my lover, and I speak Spanish to my God. And German? I speak German to my horse. All the best obscenities are Teutonic.

When Ron was fed up with Timmy's antics, he would snap at the boy with a linguistic descendant of *Passen Sie heraus auf!* (Watch out!) that came out as a single syllable with four consonant sounds: "Psowf!" There were other such phrases. Around the elevator, a pesky headhouse swivel spout might be a *verdammt Ding*, a damned thing which to Timmy's ears became the "dompa ding."

With Germans and with German, what you saw was what you got, and what you pronounced. The blocky Scandinavian tongues, and even the embroidered script of Bohemia (*Vítat až k má dvůr! Mít nějaký kapusta! Welcome to my farm! Have some cabbage!*) shared something of the frank Saxon heart of central Europe.

France, on the other hand, was untrustworthy, with a language both devious and pretentious. Suitable for lovers, if you count the disreputable kind, the roués and charlatans. What were you supposed to do with a tongue where half the syllables disappeared? Although France was more agricultural than Germany or England, there remained the ominous taint of the cosmopolitan and the risqué about her speech. Oooh la la! A slippery, elusive language, where if something was truly special, the highest praise was that you could not even say why, only that it had . . . *je ne sais quoi*.

Julian was founded by French immigrants. They were farm folk with family names such as Anville, Lavigne, Bernard, and Bazin. Naming the town was a point of contention for those first settlers. Some wanted to honor a village back home, but which one? Each family favored its own. They soon hit upon a more practical notion. A wealthy bachelor owned several farms near the new town site, a Monsieur Bahuaud. If this reclusive man would agree to move to the new town, its prospects would be brightened. They approached him with what would, in fundraising circles of later years, be termed a "naming opportunity."

The trouble was that no one of non-Gallic persuasion could pronounce his name. This might seem, at first glance, to be of little concern to folks from the country with cities named Grélières-les-Nieqes and Andrézioux-Bouthéon. But this was America the melting pot. For the town to prosper it would need to attract a somewhat broader range of white northern Europeans. It was thus decided that Monsieur Bahuaud would be honored in his Christian name, and thus was born the town of Julian.

For all that, the honoree was unimpressed. The miserly Bahuaud remained cloistered on a farm a mile outside of town. He would have reason to regret that. Thirty years later, in 1899, very old and rumored-to-be-rich, Julian Bahuaud was murdered and robbed. The perpetrators got away clean, and the crime went unsolved for years. Then things took a strange twist. In 1913 a man lay on his death bed in central Kansas, a victim of heat stroke. With what he thought were his last words he confessed to the murder of Julian Bahuaud. It turned out he'd been a bit hasty. The man recovered. He was taken back to Nebraska, tried, convicted, and lived out the rest of his years in the Nebraska State Penitentiary. There was something peculiar about Julian, all right, and maybe that included a knack for seeing justice done in the end.

Among the gandy dancers there was only one French surname, and that belonged to Mr. Armond Lavalier, who solved the problem of pronunciation by allowing himself to be called Cook. On Sunday, he got a ride to church with the Littmans.

If he had gotten a ride with one of the French families, he would have gone just a mile south of town to St. Bernard's. On this bright Sunday morning, traveling with the Littmans, Cook found himself riding three miles west, and then four north, on noisy gravel roads, to join the Germans at St. Joseph's. He sat in the rear seat, next to a fidgeting boy and a teenage girl. The boy was playing around, bothering his sister. "Psowf!" said the mister, reaching over the seat and swatting the boy.

St. Joseph's sat at the top of the hill, with only a few farm houses in sight. The wind was steady and strong, bracing on that Sunday morning.

"That is indeed a pretty view," Cook said, shading his eyes. The hills rolled off in all directions, ridge after ridge, crisp in the bright morning air. Directly in front of him, across the dirt road, a small cemetery unfolded downhill like an apron, displaying its decoration of headstones to the surrounding countryside. Some of the more prominent were inscribed with "Littman."

"Let's go in," said Ron. More cars had parked along the road. Parishioners walked by, trading awkward greetings with the Littmans, trying not to stare at the visitor.

Not a big church, but bigger than Cook expected miles from any town. It was red brick, quite tall, the right-hand steeple higher than the left. Each was topped by a sharp black spire that pierced the blue sky. The steeples were visible from three counties, or so he was informed by Carlin. Inside was even more impressive, with tall stained-glass windows that pictured full standing images of saints in rich dark hues that glowed in the morning light.

As Cook's eyes adjusted, Ron Littman whispered something. "Beg pardon?"

"I said," came the man's hushed voice, "Millie and the girl go to the choir loft. I'm down here with the boy; our pew is fourth from the front, on the right."

"If you don't mind," Cook whispered, "I'll find a place at the back." He blessed himself with holy water, and entered the empty back pew. He lowered the kneeler, and parked himself half-sitting, half kneeling, his knuckles interlaced.

From under lowered eyelids he watched the Mister and the boy go to their seats.

Soon organ music floated down from above, followed by a chorus of women's voices leading the opening hymn. Far more accomplished than he would have thought. He remembered the piano in their home and was sure it was Millie at the keyboard upstairs.

Cook narrowed focus to his hands clasped before him, ginger skin, tawny nailbeds, orange freckles. He wondered if people here made the kind of distinctions they made in other places. The kind that Cook himself made. There were plenty of Negroes in Louisiana, may God bless them, but he was not one of them. On a census form that offered only two choices, he chose White. Properly speaking, he was Creole, a singular culture that went back hundreds of years. And he was educated. Not like those Arkansas boys who were, sad to say, ignorant.

When attending Mass, Cook liked to have conversations with Jesus. He wasn't like these Protestants who thought they could talk to Jesus anytime, anywhere, and He'd drop whatever He was doing to listen. That was mighty forward.

A little girl turned to sneak a look at him. No, Jesus, you are right. These people don't know Creole from Cherokee. I'm just another Black man to them, another Negro railroad hand. I am sorry for my thoughts of superiority towards my fellow man, and I should not spit in the stew served to Ice Cantrell, even when he causes me mighty aggravation.

His thoughts wandered to the crew. Jerome was not ignorant, that was certain. Might be too smart for his own good. Or too proud. Sam was headed toward book-smart, but common sense lagged behind. It was from Sam that he learned the daughter went to a school run by nuns, confirming his hunch they were Catholic. He saw Sam wander off some evenings. He did not want to know more.

The Mass rolled through its rhythms. Cook placed coins in the collection basket but refrained from going up to the rail for communion. It ended with more adept organ-work, a sprightly spring hymn, and he was once again out in the brilliant sunshine. The ridges were already growing hazy with the heat of the day. He went to wait by the Plymouth, but Ron motioned him back to the sidewalk in front of the church steps for more tribal rituals.

"He's a Catholic," Ron kept saying to people, as if needing to justify bringing him. Cook nodded, smiled, and repeated his name. Level-YEH. From New Orleans. Yes sir. Yes ma'am. Their interest was almost childlike. "Golly, you're a long ways from home!" and "Ain't that something?"

Finally, someone changed the subject.

"Did you hear we got Lincoln Thomas Ford coming to Julian on the Fourth of July?" said a tall man.

"Everybody's heard that," Carlin answered.

"Fourth of July is wheat harvest," Ron said sternly.

"Hey Ronnie," said the tall man, adding in a mean and jocular tone, "you could take a couple hours off from making money, couldn't you?"

Ron stiffened. "Harvest time is work time." He gave the man a short stare, and turned away, with his family and Cook following.

The mood in the car was tense, for reasons that only Millie fully understood. In a rare show of affection, she reached across the seat and touched his shoulder.

He hunched over the wheel. "Do it for them. My year ain't ruined if it rains."

"Ed knows that," she said soothingly. "He was trying to make a joke."

"T'ain't funny, McGee."

"T'ain't funny, McGee!" Timmy echoed.

Cook winked to the boy. The line from the radio show. Fibber McGee and Molly.

Ron was not in a joking mood. "Psowf!" he warned, and went back to muttering. "Do it for them," he repeated. "Lazy Frenchies."

Millie was mortified. She kept her face forward, not daring a glance to the back seat. She thought of reminding Ron that his customers were mostly German or Irish, but she let it go. Her husband was a good man, a man with whom she had known hard times. The worst years were in the thirties, with a young daughter and no idea how they were going to feed themselves. She remembered his savage hunt for any kind of work. Walking the corn fields with a feed sack scrounging stray ears after the harvest. Driving thirty miles to Rock Port to scoop chicken manure all day for a dollar.

Her husband had little use for jokes. Years ago he used to say that his family came to Nebraska because his grandfather was a draft dodger. It was a line he came to regret. He was into his thirties when the war began, and expected to be drafted. He was surprised to be passed over for the specific reason that Grain Storage and Transport had been designated a Strategic Industry. Farmers were part of the same industry, but there were too many of them; they got no such exemption. During the war the government declared the need for a strategic grain reserve, and elevators were encouraged to enlarge capacity. Ron put up new bins, including the gleaming new tower at the center of his operation.

Most people understood that. But there was some whispering. Occasionally in the precincts around Julian one heard mutterings of the most hateful word in the war economy, *profiteering.*

Work was sacred to her husband, in that German way. On her Irish farm Millie learned to play the piano, to sing, and to dance. On Sundays, her father and uncles drank whisky and played cards, argued politics and literature and religion. She and brother Nicholas read poems by Yeats and entertained the family reading out plays by Oscar Wilde. It was such a contrast to the Littman farm down the road, where the father died in a farm accident and Ron and his brothers, still teenagers, worked the fields. Others might lose their farms to the dustbowl, but the Littman home place was a grim survivor. Some folks thought it an odd match, when dour Ron paid court to lively Mildred, but what did they know? She prized his fierce determination, his fierce love.

As the Plymouth crunched down the gravel road, her thoughts were softened by the view of a yellowing wheat field shifting in the wind. She loved the wheat fields—there was something spiritual about them. You plant wheat in the fall, when everything else was dead or dying, and you spend your days canning and pickling, storing up for winter. You watch it sprout bravely, such a tender green, silken in the wind, vulnerable, cheerful in the face of death. December comes and the fields are snow-covered. A blanket of snow keeps seedlings safe and warm. It seemed odd to think of it that way, but there it was. And in early spring the green came to life again, a miracle as true as the resurrection of the Lord. The sight of green wheat in spring could bring tears to Millie's eyes.

By the end of June the heads were filled out thick with seed, and when the exact right moisture was measured in them, it was harvest time. The combines stroked the fields, sending up their plumes of yellow dust, bringing the crop home. And her husband was waiting for them. The elevator doors opened at first light, and the procession of trucks waiting at the scale could stretch a quarter-mile. They didn't stop all day, and Ronnie kept the elevator open until after midnight, working eighteen-hour days, day after day. They'd fill up all the elevators and the outlying bins, and they'd send out as many boxcars as they could fill.

And it was for them. For the farmers. That's what had made him so mad. One hailstorm could cost a man his crop. One gulley-washer that leaves the ground too muddy for the combine, and wheat rots in the field. The peak of the harvest was always the first week of July. The country teams of the fast-pitch league suspended play.

Still. Like everyone else, Millie thrilled at the chance for Julian to play Lincoln Thomas Ford. Wouldn't it be wonderful to see David-Julian bring down Goliath-Thomas-Ford?

As the car neared home, she thought briefly of inviting Mr. Lavalier to Sunday dinner. But that was something she'd have to talk over with Ron, and there was no time. The family gave him friendly waves as they let him out at the camp, and he seemed pleased to be seen arriving by the other men.

Another reason for Millie's hesitance was that Sunday meant bone soup at the Littmans; vegetables simmered all Saturday in a big pot with a beef bone. They treated it as a feast. Bone soup Sunday was one thing that could make Ronnie smile. The bone was taken out before it was ladled into bowls, so there was rare teasing from father to son. "Where's that bone?" he would ask Timmy. "Where'd it go?"

The meal was, in one sense, a celebration of frugality, a nod to surviving the Depression. Millie feared that Mr. Lavalier would not understand that, and would think them cheap, serving bone soup to a guest. Her worries were misplaced. Like all good chefs, Cook knew that anybody could make a meal of prime cuts. It was bones and offal that separated the genius from the journeyman.

Bone soup. A self-created emblem for the new world. It was just as well the third-generation Silesian immigrants had no use for schmaltzy sentimentality about *Das Vaterland*; their lack of nostalgia and the Iron Curtain spared them the pain of knowing the homeland's fate. Anton Littman gave up his native soil in 1871. In 1950, those who stayed behind had no choice. The Poles, after suffering so much at the hands of Germans, were doing some serious score-settling, with Soviet blessing. At Yalta, Roosevelt had signed off on Stalin's claim to the eastern third of Poland, following the old Curzon line. In return, Poland received a generous slice of Germany. In the ethnic cleansing that ensued, Poles who were evicted from new Soviet territory in the east looked to do the same in the new Polish west. Thus were the Germans expelled from Silesia, the lights of their hereditary place names winking out one by one. While thrifty grandchildren of émigrés made bone soup in America, Schweidnitz became Świdnica, Breslau Wrocław, and Lower Silesia the *voivodeship* of Dolnośląskie.

18

DAD DOESN'T LIKE SUNDAY WORK

As Cook got out of the Littman automobile beside the camp, he saw that the boys were out playing ball. He expected, and received, a heckling as he strolled to the makeshift ball field. They hooted and hollered at him, and Cook had to remind himself that just an hour before he'd promised Jesus he would not indulge his feelings of superiority. They could not help that they were dumb as dirt.

The boys had gone crazy for fast-pitch. They loved the new ball, how big it was, how easy to hit. They relished the satisfying crack of the bat as they sent it towering into the air. But Delran was some athlete, with an arm like a howitzer, and before long the scales tipped the other way and nobody could touch what he was dealing to the plate.

Ice had been the last to get on board. He was insulted nobody played with his home-made baseballs. He got his bragging rights back when he smacked the new ball clean over the tracks right after Big Larry had struck out. After that Ice was as gung-ho as the rest of them.

Cook stopped beside Jerome, who was calling out the batting order.

Jerome gave him a sidelong glance. "Sunday at the granary?"

"One of the prettiest little churches I've ever seen. Catholic churches, I mean. Told you I could spot them, didn't I?"

"Run it out!" Jerome hollered. "You never know when somebody's going to drop one."

"You're getting to be a regular Bob Rodgers."

Jerome looked at him sharply.

Cook pretended not to notice. "Yes, that '46 Brick & Tile team was some unit." He let out a low chuckle. "I was cooking at the freight house that year, and I used to go watch the Mopac team. It was one of the only other ones that had Blacks and whites playing together. But you know that. I didn't recognize you at first, not until you told them about Ace. You've put on some weight since then. You were skinny, especially for a catcher."

Jerome grunted, and barked something at Sillman Jones.

"It wasn't your fault," Cook said mildly.

Jerome stared straight ahead. Cook could feel the body beside him winding itself tighter. He should be quiet. His intentions, however, were strictly charitable. "The play was over long before the ball got knocked out of your hands. Everybody knew it was a bad call. After the game, someone called out to the ump, 'Mighty white of you!' And the ump, he turned and laughed."

There was a long, heavy pause. Sillman Jones nubbed one towards third. Sam bare-handed it and fired to George at first.

"I think," said Jerome, slowly, "the kid, Sam, is the biggest surprise. Dreamy as he is, you'd never expect an arm like that."

Two more batters came up and went down without another word between the two men. Then it was Jerome's turn. He took a couple of practice swings and walked up to the plate. He turned on the first pitch Delran threw him and hit it about a mile in the air. It bounced high on the gravel road once, twice, three times, and then proceeded to roll halfway to the grain elevator. It was the exact same swing, and the ball landed in exactly the same place, as when he'd belted it after his fight with Ice.

While all the heads were turned following the ball, Jerome turned to Cook. "Are we getting fed today, or are you just going to stand around and gab? And I'll thank you," he added, tossing the bat aside, "not to bring up that subject again."

Unlike her parents, Carlin did not make a fuss over bone soup. She liked Sundays because most of the chores were done on Saturday, and after Mass she could have an hour or two to herself while mom looked after Timmy. She changed out of her dress, put on some shorts and a blue top, and traded her saddle shoes for grass-stained sneakers. She picked a book off the shelf above her bed, waited until Timmy was preoccupied with a toy, and slipped out into the fine sunny day.

Carlin started down the road by the elevator, glancing over her shoulder to see if Timmy was following. She frowned. What was Frank Abernathy's truck doing on the scale? She wanted to head the other way, but it was too late. Frank was waving her over.

"Hey, honey pie," he called out.

She wrinkled her nose. "You're so dumb."

"I saw you at the A&W in town last night, talking to the Krieder boys and Jack Scarborough. Ain't they a little old for you?"

Frank went into the office. Before she could think of a comeback, he called out through the door. "You might want to get off the scale, or you'll cost your dad the weight of you."

She followed him into the office, frowning. "Dad doesn't like work on Sunday."

Frank worked the scale levers with easy familiarity. He pulled a scale ticket from the cardboard box on the window sill and stamped the weight. "Oh, I'd hardly call this work. We just had a little corn leftover from what we shelled yesterday, and I told dad we may as well let Ron have it."

"It'd keep 'til Monday."

"You sound like your dad. Come on, ride around to the elevator with me."

It was stupid, but she got in his truck for the ten-second ride to the elevator. Frank parked it with the tailgate over the grate. "You reckon he'll want this in bin number three?"

"I have no idea," she said airily. Her father came out of their house, walking toward them. "You'll have to ask him."

"What are you doing with that book?"

"I was going to prop a door open," she said, with heavy sarcasm. "What do you think I'm doing?"

"Well, I'd just be careful where I walked if I was you. People been seeing those colored boys down along the crick. I don't know if they're fishing or trapping or what. Probably drinking." He plucked the book from her hand. "*Shakespeare's Sonnets*?"

"It's poetry," she said, snatching it back. "Something you wouldn't know anything about."

"Hell I don't," he said. "You can't hardly avoid it with Sister Mary Michael." A new thought hit him like a beanball. "That Negro kid had a book. Carlin, you ain't talking to him?"

Carlin made her face blank, giving away nothing. It occurred to her to be glad that Frank wasn't at St. Joseph's this morning. If Frank saw they'd brought that Mister—what was his name, Leva-yay—she'd hear no end of it from him. But now, with her father approaching, she changed her mind. She was proud of her parents for giving the man a ride. She wanted to work it into the conversation, and if Frank said something stupid she would tell him he was ignorant, and that Mister Leva-yay was as good a Catholic as anyone. And while she was at it, she'd tell him Sam had real, genuine ideas about poetry. But she swallowed all that as her father showed up with that gruff expression on his face. Frank repeated his story about the shelled corn, and Ron said the same thing his daughter had, that it could have waited until Monday.

The little cups roared to life. The tailgate was opened, the front of the truck hoisted, and the grain emptied out. Carlin used the cover of this commotion to wander out the other end of the drive-through.

She passed the train depot and crossed the narrow field on the path to the creek, and she didn't care if Frank Abernathy saw her walking there. In fact, she hoped he did. She laughed to think of Frank studying sonnets with Sister Mary Michael. He probably skipped that week. And how arrogant was that of him, just because Sam had a poetry book to think that's why she was reading poetry? She read poetry all the time. Really she did.

She got to the tree where she'd seen him perched before. Of course he wasn't here. Of course she wasn't looking for him. But if he would have been here, then that would have been fine too. It's a free country, no matter what ignorant people like Frank said. She felt another small flush of pride for her father. He was, most times, sour as rhubarb, and scolding her if she needed three dollars for new shoes if her old ones had holes in the bottoms. But she'd never heard him say hateful things about Negroes the way some of the men did. He took Mr. Levalier to church. And it was his idea to bring them apples.

And if Sam had happened to have been here today, well then, she might have happened to show him Shakespeare sonnet CXXX. He would know that means one-hundred-thirty. And she would show him where Shakespeare says his mistress is beautiful even though she's dark-eyed and wiry haired. Shakespeare was not racist. Women didn't have to have rosy cheeks, and their skin could be "dun," which means brown. Well, it didn't say "skin," it said "breasts." Carlin felt her face get warm, and then she shook her head at herself for being such a clodhopper.

She looked around at the leafy cottonwoods, the brush along the creek, the glint of water. It was beautiful in its tame way, but she wanted roaring, rushing rivers like in Colorado, or loud surf crashing onto Dover Beach, like in that poem. Sometimes she thought she could not bear an entire year more before she could strike out on her own, in college. College. The very word thrilled her. And it wasn't going to be Peru State Teachers College in stinking Peru, Nebraska. And she could say the word "breasts" in front of a Negro boy if it was in Shakespeare. For pity's sake, why did she let herself be embarrassed by things? And he wasn't here anyway, and she'd probably never see him again so why even think about him.

Some brush broke upstream. Maybe deer. She gazed where the noise was coming from, and saw that it was Sam.

19

THE SUNSET EFFECT

Ron Littman's tall silo offered a prairie combination of art and aesthetics, a late-stage expression of that vernacular architectural tradition, the wooden grain elevator. It wasn't alone. The middle of the Twentieth Century, a time of innovation and nostalgia, produced many examples of awesome obsolescence, also known as the clipper ship phenomenon, or the sunset effect.

In railroading, it was abundantly clear by the 1940s, as work of the gandies made clear, that diesels ruled the rails. In the face of this undeniable truth, the same years saw the production of the most splendid and huge steam locomotives of all time. Pundits and purists still debate whether the Union Pacific 4-8-8-4 Big Boy or the Great Northern 2-8-8-4 Yellowstone represented the apotheosis of the form.

In the skies, it was abundantly clear that jet engines would reign. And still, the Air Force went on building its most magnificent and biggest propeller-driven bomber, the P-36 "Peacemaker." It lived up to its name, after a fashion, getting mothballed without ever dropping a bomb in anger.

The gandy dancers of Julian were a living example of this phenomenon. They were the quintessence of the specialized manual labor team. The crew worked hard and they worked fast, with rhythm and with style. With Charly T calling the cadences, they were a machine made of muscle, know-how and precision. How could anyone have conceived of a more efficient operation? Apparently someone did. Within a decade, the profession would be gone. In its place would be hydraulic power machinery, and the ghost of gandy dancing would live on only in the names of the machines: spike pullers and spike drivers, ballast regulators and rail cranes, tie extractors and tie cranes.

As the gandy era came to a close, its most romantic element was the most obsolete. Machines did not need song callers to ensure precision—that was the job of the tool-and-die maker. And yet, song calling might be the gandies' biggest contribution to American culture. Talents like Charly T did not exist in isolation. The work songs—from mines, prisons, fields, and rails—heavily influenced folk music and the blues. Listen, for example, to the music of one Huddie William Ledbetter, also known as Leadbelly. Caller songs, with their special emphasis on hard rhythm and innovative rhyming, also have an ancestral claim on rap and hip-hop.

20

THE NEW ASSISTANT FOREMAN

Through a fly-spattered window, against a backdrop of summer corn, station agent Denton Henry watched the gandy dancers gather on his freight platform. Denton fancied himself a shrewd observer of human nature, and payday was a good time to observe. The men were jovial, horsing around, probably looking forward to getting a hold of some liquor. Arkansas boys, rural. He knew a few by name. The hot-head, who called himself Ice, laughing, jumping on the back of Big Larry. Wallace, the one with the wife in Omaha, coming up last.

Two cars skidded to a stop on the gravel. Moose Burdock, famous up and down the Mopac line, heaved out of the Ford. The hatchet-faced man from the other car, different story. Ivan Tarp. Timekeeper. Meddling and mean.

With two white men present, Denton felt safe joining the scene outside. Moose nodded to him once over the heads of the men, and commenced briskly. "You boys done a good job here lately. We laid near six mile of rail this week, and ought to do the same next week, if that load of ties comes in. Mr. Henry, if you could check on that."

"Will do," said Denton with a one-fingered salute.

Moose took a long look at the crew. "Stay out of trouble this weekend. No fights or rumpus to bring the police out here again, you hear?" He paused again, glancing at Ivan. "One other thing. No payroll today. Payout on Monday or Tuesday. Omaha's fault."

Amid the general outcry, Ice muscled up close to Moose. "I ain't bein' paid?"

"You'll get paid," said Moose, holding his ground. "Just not today."

"You cain't do that."

Moose's voice cranked up a notch. "Somebody got wax in his ears? I said the problem is Omaha. Your money's there. They just forgot to send it down to Ivan."

"Then Ivan can go git it!"

A smirk played across the timekeeper's face. "Liquor and jail gets expensive, don't it, boy?"

Ice took a step toward him. Ivan cracked his knuckles.

Jerome stepped between them. Denton, who'd been edging toward the door to go inside, paused.

"Mr. Foreman, we need to get paid," said Jerome. "We got obligations."

"Obligations," Moose repeated, not quite mocking. "Tell the truth, I didn't think you boys would mind, cooped up out here. Take it as a chance to save up, instead of overpaying for hooch."

Jerome remained impassive. "Our payroll is sitting there in Omaha?"

"Right in the paymaster's office," said Moose.

"So it's just a question of it being there and not here."

"Boy must've gone to school," said Ivan.

Jerome turned on Ivan. "Omaha is an hour away. You act like it's Timbuktu. You're so particular with us, docking us ten minutes for a piss. Get particular about your own job. Go get us our money."

Ivan turned red. "You let him talk to me that way, Moose?"

Jerome moved close to the foreman. "Let me do it," he said with sudden urgency. "Grace Street is ten blocks from my house. The Eagle comes through next hour—you just run me to Nebraska City." He pointed to Denton. "Station agent can wire ahead that I'm coming. I'll fetch our money, stay up home, and be back on the southbound first thing in the morning."

Moose hesitated long enough to trigger a fit from the timekeeper. "Wait a good goddamn minute," Ivan yelled. "You think the paymaster will turn over the money to him? A bad-tempered coon that tried to kill a white man? He's likely to run off with it."

Jerome visibly controlled himself. He said to the foreman, "You know I'll come back."

Moose pursed his lips.

"Crazy talk," sputtered Tarp.

For a long tense moment no one said anything.

"Well, damn," Denton heard himself say. "I'll go."

Eyes turned to him. A cheer went up from the men.

"Not my job, that's for damn sure," said Denton Henry, warming to the role. "But it seems we're at a logjam here. I don't mind the drive. I can be up and back in a couple hours."

"No, it's better I go," Jerome said, his mind searching desperately for a reason why that was so.

Not intending to help, Ivan provided the reason. "Payroll can't go to a local agent!" he bawled out. "Pay can only be released to a foreman. Payroll is next week, and that's the end of it. I'm headed home." Ivan took three steps toward his car, turned and poked his finger at Moose Burdock. "And I will report this, don't think I won't."

"One minute, Mr. Tarp," Moose said. "Any of you men object to the station agent going to fetch your pay?"

The men shrugged.

"I told you he ain't even connected to . . ."

"Any of you men object to Jerome Wallace going along to vouch for this crew?"

"He ain't a foreman!"

"He just got promoted," said Moose. "Thank you, Denton. The boys are much obliged. Keep the money in the station safe overnight, and I'll be here myself in the morning to distribute, 0900 hours." He fished a quarter out of his pocket and flipped it to Jerome. "Wallace, you're assistant foreman; there's your raise. Ivan, get out of my way before my foot reports to your backside."

"You'll rue the day," shouted Tarp, backing toward his car. "You will rue the day."

"Jerome, what'd he just say?"

"Not now, Sam."

"No, really, Jerome. What'd he just say?"

"Not now!"

Ten minutes later Denton Henry and Jerome Wallace were driving north on Highway 75 in Denton's Studebaker. The fields rolled by, the farms with their tractors and barns. Denton sat up straight in his seat, nervous and embarrassed that he'd tried to back out. When the foreman included Jerome on the mission, a fright like an electric shock ran through him, and he tried to say he'd been mistaken, that he was expected at home after all. The faces of the men turned cold. Some nodded like it was no surprise. After long seconds in which Moose did not let him off the hook, Denton righted the ship, agreed to go, and the faces turned friendly again.

Denton stole a glance across the seat, taking note of the large eyes, fleshy nose and small ears. Tiny curls of gray showed in his close-cropped hair. Minutes ticked by. The fields gave way to trees, and soon they saw a diner, a bait shop, a gas station.

"Nebraska City," said Jerome, reading from a sign. "Home of Arbor Day."

"Darn right," said Denton, eager to get past the silence. "We'll drive by Arbor Lodge on the way out of town. But first, I need to tell my wife what a fool's errand I've got myself into. We just live down on Second Avenue."

"Take as long as you need, Mr. Henry."

Denton turned onto a side street and stopped in front of a yellow house. He shut off the car, and for a moment—too long a moment—his hand hovered above the key in the dashboard. Jerome looked at him. He looked at Jerome. "I'll be just a minute," said Denton, leaving the key.

"Take your time."

A short while later Denton came out the front door, ushering a stout woman onto the porch. He pointed and waved. Jerome waved back. The woman went back inside. The Studebaker rumbled over the brick streets, and curved around the white-pillared mansion whose historic significance Denton was happy to explain. But he ran out of things to say once they were outside of town.

Minutes passed. "My wife," said Denton.

"She looks like a nice lady."

"Oh she is, all right," Denton said. "She was sure surprised to see you sitting there, I tell you."

"I'm sure she was."

"I mean, it's not every day you have a, you know . . . Damn strange sight for most folks is all I'm saying."

The Studebaker rolled by orchards and fields in silence. Finally, Jerome spoke. "Why'd you do it?"

Denton glanced over, wary. "Do what?"

"You've got no reason to be doing favors for us gandies."

"Maybe not for you," Denton said. "I've known Moose for twenty-five years. He's looking to retire soon. He doesn't need the aggravation."

"He didn't seem too worried about it."

"No, he wouldn't."

"Or getting written up by the timekeeper."

"Ivan. Well, Ivan," Denton began. There was a pause. "Well, he's from Kansas, you know."

Jerome nodded. "When we were there, place called Junction City wouldn't let us stay. Mopac had to move us to another town."

"See there. Doesn't surprise me a bit."

They passed the turn-off for Plattsmouth, and soon crossed the long bridge over the Platte River. The water was almost up to the trestle, slow-moving and muddy, prompting Denton to remark on how it'd been running high this year. The highway got wider, gas stations blossomed. Soon they were in the city.

"Poo wee," said Denton. "That does smell like Omaha."

"Stockyards."

"Don't I know it. It's good thing that Grace Street is on the north side. Excepting that it's dangerous, of course."

"I live on the north side."

"I didn't mean . . . I meant, you know, for me."

"I've been wondering," said Jerome, "if all Italy smells like that. All these Italians moving to the south side, none up north. They rather live with cow shit than Black folks."

Denton thought he should take offense. "Are you funning with me, boy?"

There was a long pause. The car stopped at a light. Jerome spoke slowly, "I guess we're about the same age."

"Come again?"

"And we both work for Mr. Mopac. So I don't see that either one of us needs to be calling the other one 'boy.'"

"Oh, hell," Denton said. "It's just a thing you say is all. Don't mean nothing by it, doesn't mean a thing." They drove several blocks, and he started again. "I don't see how any man can take offense if another man don't mean nothing by it. Golly. Whoever heard of such a thing?"

As they eased through the traffic into downtown, they came alongside the massive brick headquarters of the Union Pacific Railroad. "Not our stop, no sir," Denton said. "We Mopac boys report to Grace Street." He peered impishly across the seat. "You hear that? I said, 'we boys.' Nothing wrong with that, is there?"

"Grace Street. Yes, Mr. Henry."

"Down in St. Louis, the Missouri Pacific Building is twice this size. You ever seen Mopac HQ, Wallace? It's Wallace, ain't it? You're not gonna get upset for me calling you Wallace, are you?"

"Never been to St. Louis, no."

"Well, it is something to see, I tell you that."

They left downtown, and Denton negotiated the narrow streets that skirted the rail yards. Yard engines pushed box cars and tank cars. Train whistles shrilled. A dog ran alongside the car, barking. They came to a stop in front of a two-story brick warehouse. "Well, let's go see what kind of grief they give us, Wallace."

Inside, Denton asked for the paymaster's office. A clerk appeared, and told Jerome to wait in the lobby.

As he waited, Jerome considered it was almost five o'clock on a Friday so he wasn't likely to run into Malcolm. As if mentally conjured, his brother-in-law walked right through the lobby, wearing a green visor and carrying a cardboard box.

He leapt to his feet. "Malcolm!"

Malcolm jumped, like he'd seen a ghost. He recovered, frowned, whispered something, and hurried off, as if afraid to be seen with him. Jerome sat down, fuming. Minutes became tens of minutes, and each minute seemed like an hour. Jerome could imagine the verbal knots the station agent was tying himself into trying to explain the situation. He knew he could do it faster and more clearly. And why had Malcolm run away like that? Never mind that he was Lucy's brother, he was going to get a piece of Jerome's mind when . . .

"Jerome."

Malcolm was standing in the doorway. Jerome went to him, hand extended, repenting his harsh thoughts. Malcolm was not smiling. "Listen, Jerome," he said in a stiff whisper, "I don't know what kind of trouble you got yourself into, but there is not a lot I can do to help you now, you understand what I'm saying?"

"What? Wait."

"I thought you learned your lesson," Malcolm went on harshly. "I put my neck out for you. How could you do this to Lucy?"

"Malcolm . . ."

"Did they tell you your severance pay yet?"

"Wait . . ."

"That's where I can be of some help. I mean the union can, but I know the steward and . . ."

"Malcolm!"

Malcolm winced, shushed him, and looked around with a big fake smile on his face, apologizing to empty air.

Jerome shook him by the arm. "Listen to me. I didn't get canned. Listen to me." Jerome talked fast, but it took a while to explain to Malcolm.

When he did understand, Malcolm grinned and whistled softly through his teeth. "You hardly been out there a month, and here you are moving into management."

"Listen, do you know if Lucy is home? Can you call her?"

Malcolm looked around. "I can't use the phone for private calls. Switchboard girls will report you for that. How long you going to be in town? We can get together . . ."

"Going back tonight . . ." Jerome spotted Denton motioning from down the corridor. "I've got to go."

"You take care of business, Mr. Foreman!" Malcolm said, grinning.

Jerome joined Denton in the office of a man whose nameplate said, "Mr. Balducci." Denton gave Jerome a tiny smile: Mr. Balducci was bald as Eisenhower.

Balducci did a double-take when he saw Jerome. "What's Burdock trying to pull? He has to send a foreman to sign for the payroll."

"He's assistant foreman," said Denton. "It's on the manifest there. Tell him your name, Wallace."

Jerome told him his name.

"I don't recall seeing any foreman paperwork with that name on it. Matter of fact, I don't recall we had a colored A.F. in the whole Omaha District."

"It was recent," said Jerome.

"Recent, eh?" The man stared at Jerome for a long time. He tossed an envelope across the desk. "Well, it's your problem now. All this rigmarole just because your timekeeper couldn't get his work in on time. What's that bastard's name?"

"Ivan Tarp," said Jerome.

"I didn't ask you." Balducci gave Jerome another stare. "Sign here, Henry. You too, boy."

Denton picked up the envelope. "Pleasure doing business with you. Now we'll just be out of your hair and . . ."

"It's all there?" asked Jerome.

Balducci glanced down at the ledger. "Six hundred thirty-seven dollars and sixty-five cents. All there."

Jerome took the envelope from Denton. "There's hundred-dollar bills in here."

"I said it's all there."

"We can't make pay-out with this."

"I'm sure it's fine," said Denton, trying to take it back.

"This won't work," Jerome said. "We need tens, fives, ones."

Balducci looked up. "You a wiseacre, Wallace?"

"No sir. I'm only trying to say that . . ."

"You a troublemaker?"

"No sir."

"It's past five o'clock on a Friday, and I got some jigaboo impersonating a foreman and telling me how to make my payroll. Sign the sheet, take the money, and get the hell out of here." He pointed to the pen.

"I have to insist."

"How about if I call a couple of Pinkertons in here to teach you a lesson?"

Jerome said nothing.

Balducci stood, put both fists on the blotter and yelled, "Paskowitz!" A green-visored head popped around the edge of the door. "Take these two to the pay window, have it broken down into small bills, and show them the door. Now, if you know how to sign your name, boy, you'd best do that, or your next promotion will be foreman of shitters at the Texarkana roundhouse."

Back in the car, Denton tapped the steering wheel with the envelope and shook his head. He gave a long, theatrical sigh. "I guess we told them, didn't we, Wallace?"

"We did at that, Mr. Henry."

"Let me tell you, the real battle happened before you even got in there. If I told them once, I told them fifty times. Baldy couldn't get it through his head. Finally, he sends the girl upstairs to find out from the Roadmaster. She comes back down saying the Roadmaster said it was fine. And baldy says, 'You can't give payroll out to a station agent, you have to have a foreman from the crew to sign for it. And I say, 'That's why I brought one of them! That's what I been trying to tell you!'" Denton grinned, shaking his head. "And the girl knew. Oh yes she did. The whole time she was trying to hold back from laughing. A little cutie, too, did you see her when you came . . ." He caught himself. "Anyway, she gave me a look that said plain as day, 'Yes, he is surely a half-wit.'"

Denton took out his pocket watch. He did it with elaborate care, holding it up to the evening light.

"That is a fancy timepiece."

"Oh this?" Denton said. "Hamilton 992B Railroad Special."

"It's very nice."

"Accurate is more important than nice. Certified by the Missouri Pacific. Twenty-one jewels. When the inspector comes around—and he doesn't always tell you he's coming—your timepiece had better be on target to the second, or you're in for all kinds of trouble."

"I imagine that's true. Now as I see from your watch it's ten after six . . ."

"Six eleven. And you're probably thinking what I'm thinking, Wallace. It's supper time. I had a notion we could swing by the Dipsy Drive-In on our way out of town. They make these Dagwood sandwiches piled up about six inches thick, with roast beef, ham—hell, anything you want. And they bring them right out to your car, so we wouldn't have to deal with separate tables or any of that."

"Separate tables."

"Not that I mind, but people staring and all that. Why put ourselves through it, eh Wallace? We can get those Dagwood sandwiches on trays hung right on the car windows." He handed Jerome the envelope. "And we wouldn't want this money out of our sights for one minute, now would we? Just put that in the glove box so it's safe."

Jerome took the bulging envelope. "If it's all right I'll just take mine now."

"Whoa, there. Moose always gives out payroll. You need some cash to get the Dagwood, is that it?"

"Thirty-seven dollars even, like it says right here on the sheet, by my name." He held up the bills between two fingers, folded them, and placed them in his shirt pocket.

"I said I don't think . . ."

"Mr. Henry, I'm wanting to talk to you about this." Jerome tapped the pocket. "I've got four weeks' pay here. My house is just a few blocks from here, and my wife needs this money for bills."

"Oh no. No. No. No. No."

"She needs it real bad. It's not out of our way, and . . ."

"No. No. No. No offense to you, Wallace, but I am not driving one block further into that part of town. Not when we've got the whole payroll right here."

"Mr. Henry, listen . . ."

"No, *you* listen." Denton put his hands in the air. "Don't waste your breath. It would be irresponsible of me. No. No. No. Absolutely not. No."

FIELD NOTES

Site: Nebraska City, NE. Central Avenue Books. At the rear of the store, three small round tables with glass tops and wrought iron chairs next to a counter with a coffee machine and a small kitchen.
Subject: Irvin Beck, former employee, Missouri Pacific Railroad

Mr. Beck is tall, gray-haired, long bony face. Once a strong man, now aged and gaunt. He is having coffee and a bowl of soup. He wears a light blue summer blazer, and a hat with gold piping and the words "World War II Vet." He has recently returned from Washington D.C.

I tell him the hat looks new. He takes it off looks at it, and puts it back on his head. "You know, we're dying off at a rate of twelve hundred a day, so they had to do something quick. They found a hundred of us, and took us on a chartered jet. When we got off the bus at the mall, they had thousands of Vietnam vets there, and they made a cordon, and we walked between them to the memorial."

"I'll bet you had a big smile on your face," says the book woman, unapologetically listening in from behind the counter.

His head jerks up. "Smiles? It was *tears*, woman! Tears on everybody's cheeks." He turns to me, as if not quite sure why I'm there.

I remind him. The gandy dancers.

"Oh, lord, *those* people? Hell yes, I knew them, I was the one had to go pick them up at the police station. They'd get their pay and head straight to the bars. Well one thing and another, and they'd get to whooping and hollering and the first thing you know there'd be a fight or something and they'd end up in jail."

"Why was that your job?"

"I was timekeeper, so it was my job to keep track of them, see they did a day's work. I took down when they stopped for lunch, when there was breaks for trains to pass through. I was good at it, too. Them boys used to say, 'Can't take a shit in a corn field but ol' Irv Beck'll dock your pay.' And I'd say, 'Be quick about it, boy, or I surely will.'" He laughs.

I ask if the bars let them in.

"Oh yeah, they let them in. Money's green, not white or black, and they made good pay. Some of those little towns were dry, so they'd get rides to bigger towns. And sure enough, some mornings I had to come and take 'em straight from jail to the work site." He slurps his soup. "It was man-killing work, I'll give 'em that. You had to be big and strong. And those fellows, they were big and strong."

I ask about the game with the Hornets. He doesn't understand what I mean. I begin to explain again, and he interrupts forcefully.

"Softball? Fast-pitch? What the hell are you talking about, man? They didn't have time for nothing like that. Or inclination." He pokes the table for emphasis. "Their recreation was drinking. That was the long and short of it."

"Were you working for MoPac in the summer of 1950?"

"Might've been. Whenever it was, it didn't last too long, because then I got bumped again. In the railroads, somebody with more seniority, he can just bump you off your job, and you're out on your ass. I'm still mad about that. I tried for years to get back on. They have that pension. I *really* wanted that pension. But I ended up working at truck stops instead, until I had my two nervous breakdowns."

"Two nervous breakdowns?"

"Hands shook so bad I couldn't fuel a truck without spilling it. Word got around, and none of the truck stops or filling stations would have me anymore." He looks around, chin thrust out, but there's only me and the book lady. "That was service-related, you know," he says loudly. "And there were many of us like that. Many of us."

21

IN FIELDS WHERE ROSES FADE

Sam Washington had seen fireworks twice in his life. It was the biggest thrill he could recall. This was bigger. No, not like fireworks. More like ice breaking up in a stream on a sudden spring day, and all the crusty mud and ice being swept away by a cool blue steam. All the convolutions, all the confusions—about gravy, about streets in France—all of it swept away in the beautiful certitude of understanding. Who would have thought the meanest man on the job, Ivan the Terrible, would be the one to unlock the mystery. *"You'll rue the day, Burdock!"*

Jerome had gone off with the station agent to get their pay, so Sam checked with George, then with Cook, then with Charly T. They all said what Ivan meant was, "You'll be sorry." They acted like everyone knew that. Then why hadn't anyone said so before? Back when he was asking!

The reproaches melted away as he looked at the page again. The important thing was that he understood it now. Sam read it again, savoring every word:

> With rue my heart is laden
>   For golden friends I had,
> For many a rose-lipt maiden
>   And many a lightfoot lad.

> By brooks too broad for leaping
>   The lightfoot boys are laid;
> The rose-lipt girls are sleeping
>   In fields where roses fade.

The boy was sad. He was thinking about people who died. That was all, and that was enough. It was so simple, yet so beautiful. He smiled thinking of Carlin's streets and French kings. But she had given him the key to the second verse, when she'd tossed off, "but they're all dead now." That's what made it so sad. He thought of the foreman's speech today about moving camp next week, and a strange feeling gathered itself in his stomach—something sad and sweet and guilty at the same time. In his secret heart, 'golden friends' meant a certain golden-haired girl, one who, when they moved camp, he'd never see again.

22

PLUMBING PROBLEMS

Denton sat nervously in his car on Blondo Street, in front of a small, neatly kept frame house. He had the doors locked, the motor running, the gearshift in drive, and his foot on the brake. Two colored boys were walking up the sidewalk on other side of the street. He kept his face straight ahead, watching them out of the corner of his eye.

He pulled out the Hamilton, keeping it out of sight. Jerome had been gone for six minutes and forty-five seconds. Forty-eight, forty-nine, fifty.

At nine minutes and thirty-two seconds, the front door opened. Jerome came out, holding hands with his wife. Denton nodded, waved. He expected a wave in return. He didn't expect her to come out to the car, and especially not for them both to come around to the driver's window. Denton eased the shifter into park. He rolled his window down a little ways, then all the way.

"Lucy," said Jerome. "This is Mr. Denton Henry. Mr. Henry, my wife, Lucy."

Lucy wore a green dress that buttoned up the front. She had white ankle socks, scuffed shoes, and a shy smile. Denton stuck his hand out the window to shake. "And a very pretty wife, too!"

She put her hand to her mouth. "I am grateful to you, Mr. Henry," she said. "Being a railroad man yourself, you know how hard it is being away from your family."

"I do know," he said, although he himself drove home after work every day, and he always had.

"It means everything to us, really it does." She put an arm around Jerome, giving him a sideways hug.

"Somebody has to stand up for the working man."

"And I promise you," she went on, "that I will have Jerome ready to go and out the door in two hours, just like you said."

"I always . . . What's that you say? Two hours?"

"And not a second more," she said, laughing. "You can check it on that fancy watch of yours. Jerome said it was special."

"Yes, but . . ."

"Would you mind to show it to me?"

Denton fumbled for the watch. He heard himself prattling on about the twenty-one jewels and the railroad inspectors, and knew he was being played, and there wasn't a thing he could do about it. "Well, hell," he said at last. "You're down to an hour, fifty-eight and twenty-one seconds. Don't waste your time out here with me. Wallace, I'll see you here at twenty-one hundred hours—or I'll write you up so fast it'll make your head spin."

"Yes, sir," Jerome said, smiling and pulling his wife toward the house.

Denton drove out of the neighborhood by the quickest route. He drove with both hands tight on the wheel until he crossed into a white neighborhood. He paused for a moment to get his bearings, and realized he was only a block from O'Toole's Tap Room, Home of the Famous Roast Beef Sandwich.

The bartender was a young man, tall and slender, his hair slicked back in a duck tail.

"I'll have that famous roast beef sandwich," Denton said ceremoniously, "and a Falstaff beer. It ought to be fresh. The brewery's just a couple miles down the road."

"Yes, sir."

A few minutes later he had his sandwich. He ate it slowly, but when he'd finished it and polished off the beer, he still had more than an hour to wait. Two men came in and took stools a couple places down from him. When the boy gave them their beers, Denton held up his glass for a refill. As the bartender slid it across, Denton said, "Let me ask you. You ever get colored people in here?"

"Yeah," said the boy, "sometimes."

"Do they ever sit with white people? I mean, they come in together?"

The boy gave him a hard stare. "You got a problem?"

The newcomers had turned to look. "Oh, no, no," Denton said, speaking louder to include them. "I was with a colored man tonight, as a matter of fact. Or, he was with me. Work for the railroad, had to pick up—had an errand for the bosses."

"Union Pacific?" said the nearer one. They looked comically similar with their flat-top haircuts and blue coveralls.

"Mopac. And we should be headed for Neb City right now. I'm a station agent down that way. But I'm an old softic. Shouldn't have let it happen, but there you go. Shore leave, if you know what I mean." He winked.

They didn't know what he meant, so Denton told them. And he back-tracked from there to the fuss over payroll at the freight house. Once he got started, he found he had plenty to say.

Mel and Dave were plumbers. They talked some about a stubborn sewer drain, but mostly they wanted to hear more from him, and he was glad to oblige. Wildest day in his quarter-century with the railroad. A fool's errand with a colored man to boot. The plumbers ordered whisky. The heat of it warmed his belly, and Denton thought them great friends, and himself a fine storyteller. He realized that this too, the Tap Room, was another chapter. A man talking to men. It helped that their names were stitched right there on the coveralls. "Now, Dave . . ." he would say. Or, "Mel, you should have seen . . ."

When Denton looked at his watch, it was past the pick-up time. He called out to the bartender, and showed off the Hamilton Special, saw his bill had no whiskies on it. He thanked the plumbers warmly, and made a joke about liquid courage for his drive back to the north side.

Standing at the urinal, Denton became aware he was swaying. He splashed water on his face, and walked carefully out to the parking lot. As he was trying to get the key in the car door, they were there again.

"Wait a second," said Mel, who turned out to be much taller than Dave. "Let's have a word."

Denton waved his keys. "Have to skedaddle. Not my job, but it's what I let myself in for."

"Me and Dave were just saying, you shouldn't be going there alone. Not with all that money. Tell you what, we'll follow you. Make sure you get back safe to the highway."

"Mighty nice of you. But really, I'm all talk. It was quiet there."

"Can't be too careful," said Dave. "And we'd like to get a look at this colored woman you kept talking about."

"We'll make sure you're safe," Mel added. "And you get your man. The wife's name is Lucy, right?"

"Yeah, Lucy, but . . ." Denton stopped. He looked up. The plumbers were grinning at him. He made a sudden move to open the car door, but Dave slammed it closed and leaned into it.

"Hey, what's this?" asked Mel, putting his hands out sideways. "I thought we were friends."

"I don't want trouble," Denton said. "I'll just be going."

"Sure you will. And we'll just follow, as a security measure. Can't be too safe with a payroll to look after, can you?"

A middle-aged couple had parked and was heading into the tavern. "Hey, hi!" Denton shouted. "Can you tell me how to get to the Iowa bridge from here?"

The man detached himself from his wife and approached them. Before he could speak, Denton jumped into his car and slammed down the lock. He backed out wildly, nearly hitting the would-be Samaritan, and peeled out with a screech of rubber.

23

OHN-WEE

Carlin was wasting away another Friday night in Nebraska City.

"Hey," said Jack Scarborough, "you want a piece of gum?"

The two options were, drive slowly down Central Avenue waving at people who were sitting around on cars, or sit around on cars waving at people who were driving slowly down Central Avenue. Carlin was practicing option B, perched next to Jack on the trunk of his car in the high school parking lot. Jack took out a pack of gum, and held it out, offering.

"No thanks," she said, "I'd just swallow it."

He turned to her with a grin, and said, "You're not supposed to swallow, you're supposed to spit it out. Didn't they ever teach you that?"

She studied his grin to see if he meant that in a dirty way—and knew instantly it never crossed his mind. It never should have crossed her mind either, except maybe it did because she was bored out of her wits.

"No really?" Jack said, poking her in the side. "You swallow your gum?"

"I don't mean to," she said. "I forget it's there." That came out more snappish than she had intended. She tried again, making herself sound more stupid, the way boys liked. "Most of the time, when I'm chewing gum, I remind myself don't swallow the gum. But then I get thinking about something else, and, well, you only need to forget to not swallow for a second, and there it goes."

Jack laughed and shook his head. "I swear your brain works in the strangest ways."

A red pick-up cruised by slowly. Jack waved to them. "Hey Leonard! Hey Jim!"

"Who was that?"

"Come on, Carlin. Everyone knows Leonard and Jim."

"Neb City High boys?"

"No," he said, laughing in that patronizing way boys have. "They're from Auburn. Didn't you see the forty-four county plates?"

"If I had seen the forty-four county plates I wouldn't have asked if they were from Nebraska City, would I?"

Jack looked around. There were half a dozen cars spaced randomly in the parking lot, with kids milling around. He knew them all. Jack prided himself that he knew most of the people in three counties. Some of that came from being brother to Dave and Ernie, some of it from being a character, and some for being catcher for the Hornets.

"Maybe I'll have that piece of gum." Carlin held out her hand in a bored way.

"If you promise not to swallow it."

"I can't promise not to because, like I just said, I forget not to. Are you going to give me the piece, or do I have to go over to the Texaco and get my own?"

"Hey, I was just kidding. Sure. Here."

She took the gum sullenly.

A carload of boys came by in a Chevy. The driver waved and hollered, "Lincoln Thomas Ford!" The other boys took up the chant, and he heard, "Lincoln Thomas Ford!" until they turned the corner.

Jack waved back, smiling. He knew it wasn't that they were rooting *for* LTF. Nobody from small towns rooted for a Lincoln team, ever. Word had got around that LTF was coming to Julian. That made Jack Scarborough almost a celebrity.

"About a million people are going to come when we play them," Jack said, stealing a sideways glance at Carlin. She had her arms wrapped around her knees, and she was staring straight ahead. Didn't hear a word. Her bun had come mostly apart, so that wisps of blond were falling down around her glasses. Damn. She was the prettiest girl at St. Bernard's, the prettiest in all of Nebraska City when she took off her glasses. She got like this sometimes. Like she was someplace else, not here at all. And the part of her that was still present was easily annoyed. Sometimes Jack thought she liked being in that place—the place where she swallowed her gum—better than where she really was.

But that's what friends are for, Jack reminded himself. He and Carlin were not sweethearts. Never had been. They grew up together, but she was four years behind him, one of the little kids. In high school, after he got his car, he'd give her rides to town now and then, like he did for other Julian kids. When he graduated, she was a skinny freshman, but in the last two years she'd turned into the prettiest girl in the county, and the one with the sharpest tongue. And suddenly she was dating. She dated Johnny Miller, and she dated Ross Tedrow, and even that little Irish squirt from Pawnee City, O'Rourke. And Jack noticed some of the boys she dated were older than he was. He also noticed the boys she dated were not around very long. When she was done with a boy, brother she was done! "Don't talk about Ross Tedrow to me!" she would say. "Don't ever mention the name Ross Tedrow again!"

Jack was happy not to mention Ross Tedrow, ever. Or Johnny Miller. And he noticed that he, Jack Scarborough, was still there when the other boys could never be spoken of, and that counted for something more. If that meant just friends, it was better than banishment for life. When Carlin got moody and distant, then you did what a friend does, you sat there.

"Hey," he said. "Let's play the word game."

"I've got one," she said. "Ennui."

"Ohn-Wee?"

She spelled it for him.

"Really, that's how? It must be French."

"Bree-yah."

"What's that?"

"Nothing. I said, 'Brilliant.'"

"What's it mean, ohn-wee?"

"You have to find out. That's how the game is played, remember?"

"I know. But just tell me. What's it mean?"

A black pick-up skidded to a stop beside them. Carlin was glad for the interruption, even if it wasn't someone she wanted to see. Smilin' Jack had almost provoked her to the cruelty of telling him what it meant. She knew he'd just laugh it off. Jack only got riled up about ball games and broken-down harvesters. With everything else he just rolled along.

Frank Abernathy came around from the back of his pick-up all cool and quiet. He came to the back of the car and hopped right up beside them on the trunk with no warning. Carlin fell into Jack's lap trying to get out of the way.

"Whoa, there," Jack said, righting her.

"There's no room," she protested.

Frank pushed in anyway, and she was trapped between them like a pickle in a jar.

"Lincoln Thomas Ford," said Frank.

"Lincoln Thomas Ford," Jack agreed.

"The Fourth of July," Frank said. "Carly, you think Ronnie will come around? He's mad as hell about it."

Jack sat up straighter. "Your dad's mad about the game?"

"He's not mad as hell," Carlin said. "You always exaggerate, *Franky*. He's just worried about the wheat harvest is all. You know his motto, 'Work and work only.'"

"Well, we know he doesn't like to work on Sundays," Frank said.

"If you'd stop showing up with two bushels, maybe he could have a day of rest."

"Two bushels?" said Jack.

"Oh it's nothing," Frank said. "Just cleaning out the back bins on the farm.

"On Sundays?"

"I know it," Frank said, laughing. "My dad's crazy. Say, I heard a good one. What's black and white and red all over?"

"That's so old," Carlin said. "A newspaper."

"Huh?" said Jack.

"Like r-e-a-d all over," Carlin explained. "It's really dumb."

"No, that ain't it," said Frank, grinning. "Go ahead, ask me again."

Carlin gave a massive sigh. "All right, Frank Abernathy, what's black and white and red all over?"

Frank's grin almost split his face. "A nun in a hay baler!"

A gasp of laughter escaped Jack before he could catch it.

Carlin leaped to the pavement. "That is not funny."

"Aw, come on," said Frank. "It is so."

"And you stop laughing, Jack Scarborough. You're as bad as he is."

"Now you two don't quarrel," said Frank. "Since you're almost to the altar. When's the big day?"

Jack flushed red and thought of punching Frank.

Carlin came back in a sprightly voice, "Well, you'll sure as heck never know, Frank, because you're not invited. Isn't that right, Jackie dear?"

Jack wanted to kiss her. He could never think that fast. "That's right, Carlin dear," he sang out. But he had no snappy follow-up.

"I know someone who won't be too happy about it," Frank said. "Dwayne Buchalter. He told me you were flirting with him at the Plattsmouth game."

"He's got a pretty sorry life, if that's what he thinks that was."

"He said to tell you after harvest he'll take you to the movies."

"In his dreams maybe."

Jack frowned. "Dwayne Buchalter is a pin-head."

The conversation took a new turn, as Frank turned on Carlin, his words strangely freighted. "I'm sure you're going to want to go to the movies next week."

"I don't know," she said. "What's playing?"

Frank hopped off Jack's car, and fetched a newspaper from his truck. "See for yourself."

Carlin opened it to the page with movie ads. "Jane Wyman, *The Lady Takes a Sailor* . . ."

"The other one, below that," Frank said impatiently.

Carlin pushed her glasses up on her head. "*Pinky.*"

"Yeah, that one."

"Why do you . . ." And then she saw the smaller print. "'She Passed For White.' Oh for pity's sake."

"What?" said Jack.

Frank shrugged. "Just thought that would be of interest to you."

"What?" said Jack.

Carlin handed him the newspaper. "Just Frank being an idiot, that's all."

"You ought to be careful. People talk, you know."

Jack didn't like Frank's tone. "Hey," he said, sharply, "watch it."

Frank leaned back against his truck. "I'm the good guy, here," he said, pointing at himself. "I'm your friend. That's why I'm warning you. It doesn't look good."

"Just what are you saying?" Jack challenged.

Frank pointed at Carlin. "I'm talking about Carly here spending time with those coloreds working in Julian, like little Miss Emancipation Proclamation."

"Are you spying on me?" Carlin was flooded with indignation. "Is this Russia? Can I not talk to anyone I want in the United States of America? Did the communists take over already?"

"It ain't true, is it?" said Jack.

That was the last straw. She gave him a withering look and stalked away.

"Carlin!" said Jack.

"I can find my own ride home," she called back. "I'm not going to put up with it. And you can have this back." Carlin spit the gum into her hand and hurled it in Jack's direction.

The boys watched her go.

"God damn it, Frank," said Jack. "God damn it. God damn it."

"I'm sure I'm not the only one who'll be glad when they just pack up those rail cars and move them somewhere else."

"Yeah. Right."

"I was doing her a favor," Frank insisted. "Somebody had to say it to her face. She shouldn't be messing around with them guys."

The punch landed square on the solar plexus, knocking Frank to the pavement.

"What the hell?" said Frank, scrambling to his feet. "Oh, excuse me. I didn't know you were part of the gandy fan club."

Jack swung again, but missed. "I ain't nothing," he shouted. "Get out of here." He stalked after the redhead until Frank had gotten into his truck and squealed tires getting away. Then he slowly uncurled his fists. He was almost crying. Not only was she dating Johnny Miller and Tedrow and O'Rourke? Now Dwayne Buchalter? And colored boys too? He had nothing against colored boys himself. It was just . . . Well . . . Being a best friend was a good job, but what in the heck would it take for her to see *him* as dating material?

24

MAYBE JUGGLING INSTEAD

The tap at the passenger window nearly made Denton jump out of his skin. He looked around hastily before reaching over to lift the lock.

"What are you doing sneaking up on me in the dark? Damn!"

Jerome settled happily into the seat and gave a sigh. "I walked right up the sidewalk."

"In my blind spot." Denton put the car in gear. "Am I going towards the highway?"

"Turn right at the bottom of the hill," Jerome said. "It's lucky I found you at all. Why were you here? People in these houses just as black as the people on my block."

Denton hadn't known he was on the wrong block. He was aware that Jerome's remark would have angered some white men, but he found it hilarious. "How'd you know to come looking for me?"

"Because," Jerome answered, "it was eighteen minutes and some odd seconds past schedule, and you're a railroad man."

Now that was a respectful answer! Denton breathed easier as he slung the Studebaker into downtown, stopping for a red light. The marquee of the Orpheum Theater lit up the street like Mardi Gras. Omaha really was a nice town. He should bring his wife to the Orpheum, maybe for her birthday. The light turned green. He glanced at Jerome. "So I hope you had your fun. That wasn't fair, putting your wife on me like that!"

"Mr. Henry, you're swerving. Are you fit to drive? I smell alcohol on you."

Denton slowed the car and told himself to pay attention. "It's that Studebaker suspension. As I was saying, I hope you had your fun."

"Mr. Henry, I have a license to drive. I had a nice car of my own until I lost my job. Now, why don't you pull over down here, and you can just slide over and let Jerome be your chauffer."

"Oh, hell, I had a couple of drinks is all. I'm fine. Right as rain." Denton concentrated on the center line, and kept his speed below the limit. That should be the end of that nonsense. But it wasn't.

"Mr. Henry, you pull over now, and I will drive."

"You giving me orders now?" Denton tried for anger, but his voice came out wheedling. "We're almost to Bellevue. Once we get past the Air Force base it's just two-lane all the way. I know this road like I know my own desk."

"You are not going to pull over?"

"Nope," said Denton. "I'm fine as wine in the engineer's chair, air brakes off and easy on the throttle."

"Then you are going to find yourself sitting real close to a Black man." Jerome slid to the middle of the seat. "Because I am going to rest my hand right here, and when you swerve, I'm going to do this."

Denton screamed as the steering wheel moved against his grip. "What's the big idea? You're gonna make me wreck!"

"I'm going to keep you from wrecking, Lord willing."

"Don't ever grab the wheel when a man's driving a car." Denton tried to shove Jerome back. The car veered, and the grip hardened and straightened the wheel.

Jerome put his free arm up over the back of the seat. "It's going to be like this the whole way. Or else I can drive."

"I'm not having you drive."

"And another thing. We're going to have a nice talk. We're going to talk even if we don't feel like it, and, to be truthful, I really don't. But we're not going to have either one of us falling asleep, are we, Mr. Henry?"

"Who put you in charge of this mission?" Denton said testily. But he didn't mean it. He was a man who lived most of his life without conversation. It was something he sorely missed alone in the station all day. He remembered the plumbers, and had a salacious urge to bring up Jerome's wife again. After all he'd put himself through, Denton thought he deserved a wink and nod, man-to-man, as men of the world. But before he could think of a way to put it, Jerome went a different way.

"Now, Mr. Henry, what do you think of that Senator Joe McCarthy and his committee?"

"Um, well, sure. I think if there are communists in the government, then somebody has to smoke 'em out."

"And writers and actors?"

"Did you hear they were looking into Sinatra?" Denton snorted, and added, lowering his voice, "I could half believe it. Draft dodger for a reason."

"I like Sinatra," Jerome said. "You know that song of his, 'The House I Live in'?"

"Sure, of course," said Denton. He considered that once you got used to it, it was not so damn strange to have a man sitting right next to him. Hell, in Europe everybody sits this close because the cars are so damn small.

"That song came from a movie."

"Can't say I ever saw it."

"It's a movie against bigotry. He got an Academy Award for it."

"Sinatra did?"

"Yeah, or the guy who made the movie. Somebody did."

Denton doubted that. But still, it was nice to have a conversation like this. He was not a bigot. A serious conversation was something else. A man had serious conversations with his friend. For the first time in Denton Henry's life, having a colored man for a friend was not impossible to think of.

"Easy now." The steering wheel wrenched in his hands, and the car swerved. "You need to keep talking, Mr. Henry. Tell me what it is you do in that little white building all day."

"Don't do much," Denton heard himself say. "In the morning, yeah, but not the rest of the day. Don't tell Mr. Mopac I said so, but Julian doesn't need its own agent. If I'm being honest with you, Jerome . . . can I call you Jerome? You can call me Denton, or Dent." Henry felt full of largesse, and was taken aback that Jerome didn't answer right away.

"Mr. Henry, if you still want me to call you Denton when you sober up, then we can do that. But only so long as I don't hear you saying boy or darky or any of the rest of that."

"I'm the same man drunk or sober, Jerome." He was a fine fellow, this Jerome. He would not mind at all if Jerome visited him at the depot, just for conversation. He liked the sound of the name Jerome. Jerome Jerome Jerome. Like rowing a boat. "You see, Jerome. I'm a good driver because I'm a good drinker. It's the amateurs you have to worry about. Come by the station some afternoon. I got an extra glass. Happy to share."

"Careful!" The car swerved again, and was righted by Jerome.

"I've got it," Denton said. "With these hills you don't see the headlights until they're right on top of you."

"Mr. Henry, I have no doubt you're a good drinker, but right now you are not a good driver. You are going to pull over the next chance you get, and I am going to drive. That is the end of it."

"No. No. No. I'm fine." Denton's protest was half-hearted. He would have to give in to the absurd idea. What wounded him, though, was the tone of

Jerome's voice. Parental-like. And he'd just invited the man to his inner sanctum, his castle keep. Another swerve, and Denton considered that he was worse off than he claimed. The thought filled him with shame, and he pulled off at the wide spot in front of the Platte bridge.

"Finally," Jerome said, scooting over to the door. Denton put out a hand to stop him. "What? I'm going around."

"It's only that I wanted to say," Denton started, "that I'm sorry. I should have realized better. I mean sooner." There was a catch in his throat as he said it, and then, out of nowhere, Denton Henry was crying. And there was no hiding it. He had never been more embarrassed in his life, but he could not stop. Something that was dammed up inside him let go, and it really let go, in noisy sobs and gasping heaves. He was ashamed to look up, but when he did, Jerome's gaze was steady. Denton sniffed and coughed. "I never ever used to have a bottle at work," he managed to say. "But it just gets so damned lonely in there."

Jerome opened the car door, and came around to the driver's side.

Denton scooted himself across the seat and leaned his face against the window. He felt Jerome's hand behind his head locking the door. The seat slid back beneath him as Jerome adjusted it. He watched Jerome look carefully over the knobs and dials on the dashboard. They pulled slowly onto the highway.

Once they were on the road, Jerome said gently, "Drink can be a terrible curse."

And that was all it took to get Denton started again. He didn't know he had so many words stored up inside him needing to get out. He talked about being the skinny kid in high school, not good at sports. How hard it was to get on with the railroad. But mostly he talked about the loneliness. Some things are for men to talk about. Like for example if you saw a movie with that Claudette Colbert in it. There were only so many things you could say to your wife about that. The Cards were his team, ever since the Gashouse Gang. He said again that he wouldn't mind it if Jerome stopped by the depot. Didn't have to be a special reason for it. Just there at the station. That was where you'd find him, rain or shine. Every day but Sunday. The depot was his fortress, by gum.

"Mr. Henry. Mr. Henry?"

"Hm. Huh. What?"

"Mr. Henry, we're in Julian."

And so they were. Parked at the very fortress with the name JULIAN on it. He must have fallen asleep. He didn't remember falling asleep. He remembered talking. And crying. Embarrassment washed over him, but another part of him felt like a hundred-pound mailbag was off his back.

"You've been asleep for half an hour," Jerome said quietly. "I figure that's enough to get your wits about you. If you feel woozy, maybe you have a blanket or rollaway in your office."

Denton roused himself. "I'm all right. I'll go home."

"Whatever you say, Mr. Henry. Just don't forget the money's in the glove box. Better put it in your safe like Mr. Burdock said, before you head home. The crew is counting on you. You're a hero to them now." He got out of the car but leaned in to say something else. "Maybe you should think about some kind of hobby. Like reading books or juggling or something. Many a man wishes he had time on his hands to do something like that, to learn something. And whenever you feel like having a drink, you say to yourself no, I'm going to practice my juggling instead." He shrugged. "Just a suggestion."

25

AN EDUCATED MAN

"A nun in a hay baler? Did he really say that?"

"Yeah, he really did." Carlin hadn't intended to tell Sister Mary Michael. But she was so mad at Frank. MM's lips were trembling like she was going to start crying. Carlin caught the nun's eye, and saw it was laughter. They burst into guffaws at the same time.

"What's so funny?" said Sister Joseph Martin, bustling through the kitchen.

"Nothing," they both said at once, and broke up again.

"We're just telling dirty jokes again, sister," said Mary Michael.

"Oh, good," said Joseph Martin. "I was afraid it was something unseemly." She started up the stairs, but turned back. "Did either of you hear if the Cardinals won tonight?"

"They're probably still playing," said Mary Michael. "They're in Boston."

"Is Spahn pitching?"

"I don't know," said Mary Michael. "Carlin?"

Carlin did not know if Warren Spahn was pitching. She shrugged. Joseph Martin went on up the stairs. Carlin lifted the teabag from her cup and dropped it gently into Mary Michael's. They were sitting at the small table in the kitchen of the convent, engaging in their ritual. One teabag made two cups of tea.

"Did you mention DePaul University to your father yet?"

"No, sister," said Carlin in a repentant schoolgirl voice. "I did not mention DePaul University to my father yet. I think I'll wait 'til after harvest, when he's calmer."

Mary Michael frowned at the table. "Carlin, you have to face up to him. Waiting until November just seems . . ."

"I meant the wheat harvest. It starts next week." Carlin laughed. "You're such a city slicker."

"Oh, yes. I knew that. I just forgot. Let's practice again." Mary Michael made her voice low and gruff. "What in tarnation can you do with a major in French, young lady?"

"I can go to Paris!"

They laughed again. Reverting to schoolgirl monotone, Carlin said, "Foreign language ability can open unlimited potential. I could be a translator or a teacher or an office assistant."

"Good."

"Or a dime-a-dance girl in Le Club Jazz."

"Not so good."

Carlin loved that she could say things to a nun that most people would never dream of saying. Most people never got to see her like this, in a simple black cotton dress, without her habit. Mary Michael had short dark hair with a natural wave in it. Carlin liked to make her blush by telling her how cute she was. Rumors went around that nuns had shaved heads. She'd even heard it from her own classmates at St. Bernard's. It was ridiculous. But it could be possible, since no one ever saw the Ursuline nuns not wearing their habit. No one but Carlin. She was practically a nun herself by now. And her dad worried she was "wild." And Frank Abernathy saying she shouldn't talk to the colored boy. Who did he think he was? Her anger welled up again.

"What?" asked Mary Michael. "You're shaking your head and frowning. What are you thinking about?"

"Poetry," said Carlin. "I'm thinking about poetry."

The next morning, Sunday, Cook once again rode along with the Littmans to Mass, and this time on the way back he was invited to their home for dinner. When they arrived at the house, the missus excused herself to the kitchen, and the mister escorted him to the most formal room of the house, a parlor with the upright piano against one wall, and crocheted doilies on the end tables. Conversation was strained. They had little common interest. Ron made a good go of it, talking of the weather, of the upcoming harvest, and of the weather again. He mentioned he'd hired one of the gandies, young Sam, for a few odd jobs here and there.

Cook found himself distracted by the smells wafting in from the kitchen. Finally, he broke into Ron's discourse on grasshoppers (bad this year) and mentioned those delicious aromas. Would the mister mind if he went and asked the missus about her recipes? The mister did not mind. In fact, he seemed to jump at the chance. Ron brought the guest to the kitchen, and excused himself, saying he had to run across to the elevator for a moment—Frank Abernathy was coming by with another pittance of corn.

"Oh, Ron," said Milly, "Does he have to do that on a Sunday?"

"I told him," Ron answered. "Frank said his dad took a job in town during the week, and this was the only time they had. But you have to discount half of what Frank says."

Cook was at ease in the kitchen. Millie had a natural warmth about her, was shyly inquisitive about his background, and laughed easily. Despite Cook's invitations to informality, she refused to use anything but his surname, which secretly pleased him, although she stumbled every time she tried to say it. Eventually, with charming directness, she asked if he would write it out for her on paper, which he was happy to do. She studied it a moment, and settled into a pronunciation that rhymed with "revolver." He did not correct her. He was offered tastings of things on the stove and things in the oven. Although it was not on today's menu, fried chicken was of special interest to them both. They discussed techniques in some detail. She mentioned a restaurant in Nebraska City that everyone said was the best in the state.

"Don't buy that," said Carlin, breezing through the kitchen. "What everybody really says is that Mom's chicken is better than Uhlbrick's."

"Oh, Carlin," Millie said, blushing. "They do not."

"Really, Mr. Levalier," she said, "they do."

Cook noted that the girl's pronunciation was flawless, even if her manner was a bit sassy. She must have studied. It pleased him to imagine a gentle mother-daughter skirmish after he left, where the daughter called the mother a bumpkin ("Mr. Levolver? Oh mom, please . . ."), and the mother chided the daughter for putting on airs.

They called it bone soup. They served it with fresh bread. Fine family too. Over chocolate cake, Cook mentioned how the boys on the crew had really taken to the local fast-pitch version of softball, especially since Dave Scarborough had arranged for a farmer to come over and mow the field next to the tracks, and throw out enough straw bales to make a backstop. They had a regular diamond laid out now. Cook said one among them had played a little semi-professional ball, so they had some guidance.

His most rapt listener was little Timmy. Were they playing this afternoon? Could he come watch?

Millie said, "Those men don't want you being a bother to them, Timmy. You stay home and play with Carlin."

"I'm going out," said the girl.

"Where to, Carly?"

"No place special. Watching them play ball would be more exciting. That is if Mr. Levalier thinks it's all right."

Cook allowed as how he thought it would be. Other kids from town had started coming around to watch.

So Cook had the company of a small fry as he walked back to the gandy camp. Once there, he went out to where he had a couple chairs set up in the shade, and watched the boys play. Under Jerome's direction, they were shaping up to be a better team than he'd imagined. Delran was learning to control his pitches, and several of them could handle a bat. As he settled into a sleepy Sunday afternoon lethargy, he noticed the only one missing was Sam. He tried not to think about why that might be.

Cook loosened his belt a notch and glanced toward his mess car, wondering what he should make to show the Littmans his appreciation. And who was this white man getting out of his car and approaching him? Earnest young fellow in a black suit. The man took off his hat as he came across to where Cook was sitting. He had a thick mass of black hair combed up high on his head.

"Are you the one in charge of these boys?" the man asked, gesturing toward the field with his hat.

"Depends on how you mean that," Cook said. "You have some business with them?"

"The Lord's business," said the man, smiling. "My name's Evan Carpenter, and I have the Methodist Church a block up from Marchon's store. I expect a lot of your boys are Southern Baptist or AME, so we're not too far off the mark."

"You inviting the boys to your church?"

The man hesitated. "I was thinking, fine day like this, we could do it right here, if that's what was wanted. John Wesley himself was fond of preaching outdoors."

Cook watched the man hold his hat a while. The preacher was older than he'd first thought.

Carpenter fidgeted for a minute, and then said, "Would you like to present my idea to the men there?"

"I don't believe I would," said Cook languidly. "Look at them all out there, laughing, playing ball. No offense to your preaching, Mr. Carpenter, but can you imagine them doing anything that makes the Lord smile more than that?"

"Well, I don't know. I, um . . ."

"Why don't you just pull up that chair? Lilies of the field and all that. Mind, that one's a little rickety. You don't want to lean back too far."

The boys did look caught up in their game. Evan sat down gingerly on the broken chair. "Pleased to make your acquaintance, Mr. . . ."

Cook stood up. "My apologies. My name is Armond Levalier. The boys call me Cook, and you may as well if you like."

"Well, that other was a mouthful, so I'll take you up on that, Mr. Cook."

"Just Cook."

"Just Cook."

They settled onto their chairs and watched Big Larry hit a long fly ball that Little Larry chased down.

"I play a little myself," Evan said.

"I hear the team is real good," Cook said amiably. "I've seen the trophies in the store window. What's your position?"

"Wherever they need me. I mostly just fill in. I like to let the younger men play."

They sat for another few moments. Cook's mind drifted lazily back across his fine morning and mid-day meal. "Perhaps I should not have spoken for the crew," he said. "Since I am the only one here who has had the opportunity to fulfill my Sunday obligation."

Evan squinted at him. "You must be the one that goes out to St. Joseph's with the Littmans. You got plenty of people around town wondering about you, because, well, you know. Not many Catholics are . . ." he trailed off.

Cook let him dangle a few seconds, and then stated majestically, "I am from New Orleans. Many Catholics there." That was as far as he cared to go to explain his heritage. Around here it just made folks confused.

"Oh, right, right." Evan nodded vigorously. "I got nothing against Catholics. I do wonder about those priests, though. I don't know how a man of God should be deprived of a wife. You can't find that in any Bible I've ever read."

"So you'd pick a fight with the Pope over that doctrine?"

"I think," said Evan, staring at his hat, "that we've had too many fights over too many doctrines."

Cook felt chastened. "The Littmans were gracious to invite me to dinner."

"I'm sure you got your fill too. Millie is known pretty wide around here as a good cook."

"I would say," Cook offered blandly, "that her fried chicken is superior to Uhlbrick's in Nebraska City."

"I always thought so." Evan toyed with his hat. "Weddings, funerals, christenings. That's mostly what I do. Around here we got some Baptists, some United Brethren, Lutherans. Catholics too, of course. Nobody gets his nose bent out of shape about it."

"That's a good policy," said Cook. "I have to say this has been one of the friendlier places. A lot of towns, they see us come to town, they put out the unwelcome signs."

Evan shrugged. "I think there's a curiosity factor here. We've never had any colored folks in Julian. We've had foreigners here, mostly relatives, like from France or Germany, even New York. We're brought up to want to make a good impression to visitors. I reckon it's no different anywhere."

"It is different, Mr. Carpenter. There was a town in Kansas that told the Mopac they wouldn't let us camp there."

"Kansas," Evan repeated, seeming to chew over the word. "There was a time they called it Bloody Kansas. Before the Civil War, we had our own little war, not far south of here. Lawrence was an abolitionist town—that's what it means to be a Jayhawker, if you go back that far. Some slave owners from Missouri came over and killed some folks, and burned Lawrence down. Then the Jayhawkers went back and killed some of them. It got pretty ugly."

"You are an educated man, Reverend."

"If that's even a little true I can thank Nebraska Wesleyan University. Anyway, the abolitionists, they knew who their friends were. They had safe houses all the way up the Missouri River, and on across Iowa. The slaves ran away from Missouri into Kansas, got taken in by Jayhawkers and sent north."

"The Underground Railroad?"

Evan nodded. "It was more like a network. They had some signal—a checkered bandana on a scarecrow or something like that—to let people know they were part of it."

"That's interesting . . ."

"But my point was," the preacher continued, on to something, "it's what it made me think of when you said we were different here. In Nebraska City they even have a tourist attraction called John Brown's Cave. It's a log cabin with a cave underneath where they hid runaway slaves. Nebraska City was where they smuggled them across the river to Iowa, you know. What I'm saying is, it's something people around here know about. They teach it in schools. Kids grow up learning that we were part of history, that we were the good guys, and they take a good kind of pride in that."

"So this town, these farms," Cook gestured around, "underground railroad?"

"Some of them." Carpenter was distracted. "A good kind of pride, I like the sound of that." He stood up. "I think I have the title for next Sunday's sermon. You'll have to excuse me. I need to go write this down before I lose it. And may I quote you, about Julian being a friendlier place than most, Mr. Levay?"

"As long as you mention that I do my business with the Catholics," Cook said smiling.

"That I will do," said Carpenter, hurrying toward his car. "That I will do."

FIELD NOTES

Site: Hofstedder Farm, County Road 512, Otoe County, NE Bright ranch home on
hillside. Living room with large picture window overlooking a valley of tilled fields. An
arrow-straight rail line follows alongside a ragged line of trees and brush indicating
the path of Rock Creek.
Subjects: Eric Hofstedder, retired minister
Virginia Sweetapple Hofstedder, retired schoolteacher

The Reverend is tall and thin, with good posture and a great pompadour
disturbingly dyed to an oily cast-iron black. Virginia is shorter, rounder, prim with a
gray bun, but there is something steely about her. They sit in matching recliners on
either side of the window, giving me the couch with the view out the picture window
onto the valley.

When I say I have come to talk about railroads back in the day, the minister
gallantly defers to his wife.

"My maiden name," she says, "was Sweetapple. My father was Tom
Sweetapple, a Missouri Pacific crew boss for thirty years. We didn't see much of him
around the home place. He was, I'd say, somewhat a legend."

"A legend?"

She frowns, pursing her lips. "I'll put it plain. He had a reputation as the toughest
foreman on the line. A real son of a you-know-what." A small embarrassed laugh
from her husband.

"But he always got the job done right, and on time, so he was in high demand.
The rail workers, well, that was a different story. They were scared to death of him,
especially the colored ones—and I think they had cause to be."

"Tough and mean. You think that had something to do with the name—
Sweetapple—like he had to prove himself?"

She shrugs. "It might have."

"Thirty years is a long time," I say hopefully. "I like to think a man can change.
Maybe, by the end of his career, he might have mellowed out, become the kind of
foremen the workers love. You think that could have happened?"

She shrugs again. "I doubt it."

I turn to her husband. "You ministered to church-goers in Julian."

"The Methodists, yes. And I helped out with the Brethren, as they didn't have a
preacher of their own. Weddings. Funerals. Christenings. Or a roof needed shingles

or baby driven to the hospital. Whatever I could do. Good folks here."

"I heard you played for the Hornets."

A smile, a small gleam of pride. "We were pretty good," he allows. "I was at second base when I wasn't called away on pastoral duty."

"Do you remember the summer of the gandy dancers?"

"Oh sure," he said. "I remember that well. They wore bib overalls and cotton shirts with long sleeves, even in the heat. Hats of this kind or that. Most of the time they stuck to themselves—they didn't want trouble."

"Do you remember them playing ball?"

"Oh sure. They played near every day in the field right next to where their camp cars sat, on the side rail. Had their own gloves and so forth. Lot of talent there, by golly."

Trying to keep my voice casual: "They ever play a pick-up game with the local boys?"

"Yes!" He sits up straighter, his eyes sparkling. "Now that you mention it, we did. A Sunday or holiday I think, when everybody but me had the day off. And it was more than a pick-up game. We didn't expect much from them, but I tell you now, it was a good game. And afterward we had a picnic with them. The wives put out a nice spread in the schoolyard."

"I don't remember that part," says his wife. "You sure you're not mixing it up with some other picnic, like a church do or a family reunion?"

"I'm pretty sure it was them." He falters a little. "I could be mistaken, I suppose."

I take a long, deep breath, trying not to show my elation at his testimony or chagrin at her doubts. "You're sure about the game, though. Right, Pastor?"

"A full-on game," he confirms with enthusiasm. "No juggling or joking around— why would they? They were railroad men, not barnstormers. Except . . ." He trails off, poking the air with his index finger. "Except one of them. Yes, one had some history, semi-pro or something. He was real good, and kind of coached them up."

"Fast-pitch softball. Right?"

"Of course," says the minister.

After asking more about the picnic, to his more lukewarm certainty it happened, and her more grudging concession that it may have, eventually I make my farewells. Out on the sidewalk, I gesture to the beautiful view, and turn to give them a last wave, framed together in the doorway.

The former Virginia Sweetapple calls out, "We always wondered what became of you. Terrible, what happened to your mom and dad." The minister tries to shush her, to no avail. "They would have been able to tell you all about it. You lived right down by the tracks. Don't you remember it yourself?"

"Just bits and pieces. It was a long time ago."

"Ron was the best," the minister says solemnly. "He got those farmers from harvest to harvest, with loans to them, and deferrals of what they owed him."

"And Millie," adds his wife. "The kindest woman on earth. I knew from the Catholics she played the organ at church and sang like an angel. That must have been hard on you, losing them."

"I was very young. Honestly, I don't remember much."

"Then maybe" —her face transforms, and I catch a flash of the son of a something boss man in her— "maybe, when you come all the way back here from wherever you live, instead of this side-rail stuff about games and gandies, you should be asking folks that *knew them* about *them*."

26

YOUR FACE TOO CLEAR

Sam and Carlin were down by the creek, in the deep gulley shaded on all sides by elm and cottonwood. They did not need to speak of secrets; they shared a tacit knowledge it was better they kept it to themselves. Other people did not care about poems, did not see the beauty of poetry like they did. Other people might not understand.

With some enthusiasm, Sam was telling Carlin how he learned to read the poem right. How Ivan Tarp had shouted to the foreman that he would "rue the day. You'll *rue* the day!" Sam howled, imitating the timekeeper.

Carlin did not laugh, just grinned a sickly grin. Of course it meant "regret." She was mortified to recall how she'd blathered on about French streets and French kings. She wanted to talk about something else. "So I hear," she said, lightly, "that you've got the track finished almost as far as Paul. I suppose you'll be moving on soon."

"That's what I hear too," Sam said. "After the Fourth of July."

The truth of this settled on both of them, giving rise to an air of melancholy. Neither said anything for a moment. They were sitting in their accustomed spot, side by side so they could share the book, legs hanging down over the edge of the ravine.

Carlin spoke first, making her voice breezy. "Well, once the harvest starts, I won't be dragging around the crick anymore, that's for sure. Dad will put me to work. It's all hands on deck when the harvest starts."

"When is that?"

She found Sam's big eyes looking straight into her eyes, and it made her flinch. "Oh, you never know in advance," she said, plucking a milkweed and tossing it down the bank. "It depends on how much moisture is in the wheat. One day they do a test, and, bingo, the harvest is going full blast. Somehow all the wheat gets ripe the same day, and we have trucks backed all the way down to your camp waiting to unload. The last couple of years, Dad's made me run the scale. Sometimes Mom runs it. We stay open from first light until midnight."

Sam said nothing.

Anyway," she said brightly, tapping the book, "what other one shall we look at?"

"There's this one," he said shyly. "I think I'll look at this one a lot after I go." He handed her the book.

She read the short poem, nodding. "I see what you mean," she said, and read:

> What are those blue remembered hills,
>   What spires, what farms are those?

"Yeah," said Sam. He wished she wouldn't read the rest out loud, but of course she did:

> That is the land of lost content,
>   I see it shining plain,
> The happy highways where I went
>   And cannot come again.

"Aw . . ." she said in a teasing voice, "that's so sweet. Is Julian the happy highways you're going to miss?" Now Sam was embarrassed, which caught Carlin by surprise. She pointed to the top of the grain elevator above the trees. "I think that's what you'll miss. You really learned a lot about elevator work. Dad even said so."

"Uh huh," said Sam. "I guess I will."

"Sure you will. If you ever get tired of fixing rails, you can get an elevator job. Not that that would be a step up." She paged toward the front of the book, and stopped at random. Have you read this one?"

He looked at it. XV. "Yeah, but I'm not sure what it says."

"Let's have a look." Carlin stared at the words a long time, distracted. No more French streets or girls with lipstick. She felt so foolish. She was having trouble focusing. Okay, she told herself, *think*.

The poetry of A.E. Housman has been called wistful, bucolic, sentimental. Sometimes droll. It has never been called passionate. No poems to inspire ardor or kindle lust—or almost none. By pure chance, Carlin had chosen lyric XV, whose first quatrain veers in a sudden new direction. She sat, hunched over the book, glasses on top of her head, and began the first verse in a clear, perfect voice, unaware of the ambush. As the words unfolded, she felt an impossible heat welling up from her stomach, inflaming her cheeks. Sam's face was right beside hers. She couldn't keep going, but she did not dare to stop. She read:

> Look not in my eyes, for fear
> They mirror true the sight I see,
> And there you find your face too clear
> And love it and be lost like me.

She slowly lowered the book and raised her face to Sam's, intending to break the tension with a joke. But in the dappled summer light she saw her own face in his enormous chocolate eyes. At the same moment, Sam saw his own face staring back from her slate blue eyes, a sight he had never imagined. For a moment nothing on earth breathed. Slowly, their lips came together.

The kiss lasted less than one second. Sam's eyes opened wide in a panic. He scrambled to his feet, saying, "I got to go, I'm late," grabbed the book, and sprinted off through the trees.

27

THE NAME'S MOORE. MAX MOORE

As it turned out, that was not the week's only interracial pressing of the flesh. Another one happened two days later at Marchon Mercantile.

"Mr. Wallace," said Dave Scarborough, when Jerome came in the door.

"Mr. Postmaster."

"I am afraid that I don't have any letters here with your name on them," said Dave, "just got the mail an hour ago."

"I'm here for Mr. Mopac today. We need wire."

"What size wire?"

"Whatever you got."

They were working four miles up the track. The foreman had pulled Jerome off the spiking job, and told him to take the track cart back to Julian, find some wire at the store, or borrow it at the grain elevator if he had to, and get back as quickly as possible. They'd run out.

Dave plucked the two rolls off the shelf. "What's the urgent need?"

"Slow orders," Jerome answered, feeling like a true gandy for the first time. "We need to hang slow orders and stop orders from the telegraph poles. If you nail them, the signs break up."

"And one thing you don't want," Dave added, "is for the engineer of the Red Ball Express to be wondering whether he's got a slow order or not. Charge that to the Mopac account?"

"Yes, sir."

"Sign here. And it's Dave Scarborough."

"Pleased to make your acquaintance, Mr. Scarborough."

"Dave."

"Dave."

Dave put his hand across the counter, and Jerome shook it, feeling conspicuous. He saw Dave's smile, and knew the postmaster was making a point to someone else. He looked around. Ron Littman had come in after he had, and was getting his mail out of a cubicle in the wall of mailboxes. But the grain man didn't need a lesson. After all, Cook got Sunday dinner there. And just yesterday, Jerome had crossed paths with the grain man on Main Street. Jerome had asked, and gotten reassurance, that Sam was not being a pest coming around the elevator too much. No, Littman had said, the boy has helped him out when he needed it. He said he had another job for Sam, if Sam wanted it.

The only other people in the store were a couple, a tall man with thick glasses, and a short woman. They hadn't moved since he'd entered the store. He remembered them from when he came in that time with Ice. The man had held forth like the preacher. The handshake must be for their benefit. Jerome took the wire and the receipt and was about to leave, but Dave wasn't done.

"I believe you know Ronnie," he said, indicating the grain man.

He did. They made awkward nods to each other.

"Additionally," Dave said, "I want to introduce you to Mr. Henry Benkleman. Hank Benkleman, this is Jerome Wallace."

"Mr. Benkleman."

"Wallace."

There was no move on either side toward a handshake.

"Hank is a certified umpire for the country league," Dave went on in a sprightly voice, "best umpire in the state. In fact, just the other day Hank was allowing as how, if he was to call a game between the Hornets and your crew, he'd call it fair and square. Isn't that right, Hank?"

"Ye . . . yess." The word came unwillingly from Hank's lips.

Jerome heard the spite in Dave's exuberance. The tall man was not happy to be fraternizing, and Dave was forcing the issue. That was the only explanation here, and Jerome was ready to play along. He said, "Is that right? Isn't that something? If we ever had such a great opportunity, it would be good to know we had an honest man behind the plate."

"How about the Fourth?" Dave popped in.

"What's that?" said Jerome.

"What's that?" said Hank.

"Fourth of July, week from today. The gandies have off for the holiday."

"That's impossible," snapped Hank. "Lincoln Thomas Ford is coming on the Fourth."

"Oh them." Dave waved a hand. "That's at two. No reason we can't have a little bat-around at noon. An exhibition. Three innings. For fun. We can still whip LTF after that. Mr. Wallace?"

"Jerome."

"Jerome. Think your crew would agree to that?"

Jerome's mind raced. He was plotting to get to Omaha on the Fourth, one way or another. A game was out of the question. But something held his tongue. Jerome had concluded some time ago that white people fell into four groups. There were outright racists, and passive racists. There were good folks who were not bigoted, but had heard the stories and had some fear. They avoided confrontation. Then there were the fourth category folks, outspoken anti-racists. This type was extremely rare, and mostly consisted of preachers and politicians. And this groceryman, Dave Scarborough.

"Well," Jerome heard himself saying, "Noon on the Fourth of July?"

"Wait," Hank said. "Let's not be hasty."

"It'll be fun," said Dave. "Real entertaining. Don't you think so, Ronnie?"

Ron Littman frowned. "You know what I think, Dave. I'm all for fun and games, as long as it's not harvest time. If it's harvest time we get the crop in."

"Aw, Ronnie," said, Dave, smiling. "It's just one day, a few hours . . ."

The door banged open. A short, thick-waisted man in a striped suit came in, followed by a tall girl in a tan dress. Her hair was piled up on her head, and she held a steno pad.

"Say, there." The man glanced around quickly, and addressed himself to the one in the apron. "I'm looking for a town around here by the name of Julian."

"You found it," said Dave.

"I was afraid of that. Can you direct me to someone connected with the Julian Bees?"

"Hornets."

"What?"

"Julian Hornets. I'm as connected as anybody, I guess. Dave Scarborough."

The man's face lit up. "Scarborough! Pleasure to meet you. State batting champ—mmm, what year? That goes back a ways now. Up in Lincoln, we were hoping you'd play for the University."

"You got the wrong Scarborough, Mr. Thomas."

"What? Ha." He gave a short laugh and turned to the tall girl. "He thinks I'm H.T. These gentlemen think that Harold Thomas has time to come here to set up a game for his team. They got a pretty high opinion of themselves." He turned back to Dave. "The name's Moore. Max Moore. And this is my assistant, Maureen."

Maureen did something between a nod and a curtsy. "Hello."

"Dave," said Dave, nodding in her direction and turning back to Max. "You meant my brother, Ernie. Ernie had the batting title."

"That right?" said Max Moore, no longer interested. "Can one of you show us the ball field?"

"Sure can," Dave said. He untied his apron and draped it on the counter, proclaiming, "Ladies and gentlemen of the high opinion of ourselves, Marchon's is closed until further notice."

They all shuffled out the door. Dave came last, flipping the 'Open' sign around and pocketing the store keys. The brand-new black Lincoln Cosmopolitan made everyone pause to look. Not exactly shiny, not after its trip down the gravel road, but still a beautiful machine. Max ran a finger across the fender and looked at it with disgust.

"Remind me to have this washed," he said to the girl.

"Look, Max, they've got their trophies right in the store window. Isn't that cute?"

"Terrific. Let's get going, honey."

Dave put a hand on Hank's back, propelling him forward. "Mr. Moore, this is Henry Benkleman. He will be the umpire on the Fourth. I just want you to know, there isn't a better . . ."

"Whoa. Stop right there." Max gave Hank a cursory glance. "Is this a joke?"

"No, it's . . ."

"Did you think Harold Thomas was born yesterday?"

"No, it's . . ."

"Nice try. No way we're going to let some local yokel steal a game from LTF," Max said, adding, in Hank's direction, "No offense."

Hank bridled. "When I call a game . . ."

"I said 'nice try'," said Max, cutting him off. "Okay, here's how it works. We book an ump out of Omaha—not Lincoln, not Nebraska City—that way everyone knows he's neutral. I'll handle that, it's on my list. The teams will split the cost."

"Cost?" said Dave.

"Don't worry, we'll take it out of the profit."

"Profit?"

Max Moore looked around at each person, his gaze lighting lastly, and curiously, on Jerome. He shook his head, as if to clear it. "I'm in kind of a hurry here. Lot of things on my list. Can we talk in the car? Maureen, hop in the back seat, honey, and let the grocer sit up front."

Jerome pulled the cord and backed down the choke of the small gasoline engine on the track cart. He sat on the edge, engaged the gear, and off it went.

The work site was miles away now, so the crew had to pile onto these carts to get there and back. Back when he first got wind of the rail job, he'd pictured himself, not pleasantly, pumping one of those hand carts with the big lever in the middle, like in the movies. He was relieved to find out they'd been motorized.

He opened the throttle as far as it would go, and felt the wind in his face. He had dawdled too long at the store. The foreman would be having fits. But he'd been roped into the conversation with the umpire, and then was curious as everyone else about the sneering Max Moore. As long as he got the wire to Burdock before the noon freights, they'd be all right. And what news he was bringing! They'd been challenged. A real game, on a real ball field. The boys would be excited. As the green and golden fields rolled beside him, Jerome indulged himself in strategy. He'd play catcher, so he could keep an eye on everyone, and manage the team. Delran would pitch; that would be an adventure in itself. Big Larry on first. George at second? Or would he be better used in center field? Sam could play the corner, and who at short? Well. Ice thinks shortstop is the glamour position, so he would claim it, no matter what Jerome said.

Jerome filled in the rest of the positions, and started thinking about batting order. He wondered how the opponent planned their line-up.

The word "opponent" struck a false note in his mind, and he wondered why. Something began to curdle in his stomach, a feeling like guilt. For what? And it slowly came to him. He recalled Dave's words. "For fun! Entertaining!" And worst of all, "exhibition." Who was he kidding? The Lincoln team was the opponent. They were the minstrel show.

Jerome eased the throttle down on the gas motor. He was suddenly in no hurry to get to the job. Because these boys would not know. No matter how he told them, they'd think it was going to be a real game. They hadn't been on the barnstorming circuit. They didn't know how it was. These things followed a formula. For the first two innings the colored boys were expected to clown around, show off, and mess up on purpose to make people laugh. His boys didn't have any routines, and Jerome was in no mood to teach them any.

It was like that fish story Charly T had told him about gandy dancing coming from the courtship step of the male goose. It had sounded good, and during a work break, he'd been passing the story on to Sam when Burdock happened to walk by. The foreman grinned at him, then tipped his hat and said, "That would be fine, except for your lining bar and your spike maul are made by the Gandy Manufacturing Company of Chicago. That might have more to do with it." Jerome endured the foreman's jeers with grim good humor, but inside he was furious with Charly T. That goose story was the kind of the thing keeping them down, the Black man putting on the clown clothes. No, by God, his team would march out on that field and play straight up, and may the best team win.

Jerome was not entirely at ease with this either. Dave Scarborough was going to be promising everyone an exhibition. Maybe to Dave that just meant a game, but the small town folks would be expecting something else. This town had been good to them, and that postmaster was a true man. The gandy crew would be packing up soon. Jerome wanted to leave on good relations. But, damn, he was not about to play Bojangles in Julian or anywhere else. Never again. A new thought occurred to him. Why did he need to worry? If he could get away to Omaha, the exhibition could play out however it went—without him.

28

WHAT IS BOTHERING MAUREEN

Maureen Fallon was not Max Moore's secretary for her typing skills, she knew that. But contrary to what people thought, she was not his mistress. He liked to act the big shot and throw his weight around, but alone with her he was really kind of shy. At holidays, well, it was a little different then. Max Moore was one of those holiday party gropers. The rest of the year he was all right, but at company parties, Katie bar the door! Last Christmas he caught up with her in the hallway coming from the women's room. She'd stood for it long enough to let him run his hands over her garter stays through her skirt, and that was more than she should have.

This was as far afield as she'd ever traveled with him, and her mother was not happy. As she showed her mom on the map, they weren't going to Calcutta. They weren't even leaving Nebraska. And Mr. Moore was a perfectly respectable man. She didn't tell mom about his party habits, of course.

Something else was bothering her today, and she didn't know exactly what it was. She had a sense of unease, a worry deep in her stomach. She should be happy. She was getting out of the boring dealership for a whole day, and all she had to do was put up with Max. It was a beautiful day, sunny and warm, with fields of golden wheat waving in the breeze. Nebraska City was where people from Lincoln and Omaha went on weekends to visit orchards and have picnics. She remembered a grade school trip where they toured the big white mansion of the man who founded Arbor Day.

On the ride down from Lincoln he was talking about a restaurant in Nebraska City famous for fried chicken. He'd said if she was a good girl, on the way back he'd buy her lunch. She hoped he meant 'good girl' in a general way. But if he got ideas she could handle him. That wasn't what was bothering her. She couldn't put her finger on what it was.

The country store with the trophies and bats in the window was just darling. The people inside were like the cast of a play about good country folks. There was even a kindly Negro. The grocery man, who was riding along now to the ball field, he seemed nice. She wanted to talk to him, but Max never let her get a word in edgewise. And there wasn't time anyway because they were already there. They parked by a brick school and walked across a playground, approaching down the third base line. The field had a bank of white-painted bleachers on either side. The dugouts were only two steps down from the field, and the scoreboard had neat little rows of nails to hang every inning's scores.

"It's absolutely charming," she said.

Dave smiled to her. "Thank you. We like it here."

Of course, Max didn't find it charming. He was even more of an ass than usual. "Nice practice field," he said. "Where do you play your games?"

Dave gave a forced laugh. "It's not much, I admit, but . . ."

"Not much? Where is right field?"

Dave laughed again. "It's a short field, all right."

"Short field?" Max said, stomping out to the mound. "My back yard is deeper than that."

"You see, the property line is right there. No room."

"Maureen, did you hear that? No room! What do you call all that out there?"

Dave looked. "Why, I'd call that a hay field. What do they call that in Lincoln, Mr. Moore?"

A giggle escaped Maureen, and Max gave her a death stare. He took off his hat and wiped his brow, and that made her want to laugh again. The bald spot was not covered the way he liked it to be.

"And these grandstands. What do they seat, two hundred?"

"If you don't mind being cozy," said the grocer, giving Maureen a smile.

She liked that he didn't let Max rattle him. Max rattled a lot of people. It was about his only talent. She'd bet this Dave had been in the service. He stood up straight the way veterans did, and wasn't thrown off when someone talked tough. She pictured him in a uniform, and swooned a little. The unease gripped her stomach again, and she pushed it away.

Without warning, Dave took off running into right field. Maureen thought he was trying to show how deep it was, but he ran all the way to the fence and climbed half way up it, waving his arm back and forth. Way out across the field, a tractor was pulling some kind of plow thing. He got off the fence and trotted back to the infield, grinning.

"I thought he might be working there today," Dave said. "Mr. Moore, Miss Fallon, here's the man you came to see. And you'll come back on the Fourth to see him in the line-up."

Maureen smiled. He remembered her name, and called her Miss Fallon. The tractor lumbered in their direction. Max looked at his watch, then looked unhappily around the ball field. "Boss's not going to like this," Max said sideways to her. Then, to Dave, "There any way we can get a couple rows of folding chairs? Maybe from that school over there?"

Dave considered. "Generally, people just stand along the foul lines if the bleachers are full."

The tractor was taking its time. Finally it swung to a slow stop outside the right field fence. They heard it throttle down. Maureen watched Max being Max, stepping from one foot to the other, balling one fist into the other hand, looking over at his car. He could be the devil for impatience. It had better be President Truman driving that tractor. With infinite slowness the man climbed down off the seat, and ambled around the fence toward them. Dave must know Max was getting annoyed—it's not as if Max was trying to hide it. The grocery man went out to meet the farmer in the overalls, took him by the shoulders, and pushed him toward Max and Maureen.

"This here's the man you wanted to meet," Dave said with enthusiasm. "Owner of all those batting records, and my brother, Ernest Scarborough. Ernie, this here's Mr. Moore and Miss Fallon, representing Lincoln Thomas Ford."

Maureen could see the resemblance. Dave was taller, his face more open and expressive, but they had the same strong jaw. The farmer brother barely nodded, and looked like he didn't want to be here either. Her heart clutched with his pain, whatever it was, and inside her head she begged Max not to be rude. It seemed he half-heard her.

"You're the man, eh?" They shook hands briefly. "I always thought you'd be, I don't know, bigger."

"He hits plenty big," said Dave. "Your boys had better watch out for him on the Fourth."

"Whatever happened to you?" Max said. "I heard the Cubs signed you to a deal."

Ernie shrugged. "Oh, you know. The war."

"Oh yeah. The war. Wounded?"

"Somewhat."

"Too bad." He turned to Dave.

Maureen could tell he was done with farmer brother, and done being nice. It was time to talk turkey.

"Listen, we got a problem, a math problem. Lincoln Thomas Ford isn't coming all the way out here for the love of the game, if you know what I mean. At fifty cents adults and two bits for kids, times your grandstand capacity of two-hundred, we're looking at a total gate of a hundred dollars, maybe."

"We didn't think about any gate."

"I know you didn't," said Max, "so I'm thinking for you. Let's say we get receipts of one hundred dollars. Then there's fifteen dollars for the ump . . ."

"Fifteen dollars for an ump?"

"To come down here from Omaha, you bet. And we'll have to toss fifty to some charity."

"Charity?"

"You really don't know how it works, do you? Lucky I came down here today. Got to be a charity. Thomas Ford supports the community, all that jazz. Now, about the . . ."

"What charity?"

"Some charity, any charity," Max answered, casting around. He looked at Ernie. "Disabled vets. That's a good one. We're going to need it with the new war in Korea. But the point is, what's left over is not hardly worth our while . . ."

"What new war in Korea?" Ernie said, his voice loud and unsteady.

"Haven't you seen the morning paper? Communists pouring in from the north. Our side's getting overrun. Oh, it's a hell of a mess. Truman says we're not going in, then says we are. Probably be a call up any day."

"A call up?" said Ernie.

"Naw," said Dave, touching his brother's arm. "There's no call up."

Maureen's mind was exploding. Korea! That was it! That's what was bothering her. It was on the radio this morning while she was getting dressed. She had heard it and not heard it. It was frightening. The farmer was taking it bad. He looked stricken. A mental condition from the war. Instinctively she tried to help. She took a step toward Ernie, made him catch her eye. "They said there wouldn't be any more call ups. I heard it on the radio."

"Don't you believe them, honey," Max said blithely. "I always said the war wouldn't really be over until we took out Russia. Lucky we've got the atom bomb. Korea's just the start, mark my word. What? I got something on my face?"

Maureen was frowning, making shushing noises, and Max just sailed right on.

"Let's not talk of war," said Dave, guiding his brother a few steps away. "Ernie, are you feeling up to finishing that field?"

"Yes," said Maureen. "Let's talk about the game. Talk about the game."

"What's gotten into you?" Max said to her under his breath. Louder, to Dave, "Yeah, the game. So as I was saying, we got a problem with the gate. Not to mention you don't even have a fence around the place, so how do you charge admission? So I got a plan. What we do is, we make it all donations."

"Donations?" said Dave.

Maureen could tell they were hardly listening. Dave was walking his brother back toward the tractor.

"Yeah," said Max, trailing them, shouting to their backs. "You make the game free entry, then you ask for donations. You take in more than the other way, you'd be surprised. What you do is, after the second inning, you make an announcement for disabled vets, and you pass the hat. Or in our case buckets."

"Buckets?" said Dave.

"Shiny tin buckets," said Max. "They got LTF painted right on them. I got a couple rattling around the trunk. I'll show you right now."

"I HAVE TO SIT DOWN."

Finally, even Max had to notice. The brother's voice so unnatural, loud and strained. Dave walked him toward the dug-out.

Maureen kicked Max on the shin, as hard as she could.

"Ow!" he said, hopping on one foot. "What'd I do?"

"You . . . You . . ." Maureen could not think of a word bad enough to call him.

Dave had been talking softly to his brother. When he turned back to them, he was no longer trying to keep up any pretense. Tears sprang to Maureen's eyes. In all her life she had never seen anything so sad as those two brothers' faces, one plainly terrified, the other asking someone, anyone, for mercy.

"Let me give you a ride," Max called out, solicitous at last.

"I think it's best we're left alone," said Dave.

"It's no trouble."

Maureen spun Max toward the car, saying, "Shut up, Max."

The last glimpse she had of them, as the car pulled away, was two figures in the corner of the dug-out, huddled together as if against a snowstorm.

29

SAM COOPERS THE CAR

At the intersection of poetry and history sits the boxcar. Today's top-loading grain cars are merely efficient. The boxcar, like the gandy dance, was an emblem of the railroad America. The Okie Airstream, the Hobo Hilton. In its primary function, it was the love-knot between grain elevator and railroad, essential to each. Every country elevator had a fat articulated spout hanging out of the side above the rail. You don't need to be Sigmund Freud to raise your eyebrows when the dangling pipe is turned upward, inserted in the boxcar door, mounted and rigid. Or when you hear the hoarse roar of a cannonade of grain dropping down the sluice from ninety feet up and shooting into the shadowy depths of the car. Once loaded, the cars are eased on down the side track by the grain men, where they wait, big with seed, for the call of the freight train.

The standard boxcar was forty feet long, eight feet wide and ten high, with six-foot wide floor-to ceiling doors on each side. The iron doors were top-hung on tiny iron wheels that frequently failed to roll, due to dents, age, or rust. Ron Littman spent as much breath cussing stuck boxcar doors as he did cussing stuck boxcar wheels.

In order to transport grain, the boxcar needed an interior barricade. These walls were rebuilt for each filling using heavy planks nailed up from the inside. The Missouri Pacific provided the boards free of charge. They arrived on flat-cars, stacks of them tied down with ropes. Borrowed from barrel-makers, the term "coopering" was used to describe the job of making the boxcars fit for hauling grain.

This is how Sam found himself, on a Wednesday evening, lifting the heavy planks, one after another, off the flatcar and easing them down to lean against the car. Ron had given him leather gloves. The boards were splintery, with nails sticking out every which way.

Sam leaned ten boards, then hopped down and started stacking them in a crossways pattern, as Ron had showed him. He tried not to think of anything but railroad timber, but that was hard to do. After seeing himself reflected in Carlin's eyes, after that moment between them, he had vowed to steer clear of the creek, the elevator, and anywhere that girl might be. When he got word from Jerome that Ron wanted to see him, fear flared inside him. When he saw Timmy with his dad he had the worst scare. For a moment he was sure the boy had seen them.

But it turned out Ron just wanted Sam to unload and stack planks. He didn't mind that at all. A full day of gandy dancing was hard work, but there were plenty of breaks waiting for other things to get done, or for trains to come through. In the evening, after a big meal, he was ready for more. He liked the money part of it, too. Every time he got paid out of that cigar box the elevator man kept in the office, Sam thought of how proud his own dad would be.

As he climbed back onto the flatcar, Sam saw Frank Abernathy walking towards him, a sideways grin on his mouth. Sam wished he had his shirt back on. Sure enough, Frank fastened on that first thing.

"Showing off your muscles for the girls?" Frank looked around in a stagey way. "Too bad no girls are around here now. White girls like to look at that."

"It's hot out," said Sam.

"Yes it is," said Frank. "Don't let me slow you down. You go right on, I'll just sit here a bit." Frank hopped up and sat on the edge of the flat car.

Sam went back to stacking boards.

"I could tell you how to do that better. I unloaded thousands of these. First off, you don't have to line them up like that. Just throw them all off at once." He took one board off the pile and sent it clattering onto the gravel, and Sam had to dance out of the way. Frank sat down again. "I never liked stacking timber. Looks like Ronnie figured out it's a job for unskilled labor. I bet you don't even know what these are for, do you?"

Sam did know. Ron had explained. But as soon as Sam started, Frank interrupted.

"Knowing how it works is not the same as doing it. Ronnie will be having me coopering first thing tomorrow, I'll bet on it. He's going to want a dozen cars at least ready for harvest. Bet you don't know why it has to be done early in the morning."

Sam allowed as he did not.

"How hot do you think a boxcar gets sitting in the sun all day?"

"Pretty hot," Sam said, turning to go back to his pile.

"Been measured at a hundred thirty-five degrees. Too damn hot to work inside of, that's for sure. For a white man, anyway." Frank went on, not letting up. "I hear you boys been playing a lot of fast-pitch down there. I heard, in fact, we've got an exhibition with the gandies before Lincoln Thomas Ford on the Fourth. Their man was down yesterday to see the field. Going to be a great show, that's what everybody's saying. You been practicing your tricks?"

"I generally play third base," Sam said.

"You think you boys are pretty good?"

"We're okay," said Sam.

"Let's make it a friendly wager. When we get down to business, after the farting around, who's gonna score more runs, the Hornets or the Gandies? How about five dollars, straight up? My team and yours."

Sam paused from stacking. "I promised my daddy I wouldn't gamble."

"All right," laughed Frank. "You got me. How many runs do you want? How about four and a half? I win if we win by five; you win if you lose by four or less."

Sam started to repeat himself, but stopped mid-sentence. He didn't know how long Ron had been standing there.

"Frank," Ron said gruffly, "I sent you out here to help unload. Sam, has he done a single thing?"

Sam considered. "Maybe a little."

"I'll bet," Ron said. "When you get them stacked, come over to the office and we'll settle up. Twelve dozen board, penny a board, that's $1.44. We'll make it one-fifty. You," he pointed to Frank, "stop pestering him."

When Ron left, Frank started in on Sam, red-faced and angry. "He's not so smart. He's supposed to be mister businessman. Hell, I can run rings around him any time I want." His voice turned spiteful. "Where's your poetry book, boy?"

Sam didn't answer.

"Isn't that what you like to do, bring your book to show off to the white girls? White girls love poetry, is that something you heard?"

Sam went back to stacking planks.

Frank hopped to his feet, standing on the rail car, talking downhill. "Look at me when I talk to you."

Sam looked up briefly, and resumed stacking.

"Because I tell you what. Truman can integrate the army if he has to. We can have exhibition games from here to next year, but some things are never getting integrated. In fact, you'd better be watching your step around this town.

I'm not saying anything bad will happen, but it could, and it could be real bad. Just a friendly warning."

Neither of them saw Jerome approach. But suddenly he was right there. He wore a tight smile. "Everything okay here, Sam?"

"It's okay."

Jerome shaded his eyes up at Frank. "Everything okay with you? You seem somewhat excited."

"Just giving your boy here some free advice. One time we found a skunk hiding in the woodpile. Had to kill it, and it stunk the place up good." Frank tried a smirk, but Jerome's steady eyes made him look away. He jumped down from the flat-bed and started up Main Street, calling back, "You stack all those good, and don't dawdle over it, or we won't be paying you."

Jerome nodded to Sam, and continued his walk down the tracks. His destination: the train station.

"Oh, there's the man!" Denton Henry said theatrically as Jerome came through the door. It was their first meeting since the Omaha trip. Denton swiveled in his chair. "There's the man made me sit outside in the dark with the whole crew's pay, liable to be hit over the head or robbed or something. Well, I hope them boys appreciated it is all I can say."

"Thank you, Mr. Henry. They did."

"Well, that's good, because Ivan Tarp was none too happy, I can tell you that!" Denton chuckled broadly. "What can I do for you? Burdock got another crazy idea? Needs me to get him out of another fix? What is it this time, Wallace?"

"No errand, Mr. Henry," Jerome said. "Just taking in the fine evening. Thought I'd stop in and say hello. Mind if I sit down?"

"Well, I am awful busy, what with the harvest coming. This will be the first harvest where we'll have to back every boxcar in and out from the south." He wagged a finger at Jerome. "That's on account of you boys' Pullmans sitting out there . . . I mean the gandy crew. No offense."

"None taken."

"If you don't mind if I'm working while we visit, then sure, pull up one of them chairs from the other side there. That was the waiting room back in the day. Used to be a partition right across here, but I took it down."

The telegraph clicked to life. Denton tilted his head, listening, and then put thumb and forefinger to the small device and clicked a reply.

"Fine skill to have," Jerome observed. "All I know is S.O.S. and I'm thankful I never had to use that."

"I'll bet you are. So I suppose you've heard the big news?"

"Which big news is that?"

"Korea," Denton said. "We got another shooting war on our hands, and this one could bring Russia and China into it."

"I hope it doesn't come to that."

"Nobody wants it to come to that, but these communists, you know. They want to take over the world. And I'm not sure Harry has the stomach to stand up to them. What other big news is there?"

"Not as big as that," said Jerome, glancing out at the fields. "But some folks were pretty excited that the man from Lincoln came for a visit. And it looks like the gandy crew will have a game with the Hornets too."

"Oh, yeah yeah yeah," said Denton, nodding. "I had heard that. I didn't know your boys . . . ah, your gang knew any tricks like that. Some of them must have pretty good tricks with a spike maul, those gandies always do. But baseball?"

"We thought we'd just make it a regular game," Jerome said patiently. "Without any tricks."

"Oh, sure sure sure." Denton was nodding again. "Mrs. Henry never wants to come to Julian on any account, but maybe for this she'll change her mind. A chance to see Lincoln Thomas Ford. And to see how you gandies handle a bat."

"Actually, I might miss the game myself."

"Well, it's probably more fun for the younger men anyway. Old guys like you and me, well . . ."

"Mr. Henry, I am wondering." Jerome leaned forward. "No, I am asking. I want to be with my family on Tuesday, the Fourth. Could you see clear to get me to Nebraska City Monday afternoon for the train?"

Denton sat back, smiling broadly, waving a finger at Jerome. "I might have known it. I did know it. First thing I asked when you come through the door— what trouble you want to get me into this time? Well, you put one over on me in Omaha, but I'm a pig's ear if it's going to happen again. Oh, no." Denton laughed loudly, as if putting the matter to rest.

Jerome pulled his chair one step closer. "Mr. Henry. Denton. What you did helping me out in Omaha was the decent thing to do, and for that I am—all the boys are—in your debt. But you also know, if you remember, that I did you a turn on the way back."

Denton's face reddened to the roots of his sandy hair. "I don't know what you mean."

"I think you do know what I mean, and I'm ready . . ."

"You're trying to blackmail me, is that it?"

"No, sir. I was just saying I'm ready for that to be never mentioned again."

Denton thrust out an arm, holding his hand in the air. "Look at that. Steady as a rock. If I gave you the impression that I am anything but . . ." He jumped up, agitated. "You want to smell my breath?"

"No, sir, I do not."

"Well, then." Denton stared fiercely at him.

Jerome stood up. "I won't take up more of your time. You're a busy man."

"Not that busy," Denton said, in a sudden change of tone. The station agent got up and walked across the forlorn ghost of a waiting room, his heels clicking on the black and white tile. A framed passenger schedule still hung on the wall. He stared at it, and when he spoke, his voice was quiet. "There was this week one winter, it must have been ten below zero every day, with snow piled up to here. And Ronnie comes over from the elevator and he says, 'You got yourself a lunch?' and I said, 'I got my sandwich right here.' And Ronnie says, 'Put that sandwich away, you're coming over to the house for soup.' And all that week I went over there, and Ronnie's wife served up that beef-bone soup she makes. Hot soup on a cold day. And conversation. I just can't tell you."

There was a pause. Jerome said, "So, after that? You and him quarrel?"

"What? Oh, no." Denton laughed sourly. "The weather got warmer is all. The snow melted, and I went back to my sandwiches."

"You ever think of bringing him a sandwich?"

"Oh, no, no, no. That would be too forward. And Ronnie's always so busy over there, running around his bins and boxcars."

"Man has to eat lunch. Nothing forward about two men sharing lunch-time."

Denton thought about this. "No, I guess not. It's just, people here, you know. You get to doing things one way and you need a reason to do them some other way."

"Like a snowstorm."

"I guess."

Jerome had one hand on the doorknob, but let it drop. "Last week I saw a man step out against the way things are done, for no profit for himself and to the benefit of fourteen hardworking men. For that you should be proud of yourself, Mr. Henry. As for the holiday, I think you know what a ride to the station would mean to me and my family."

The station agent didn't answer.

Jerome drew a red bandana out of his pocket and shook it out. "You recall telling me about the old days when this was a flag stop depot for passenger trains."

"Yes."

"I'm going to leave this here on the window sill. I want you to consider what I'm asking. If you decide you can help a man see his family on the holiday, you tie it to that flagpole out front. If not, no hard feelings." The red cloth seemed accusing against the muted colors of the station. Jerome took a last look at it, at Denton, then closed the door gently behind him, and headed back to the camp.

30

BOYS ON THE BLEACHERS

Thursday evening the Hornets took care of Weeping Water in the last game before the wheat harvest break. It was a league game that counted in the standings, but the Hornets couldn't help thinking it a tune-up for Lincoln Thomas Ford. Jack Scarborough was the unlikely star, banging out three hits and knocking in four runs. After the game, after shaking hands with Joe Turko and the Weeping Water boys, after the families and fans had left, none of the Hornets were quite ready for the evening to end. There was still plenty of light, the best light of the day, the gentlest light. Randle Bazin, who only lived just down the block, said he had a case of Storz Triumph on ice, and went and got it. The boys spread out on the home grandstand, leaning back, all of them but the minister sipping a beer.

"Going to be a full moon tonight," said Ken Mills.

"Be bright enough to play a game," said Randle Bazin.

"A moon like that," said Ken, "you'd have to be careful not to mistake it for a fly ball."

"I lost it in the moon!" Randle said, hamming it up.

There was some joshing on the idea of fast-pitch by moonlight. Jack laughed along, but he wished the boys would talk about the game some more. It wasn't his place to bring it up, that would be bragging. Somebody else should bring it up, say he got lucky on that bloop single to left, tell him he'd better save some of that for LTF. That's what he did for the other guys. The irony was cruel: since he was the guy who did that for everybody else, there was no one to do it for him. At least Carlin was there to see it. She had pumped her fist to him when he was standing on second after his double.

The conversation lagged. The boys sipped their beers and looked out across the shadowed ball field. Evan Carpenter eventually started in on some notion he had about why people here were nicer than most folks, even to the gandy crew. Something to do with Bloody Kansas and the Underground Railroad.

Jack thought the minister's theory was pretty good, but maybe too optimistic. You only had to look at Frank Abernathy's face. Frank was just waiting for an opening to spout something sarcastic. And then if anybody laughed with him, he'd play it up, and make people uneasy. It could ruin the whole evening. Dave—the new Dave—would probably cut him down to size pretty quick. Word had gotten around about Dave's tussles with Hank at the store. And, of course, Dave was the one who got up this exhibition game with the gandies. Jack corrected himself: it wasn't a new Dave, just a side of him that nobody had seen before because there'd been no call for it. Genial Dave had lately shown himself to be a man intolerant of intolerance. And that was a good thing, as far as Jack was concerned. He thought that mostly out of the awe he held for his brother, but if you thought about it, it was the right thing, too.

But Dave was off his feed tonight. Everyone on the team noticed how subdued he was, and Jack, like everyone else, thought it had something to do with Ernie, who hadn't shown up for the game. They moved Kenny Mills to center field and put Evan in right, where most hits went right into the hayfield anyway. They did tonight too—Weeping Water had three dingers. The Hornets still won, thanks to Jack. He had an idea that Ernie's relapse was because of Korea. He felt guilty for not stopping by the farm and asking Lucine if there was anything he could do, run errands to Neb City or something.

Just as Jack was thinking this, somebody went and started talking about the invasion in Korea, and what was Truman going to do, and the Chinese and all that. Great. Now they'd never get back to talking about the game. Jack knew it was selfish of him, but damn it. Three hits! Four ribbies! At least Frank's snarl had eased up now that they moved past the topic of colored people. Frank had missed his chance to be a knucklehead, and Jack was glad of it.

"I heard there's a wild party going on out here."

"Hey, Ronnie," said Dave, rousing himself. "Have a beer, pull up a base. Hiya Timmy."

"Thanks, I will." Ron took a beer from the case, pierced the top with the church-key, and had a seat on the bleachers. The guys all said hello.

Ron was a few years older than the players. And Frank was the only other Catholic, so they went to different church picnics. But, in some ways, Ron knew them better than they knew each other. They were farmers, and he was their dealer, their grain dealer. He wrote the checks that were their livelihood. He listened on the radio every morning to the market reports from the Chicago

Board of Trade, and scribbled prices on a chalk board in the office. His profit margin was a penny per bushel, sometimes two pennies. The farmers all knew it took hard work to earn those pennies. But they also knew pennies added up, not to mention what he made on selling them seed stock, fertilizer and pesticide. No wonder he was always expanding capacity, putting up more bins. That back quonset must be sixty yards long.

Ron must have been feeling feisty tonight. He turned on Jack and said, "Where'd you learn to hit like that?"

Caught by surprise, Jack could only squeak, "I don't know, Ron," and everyone laughed.

"About time you outhit the mailman."

This was a good-natured poke at Dave, who was thought to have the easiest job in town, starting with his duties as postmaster.

Ron could be damn funny when he eased up, like in late afternoons when men stopped by the grain office for a beer. When he leaned back in his swivel chair, his feet propped on the bottom desk drawer, the work day was over. He could tease and be teased.

"Hey Ronnie," Frank said with a malicious grin, "whyn't you tell them what you were telling me the other day?"

"You mean when I cussed you for loafing when you said you were working?"

"No, I mean the part where you said having an exhibition game with coloreds was all foolishness."

"I say the harvest should come first. It's nothing to do with the coloreds."

"You said it was foolishness piled on foolishness."

"You all know what I mean."

No one challenged him on that. Every farmer there, at some time or another, had gotten into some trouble—too little rain, or too much, or too much at the wrong time. And every one of them had been able to put off paying a bill, or had got an advance on a crop in the field.

Finally it was Dave who spoke, and his voice was gentle. "Ronnie, we know you got everyone's best interests in mind. But it doesn't look like the wheat will even be ready by Tuesday. We got a chance to have a game people will be talking about fifty years from now. And besides," Dave's voice got tighter, "those city boys are badly in need of a whupping, if the man they sent down here is any indication."

Jack glanced sharply at his brother. So something had happened out there at the ball field. He knew that was the day Ernie got worse, the day the news broke about Korea. And again, as soon as Jack thought about Korea, somebody said it out loud. This time it was Dave.

"And now it looks like we got a shooting war in Korea."

"Truman says we're only going in as advisers," said the minister.

"I hope that's true, Evan," Dave said, smiling sadly. "But everybody thinks we'll have to go full in. So there's also a chance not all of us will be sitting here a year from now. If I was over there, I would be happy looking back to the day we beat the state champs."

Everybody looked around, spooked. For an instant Jack was angry with his brother. Why'd he have to put it that way? A chill went through him as he realized Dave's comment applied most to him, the youngest one there. Him and Frank.

Frank got himself another beer. "If they come after me, I think I'll be a draft-dodger. Or maybe I can get a federal exemption, since I'm working for Ronnie."

There were a couple of smirks, but to Jack, this was a low blow. It was Frank trying to get back at Ron for calling him a loafer. Ron himself stood up, finished his beer, and tossed it in the direction of the trash barrel.

"Come Tuesday," he said, "if the wheat has turned, I'll be open for business. And if nobody comes, I'll be there five AM Wednesday, looking forward to hearing how you won. Best of luck against Lincoln—and against the railroaders too."

"Where will you be Tuesday if the wheat hasn't turned?" said Ken Mills.

"Right where you're sitting now, Kenny."

That eased the tension. As Ron and Timmy set off toward home, Frank made some comment under his breath. Jack didn't even hear what it was he said, but he'd had about all he could take. He took off his cap and used it to whip Frank about the head and shoulders, chasing him from the stands. "You're a turd, Abernathy, a Grade A turd. That was real good of him to stop by tonight. How Ronnie puts up with you is a sheer mystery."

Over at the gandy camp, Cook looked up from his rocking chair to find Sam hesitating at the doorway. "Well, come on in, son."

"I come for flour. You have some you can spare?"

Cook smiled. "Of course I have some I can spare," he said, heaving himself up. "Did she say how much was wanted?"

Sam was embarrassed for forgetting, so Cook tried to help him out. "Did the missus give you a measure cup?"

"No. I was just . . . she said she'd need quite a bit."

Cook laughed. He calculated how much she might need if she was baking bread, or making pie crusts. Then he doubled it. He went to the stores bins in the next room, doled out six cups of his best white flour into a wrinkled paper bag. He folded the top and handed it ceremoniously to the courier.

"You tell her, if more's needed, there's plenty here. What's she in the middle of that she ran out? Did she tell you that?"

"No, she never said." Sam took the bag, thanked him, and was off.

Cook was pleased with himself as he eased back into the chair. He imagined her face as she got that heavy bag from Sam, and falling over herself to say she only said one cup! A wave of doubt crossed him. What if she sent some of it back? He should have told the boy expressly to make sure she kept it all, with his compliments. He liked the sound of that. He pictured himself in chef's whites, striding across a packed dining floor, with people looking his way and pointing. The Littmans were at a special table near the front. They were nervous, not used to fine dining, and the hubbub of New Orleans was almost too much for them. He put them at ease with some banter about the Quarter. Of course they loved every morsel, and told him so when he stopped by to say hello. And when the mister asked for the bill, he would come out of the kitchen again to make a small, self-effacing bow. He would be heard to murmur, *"Avec mes compliments."*

31

THE HOME OF ARBOR DAY

Saturday brought the new month, but the routine was the same, with Moose working the crew until a little after noon. When he told them to knock off, he added pointedly that he'd see them Monday morning, the regular work day before the Fourth of July holiday. The gandies ran the carts at full throttle back to the camp, eager to practice. They only had three days left to get ready to play the town team, and play them on a real ball field. Things seemed to be falling into place. Delran was finding his control, Big Larry was a hitting machine, and the fielders mostly stopped the balls that were hit at them. Even Jerome, who told himself he should know better, was beginning to think they had a chance—which made his decision, if the station agent gave him a decision to make, all the harder.

As the others were grabbing mitts and running out to the hayfield, Jerome told them to start without him. He had an errand to run at the store. Marchon Mercantile was busy, as it tended to be on Saturdays. As soon as Jerome came in, Dave stopped what he was doing and hurried to the mail room.

"I figured you'd be coming for this," Dave said, and handed over a package. It was almost flat, and wrapped in brown paper. "Here you go, one mystery parcel."

It was an invitation to talk, but Jerome felt quietly private of his new possession. He said his thanks and started for the door. Before he could get there, Dave used him as a billboard, announcing that everyone should come out and see the exhibition against the gandies at noon of July Fourth, before the game with Lincoln Thomas Ford. Jerome waved to the townsfolk, feeling foolish.

He veered past the train station on the way back. It had been four days since he'd made his flag-stop challenge to the station agent, four days of no signal. Jerome was partly relieved by that. If he had no ride to Neb City on July

3, then Lucy would have to understand, and he'd be here for the game. His gut curdled at the thought of it, though. He'd as good as promised her he was coming. Jerome was so caught up in his thoughts, his mind didn't at first register what his eyes were seeing. A band of red tied twice around the flagpole like a bandage. His ambivalence dropped away. He sprinted to the flagpole, joyfully unwrapped it and came through the station door waving it. He was going home to Lucy and JJ!

Denton Henry wheeled around in his chair and greeted him brightly. "Maybe you got a different color handkerchief? People around here are going to think I'm pinko, putting out the red flag."

Denton was in a chatty mood. He ordered Jerome to pull up a chair and plunged right into some story about his fight with the roadmaster in Omaha. "I told him we got no room here, with you boys camped and Ronnie stockpiling boxcars for the harvest. I told him to park those ties up at Paul where they could do some good. You boys are almost to Paul now, aren't you?"

Jerome affirmed that they were.

"See, that's what I told the roadmaster, but he's got wax in his ears."

Jerome bided his time. He was happy to play it this way, as if they'd been best friends for years. You never knew what you were going to get with Denton Henry. He gradually maneuvered the conversation to the close shave it was going to be from quitting time Monday for him to catch the train in Nebraska City.

Denton agreed, and brandished his railroad watch to show how meticulous he would be. "How are you getting back?"

This was the opening Jerome had hoped for. Morning of the fifth, he explained, the southbound Eagle got into Nebraska City early, and since Denton would be driving to Julian that morning for work anyway . . . he shrugged. He hadn't dared to look up while putting his plan on the table. When he did, Denton was smiling.

"Don't go blaming me when you miss morning muster."

Jerome grinned. "Mopac said they'd fire us if we miss work on Monday. They didn't say anything about Wednesday."

"Ivan will dock you."

"He surely will," Jerome agreed, laughing. He grew serious as he got up to leave. "One thing I'd appreciate, and that's if you wouldn't mention this arrangement to anyone. I'm going to tell the boys it's a family emergency."

"Gotcha. That'll give us an excuse to be in a hurry. I'll keep my motor running, yell at you to come on and make it quick, that news came over the telegraph, I got to take you up to catch the Eagle. Your wife's name is Lucy, right? I need to have my facts. And your boy, is he Jerome too?"

"We call him JJ." The station agent's enthusiasm for the lie made Jerome feel slightly ill. "Well, thank you again, Mr. Henry."

"Oh, call me Denton. Hey, just thought of something. I have to run up to town this afternoon. Coming back tonight. If you need anything from Neb City, you can have a ride."

Jerome declined, eager to get away. It pierced his heart to picture himself lying to the boys on Monday, saying he couldn't be there for the game. It occurred to him he needed to break in another catcher; the job was no cakewalk with Delran pitching. Maybe Little Larry. When he got to the camp, the field was empty except for George and Sillman Jones, who were having a leisurely catch. George explained that some of the track had slipped. The foreman came in his car in a big hurry, and took five gandies to go fix it, including Delran and Big Larry. No telling when they'd be back.

Jerome felt a surge of guilty relief. He didn't want to face them right now. He spotted Sam, and a new thought hit him. He tapped the package against his hand and said, "Mister Sam, you still want to show me that place in Nebraska City, that place with the Underground Railroad?"

Sam hesitated. "Sometimes Mr. Littman, he has work for me, and . . ."

"Well maybe we can sneak out of here before he does, if our ride hasn't left yet. Now use those fast legs of yours, run down to the depot, and find the agent, Mr. Henry. You tell him we will take that ride he offered, if he's still offering. You got that?"

A few minutes later they were on the highway to Nebraska City in Denton's Studebaker Champion. Along the way Denton decided that their visit to the county seat had to begin with the famous shredded beef sandwich at Dinty Moore's.

Jerome was expecting a homey cafe with its name painted on the window, and lemon meringue pies under glass. What they got instead was a dark tavern on the side of a building around the corner from the main street. The place was maybe ten feet wide, the entire length of it taken up by a wooden bar and fifteen stools. Above the bar stretched a dingy mural, a prairie scene where a plucky Indian on a pony aimed his arrow at charging buffalo.

There were only four customers, solitary men strung out along the bar. Denton knew three of them, and should have known the fourth, according to the other three, a stocky man who went by Zebby. Denton introduced them as men of the Mopac rail crew. Jerome saw the drink of choice was beer from a tap. He ordered RC Cola for himself and Sam. And of course, the sandwiches. While the barman dished them up, Jerome fielded questions about the job. Which side of Paul were they on now. How they managed to run trains through when they were fixing the line.

The sandwiches slid in front of them on pieces of newspaper. Denton beamed in anticipation. The object of everyone's adoration was a circular bun with grayish meaty gravy oozing out the sides.

Jerome took a bite, and said, "Mmmm, mmm mnn. That is good, isn't it, Sam?"

Sam mimicked Jerome, saying, "Mmm."

The barman nodded. "We been serving that shredded beef since 1911."

"Folks always say," Henry put in, "the secret is that Hanratty has never washed the pot. He just keeps adding more stew beef."

Hanratty grinned. "I ain't saying one way or the other."

The shredded beef on a bun, the pride of Nebraska City. Fifteen cents each, or two for a quarter—and the plural, apparently, was beeves.

As Jerome was finishing his sandwich the man at the far end spoke up.

"Them camp cars," said Zebby. "You boys will be moving next to Nebraska City?"

Jerome kept his voice flat. "I expect so."

"Some of your boys stirred up some trouble here a week or so ago."

"Some trouble was stirred," Jerome answered.

"You saying you were one of them?"

"Aw, Zebby," said another man.

Jerome secretly tightened a grip on Sam's knee, enjoining silence. "Neither of us two were there."

Denton Henry stood up, agitated. "Moose Burdock took care of that. And if you know even a little about Moose, you'll know that's the last of it." He paused and looked around. "This crew has caused no problems at all in Julian. In fact, this one," he pointed to Sam, "he's working odd hours for Littman Grain."

"What's Ronnie paying you?" asked another man. "Two cents an hour?"

"Penny a board," said Sam.

This, apparently, was the funniest thing anyone had ever said at Dinty Moore's. Penny a board from stingy Littman! Zebby turned back to his beer.

Denton and the barman each took a turn praising the shredded beef, and then turned to Jerome. He was running out of things to say. Finally, he came up with, "A sandwich this good, pity you don't have tables so families can eat."

"Families eat the hell out of them," Denton said happily. "In this town, come supper time, wife doesn't feel like cooking, she says, 'I don't feel like cooking, you go on down to Dinty Moore's and pick us up some beeves.' I always tell Hanratty here, he could make a million dollars with outlets in Omaha or Lincoln, but he won't listen."

"You know what I always say about that," said Hanratty, winking.

"You always say," said Henry, lowering his voice, "that it won't work, because no place else has wives as lazy as the ones here."

This was the second funniest thing ever heard at Dinty Moore's. Jerome couldn't help himself. "Women welcome here?"

"Oh sure," said Henry.

"Everybody is welcome here," said Hanratty, looking pointedly at Zebby.

Zebby picked up his change and made for the door. He let the screen door slam behind him.

A few minutes later they were out the door themselves, with Jerome careful not to forget the parcel he'd set on the bar. Henry confirmed plans to pick them up in three hours behind the Court House.

Jerome led Sam down Central Avenue to the Missouri Pacific station. He wanted to be sure of its exact location, and to recheck the timetable on the wall. Sam said John Brown's Cave was at the other end of town, so they headed back up Central. Sam kept getting distracted by the store windows. Damast Clothing. Brown Shoe Fit. Wenzl's Hardware. Sam would stop and point, saying, "Look at that. Look at that."

Sam had a way of being wholly absorbed in whatever was right in front of his face. He didn't notice the people who stopped to stare at them. Jerome noticed. He wondered how many Hanrattys there were, and how many Zebbys. He told himself to give the place a chance. Based on the sample so far, that only one in six were outright bigots. Pretty good for a white town.

Watching the boy, Jerome felt a surge of affection. Sam had grown up poor as dirt, but it seemed the boy had managed to miss most of the cruelties of life. He spoke with reverence of mother and father and grandparents and school teacher. He'd been off looking at churches that night while the rest were fighting and getting thrown in jail. Still, Jerome worried. Sam got teased; sometimes they called him a sissy on account of the poetry book. Jerome had no intention of being a gandy past this one season, if he could help it, and he hoped Sam would get out too. He patted the parcel against his thigh as he walked, thinking somehow it might help.

They reached Tenth Street, where a three-story hotel took up half a block. It had fancy double doors, and a gleaming Coffee Shop next to the lobby. An L-shaped sign hung above the sidewalk with the words HOTEL and GRAND.

The doorman had big silver epaulets on a smart maroon uniform. He saw Sam staring up and said, "That's Hotel Grand, not Grand Hotel. A lot of folks get it backwards." He was the first Black person they had seen in Nebraska City, a trim man with a salt and pepper hair. He said his name was Luther Martin, and added, in a practiced way, "Not Martin Luther. Folks get that backwards too."

Jerome started introductions.

"Oh I know who you are," Luther Martin said, still smiling. "You being here, and you being colored, and you being not known to me, it means you're on the Mopac crew."

Sam wanted to know about the hotel, how many rooms and if it had an elevator. The doorman gladly obliged him. He had to get back to the desk, but he wanted them to know there was a Southern Baptist and an AME in town, and the boys would be welcome at either one. It was nice to make their acquaintances, and to please give his regards to Mr. Cantrell.

"Mr. Cantrell?" said Jerome. "You mean Ice?"

"Mr. William Cantrell."

"How do you know him?"

The man smiled. "I try to do a favor when I can. Must be lonely out there. If a man need a little whisky to be of comfort, Luther Martin can help him out. We've got a fine selection here at the Hotel Grand. Of course," he added, "we do that business out the back door. You know how it is."

"He knows Ice?" Sam said, after he was gone.

Jerome shook his head. "You never know how people come to know other people."

No sooner had he said that than a girl's voice called out from across the street, "Sam!"

They stammered hellos to Carlin, trying not to stare at the black-clad creature that seemed to levitate beside her. Black veil, belted black dress with a skirt that hovered just above the sidewalk. Only the face and hands showed there was a woman under there. There were nuns in Omaha, but Jerome had never seen one up close.

"That's so great I saw you," said Carlin. "I've been hoping you could meet."

"Sister Mary Michael, this is Mr. Wallace."

Jerome was surprised she knew his name. He shook hands with the sister, noticing her smile and lively eyes. She was younger than he'd thought.

"And this is Sam Washington."

Sam grinned sheepishly, staring at the sidewalk. "Hi."

"Carlin tells me you're a Housman fan."

"Yes, ma'am."

"Me too. 'High the vanes of Shrewsbury gleam' and all that. It's just lovely."

Ex ex vee eye eye eye.

"What was that?" said the sister.

"It's the number in the book!" Carlin cried. "He knows them all! Say it again."

Sam didn't know he'd said it out loud. He repeated the letters while Carlin smiled. "Twenty-eight! Right, Sam?"

"Yes."

"See?" Carlin said, turning to the sister. "He knows them all. It's going to be so boring in Julian when they leave."

"You'll still have your fast-pitch team," Jerome said, trying to guide the conversation to an end. Everybody on the sidewalks was staring at the nun and the Negroes.

"Yeah, we still got them," Carlin said, with a trace of sarcasm. "Only my Dad doesn't even want them to play Lincoln Thomas Ford, because of the stupid wheat harvest. Tomorrow may be my last day of freedom for weeks."

"Well," said Sister Mary Michael, clapping her hands brightly. "It's so nice to have met you both. We should be getting along, shouldn't we Carlin?"

32

ANOTHER ROADSIDE ATTRACTION

The museum was not what Jerome expected. He wasn't sure what he had expected, but not this gaudy sign ringed in lights along the highway: JOHN BROWN'S CAVE. Or the souvenir shop with the AUTHENTIC INDIAN BEADS and the rack of postcards. A card showing HOTEL GRAND caught his eye. He squinted to try to see if there was a colored doorman in the picture. Another card featured a pillared white mansion, and on another, there was the dazzling sign of this place, lit up at night.

The woman at the counter remembered Sam. "You said you were going to bring your friend," she said cheerfully.

Jerome paid the admission, chiding himself for expecting something dignified. For them, this was no different than World's Largest Windmill or See Seven Counties Lookout—something to lure people off the highway. Jerome smiled to the lady and followed where she pointed, to a path out the door. With Sam in the lead they circled around to a one-room log cabin with helpful signs in capital letters. Inside, the floorboards creaked, and dummies of white people stood there decked out in TYPICAL HOMESTEADER CLOTHING. A wooden baby rocker sat on the floor with a doll in it, right next to the mother dummy. On a shelf of old books, Jerome noticed one with tape on the spine with BIBLE written on it, only the tape was half torn, so the real title showed underneath, something about grammar.

He felt like he was back in Dinty Moore's, only instead of shredded beef it was washboards and weathervanes, and instead of Denton and Hanratty, it was Sam wanting his approval. In North Omaha it was called 'Uncle Tomming,' and Jerome never cared for it. But there was something of the same innocence at work back at the tavern and here with Sam, and it would be cruel to let the boy down.

"Yes, sir," he said. "That sure is something. Mmm hmm."

With Sam in the lead, Jerome left the cabin and circled around to its other side, where WATCH YOUR STEP pointed down a damp set of stairs to

WATCH YOUR HEAD over the basement doorway. They went down. Inside, it was dim and dank, and they had to duck their heads under the log joists. Small slants of light came through the floorboards they'd just been standing on.

"This way," Sam whispered. He led Jerome down a dim tunnel. As it curved, the light from behind grew dimmer, until they were standing in utter, absolute blackness. Jerome didn't know Sam had stopped and ran into him. "Sorry." His voice echoed strangely.

Sam whispered, "Spooky!"

They moved on, feeling their way by the handrails, and they saw a hint of light ahead. They came to the place where the tunnel widened into a cave dug out on one side and propped up with timbers. At a crude table sat a dummy of a mammy holding a child, a red bandana over her painted-on curls. A skinny man-dummy held up a lantern, and, even in the clumsy hand of a bad artist, the man looked scared. The scene was dimly lit by a single bulb, red tinted, by which one could barely see the RUNAWAY SLAVES sign.

Jerome felt Sam beside him, still as a ghost. They stood for several moments, unmoving. The only sound was an intermittent drip of water echoing from somewhere in the tunnel. Eventually they moved on, following the damp corridor as it continued turning, and it almost got pitch black again, but not quite. They could see light coming from the far end. The tunnel opened out at the bottom of a ravine, where a wooden walkway crossed a small stream. FROM THIS GULLEY SLAVES WERE SMUGGLED AT NIGHT TO THE MISSOURI RIVER TO MAKE CROSSING TO IOWA.

"This gulley, huh?" Jerome looked around. It resembled the one by Julian, maybe ten feet below ground level. That was something to think about, people making their way to freedom up this very ravine. The path followed the ravine a ways, and then a set of narrow wooden stairs led them up to a small meadow. They walked along the path to an open-sided barn with old farm equipment, PIO-NEER THRESHER and HORSE DRAWN HARROW. The other building said SCHOOL HOUSE, though it looked to Jerome like a recently dashed together shack. Inside, on one wall was a copy of the famous picture of JOHN BROWN, the one with his arms spread out, his beard flying, and the fanatical look in his eyes.

On the other wall was a portrait of a plain-looking young man in a frock coat, with an inscription below.

"Read it to me," Jerome said, "I can't see that print."

JOHN HENRY KAGI

"John Henry Kagi lived in the log cabin with his sister Barbara Kagi May-hew and her husband Allen Mayhew. Operating the crucial river stop on the underground railroad, Kagi and the Mayhews helped many runaway slaves to freedom. Kagi joined the abolitionist side in the struggles of Bloody Kansas, and was severely wounded in a duel with a pro-slavery judge. A trusted advisor of John Brown, Kagi was second in command at Harper's Ferry. He was shot dead in that skirmish while attempting to retreat across the Shenandoah River. He was twenty-four."

A thought came to Jerome—one that he wasn't used to having, given his years of experience with them. There were white men who entered into duels for his people, who got shot dead crossing rivers for his people. It took a war to stop slavery, battles where tens of thousands died. He looked again at the young man in the picture. "He was twenty-four."

"Jerome?"

"Yes. I'm coming."

"Jerome, look at this."

Sam was staring at a framed piece of newsprint, yellowed and crumbling at the edges.

"What's it say?"

"Jerome, look at this!"

Jerome looked. It was a map. He recognized the Missouri River, and the state borders. Lawrence was at the bottom, Tabor, Iowa, at the top. In between was a line of dots, and next to each dot, names in tiny script. The caption said, "Route of the Underground Railroad."

Jerome said, "That is something," and started to turn away, but Sam yanked him back. "Look at it! Starting right here."

Jerome focused on the dot by Sam's fingernail, and started reading the town names upward, squinting to discern the type. "Leona, Hiawatha." Then, with growing comprehension, the first one in Nebraska, "Falls City." Chills went down his spine as his eyes climbed dot by dot: they'd put down rail through each of them. Finally, "Auburn, Julian, Nebraska City."

"We're building it," Sam breathed. "We're building the Mopac right on top of the Underground Railroad."

"I guess we are at that," Jerome said, laying a hand on Sam's shoulder. "I guess we are at that."

They stood there a long time, rereading the tiny legend up and down that faded piece of paper.

Sam bought a penny postcard of the log cabin on their way out. It was something worth having, after all, and the garish highway sign didn't seem so awful now. Just past the parking lot, in a patch of grass shaded by trees, sat a picnic table. From the clock in the shop, they still had forty-five minutes before meeting Denton Henry. Time to rest after all their wandering. Time for a gift. The brown paper parcel was grimy from him carrying it all day. Jerome said, "This is for you," and handed it to Sam.

"Really?" Sam said, staring at the thing in his hands. He worked carefully, as if not wanting to injure the wrapping. It was a book with a plain cover of mottled yellow, twice the size of the Housman.

Sam saw the words on the spine, and read out loud, "The Weary Blues." He opened it, and delicately thumbed through the pages, seeing titles with the words "Negro" and "Black" and "Harlem." He tried to concentrate on one called, "Aunt Sue's Stories," which began:

> Aunt Sue has a head full of stories.
> Aunt Sue has a heart full of stories.

His eye skipped ahead to

> Black slaves
> Working in the hot sun.

He thought of himself out on the tracks, the sun burning down, and Charly's songs of her biscuits. No that was Sally's biscuits. Sam felt dizzy; he couldn't process the words. He looked into Jerome's eager eyes. He said, "That's real good."

"This is the poetry of a Black man," Jerome answered. "A living Black man, a man that Black folks and white folks respect as one of the best of our times." He took the book from Sam. "My daddy gave me this book, and now I'm giving it to you. It's different, it's jazz." Jerome read, looking up eagerly after each line:

> The rhythm of life
> Is a jazz rhythm,
> Honey.
> The gods are laughing at us.

"That's nice," said Sam, nodding. "That's real nice."

Sam was Uncle Tomming him. He, Jerome, was suddenly on the other end, trying to nod and smile Sam into loving something. Jerome blew air out of his cheeks and handed the book back to Sam. "Someday it's going to be real important to you."

"It's important now!" Sam exclaimed. He was aware of Jerome's disappointment, but unable to find words; it was too overwhelming. He turned the book over in his hands. "It's important because you gave it to me."

"You just be sure and read those poems."

"I will," said Sam. "I promise I will."

33

LECHERS, AND OTHER INSULTS

To the credit of its proprietors, the AUTHENTIC INDIAN BEADS on sale at John Brown's Cave came from Arizona, not Japan, though the Japanese miracle was gearing up, with the help of American entrepreneurs. But what of the original Americans who populated this gentle region along the Missouri River?

Nebraska history does not begin with Lewis and Clark.

The pre-Columbian inhabitants of North America were neither savage killers nor enlightened communitarians—or rather, they were both. In the centuries before Columbus, clans and tribes engaged in wars and intrigues every bit as complicated as those of the princes of Europe. And, as in Europe, there were occasional losers, and there were perennial losers.

The tribe known as the Oto must be counted among the latter. They were originally a part of the Chiwere group that broke off from the Eastern Sioux nation of the Great Lakes and migrated southwest. It is supposed they were lured by the prospect of buffalo, belying the tribe name Hotonga, "Fish Eater." The migrating nation soon had its first split, one that left half the group parked in Wisconsin, as Winnebago. The rest of the nomads moved on, but then another split occurred. The resultant pair of tribes were the Iowa and the Missouri, who settled in the places where their names would lead you to suppose.

The Missouri faction stopped where the Grand River meets the Missouri, and took the name Neutache, "live at the river mouth." Then an interesting thing happened. The son of one Missouri chief seduced the daughter of another Missouri chief. I will leave it to some other bard to pen the tragedy with a raven-haired prairie girl sighing, "Wherefore art thou Ahrowha?" The actual fate of the young woman is not known. What did come to us is that the seducer, his father, and the rest of their clan, were banished from the tribe, branded with the name, Oto, short for *Wat 'ota,* "lechers."

As origin myths go, it's nothing to write to Great Spirit about, although it did take a fateful twist. Sometime after this split, the remaining Missouri entered into an unwise campaign against the Osage, a tribe with a brutally high batting average. The remnants had to flee west to rejoin the spurned Oto. Even reunited, the Oto were never very good invaders, and bounced around both sides of the Missouri, routinely chased off by the tribes already living there.

At the time of the white invasion, they were living on the western bank of the Missouri, at the place where the twin Table Creeks met the river—a small band, grudgingly tolerated by the Great Pawnee Nation. The place was called Cherry Run by Sergeant Charles Floyd, who, a few weeks later would have the dubious distinction of being the sole fatality of the Lewis and Clark expedition. Later names included Table Creek, Kearney City, Greggsport, Prairie City, and—as of 1854—Nebraska City.

The Otos fared no better with the white man than they had with the red. In 1817 they signed a treaty ceding rights and lands in exchange for the promise of no further concessions. They did so again in 1830, in 1833, and in 1836. The final blow came in 1855, with the Treaty of Nebraska City. A monument just outside of town celebrates the treaty for "establishing permanent friendly relations" with the natives, who were, as part of the friendly treaty, summarily deported to a reservation. The principal signatory for the white men was James W. Denver himself. Signing the scorecard for the losing team, Chief Chianaka. Listed as "interpreter," none other than J. Sterling Morton, founder of Arbor Day, the most glorious of Nebraska Citians, who rose to the dizzying height of secretary of agriculture in the second Cleveland administration. In a memoir from his later years, the "interpreter" Morton will poke good-natured fun at the sound of, and his own total ignorance of, all Native American tongues. Anyway, in the year of the Treaty of Nebraska City, in honor of the recently departed permanent friends, Nebraska City became the seat of *Otoe* County.

Perhaps old Chianaka had the last laugh after all. Maybe his mark on the Treaty of Nebraska City was not a concession but a curse upon the land that had never been very good to the Oto after all. For what else could explain how Nebraska City, with all its advantages, would lose out time and time again in the pennant race for state dominance? The perennial winner was a place named for another banished tribe, the Omaha.

And what else could explain how, after all the build-up, the Julian Hornets would suffer the insult of being snubbed by Lincoln Thomas Ford? It happened that same afternoon Jerome and Sam visited Neb City. Adding to the affront, the blow was delivered by telegraph in all of four words.

"By telegraph!" Jack exploded. "Let me see that."

Dave handed it over. The word would get out soon enough, but Dave figured Jack should hear first, and from him. So he had taken his pick-up down to the home place where Jack still lived with their parents. Fortunately, Mom and Dad were in Neb City, so Jack wouldn't upset them with his cussing and storming around.

For the moment Jack was calm, squinting at the page. "What's that mean, 'facilities max'?"

"That's the man they sent down here." Dave stood beside him and read out loud. "NO GAME INADEQUATE FACILITIES," he paused, "MAX." Jack started to sputter, and Dave continued, "I think what it came down to was money. He talked about making it a free event, but . . ."

"Free?" said Jack. "As opposed to what, charging admission?"

"I know," said Dave. "He mentioned something about charity for disabled vets, but I think they were looking to make out for themselves, primarily."

"It's not about money," Jack cried righteously, "it's about who's the best fast-pitch team in this state."

Dave let the storm blow over, then said he needed Jack's help. Phone calls had to be made. He divided up the job between himself and Jack, so everybody got the word at about the same time. Dave paused and looked up. "You think we should go ahead with the exhibition game?"

Jack frowned. "That *was* the exhibition game. Oh, you mean with the railroad crew?" He laughed shortly. "That's a good one."

"Why not?"

"I'll tell you why not," Jack said. "Everybody is going to be so damn mad they're not going to be in any mood for clowning. We go from playing the best team in the state to playing a rail gang that's never played one game?" Jack stared at his brother, shaking his head. "And if you need reason number two, we'll likely be in full-on harvest by Tuesday."

"It is a holiday."

"Holidays don't matter to Ronnie Littman. When the wheat is ready, he'll be open."

"I suppose," said Dave. "Still, it's a shame."

"I agree," Jack said in a perfunctory way. "The real shame here is Lincoln Thomas Ford."

After Dave left, Jack sat at the kitchen table, the telephone in front of him. His first call was to Hank Benkleman. That one was tricky. Jack didn't even know if Hank was planning to show up—he'd been mighty aggrieved that they wanted an Omaha umpire, and was not happy to be relegated to the gandy game.

Hank harrumphed on the phone, and Jack could picture him nodding his heavy head. He'd known all along those big city types were scoundrels. Never trust any of them as far as you could throw them. "And I presume, then," Hank said gravely, "that the game with the rail workers has become the main event. But I warn you, I will not be a part of any dog-and-pony show. If it's a real game, fine. However . . ."

This caught Jack by surprise. "Naw," said quickly. "That's done too. You know, the harvest and all."

Jack crossed off "4Eyes" from his list. Five names were left, but it only took four calls, on account of the Bazins were on the same party line as Chick Beadle, and Chick's wife picked up halfway through the call to Randle. In each call Jack aired his righteous outrage, but folks took the news in stride—almost as if nobody really expected the game to happen. They all said what about the colored boys. Jack felt a little guilty saying that was scuttled too. Maybe it wouldn't have been so bad to play them. He remembered that Friday in Nebraska City, when Frank Abernathy accused Carlin of getting chummy with that Black boy, and he felt a pang of emotion that wasn't easy to pin down. It was not that he minded if Carlin was friends with a Black boy. It wasn't about being Black, it was about being with Carlin, same as if it was Johnny Miller or Ross Tedrow. He told himself that was true, and he tried to believe it was.

Cook was in a sour mood. Here it was Sunday morning, and he'd had no invitation to go to Mass, which meant no invitation to Sunday dinner either. Ever since he'd sent over six cups of flour, he'd been looking forward to seeing the family again, to letting the missus thank him for his largesse. He had a real hankering for bone soup and civilized conversation. He wasn't going to get either one at the camp. Ice and some of the others had got hold of liquor again, and they would be snarling with hangovers when they got up.

To compensate himself for these injustices, he made himself a large and perfect omelet, and a pot of chicory-flavored coffee. As he was taking the frying pan off the gas, he spotted Sam sniffing the air outside. He sighed, went to the door of the cook car, and told the kid to come on in and sit down.

"You sure?" said Sam, lingering at the door.

"Sure I'm sure. Come on in here now. The others won't be up for a while." The large omelet became two modest omelets. He tossed the kid a few slices of bread and poured two cups of coffee.

"Jerome's up," Sam said, sitting down.

Cook was not about to get out another plate. This loaves-and-fishes was stopping with Sam. "We'll just let him be Martha and you can be Mary today."

Sam concentrated. "You mean by that Jerome should be serving us?"

"No," Cook laughed. "Only that you got the better part. That's good, though."

Cook watched the kid inhale the omelet, and took some satisfaction in that. When Sam asked if he was going off to church with the Littmans, Cook tried to sound nonchalant.

"Not today," he said. "I saw the family drive by at six this morning. Headed to the early service, I guess."

Sam nodded. "Because of the harvest."

"Say again?"

Sam explained how Ron was crazy about the harvest. Apparently it was like a race, with all the runners twitching at the starting line. There was some starting gun somewhere, and then everybody went pell-mell trying to bring grain to the elevator the fastest. He wasn't sure why they did it that way, but it's all anyone was talking about this week, besides of course the games that got cancelled.

Cook felt his spirits lighten. He didn't fully understand the details, but he did understand that there was a *reason,* a business reason, why they went to the early Mass, and why they may have overlooked his generosity to them. And then, of course, there was the cancelled game. "Did you see what happened last night?"

"Not up close," said Sam. "I know Jerome was mad at Ice."

"Yes," said Cook, "he would be."

Last night as it was getting dark, a white guy came poking around camp. Cook recognized him as the manager up at the store, a friendly man who had insisted, on one of his trips up there, that Cook try a sample of their air-dried beef. Last night the man talked to Jerome for several minutes. While they were talking, word spread among the crew that the game with the local boys was cancelled. Then Ice had to get up and make some noise about it. Being on the far side of tipsy, Ice made more than a little noise, and for a while Cook thought Jerome was going to be physical with him. But the store manager was unflappable, apologizing with a sincerity that even melted Ice.

Cook didn't get involved. He didn't care to know about all that. This was his third summer out in the camps, his second with Ice and Delran and Big Larry. He'd noticed that just before it was time to strike camp and move on, folks got on edge. One time in Sedalia, Missouri, the boys had gotten the idea to try to win money in a bare-knuckles fight competition some white man was staging. Cook knew that would turn out bad, and it did. Well, inside a week they'd be set up in Nebraska City, and Cook would see what that would bring. In the meantime, Sam thanked him with great enthusiasm for the breakfast, and went off to do whatever Sam did on Sundays, which Cook also did not care to know about.

34

EDGE OF THE ABYSS

Sam sat on the edge of the ravine by the low-hanging tree, studying the mottled cover of his new book. Jerome had given it to him, and he felt the weight of his promise to study it. He'd never heard of anyone named "Langston." He practiced saying it out loud. He opened the book, intent on reading slowly. But he found himself rifling through the poems, as if the words were hot to the touch, or a hole he could tumble into. He thrilled to, "This strong young sailor" who "carries/His own strength/And his own laughter . . ." He paused over dangerous rhymes.

> A dancing girl who eyes are bold
> Lifts high a dress of silken gold.

He wondered if she was coming. It probably didn't mean anything when she said she was going to be so bored on Sunday. He had dithered a long time over which book to bring. It seemed safer to stick with the old one, with its daffodils and hedgerows. Then it had come back to him, that moment when she'd read "Look Not in My Eyes." It seemed all poetry books carried dangers. He was eager and nervous to show her this new one.

She did come, and her first words were, "That's a different book." She was wearing a dress that came to her knees, and had a wide pocket stitched to the front of the skirt.

Sam looked around. "Where's your brother?"

"Oh, he'd rather watch gandies play ball," she said. "What's that book?"

"Jerome gave it to me. It's by a Negro poet. Langston Hughes."

"Oh! Let me see." She plopped down beside him, and together they admired it. She said the texture of the paper showed it was an expensive book—it was made to look old-fashioned, like parchment. As she paged through it, Sam almost snatched it back, afraid she would just start reading out loud from anywhere. The title "Nude Young Dancer" paraded before them, and she got it. She moved on quickly, seeking safer landings.

"Hey," she said. "Here's one for you. For this week." She read:

> Got a railroad ticket,
> Pack my trunk and ride.
> And when I get on the train
> I'll cast my blues aside.

She looked up with a bright smile that faded gradually. She closed the book. "I'll probably never see you again."

"I guess not," said Sam.

"That's sad." She sighed. "I'm going to college."

"That's good."

She picked a leaf from a tree branch and tossed it in the ravine. "I was thinking how it's sad to meet a person and never see them again, and nothing you can do about it. In college it's better. You make friends with whoever. I'm going to DePaul University. That's in Chicago. Mary Michael went there. She said you were nice, by the way. And she said you should go to college too. Not DePaul," she added quickly, then reset her course. "I mean, you could if you wanted to. But just anywhere. She said to tell you, if you can read Housman, you can go to college. I'm glad I remembered; she'd kill me if I forgot to tell you. Anyway, since you're going, I thought of a good-bye present. It's not a book or anything, just something you can remember Julian by. Stand up. Close your eyes."

"What about my book?"

"I'll put it right here." She slid the book into the pocket on the front of her dress. "Now close 'em!"

"Okay, but . . ." He jumped when he felt her cool hands on his forearms. She was guiding him. He was walking. He snuck a peek through squinted lids but only saw the path.

"Now you can look."

He opened his eyes to a field of ripening wheat, the railroad tracks, the train station, the long back bin.

"You get it?"

He gave an embarrassed laugh.

"You're looking right at it!"

"I am?"

She laughed again. "The elevator. I'm giving you the elevator!"

"You are?"

"You love high places. I'm going to send you up to the top. On the man-lift. It's easy. See that window way up in the top there? You're going to look out and see where we are now." She started off at a quick pace, saying over her shoulder, "There's one on the other side where you can see the whole town."

Sam plunged after her, saying, "Won't your dad get mad?"

"Dad's not around," she said breezily. "It'll only take a couple minutes. Come on."

They hopped across the main line, gleaming with the crew's handiwork. They went by the back bin, its door hanging open as usual. Sam had to resist the urge to go inside and check the piles of corn there, but that was something he had to do alone. Soon they were inside the elevator, walking over the grate where the trucks dumped. Sam was now familiar with this terrain, after his odd jobs for Mr. Littman. The interior was dim, and it took a moment for their eyes to adjust. The lift sat waiting, an open-sided metal cage, with a rope coming up through a hole in the floor.

He looked up the impossibly long shaft to the tiny glimmer of light far above. Terror and excitement seized him together. This was crazy. It was so high. She looked so proud—he couldn't disappoint her. He would never have this chance again. But this was crazy.

"It's really simple," she said, hopping onto the lift. "This is the brake. It's the opposite of a car. When your foot's off, the brake is on. You can only move if you're stepping on it." She stepped on it, this time slowly, so instead of ramming up against the railroad spike, it eased there with a sickening whine of metal on wood. "Grab that bucket. You're going to need the extra weight." She hopped off to make room for the bucket of sand. She looked him in the eye. "Ready?"

He looked into hers. "Yes."

"Okay, get on there. When you get to the top just get off. It's not going anywhere. The windows open. It's real dusty. Don't touch any of the equipment. Don't stay too long. If I knock on the leg like this"—she knocked on the tin shaft—"you'll hear it up there. That means come down right now."

"You said your dad was gone."

"He'd be a grouch about it, but that's all. Just don't fall off and kill yourself." She added, smiling sweetly, "That would make him mad."

Sam got on the lift. His hands trembling, he slowly began to pull on the rope. He used all his weight. Nothing moved.

"The brake," she said, with a little stomping motion. "Push it in slow."

He pushed it in, not slow enough, and the lift went skyward, with a bone-jarring stop after six inches. Sam leapt off in terror.

Carlin frowned at the lift. "The bucket's not heavy enough." She poked his rib with a fingertip. "You are awful skinny. It's lucky for you I forgot to pull the safety bolt."

Sam blinked at the enormity of the understatement. "I guess I can't go up."

"I guess not," she said. "Come on, we need to get it back to floor level anyway." She took the big step up, and motioned him to do the same. He got on behind her, straddling the sand, careful not to let their bodies touch. She footed the brake and they sank to the floor.

"Wait a second," she said. "Stay on, but put the bucket on the floor."

He did so.

"I just want to try this. Hold on."

There was nothing to steady himself but the steel crossbeam above him. He reached up and held on. She eased off the brake again, and pulled on the rope. They went up a few inches. "Ha," she said. "Got it right. We're still kind of heavy, though. Guess I'm too fat."

"Let me try."

"Okay."

Sam thought she was going to get behind him, but instead she hunched her shoulders with her arms down at her sides. "Just reach around," she said. "I'll do the brake."

He reached around and above her, arms encircling, trying not to touch her. He pulled on the thick rope. He sensed the movement of her leg pressing the brake, and felt the lift go up.

"You're strong," she said.

"It's easy."

She took out the safety bolt and sat it on a beam. Sam pulled the rope and the platform rose two feet, four feet. He did not know if they were just testing her theory, or if they were really going up together. She said nothing, so he continued to pull, and the lift continued to rise. It was not easy, but it was not hard, either. Sam could feel the pull of the counterweight. When he paused, the lift would drift downward. One time, when Sam was small, his dad got the use of a rowboat, and took him out on a lake. Sam was terrified of the water, but watching his father calmed him. He sat in the bow, mesmerized by the flow of his father's arms and torso, leaning forward then pulling back with long, steady strokes. He thought that must be the finest feeling a man could have, smooth and powerful. *He feels the whole pond through the oars*, Sam remembered thinking.

Sam could feel the whole elevator through the rope. He was half a head taller than Carlin. He gripped the rope with one hand above her head, and pulled down, past her forehead and face, and let go as the other hand enclosed the rope above her head. He knew they were moving. But if he closed his eyes it felt like he was just pulling a long rope through a hole, easy as you please. They had climbed to where the shaft became narrower, the walls closer, but there was still room to fall off on either side. It was dark, but not black like John Brown's Cave. A little light filtered in from above, and it slowly got lighter as they climbed.

Carlin giggled. "I guess we're going all the way."

Sam slowed down. "You don't want to?"

"I haven't put the brake on, have I?"

Sam gave a nervous laugh. He concentrated extra hard not to let his arms brush against her. She was trying to help, leaning back against him to give him more room. She was leaning back against him.

The light became stronger, and in another moment the floor of the head-house dropped down around them, and the crossbar of the lift bumped to a stop against the pulley. They stepped off into a small room with a peaked roof, six feet wide, twice that from window to window. All around, at head level, were oval metal openings that fed fat steel tubes. The tubes narrowed to a foot in diameter, made sharp angles and went down through the floor. They un-nerved Sam. It was like being surrounded by giant baby birds, open-mouthed, demanding food.

"And this," Carlin said, leaning on a bright red spout mounted on a central pivot, "is what Timmy calls the dompa-ding. It's supposed to put the grain in the right hole, but half the time it dumps it on the floor. Dad *rues the day* he installed this thing." She made a face at him, scrunching her nose cutely on the famous phrase.

Sam grinned back, and almost called it the momma bird, but was afraid that would sound stupid. Dust lay inches deep everywhere. The floor, the beams, the tops of the open mouths—everything was deep in dust. Even the electrical wires crisscrossing above had an inch of dust riding them. The air felt thick and heavy.

"Come on, look."

Sam ducked under the red spout, following her to the back window, stirring up dust as he went. The window was regular size. Funny—it looked so tiny from below. She tried to lift it, laughed because it was locked, and pushed it open. The cool air reminded Sam his shirt was damp with sweat, embarrassing him. But the view! He had often looked up at birds and wished he could see what they see. The boxcars looked like toys, like he could reach down and pick one up. The train station looked like a dollhouse.

Sam's eyes followed the dark green meanderings of the creek. Beside them, gleaming like steel ribbons, ran the rails of the Mopac main line. He stuck his head out, trying to see the camp, but it was hidden by trees. The rolling hills were a patchwork quilt of green and gold, crisscrossed with dirt roads where plumes of dust rose behind vehicles as they went along.

"Now come look out over here."

Sam followed Carlin to the other window, which created a nice breeze when opened. Julian was at their feet, a dollhouse town. The shingled roof of the office was right down there, with the clean white of the truck scale stretching out each way in front of it. Up the block he saw Marchon's store and the tiny gas station.

"See that square red building," Carlin said, pointing. "That's the Julian School. And to the right of it, those white things?"

"Yeah."

"That's the bleachers where you were going to play ball, until Lincoln Thomas Ford did us a nasty. They should've just gone ahead with your game."

Sam stared off into the tree tops where she was pointing, but his real attention was focused much closer. As she said "your game," she'd put her hand on his arm. It rested there, light as straw and heavy as a brick. Before he could think of what to do, she pulled him to face her, pecked him briefly on the lips, and pulled back, grinning mischievously. "Sorry. I just had to do that one more time."

Whether the buss was intended as initiation or a valediction, he would never know, because of a faint but insistent tapping from some part of the machine.

"Oh brother," Carlin said, rolling her eyes.

"What?"

"Nothing, it's fine. I was hoping we'd get out of here without theatrics."

A muffled voice—somebody hollering up the shaft. Carlin got down on her hands and knees, listening. Another distant shout.

"Oh for pity sake," she said, throwing her hands wide in frustration. "It's Frank."

Sam felt sick, but Carlin seemed merely aggravated. "He's always coming around with his little bit of corn on Sundays." She yelled down the shaft. "Frank! It's Carlin! Don't turn on the leg! You hear?"

More indistinct hollering from below.

Carlin jumped up, brushing the dust from her skirt. "He'd better not turn it on. You think its dusty now, wait 'til that thing starts up. Be just like him. I'll get the windows." She went to the back one, but hesitated, staring out at something. After a thoughtful pause she closed it and went to the front window, tilting her gaze downward. She stood there, shaking her head, and said softly, "I don't believe it."

"What?" Sam went to the window. He saw a truck sitting on the scale. Three more trucks were lined up behind it. Their cargoes glowed golden in the sun. Drivers were getting out, shaking hands. Bits of banter drifted up to them.

"Wheat wasn't supposed to turn until tomorrow at the soonest. Oh brother." Carlin closed the window, still shaking her head. "We're in for some fun now." She took his hands into hers, and spoke intently. "Listen, Sam. Don't worry. I brought you up here to see the view before you had to leave town. That's it." She paused, eyes locked with his until he nodded, and then nodded back. "Good. I can handle them. I'll get a lot of stupid teasing is all."

A hum electrified the air, followed by a rumbling that started soft and built to a roar. Dust rose around them like a ghostly specter summoned to life.

Carlin turned around, hands on hips. "He is such a brat!" she shouted, "I told him not to turn on the . . ."

Sam looked behind her, where the momma bird, strangely, had come to life. Its beak perked up six inches, and began to revolve briskly on its axis. Before he could warn her, the spout hit the back of her head. As she sprawled toward him, he watched her glasses hop through the air, land on the lift platform, and skitter over its edge to the blackness below.

"I'm okay," she said, regaining her feet in the dusty haze. "Just a bump. That Frank, I swear I'll . . ." She paused to stare at her hand. *Wet?* She frowned at the blood a long moment, brows knit, and began to sway. Sam reached to steady her, and then caught her as she fell.

35

LIARS

Sam gathered Carlin onto the lift, while the spout, like an unhousebroken dog, began pouring grain onto the floor. The error awakened the ghost in the machine: red lights flashed on and off. A buzzer made deafening shrieks.

Sam put his foot on the pedal, and started down. He kept her cradled against him, her bloody head against his shirt, her body curved into his. After a few seconds the buzzer stopped, the roar of the leg died away. Sam fought to keep his wits in the darkness. He proceeded carefully, keeping his arms around her, her weight against him, knowing that if her knees buckled, she could slip right off the edge.

"Talk to me," he whispered. "You should try to talk."

"It . . . it surprised me, is all. The blood, I mean. I'm okay."

But she didn't sound okay. "Talk," he said. "Say anything."

A strange small giggle came from her. "This is how I used to go up with dad," she said. "Only I was shorter then, because I remember his hands being higher."

Sam thought of her as a big person. Not actually big, but her gestures, her confidence, the way she talked—she commanded a lot of space. But now her voice sounded tiny in the darkness, and her body seemed almost nothing against his.

She tensed. "We . . . I . . . My glasses. We have to go back up."

"They fell off the edge."

"What? Where? Down the shaft?"

"Uh-huh."

"Oh, no. I'm blind as a bat." She took a quick breath. "But, listen. I can handle them. Nothing bad is going to happen. You hear?"

"Yeah."

"Nothing."

Her voice wasn't as confident as her words. Hand over hand Sam lowered them toward the white men he knew were waiting below. The light leaking upwards reminded him of John Brown's Cave, the glint coming from up around the bend, where the tunnel came out in the ravine. He thought how scared those freedom-seekers must have been, thinking what might be waiting for them out there, but knowing there was no turning back.

The dull luminance rose to meet them. The ceiling was at their knees, their shoulders. The lift landed with a small thud. Sam replaced the safety bolt, and looked around the dim dusty floor for her glasses. No luck. When he looked up, there was Frank's truck over the grate, and a ring of white men clustered around it, all squinting into the gloom. The only sound was the dribble of corn from the tailgate.

Carlin gathered herself, took a deep breath, and stepped off the lift. "Come on, Sam," she said in a clear voice. She strode briskly past the men, toward the big open doorway, holding up a hand to ward off Frank. Sam trailed behind.

"Tell me this ain't true, what I'm seeing," Frank said with high emotion. "Tell me it ain't true!"

"Don't even start with me, Frank Abernathy. I've got nothing to say to you." But when she stepped into the glare outside, she shaded her eyes and took a stagger-step sideways. A collective gasp went up, and the men rushed out of the elevator. The sunshine exposed the blood on her hands and her dress, and the ugly knot of dark red at the back of her head, and the two trickles down her neck. Also, the stain on shirt of the colored boy.

"It's nothing," she said. "Somebody—Frank—turned on the . . ."

"She's been attacked," bawled Frank. "Grab him!"

Two white-haired boys leaped forward and took hold of Sam.

"No," screamed Carlin. "He didn't do anything. Buchalters?" She squinted, and joined the fray, prying at a plaster-casted wrist. "Dwayne! You let him go." She looked wildly around, stopping on a stout figure. "Jack, is that you? Help me, Jack!"

For long seconds Jack did nothing, and Carlin fought to pull the arms from Sam.

Ron Littman came at a sprint from somewhere. "What's going on here? Carlin, what happened?"

"Nothing," she said, letting go of Dwayne. "An accident. I just . . ." But the bright sun, the injury, and the exertion caught up with her. She staggered forward, and her father rushed to catch her.

"He did it," Frank howled, pointing to Sam.

"Where are you hurt?" Ron asked.

"Just bumped my head. A little dizzy. I'm fine."

"It wasn't me!" Sam cried out from between Buchalters. "The thing, up there! The dompa-ding."

But all eyes went to the dark red stains on his shirt.

"He's talking crazy," Frank said. "He's a sex-maniac. They all are!"

Ron glared around at everyone, as if daring them to say something. He put his arm around Carlin's shoulders, said, "Let's get you home" and turned toward his house.

"I got a witness!" Frank's voice went up an octave. "And he's right here." Everyone stopped, eyes wide. Frank pointed. "Timmy! Timmy saw them."

"Tim?" Carlin said, looking around wildly. "I lost my glasses, is that you?"

Timmy emerged slowly from behind some men.

"Okay, Timmy," Frank said hurriedly. "You told me you saw this guy all over your sister, didn't you?"

Tim stared at Carlin, at the splotch on Sam's shirt.

"Come on, Timmy, like we practiced it." Frank sang, imitating a child voice. "Carlin and the Black boy sitting in a tree, K-I-S-S-I-N-G."

Hearing it, Tim wondered, as he did the first time Frank cornered him to sing this strange song, why *spelling* was part of it.

"Come, on," Frank prodded, "You saw them, right?"

Timmy waited for the next part, the saw-them-what or saw-them-where, but everyone just stared at him. In the glare of gazes, he tried to move it along. "Yeaahhhh . . ."

A quick stirring, audible gasps from the farmers. And then, unaccountably, Carlin was yelling at him. "He's lying," she shouted. "He's just a little boy!"

"He seen what he seen," Frank bellowed. "And he," pointing to Sam, "is gonna pay for this."

The circle of men constricted, and Timmy, in a moment to be replayed in future nightmares, thought they were coming for him. But they turned on Sam.

"Nobody does nothing," Ron Littman commanded, waving his free arm. "Stand down. I'll be right back. Carlin, come on. And Timmy! Home! Now!"

Millie could never have imagined this homecoming parade. Carlin bloody, woozy, but fighting her father's grip. Timmy full-on bawling, giant inconsolable heaves. Her husband holding too tightly to one, and yelling too harshly at the other, possessed by a muted and strangely incoherent rage.

Timmy flew into her arms, but she could only hold him a few seconds before letting him down, turning to Carlin, whispering, "Where are you bleeding?"

"Mom, mom." Carlin, agitated, "My old glasses. Where are they? I gotta go back . . ."

"You gotta nothing," said Ron. "You're staying right here."

"You've got to save Sam . . ."

"I'll take care of it," he barked. But Ron was, for once, gripped by uncertainty. One of his children was lying, and too much depended on which one. He tarried to see the bandaging of Carlin's wound, a half-inch cut at the back of her head. "You," he said gruffly to Tim. "Be quiet. You weren't hurt. Stop crying."

But Timmy was unable to stop crying.

Jack Scarborough had been horrified to see Carlin stagger out of the elevator, dazed and bloody. And that Black boy skulking behind looked guilty as hell. If the Buchalters hadn't grabbed him, by God Jack would have. But then, confusingly, there she was, clawing at Dwayne, screaming to him for help. And he would have. He really would have. But then Ron burst in, to his relief. But Ron had taken Carlin home, and now Frank was throwing out orders like a boss man.

"Hold him tight. Bring him over here." Frank had bailing twine. Sam tried to fight, but Big Bobby had him firmly from behind. While Jack and the other men gaped silently, Frank tied Sam's hands in front of him. The redhead strutted in front of Sam, his voice like a radio-show lawyer. "She resisted your vile advances, so, in an animal rage, so you hit her on the head."

"No! We went to look out the windows."

"That's the weakest alibi I've ever heard," Frank crowed, warming to the role. He swooped in to pick up something on the gravel. "This is what done it," Frank announced, holding the book aloft. "He got her all worked up with words, and he used it to take advantage."

Even with hands tied, Sam's eyes flew to the book, terrified. If Jack opened it, found the brazen lyrics—they would kill him for sure.

Bobby Buchalter didn't care about books. His new idea was worse. "How about we see how fast he can run?" He pulled Sam to the back of Frank's truck, and began working the rope through the latch.

It took Jack's mind full seconds to catch up. *How fast he can run . . .* tied to a tailgate? A joke, right? But at the same time, Frank's accusation hit Jack in tender spot. A book. Words. That was *his* territory, what *they* talked about.

For a moment, a small evil part of Jack wanted to see Sam running behind the pick-up.

"Here's your poetry." Frank held the book up to Sam's nose, grabbed a hunk of pages and tore them crosswise, and hurled it to the ground. Face to face with Sam, he said, "How ya like that, boy?"

Sam's foot shot out, slamming Frank's knee.

Frank hopped backward with a howl. He took one limping step forward, and said coldly, "Come on, Bobby, let's go for a ride." He got in the truck, slamming the door.

"Woo-wie!" went Bobby, as he and Dwayne piled in from the other side.

Jack flashed a panicked look to the other men. He didn't know them, but they seemed to know the Buchalters. Wheat must have turned at Plattsmouth. They looked thrilled. Bleeding blond girl. Sex-crazed Negro. Vigilante justice. What a show!

"Wait!" Jack shouted. "Wait a god-blamed second here."

But he was too late. As in a dream, there was the pick-up trundling through the elevator with the colored boy dancing behind it, hands tied to the tailgate. It went down the incline on the other side and out of sight. They heard the spray of gravel as the motor gunned.

"Oh my God," breathed Jack. "Oh my God, oh my God."

In seconds the truck came into view again, careening around in front of the office. Frank drove it past the line of trucks, and skidded to a stop.

"That oughta taught him," Frank called, leaning out the window. But his voice was shaky, and Jack saw fear in his eyes.

A pause. Then a guffaw, and soon the farmers were laughing.

"What the . . . ?" Frank and the Buchalters poured out of the truck.

There, perched on the back bumper and grasping the tailgate, was Sam.

"Damn it all!" Frank threw his hat to the ground, to more laughter. "I'll show you, you . . ."

Sam tumbled off the bumper, landing on his back. In a blur of speed he leapt to his feet, teeth and fingers clawing at the knots. In seconds he was free. He faced Frank, crouching. "I didn't hurt her," he said, "But if you want to fight, Mr. Abernathy, do it fair."

The formality caught Frank off guard. He took a step back, trying to frame his outrage, but only managed, "Like you were fair to that girl?"

"He's a thief," Sam said, appealing to Jack. "He's stealing, and I know he is."

"Dwayne!" shouted Frank. "Help me get a hold of him. Don't let him get away."

Dwayne inched forward, unsure. Sam was ready for them this time, and he had a wild look in his eye. With Sam's eyes on Dwayne, Frank charged in, and got a roundhouse hook that sent him sprawling. One-armed Dwayne backed off.

A blast split the air. The topmost steel of the elevator rang with the ricochet of buckshot. Red-faced, Bobby Buchalter turned the double-barrel shotgun on Sam. "You don't ever hit a white man. You call him sir! We'll show you what comes of assaulting a woman."

"I never . . ."

"Shut it! One more word out of you, and they're gonna be scraping parts of you off the gravel. Frank, get some more of that rope. And do it right this time. We're gonna have a regular track meet, right up Main Street."

"No."

Everyone looked around.

"No," Jack Scarborough said again, stepping forward. He felt as if he were coming out of a dream in which he'd been unable to talk or move. As they moved toward Sam with the rope, Sam and Jack locked eyes, and a number of hard truths hit Jack all at once. One, he never believed that boy would hurt Carlin. Two, it was jealousy, not justice, that had kept him rooted. Three, a flashback to the Julian schoolyard, where he is the frightened weakling, cowering before Big Bobby Buchalter, praying for his big brother to come put the bully in his place.

But this wasn't the playground, and Dave wasn't here.

"This has gone far enough," Jack said. "You scared him good, Bobby. Now put that thing back in the truck."

Frank turned on him. "You think we're kidding? That boy attacked Carlin. Justice says we got to . . ."

"Justice can wait."

"I am justice," Bobby said, waving the gun to show why. "And I got a half a dozen witnesses will say that he came after me with a knife."

Jack swiveled on the farmers with a cold stare. "And I got the same will say you shot him in cold blood, or go to jail for lying."

Bobby motioned with the muzzle. "Back out of the way, Scarborough."

Jack kept moving forward, slowly, his talent for chatter facing its ultimate test. "Now Bobby, if there's cause for the sheriff to come, we'll get him here in a jiffy. This guy is Mopac, he's not running away anywhere." With all eyes on him, Jack's peripheral vision registered movement. One was Timmy, returned, his tear-streaked face next to a truck. Something else moved stealthily behind the trucks. *Eyes on me*, thought Jack, boring into Bobby's gaze, *eyes on me*. Jack opened his palms. "Isn't it better to put the gun away? Prison's no fun, from what I hear. Dwayne," he called out, his eyes still locked on Bobby's, "Dwayne, you and me, rivals, yeah, but I always figured you for a stand-up guy. You don't want to be a party to this."

"C'mon, Bobby," said Dwayne. "This has got out of hand."

"Shut up, Dwayne." Bobby lowered the gun slightly, then swung it quickly in response to a movement.

"Timmy," Jack shouted. "Get down!"

For a sickening second the gun barrel swung towards the small boy, and Jack tried to scream, anticipating another blast. But none came. A dark hand flashed from behind Bobby, gripping the gun-barrel, yanking it sideways. Another hand grabbed the stock. Bobby held on, and for long seconds the two big men were face to face, immobile as stone statues, each trying to muscle the shotgun away from the other. Using his enormous weight, Bobby appeared to be twisting the other man over backward, and a sneer started to cross his lips. But suddenly Bobby was on his back, with Jerome towering above, pointing the gun at his face.

36

GUN, FLOUR, CROWBAR, PENNANT

Jerome waved the gun around, a wordless warning to all. Without taking his eyes from Bobby, he called out. "Sam, are you hurt?"

"No, sir."

He kept the gun on Bobby, voice cold with rage. "You tried to drag that man behind a truck."

"Just for fun," Bobby pleaded. "He wouldn't get hurt by it."

"Not hurt by it?" Jerome's voice shook. "Do you hear what you're saying? And the rest of you." His look raked over the farmers. "You were going to stand and watch it happen?"

"He attacked Carlin!" shouted Frank. "That's her blood on him."

"I didn't," said Sam.

"Who fired that shot?" Ron called, bursting into the group.

"Look out!" shouted Bobby. "He's got my gun!"

"I asked who fired it."

"Bobby did," said Jack. "And he was fixing to do worse."

"Ronnie, I was only acting . . ."

"Shut up, Buchalter." Ron took in the situation, did a double-take at Tim, and shouted, "Get home now!"

The entire assembly turned to watch the stubborn boy.

"Run!"

And Tim ran.

Ron turned to Jerome, and made a soothing gesture. "I think you ought to give me that. I won't turn it on you, I promise. You and Sam go back to the camp."

Jerome took a long moment, staring at the ring of white men. "And then what? How long till they come for us? I'm going, and I'm keeping this in self-defense.

Get the foreman. I'll hand it over to him, as long as there are witnesses." He took a position beside Sam, and gestured for the farmers to make way.

"You'll both be dead by sundown," taunted Frank. "Look at this shiner, Ronnie. He did that."

"What?" shouted Jack. "You had rope, and you were going to . . ."

"And you're a coon-lover," Frank over-shouted him, "just like your brother. I got cold-cocked. Ask anybody. Didn't he hit me in the eye?"

The farmers nodded. "She tried to run to him for protection," one added.

"That's a lie," stated Jack.

Jerome silenced them with a wave of the gun. He had one arm around Sam's shoulders and the other on the trigger. "Nobody move. Nobody come near our camp. I warn you."

"Wallace. Wait."

All eyes swung to the doorway of the elevator. Denton Henry came forward. "Wait," he said again. "That's not your best play. Word gets out you're holed up with a shotgun, only bad things will come of that." He crossed to stand beside Ron Littman, moving gingerly around Jerome. "I was late to this party, Ron, but I saw enough, and the only one speaking rightly is Scarborough." He faced Jerome. "You know I'm your friend. If Ron says he won't turn that gun on you, his word is gold. Give it to him. Go back to the camp, and tell the men to stay in the bunk cars. I'll call Mr. Burdock."

"You forgetting Carlin?" spluttered Frank. "Even if she tries to cover for him, he still done it. You going to stand for that?"

"Shut up, Frank," Ron said.

Jerome gave a long, slow exhale. The station agent wasn't wrong about the prospects of a Black man holed up with one shot left. And he'd be endangering the rest of the crew. Still, he hesitated. What they tried to do to Sam had awakened the horror of dead Will Brown, dragged around the streets of Omaha. Every molecule of him screamed not to give up the gun. Reason slowly overcame wrath. Finally, looking Denton Henry in the eye, Jerome handed the gun to the grain man.

"Thanks, Ron," Bobby said, popping up from the ground. "Gimme my gun, and we'll take these two to jail."

Ron gripped the gun by its barrel and in a sudden vicious stroke smashed it against a truck bumper. The wooden stock went spinning across the gravel. He handed the barrel to Bobby. "Get in your truck and get out of here."

Bobby stared it. "That's a Winchester 21. You know what I paid for that?"

"Don't you ever pull a gun, not on my property. Go on. The rest of you Cass County bums too. Your wheat ain't welcome here." He shoved Bobby towards his truck. "I said, out of here!"

There was a moment, a short moment, when it looked as if Bobby might go after Ron. Even with a gun barrel as a weapon, it would have been a bad idea. The rage of Ron emanated like a beacon. He was practically levitating.

"C'mon, Dwayne." The Buchalters got in, wheeled the truck around, and headed for the highway, followed by the sullen Cass county bystanders. One by one the grain trucks, brimming with wheat, trundled down the road.

Jack said quickly, "Is Carlin okay?"

"We think she'll be fine. She told me how it happened." Ron glared at Frank.

Jerome turned to Jack. "That was real brave or real foolish, what you did."

Denton jumped in, explaining to Ron, "This man," he said, gripping Jack's shoulders, "this man faced down that shotgun bare-handed. And *this* man took it away from him. That's what I call courage."

"I saw you around the back," said Jack.

"He's like John Henry Kagi, right, Jerome?" Sam put in. As the white men looked around in confusion, Sam scooped up his book, and slid it in his pants.

Frank broke in, his voice shrill. "Am I the only one who gives a whit about Carlin? If not for me . . ."

Ron wheeled on him. "Frank, did you turn the spout when you knew there were people in the headhouse?"

"Well, uh, I . . ."

"Knowing full well how dangerous that is."

"I thought it was you up there," Frank said, "and being we're in a hurry with the wheat and all, I thought if it jammed you'd be up there to fix it."

"And the spout take my head off? Is that what you thought?"

"You're getting on me?" said Frank, trying for outrage. "It was your daughter went up there with him."

"He's robbing you!"

Sam planted himself in front of Ron, talking fast. "He's robbing you. He's taking your corn, and selling it back to you. He's getting it from the back bin."

"That's crazy," said Frank.

"I can prove it," Sam said. "The flour." He almost dragged Ron to the back of Frank's truck, where he scooped out a handful, rubbing it in his hands. "See—it's flour." He reached his hand across the truck bed, and held it up.

A smudge of white shown against Sam's fingers. "I figured he was cheating you, so I spread flour in the back bin."

"Ronnie, you ain't listening to him!"

Ron was listening all right. Sam led everyone in a strange procession to the long quonset bin on the other side of the track, to the back end piled high with corn. Even Timmy, who had never quite managed to run home, trailed along, keeping out of his father's sight. As their eyes adjusted, they could see where the pile of yellow corn had been sprinkled with white dust. A pure yellow place stood out in the middle where corn had been scooped off the surface. The shovel stuck up like a flag pole, marking the spot.

"I heard noises over here on Saturday nights," Sam said. "And he kept bringing in corn to sell on Sundays. I got the flour from Cook. I knew he wouldn't see it in the dark."

Ron turned on Frank. "You're stealing from me?"

"No," said Frank, backing up, "he's lying."

"After all I've done for you?" Advancing on Frank, "Selling me my own grain?"

Frank snatched a crowbar laying on the floor. He waved it with both hands. "Don't make me hurt you, Ronnie."

"Psowf!"

As fights go, this was not much of one. Ron stepped toward Frank, ducked a wild swing, and de-crowbarred him. Then he knocked Frank down, knocked him down again when he tried to get up, pushed him, rolled him, and kicked him across twenty yards of concrete floor, cussing a blue streak the whole way. As Frank cowered in the doorway, Ron told him never to set foot in Julian again. Frank got up and ran.

"Well, that's that," Denton Henry said grandly, "and that should be the last we see of him." As if he'd been the one to unmask Frank's perfidy; as if he'd kicked the crap out of him.

"I should've known they never had so many bits and bobs of corn out at the home place." Ron shook his head, angry with himself. He turned to say something to Sam, a compliment, maybe, or perhaps a word of thanks, but he got distracted. "Timmy," he shouted. "I told you get home!" He shook his head again. "Everybody go home. We've got a harvest to manage."

Denton fell in beside Jack. "Come on over to the station sometime. We can compare war stories."

Jack nodded, and hurried to catch up with Ron and Timmy. Someone was going to tell Carlin how it all went down, and he thought it might as well be him. No, it had to be him. He didn't know why, but it had to.

Jack had never seen Carlin's room. It was small, and seemed smaller for the multi-color maze of felt pennants adorning the walls. St. Louis Cardinals (red), Lake of the Ozarks (blue), St. Bernard's Academy (dark blue), Nebraska Cornhuskers (red again), John Brown's Cave (black). She was propped up in her bed, wearing a flannel nightgown (green, plaid). A white bandage encircled her head, but she was far from acting the invalid. When Jack knocked and came in, he was met with, "Why didn't you help me? I said, 'Jack help! 'I got my hands full here,' and you stood there like a stump."

"I did help," he said defensively, "I mean, later."

"Is Sam all right? I heard a gunshot."

"He's fine," Jack said, working to keep anything like a sneer out of his tone, "in fact, he's kind of a hero. Did you know Frank was stealing corn from the back bin? Stupid question. Well, Sam figured it out, and got flour from I don't know where, and . . ."

"The gunshot?"

"Bobby Buchalter being an ass wipe. Jerome snuck up on him, and got it away. Your dad smashed it on a truck bumper."

"And what were you doing all that time, for pity's sake?"

"Trying to keep people from getting killed, mostly!" It sounded whiny and shrill. Jack wished it was someone else telling the story, someone like the station agent who could grab his sleeve and call him a hero.

"Sam's back at the camp? Nobody called the sheriff, nothing stupid like that?"

"He's *fine*." This time his tone did betray him, and Jack couldn't keep himself from plunging on. "You and him . . . Sam. You're not, you know?"

A long, crushing stare. "Not you too, Jack Scarborough. I expect better from you. I wanted him to see the town from up there, that's all. And I could have made it okay, I could have shamed those perverts, if only Frank hadn't . . ." she waved a hand to her bandage, too impatient to spell it out. Her composure suddenly folded, and she was near tears. "Why didn't you *help* me, Jacky?"

Jack left soon after, amid stumbling apologies and attempts to explain. As he got in his truck, he realized it wasn't even one o'clock, and the wheat had turned. The harvest! He had to get home.

Jack spent the rest of Sunday following the combine across the fields, and trucking loads of wheat back to Julian. Plenty of time to go over it again and again in his head. He had done the right thing. Eventually. But he had failed her in the moment, and Sam could have died. But he didn't, he thought, trying to console himself. The gandy crew would be gone before week's end, and everything would all get back to normal, except he wouldn't have to look at Frank's ugly face anymore. Why did Jack still get that sickly feeling when he thought of Carlin?

37

BROTHERS HAVE A BEER

While Jack fretted and trucked grain into Sunday evening, the story of Carlin and the gandy spread swiftly, over telephone lines, across fences, and in the lines of trucks waiting to unload at elevators across at least three counties. The punch line, served up in a dozen ways, went something like this: That Ronnie Littman, you can take your chances with his daughter, but God help you if you steal his corn. The laugh line was followed by more sober accounts of that drama at the elevator. The bigotry that inflected these stories was tempered, at least somewhat, by the bravery of the older gandy getting the shotgun, and the way the younger one used flour to turn the tables on the Abernathy kid. Some things, a man just had to admire, no matter who did them.

And as for Carlin, well, what could you say? Everyone knew she was headstrong. A real handful, that girl. She probably should have known better than to go up a lift with that boy, but everybody knows you don't turn on a swivel spout when someone's in the headhouse. Get somebody seriously killed that way. That Frank was an ornery piece of work, but you didn't figure him for the kind who'd turn on a swivel spout, or drag a man behind a truck.

Oh, and how about that Scarborough boy, standing nose to muzzle with a Winchester side-by-side? Damn fool thing to do, but he must have stones the size of Mount Rushmore.

Jack stayed in his truck when he brought loads to the Julian elevator. He did not want to hear the gossip, and he did not feel like a hero. After taking the last load to the elevator and dumping it under the glow of naked bulbs, with Ron nodding curtly to him like it was any other harvest day, he wheeled the grain truck over to Dave's house.

"The man of the hour," Dave said, greeting him at the door. "The man that faced down Bobby Buchalter."

"You heard about all that?"

"I heard it about six ways from Sunday, and the store isn't even open today."

"You got a cold one for me?"

The house was calm, Dave's wife and kids in bed. The brothers sat on the screened-in back porch and had a quiet beer. Dave took the porch swing, Jack the overstuffed chair that used to be in the living room. It didn't take much coaxing for Jack to tell the whole story. He'd been rehearsing it all day in his head. Dave just kept shaking his head, rocking gently on the swing, and smiling.

"You know when it really hit me?" Jack said, doubling back to the middle of the story. "It was when Bobby said, 'It'll be a track meet, right here on Main Street.' I thought he was joking. Then I thought: this isn't your Main Street, Buchalter. You don't get to do something that will shame us for a hundred years. That can't happen in Julian." As he said it, he realized it sounded like the story Dave told about Camp Rucker. Jack wondered if his brother was thinking the same thing. Dave's little smile meant something. "What?" Jack said.

"What what?"

"You. Something in what I said. What is it?"

"Nothing."

"But?"

"Nothing. Only . . ." Dave set his beer on the table in front of him and stopped the swing. "Only something still doesn't sit right with you, and I think I know what."

Jack shrugged. "I asked her about him, and got my head handed to me."

"And?"

Jack snorted. "You think they went up to the headhouse for the view?"

The sarcasm didn't stick. "That's the only reason I can think of," Dave said. "Think about it logically. You know it wasn't that boy's idea to go up the lift. And if—let's just say if, though I don't believe it for a second—but if there were any ideas of cootchy-cootchy . . ." Dave took a sip of his beer. "The headhouse of the grain elevator is the last place anybody'd go. A rickety lift to a cramped mess of machinery six inches deep in dust? Doesn't pass the stink test."

"You didn't see the way her cheeks went red the second I asked her."

"And?"

"And no matter what she says, she has some kind of feelings for him."

"And?"

"Stop saying that. What do you mean?"

Dave put his feet down to stop the rocking swing. His voice became serious. "I mean, there's all kind of feelings in this world, and we're all entitled to all of 'em. If you have to ask yourself why you get bent out of shape when it comes to Carlin and Sam, but not when PD Klyber's joshing her, there's some other hard questions you need to ask."

"Damn it, Dave, why do you always go there? You bend over backwards to take their side. Everybody's saying so. Ever since that crew came to town, you've been a different person."

"Before that crew came to town," Dave answered, "I didn't need to be a different person." Dave said it in a calm voice, pushing with his feet to make the swing rock again.

Jack was ashamed of his outburst even as he'd said it. His brother was the best man he knew, or would ever know. "I did the right thing," he said quietly.

"You did do the right thing," Dave said, with emphasis. "And everyone in three counties knows it, and I couldn't be prouder of you. And I love the part where Ronnie smashes that Winchester." He stood up with a short laugh, and plucked up the empty can. Jack stood too. The brothers went outside and put the empties in the garbage. Jack climbed in the cab and cranked the engine. Dave hopped onto the running board, and spoke through the window. "I've said all along, the only thing we owe them or anyone else is a fair shake." His voice became quieter. "And I know full well, sometimes that can be damn hard to do."

38

GAME ON!

Monday, the Third of July, dawned clear and bright, a perfect wheat harvest day. The radio said there was a chance of rain in the offing, adding a sense of urgency to the process. All day long the trucks came, one after another, to Littman Grain. If anyone thought Ron Littman was going to keep his daughter hidden away after what happened, they were disabused of that notion. The way it played out, with Frank disgraced and banished, served wholly to exonerate Carlin. His daughter was not a liar. And the gandies were leaving this week, anyway.

Carlin worked the truck scale, making her the first thing a man saw as he climbed down out of his truck, and entered the office. And she was a sight to see. She wore a red kerchief on her head, with wisps of blond hair peeking out the corners. Only if you looked carefully could you see there was a bandage underneath. She had a red-checked shirt, tied off at the tails to where it showed a stretch of midriff above her jeans. A thought passed through many truck drivers' heads that day, along the lines of, *I sure wouldn't mind a trip to the top of the elevator with her.* Carlin, bright and chipper, looked each man in the eye, the round wire frames of her old glasses adding 'cute librarian' to the picture.

A quarter-mile to the north, Moose Burdock stood outside the camp cars and told the gandy crew they'd taken the track about as far as it needed to go before the next big rip and run. He told them to spend the day packing up the camp. Tomorrow was the Fourth of July holiday, and Wednesday the switch engine would be coming to haul their camp cars to the rail yard at Nebraska City. He added that certain weekend goings-on had no connection to the timing of this move. Nevertheless, they should stay in camp, and not to go running their mouths about anything, and especially nobody needed to say anything to anyone in Omaha about anything in Julian. The foreman stared down the timekeeper during this last part of his speech.

The crew had packed up the camp enough times, and needed no supervision. Moose and Ivan took off in their cars, and the gandies went to work. Despite what Moose said, Sam found himself a reluctant celebrity. The boys caught wind of what happened, and had pried the story out of him. The part about going to the top of the elevator had the gandies grinning and hooting. That Frank, who charged them five bucks for a ride to town, was a thief, surprised no one, but Sam's way of proving it impressed them all.

If there had been a church and a service handy on Sunday, Jerome would have been there, down on his knees and giving thanks. For a few minutes he had seen his world tottering on the edge of abyss, watching Buchalter train a shotgun on Sam. But even when he got the gun away, or because of it, he knew he might not live to see a new day. In those awful moments he thought about JJ. He thought about his house on Blondo Street. Most of all, he thought about Lucy, the horror of her coming to identify his body, the lies they would tell to justify killing him. He was thankful for Denton's help. He thought about Jack stepping in front of that gun.

Jerome watched the other boys tease Sam while they loaded the tool car. He marveled that Sam could come through it all with such apparent ease. The sheriff had showed up the night before, blunt and suspicious, and might have made trouble. But he knew the foreman and he knew the station agent; he knew Ron Littman and all three Scarboroughs. And the Buchalters by reputation. Against his general inclinations, and seeing as how the crew was leaving in a day, he went away without a fuss.

By ten in the morning the trucks were backed up all the way past the camp, a dusty convoy of all sizes, shapes and makes, all with golden piles of wheat brimming over the tops of their boxes. The farm boys sat in their trucks and stared at the gandy dancers doing their clean-up-and-put-away business. The gandy dancers sometimes paused to stare back.

At noon, when Cook said break for lunch, Jerome ate his sandwiches fast, and started down the row of trucks toward Main Street, feeling their farmer eyes on him. He thought he got away clean, but after twenty steps he heard someone trotting up behind him. He hoped it wasn't Sam—that boy should keep a low profile. And he hoped it wasn't Ice, on general principle.

George came along beside him, pushing his wire-rimmed glasses up on his nose. "Moose said stay around camp. You going up to the store?"

"I am," said Jerome.

"Me too," said George. This gandy was a mystery to Jerome. Quiet and serious, George spent his downtime poring over newspapers. Jerome couldn't feature him being one of the drinkers, but he'd been at the center of the scuffle with the white boys in town.

The store was busy with a noontime rush. Jerome saw Millie and Timmy. He gave a respectful nod, but said nothing. Hank Benkleman was there too, along with a bevy of folks Jerome didn't know.

"Mr. Wallace," Dave called out to him in a loud and cheerful voice. "And Mr. Baseball."

George grinned, and said, "Hi Dave."

Jerome did a double-take. *Mr. Baseball?*

"I got your newspaper right here," Dave said to George. "DiMaggio got his two-thousandth hit, you see that?"

"Hank Thompson had an inside-the-park home run."

Dave laughed. "You and your Giants. They're not going to catch the Whiz Kids. You see what that Richie Ashburn's been doing? He's from Nebraska, you know."

"The Phillies will choke," George said, with offhand confidence. "It's the Dodgers I worry about." He handed over a nickel and Dave slid the Nebraska City News-Press across the counter. The bold headline drew their eyes: "First American Troops Arrive in Korea."

"Hope the news is better on the inside," Dave said. He turned to Jerome. "I'm afraid there's no mail for you."

Jerome had to gather himself. Why had he assumed George's newspapers were leftovers from somewhere else? "Cellophane tape?" Jerome managed. "Do you sell that here?"

"Right there on the shelf behind you."

Jerome reached for the roll.

A grain truck rolled to a stop in front of the store. The motor was left running, and Jack came plunging through the door. "Hey Davy . . ." Seeing Jerome, he stopped short. "Hi. Uh. Again."

"Nice to see you," Jerome said, with some formality.

"Uh, yeah. You too."

Dave smiled. "What's the word, brother?"

"I was just going to ask you," Jack said, sounding distracted, "to throw some dried beef on bread with mustard, and make another one I can take out to dad on the combine. He won't stop for love or money, especially now they say rain's coming tonight."

"Rain?" said Hank Benkleman. The word rang like an alarm through the store.

"Yeah," said Jack. "It's not supposed to be too bad, though. Wichita got twenty-nine hundredths, and they're expecting the same in Topeka. Maybe we'll get a rain day."

"I'll get sandwiches as soon as I ring up this man's tape." To Jerome he said, "All the activity down there, looks like your crew is about to move on. They picking up your cars tonight or tomorrow?"

"Nothing moves on the Fourth except passenger trains," Jerome answered. "It's the one union rule they manage to uphold."

"We hope it's just a rain day," Hank intoned soberly, "not a wash-out."

"A rain day," Dave explained, "is when you get enough rain that you have to let the field dry out a day before you can get the combines back out. A wash-out is when you lose crops because it's too muddy. Wait a minute." Dave snapped his fingers. "Tomorrow's Fourth of July. Mopac has the day off. If those showers make it a rain day, the farmers won't be working either. We could play that exhibition!" His excitement carried over into his next question. "You'd be available, wouldn't you, Hank? Say, at noon?"

Hank coughed, paused, coughed again. "After what happened this weekend, I hardly think it's appropriate to talk of . . ."

"So we need to find an umpire," Dave said harshly, cutting him off. He turned to George. "Mr. Baseball, your gandy team ready?"

"We've been ready," said George.

Dave was animated, almost manic. "Jack, you're hitting lead off. Spread the word down at the elevator. Oh, yeah. Sandwiches." Dave went to the meat counter, yanked out a tray of dried beef. His hands flew, making sandwiches in record time.

Jack's head was spinning. Lead off? A game. After all that . . . *against the gandies*? Fourth of July? "Wait a minute, Dave. Let's think about this. Are you sure?"

"You got a problem, Jack?"

"It's just, well. I don't know if the boys will want to give up their rain day for . . . for . . . they're not even a real team. I'm sorry," he said to Jerome and George, "but we were all set to play Lincoln Thomas Ford."

Dave nodded, appearing pensive. "Mr. Baseball," he said at last, "could you lend my brother that newspaper for one second? Page eight, sports headline."

Jack opened it, aware of everyone's eyes on him. "Cards Sweep Braves."

"The other one."

"For Disabled Vets."

"That's the one. Read it out loud."

Jack cleared his throat. "Two of the region's best to tangle Tuesday as the peerless Lincoln Thomas Ford fast-pitch nine travel to Des Moines to take on Iowa's top team, Aldheiser Oldsmobile for a July Fourth exhibition." Jack lowered the paper, the enormity of the betrayal washing over him. "Des Moines?" he said slowly. "Iowa? Why those . . ."

"Keep reading, brother."

"A crowd of more than eight hundred is expected to watch the visiting state champion Forders duel the Aldheiser Tigers. The patriotic players will sacrifice their summer holiday to raise money for disabled veterans." Jack looked around, his face hot. "Those crumb-bums! Those wart hogs!" Jack had plenty more, but there were women present. "Those lying sacks of sorghum!"

Jack threw the paper aside. George made a nifty catch before it hit the floor.

Dave nodded again. "Looks like the joke's on us, doesn't it? Meanwhile, we've got a chance to show that the Hornets don't go back on our word. We owe these fellows a game."

Hank broke in, "I did not say I wouldn't do it. However, if the rains miss us . . ."

"Yeah, yeah," said Dave, impatiently. "The harvest, the harvest, the harvest." The waxed paper folded itself expertly around two sandwiches. "But if Wichita and Topeka are getting less than a half-inch, I'm forecasting a rain day for Nemaha and Otoe Counties." The sandwiches sailed across the store for Jack to catch, one after the other. Dave turned to George.

"Mr. Baseball? Mr. Wallace? Noon tomorrow? Ball field up on the hill?"

George smiled. "We'll be there."

"Well then," said Dave grandly, "Game on!"

39

SNAKES IS WORSE THAN GATORS

Jerome had it all lined up. In three hours, Denton Henry was going to come charging into camp with news of his family emergency. He would hustle out of there, and be home with Lucy and JJ by dinner time. But he hadn't been prepared for how the crew would take the news the game was back on. There was so much whooping and hollering you'd have thought they all got a raise. Jerome couldn't take it. He walked blindly away, down the track, until he was alone at the edge of a swaying wheat field, ripe and awaiting the harvester. He plucked a thick head off a stalk. The grains were golden, tinged with red. He brought it to his nose, savoring the smell. He broke off a couple kernels, tossed them in his mouth, and chewed. The stuff of bread, all right.

From this spot he had a panoramic view across the wheat field to the train station with the elevator buildings behind it, trucks lined up to get on the scale. A haze of grain dust hung in the air. He found it oddly touching, their common resolve to get the grain harvested, as much and as fast as humanly possible. He felt guilty wishing for a good hard rain, a rain that would give them what they call a 'wash-out,' and wash out the game as well. So he wished for no rain at all. Let them work right through the Fourth of July and every day after until they've got every kernel picked and sent off to wherever it goes in those boxcars. Just not a light rain, please God. Just not what they call a rain day. The boys would get over their disappointment; in a week or so they'd forget all about it. If there was no game, he could not be a traitor.

Jerome looked past the field to the gulley of the creek. It reminded him of the one in Nebraska City, the place where he came out of John Brown's Cave. Julian, too, had been on the Underground Railroad. And these other little towns they'd run track through. They were building the Underground Railroad, Sam had said, putting it above ground. That was a poetic way to think. The stuff was rubbing off on the kid.

At least he'd gotten that cellophane tape. He would tape up those torn pages in the Langston Hughes book. When he saw Frank's truck careen around the elevator with Sam clinging to the back end, it had twisted something inside of him. He stared into the ravine, imagining former slaves trailing warily at night. John Henry Kagi. Sam remembered the name of the boy who died at Harper's Ferry. Jerome smiled, remembering how Sam had compared Jack to Kagi.

"You reckon there's snakes down there?"

Jerome jumped. He turned to find Cook beside him, staring at him from his rheumy eyes. "What are you doing out here?"

"That's pretty obvious. I followed you." Cook plucked a head of wheat and brought it to his nose. "You were the only one not smiling back there."

"It's not even a real game."

"Don't like gator meat. Got a wild taste that doesn't sit easy in the belly, no matter what you do with it."

"I promised my wife, Cook. I set it up with the station agent for a ride to the train today. My boy's expecting me. I can't let them down."

"I expect not. Now, snakes is even worse than gators. More gamey. Make an exception for eels, though. Ugly as they are, eels are fine eating."

"They're undefeated, and we've never played a single game. It was a farce to begin with."

Cook had been staring out across the fields. He turned to look Jerome in the eye. "You got to do what's best for your family. But be honest about it. Our boys probably get beat either way, but without you it *will* be a farce. Face up to what you're doing, that's all I'm saying."

"George can run the team. He's Mr. Baseball."

"George can not run the team. You're the only one."

In spite of everything, Jerome's vanity was soothed. "You really think we have a chance?"

Cook shrugged. "Delran can pitch. Big Larry can hit. I've seen worse. That's why they play the games—isn't that how the saying goes?"

"Huh."

"Do what the Good Lord tells you is right. Meanwhile, I've got to make a respectable house call. I've got my own mess to clean up."

"Your own mess?"

"Last week," Cook said, shaking his head, "when Sam asked for the flour. I thought it was for the missus. Never dreamed he'd use it to lay a trap the way he did. When I didn't hear from her, my pride got the best of me, and I sent over a note asking did she like the flour and what did she make. She's probably figured out where that flour went to, but it's my place to apologize."

Cook left, retreating from the wheat field. Jerome watched him all the way until he disappeared at the grain bins. "My place to apologize" echoed in his ears. Clouds were gathering in the south. "What the Good Lord tells you is right" rang in his head. Jerome, who wasn't much for praying, made a brief impious prayer for a good hard rain—or else for none at all.

40

OTOE COUNTY EXCEPTIONALISM

Jerome's prayer was not answered, as prayers so often aren't. Or maybe it was, but in a different way than he thought. That happens too. The early morning hours brought a fast-moving line of thunderstorms that made some noise, discharged a quick soak, and moved on to Iowa, where it gathered strength, and crossed over Des Moines just in time to rain out a much-anticipated exhibition game there. Julian dawned crisp and wet—just wet enough to keep the combines at rest. A perfect rain day, in other words. Game on.

For uniforms, the gandies all had T-shirts that were more or less white. As they started up Main Street for the school yard, a curious thing happened. One by one, every little kid in town joined them. By the time they made the three blocks to the school yard, it was a full-on parade, with children prancing and gandies laughing. All except for Timmy, who trailed behind and spoke to no one.

Moose Burdock guessed it must be true about him going soft. That was the only way to explain why he would spend his holiday watching gandies play fast-pitch. Gandies. As if he didn't get a bellyful of them all week. To add to that, he was sitting next to a lame colored man who thought he invented the game. Damn song caller dragged him out here early to get the best seats. And the best seats, Moose dictated, were right behind the home dugout, elbows resting on the half-shed, right over the players' heads.

Charly T wanted to sit behind the gandy bench, but Moose put his foot down. "How would that look?" he scolded. "With me sitting right there, folks would think this was a Mopac team. All I need is word getting to Omaha I'm out here running my own barnstorming outfit. They'd love that."

"Don't forget you got to pay off our bet."

"I'll pay it off right now," said Moose, annoyed. He stood up.

"No, no," said Charly. "Later. Has to be in front of the crew."

And he had agreed to make a fool of himself to pay off a bet. If that wasn't the definition of soft, he didn't know what was.

The Hornets came from around behind the stands, stashing bats in the dugout and taking the field to shag flies.

Charly pointed. "Isn't that the grain man?"

"I'll be damned," said Moose. "He was a hell of player in the twenties. They called him Speedo." The old uniform still fit, but the script of "Julian" had old-fashioned curly letters, and the red was faded to pink. Moose had to hand it to him. A lot of men, something like that happens to their daughter, they'd make themselves scarce. Ronnie was suiting up to replace Frank.

The Hornets all knew Moose, and many a holler came in his direction. Dave called out, "I hear you gave 'em a light day to get ready for us."

"That's right, Scarborough."

"Is that Ernie Scarborough?" asked Charly.

"No, that's his brother, runs the store. Ernie's in center field." Moose squinted, trying to get a better look. He'd heard Ernie was having a spell lately.

"The boys are here."

Moose looked where Charly pointed. Out past the left-field fence, coming through the schoolyard, was a rag-tag parade of gandies and children. About half the team had baseball caps. Little Larry wore a pork-pie. Ice led the way, smiling and nodding in that scary way of his.

The bleachers were filling in around Moose and Charly. Millie's brother, Nick Reilly, rolled in and sat behind them. Nick had worked for the Missouri Pacific years ago. Moose turned around and said hello.

"Twenty-three hundredths," said Nick.

"I heard twenty-one," Moose answered. "Just enough to keep the dust down."

"Just enough to keep the dust down," Nick repeated. The air was bright, a few stray clouds drifting by. It was cool for the Fourth of July, upper seventies, the scent of rain still lingering in the air.

Moose introduced Nick to Charly T. The men shook hands, and Nick expressed his admiration for song callers.

"Who's that?" added Nick, pointing out a young woman alone at the top of the bleachers. "She with Mopac too?"

"Never seen her before," said Moose.

Nick frowned. He thought he should know everyone in Julian, especially an attractive young lady.

Moose watched the gandies amble toward the field. He saw them get intercepted by a blond girl and a black-robed figure who gave them several somethings that the men laughed to receive. The mystery was revealed when the gandies got to their dugout. They all whipped off their shirts and took turns writing on them. Carlin and the nun had brought them laundry markers. Ice was first to finish, and held up his shirt proudly to Moose and Charly.

"**GAN**dies." He had run short of room.

Moose saw the reactions of the Julian boys in the field. One by one they stopped whatever they were doing, and stared, slack-jawed at the visitors.

A soft, "Damnnnnnnn . . ." came from somewhere on the field.

It wasn't the shirts they were looking at, it was the shirtless physiques. To a man, the gandies were broad-shouldered and chisel-chested. From the ebony of Ice to the chocolate of Sam to the caramel of Big Larry, their taut skin bulged and rippled with muscle. Moose saw it, laughed, and shouted to the home boys, "What'd you think they been doing all summer, picking tulips?"

"Come on." Dave waved his team in. "Let them take some field."

The visitors spread out across the diamond and the outfield, to a smattering of applause. Each shirt had "Gandies" in a different scrawl across the front or back. Moose decided he liked it.

On the visitors' side, a group of nuns was filing into the mostly empty bleachers. Charly T giggled quietly beside him.

"What?"

"They got to root for the Black folks, right?"

Moose laughed. "Strangest cheerleaders I've ever seen."

The nuns took up residence in the front row, leaning their elbows on the top of the dugout. The line of black-veiled heads with linen-framed faces gave the dugout the look of an altarpiece of a very unusual church.

"Grounders, that's it," Charly said. Jerome was tossing balls in the air and smashing grounders. The boys had never played on grass. They were used to the crazy bounces of the pasture. Sure enough, balls were scooting right under their gloves. Jerome kept yelling for them to get lower.

Moose never would have figured Ice for a short stop, but there he was, doing a fair imitation of one. Washington at third base had to be a weak spot, but Moose put that thought on hold as he watched Sam snap the ball to first, where Big Larry had a lot of reach. Charly didn't think they should waste George at second, but conceded the Jones-Bones-Little Larry outfield did have a nice ring to it.

The home stands were over half full, Moose noted—quite a showing on one day's notice. Benkleman strode out on the field, carrying his face mask in his hand. Dave and Jerome joined him behind the plate. After a couple of minutes, Jerome waved his team back to the dugout.

Hank stood on home plate, hands on hips, surveying his kingdom. Finally, he cleared his throat, stood up tall and said, "Today's game is an exhibition, and will not count in Country League standings. We'll go seven innings. The fifteen-run mercy rule is in effect, if that should be the case." Some sniggering came from the stands, where a lot of people were sure it would be the case. "Before we start the game, the Reverend Carpenter will have a word of prayer. Will the teams come out, please."

Some of the home folks thought this was too much. They only had prayers for league championships. Hank was grandstanding, that's what it was. Everyone knew he was still mad about Lincoln Thomas Ford wanting to bring in an Omaha ump. The players came out and lined up, Hornets in their red with white trim on the first-base line, Gandies in their bespoke whites along the other.

Nearest home plate, Jack Scarborough was face to face with Sam for the first time since Sunday. Sam smiled shyly at him, and Jack felt a fresh wave of guilt. For all his ballyhooed bravery, what Jack remembered was how he froze when Carlin begged him to help, how he failed to stop them from trying to drag Sam behind a truck.

Evan Carpenter went to the pitcher's mound. He took off his baseball cap, showing his upswept mane of black hair. The players and fans followed suit. He stood tall, handsome in his red uniform with "Julian" embroidered across the front. He bowed his head and began, "Lord God of Creation, we thank you for this beautiful day, and the chance to honor you playing the game we love. We welcome our guests, and wish them luck on the next stretch of rail. You know, the other day I was remembering . . ."

A restless ripple went through the crowd. Nobody wanted preaching.

"I was remembering back in the thirties, when I was a kid, when times were hard. In those days, we used to see a lot of unfortunate folks riding the rails. Hobos, Okies, whatever you want to call them. All of them hungry, some near starved to death. I remember how the women up and down the railroad would feed them. The farmers didn't have two dimes to rub together themselves, but they always had chickens, so they always had eggs. I don't remember a one of those poor folks ever being turned away without at least a fried egg sandwich."

This brought nodding in the bleachers. People did remember that.

"And it was only a few generations before that," Carpenter went on, "people here were part of the Underground Railroad, helping slaves get north. A noble cause, if ever there was one. So it seems to me—and I say this in all humility—here in Julian we are different from a lot of places when it comes to strangers who don't look like us. Unlike most places, we don't have a history to live down. We've got a history to live up to.

"And, good Lord, we ask you to remember our white soldiers and our Black soldiers bound for Korea. Let the struggle be brief, and the cause be just, and victory be ours, we humbly pray."

Prayers seldom had an effect on Jack, but this time he had a lump in his throat. It seemed the only thing to do, in the silent moment after the amen, was take a step forward and shake hands with Sam. What Jack didn't foresee was the swinging gate effect of his gesture, making players on both sides think it was planned, and they had better get their butts out to shake hands with the player across the way.

Jerome and Dave Scarborough shook hands.

"Mr. Wallace," said Dave.

"Mr. Postmaster."

Dave pointed with his chin over Jerome's shoulder. "Looks like you got visitors."

41

THE SHORT PORCH

Jerome turned around to see where Dave was pointing. It was Lucy! Smiling, waving, carrying JJ, making her way into the bleachers. Behind her was Malcolm, and Malcolm's wife, Vera. Malcolm pinched the corners of his own shirt to make fun of Jerome's, and laughed. Behind came Denton Henry, shepherding them along. The new arrivals joined the nuns. The station agent met the stares of the home side by smiling and waving.

Jerome sprinted to the stands. He took his son to his chest and hugged him, and squeezed his wife's hand, saying, "Lucy, Lucy." He shook hands with Malcolm and Vera, and then his glance went to the all-smiling Denton Henry, the benefactor for this wonderful turn of events.

After his conversation with Cook at the edge of the wheat field, Jerome had gone to the Julian station to call off their scheme to pretend he had some emergency at home. Against company policy, Denton had let Jerome use the phone to call his wife and tell her, painfully, he was not coming home. He could not let these boys down. He had to play the game. Lucy was not one to holler or make a scene. She just said she had trouble understanding that, and Jerome said he knew she would.

Jerome had jotted his home number on the well-scribbled desk blotter so he could say it clearly to the operator. A little while after he left, the station agent broke company policy again by calling it. The station agent had a plan.

"Jerome, come on," George called.

Jerome tore himself away, circling back into the dugout, where his team was standing, waiting for him to lead them.

Hank Benkleman took three mighty steps from home plate towards the pitcher's mound, pointed his mask to the noon-day sun, and shouted, "Play ball!"

The Hornets took the field. Chick Beadle was in good arm, but Jack noticed he wasn't warming up as seriously as he would for Plattsmouth or Peru. "C'mon, big guy, bear down, bear down," he called.

Sam ventured uncertainly onto the field.

"He's got the kid leading off?" Moose scratched his head.

"Fastest guy on the team," breathed Charly, gripping the top of the dugout with his knuckles.

A murmur swept through the stands. Fingers pointed. Nick Reilly frowned. "That's not the one went up the elevator?"

"That's him, Uncle Nick," came a voice from two rows back.

Carlin had been tempted to join the row of nuns on the visitors' side, but her mother's warning look made her think better of it. She was sitting with her mother and Tim.

"Why, he's just a boy," said Nick.

"I know! You'd think he was Al Capone." Carlin, seeing the stares, put on a fake smile and gave Miss-Apple-Blossom waves to the crowd. Millie discreetly pulled down her daughter's arm, fixing her with a stern look.

Sam saw Carlin's wave, and thought, with horror, it was for him. He had begged not to bat first. But Jerome said the sooner they got it over with, the better. The catcher, Jack, grinned up at him from his crouch. He smiled back, trying to ignore the staring and pointing. He took a couple of practice swings. The umpire settled in.

"You-can't-hit-you-can't-hit-you-can't-hit."

"Can it?" Sam turned to Jack.

"Strike one!"

Jack grinned again, mouthing the word "Rookie." Sam grinned back. The pitcher went into his wind-up.

"Easyout-easyout-easyout."

"Easy how?" Sam turned again.

"Strike two!" shouted Hank.

"Time!" Jack stood up, took a step in front of the plate, and lobbed the ball to Chick. While fiddling with the laces of his mitt, he said under his breath, "I'm distracting you." A glance up met two big chocolate eyes. Hank bent to dust the plate, hiding a smile. Jack whispered, "You're supposed to ignore me."

"Oh, yeah, okay, okay," said Sam whispered back.

Jack pulled on his mask and squatted. Sam cocked the bat, stared fiercely at the pitcher, and waited for Jack to chatter so he could ignore him. The ball whipped by. A cheer went up as Hank jerked a thumb hollering, "Strike three!"

Charly T turned to Moose. "Stage fright."

"Maybe a little," said the foreman.

Returning to the dugout, Sam got a look of disgust from Ice, who snatched the good bat from his hands. Ice stalked to the plate, and digging in, said, "Don't be throwing that cracker talk at me."

Pause. "How'd those duct-tape balls work out?"

Ice ripped the first pitch foul over the home stands.

Hank handed Jack a new ball. Jack gave it a toss in the air before throwing it to Chick. "Hard to figure how a man could miss something that big."

Ice was early on the next pitch, and nearly killed Little Larry in the dugout. A gasp went up as the ball thunked the wood and caromed back onto the field.

Jack set up for a pitch way outside, but Ice didn't bite. He stepped out and took a practice swing. "You better keep it away, fat boy."

"Next one's right down Broadway, scarface."

Chick got the sign to bring the heat, and nodded shortly, with a small malicious smile. Chick was no palooka. He'd pitched for the great Julian High teams in the Ernie Scarborough era, and he had expected a scholarship from the university. The offer never came, and he spent two years as a Peru State Bobcat before shipping out with the Signal Corps. He never got over the slight, and that's what gave him the extra bit of mean it takes to be a great pitcher. He whipped it underhand harder than he'd ever thrown over the top, and moving from sixty-feet six-inches to forty-five feet was almost like handing him a license to kill. He opened the throttle and gave the sneering dark fellow his come-get-it fastball.

Ice almost got it. Nobody insulted his face without ret-ri-bu-tion. He focused his rage on the pitch, but got under it, and threw the bat in disgust to trot out the fly ball.

"Can of corn," said Nick Reilly.

It looked routine off the bat, but somehow the ball dropped two steps in front of Ernie Scarborough in center field. And there stood Ice, clapping fiercely on first.

The crowd groaned and went silent. That was no dying quail. That was a ball Ernie should've had. The brittle way he threw to Evan Carpenter, in at second where Frank usually played, had everyone shaking their heads. In the dugout, Dave looked to the far end at Ron Littman, the unwilling last-minute fill-in.

George, batting third, did a curious thing.

"He's not left-handed," said Moose.

Charly T giggled and clapped his hands. "I get it, I get it."

"Blind-bat, blind-bat," chirped Jack. "Can't-hit, can't-hit."

George ignored him, choked up on the bat, and studied the lanky gun-slinger. He didn't move as the first pitch sailed by for a strike.

"Schoolteacher, schoolteacher. Can't see that thing."

George watched another pitch.

"Ball!"

"No favors for four-eyes, Hank."

"Low and you know it," grumbled the umpire.

Another pitch missed inside. The bat had not left his shoulder. The kid was playing for a walk. Jack signaled Chick to bring it down the middle.

George turned on it, and with a compact swing neatly jerked the ball into the hay field beyond right. George followed Ice around the bases, looking non-chalant compared to his showboating teammate.

"How you like that, fat boy?" Ice said, stomping on home plate.

Jack pretended not to hear. The faint smile of the bespectacled kid annoyed him more. The nuns and Black folks cheered; the rest of the crowd gave a grudging clap.

"Didn't know George was a switch-hitter," said Moose.

"Hey, boss?" asked Charly. "You ever met a spiker who couldn't hit from inside or outside the rail? You got a whole crew of switch-hitters."

And so they were. Big Larry, normally a free-swinging righty, went to the other side and choked up. Jack barely had time to call him "Tree Stump" and "Man Mountain" before Larry yanked it out to right, the same way George had.

As Jerome strode to the plate, Jack knew he had a problem on his hands. This was their clean-up man, and his pitcher had smoke coming out his ears. All Chick would see was the salt and pepper hair. "Time out." Jack stood up. He gave Jerome a chin nod, said, "Scuse me second," and went out to the mound.

Malcolm clapped his hands. "Jerome's up!" He bent over to JJ in Lucy's lap, pointing. "Daddy's up to bat!"

"Daddy's up to bat!" the boy repeated, clapping.

Lucy rocked her son on her knee, her head in a swirl. It had all happened so fast. There she was, standing in the kitchen, phone in hand, with her stomach sinking right through the floor. Jerome had just told her he wasn't coming home for the holiday because he had to play a game with the boys. *The boys?* He'd always just wanted to get away from those bandy gangsters, or whatever they were called. And now he could not let them down—over a game? What about his family? What about his boy? She didn't say of that, of course, especially since the station agent was letting Jerome use the phone. But it was worse than being angry with him. For the first time, she doubted him. For the first time she gave weight to Malcolm's winks and smiles about the wild life. The twenty minutes after she put the phone down had been the worst of her life. She'd wandered around the house bumping into things—ironing board, nightstand, grandpa's rocker—feeling like she'd never seen them before, like they belonged to someone else.

When the phone rang again she ran to it. But it wasn't Jerome. It was the station agent, the one who'd brought Jerome home that time. He talked fast, and she had trouble understanding. Something about her taking the train to Nebraska City. Something about him coming to pick her up. An instinctual wariness took over, like when a stranger showed up at the door, so excited to dump dirt on her rug so he could clean it with that Kirby vacuum. She told Mr. Henry that it sounded nice, what he said, but could he please call Mr. Malcolm Freeman, also with the railroad, and explain the plan to him.

And here she was, with JJ on her knee, Malcolm and Vera beside her, and Mr. Henry a row behind. The sun was high in a beautiful blue sky, the grass as green as grass could be, and her husband up to bat.

"They best look out for Jerome," Malcolm said over his shoulder. "Back in the day, he played with Ace Hill."

"Chick will settle down," said Denton Henry.

Lucy wasn't listening. She was staring at the boy kneeling up at the end of the dug-out, they young one who'd struck out. She didn't have to ask. She knew that was Sam, the one who had inspired her husband to give away the book he cherished above all others. Seeing Sam's face, she somehow understood, and she found forgiveness in her heart.

On the other side of the field, Charly T was frowning. "No! No! Why isn't he batting lefty? He's seen how to do it."

"He's no double-side spiker like them others." Moose paused long enough to watch Jerome open up and take the first pitch the other way, sending it about a mile over the right field fence. "But it looks like he can handle a bat some."

As the ball sailed over his head, Kenny Mills threw his glove straight up trying to intercept it—a gesture of futility that brought uneasy laughter from the crowd. It was the coloreds who were supposed to do the clowning, and the Hornets to hit dingers.

Jack trotted to the mound a second time. He stood beside Chick, one hand on his hip, watching Jerome round the bases. Beadle, red-faced and furious, cursed to himself while hurling the ball into his glove.

"Good thinking, Chick. You smoked out their ringer."

"Lucky shot," fumed Chick.

"Maybe." Jack scratched his nose. "Say, Chick, you know there's catfish in Rock Creek?"

Chick stared at him. "I reckon so."

"You ever had any?"

"I dunno. Spect so."

"Those railroad fellows love catfish. They been going out on the crick with their poles, pulling out some fine ones for their cook to fry up."

"What in the hell are you talking about, Scarborough?"

"I'm talking about *fishing*, Chick," Jack said tersely. "Like maybe you don't have to challenge every damn batter."

Chick's mouth was tight, but he nodded curtly.

This plan worked better. Chick threw outside, neck-high, in the dirt. Delran was so eager to get in on the home run parade that he flailed at all three, and looked bad doing it. But Little Larry waited out a walk, and it took a nice grab deep in the hole by Randle Bazin to end the half-inning with a flip to the minister at second.

42

THAT ALL YOU GOT?

WELCOME TO JULIAN!	1	2	3	4	5	6	7	8	9
VISITORS	4								
HORNETS									

As Jack strode up to the plate, he didn't like what he saw in his own dugout. The Hornets looked stunned. He had suspected that Dave made him the lead-off hitter as a joke for the home folks. But he had been the best hitter against Weeping Water, and this was a serious game now. It was up to him to turn it around. He took practice swings, and glared out at a pitcher with the longest arms he'd ever seen. That fellow could drop the ball into the catcher's glove just by leaning forward.

Delran was still mad about striking out. He barely glanced at the sign. He rushed his wind-up and cannoned the ball with everything he had. Jack tried to jump back, but he never had a chance. The pitch caught him square in the ribs with an explosion of pain that put him on his back, and filled him, for one long instant, with a murderous rage. The spectators sprang to their feet as if on strings, and players from both sides vaulted onto the field.

For several seconds the world hung in balance. Then Jack popped up, shouted, "That all you got?" and trotted down to first base. The volley of cheers salved his burning ribs, and sent both teams back to the dugouts.

Jerome went to the pitcher's mound. "Delran," he said in a low voice. "Delran. Look at me." The kid had only learned underhand a few weeks before, and never been in a real game. His eyes were wild. Jerome put the ball in Delran's glove and held it there. "Delran, concentrate. Concentrate." When the boy's eyes finally met his, he said, "Do not hit another batter. Are you hearing me? Delran?"

"Yeah."

"I don't care if you serve up lollipops and ice cream. The score doesn't matter. What matters is that you do not hit another batter. You understand?"

"Yeah."

"You sure?"

"Yeah."

While this was happening, another conference was going on in the Hornet dugout. Ernie Scarborough sat on the bench, forearms on knees. Dave sat down beside him and said quietly, "We're going to need you, Ernie."

"They say we're going to use the A-bomb in Korea."

Dave paused, watching Jerome calm down his pitcher. "Korea's a terrible thing, God help 'em," said Dave. "But if it has any meaning at all, if we're fighting for anything, it's right out here on this field."

"Ronnie can go in."

"Not if I can help it," said Ron from the end of the bench.

On the field, Jerome took his crouch for Delran's second pitch. Little Randle Bazin approached the plate warily. "I got a wife and kids to think of," he said out of the corner of his mouth.

"Just a friendly game," Jerome answered, punching his mitt. A chastened Delran focused on that mitt, as Jerome told him to. Bazin watched it float by for strike one. He thought it must be a trick, and laid off a second pitch. Another marshmallow. Strike two. When it came just like that again, the singles hitter took a home run swing. The ball sailed high off the bat. Bones made it an adventure in center field, but held on to the ball.

Dave took his time walking to the plate. Jack was dancing off first, chirping, trying to distract the pitcher. Dave settled in, and said, without looking back, "Mr. Wallace."

"Mr. Postmaster."

Delran served another cupcake, and Dave stroked a single with an ease that reassured the home fans. Scarboroughs on first and second, with the big stick coming to the plate. They laughed at themselves for fretting over four measly runs. But wait—Ernie'd let the ball drop. Which Ernie was scuffing his cleats in the batter's box?

Moose Burdock was surprised to find his loyalties conflicted. Like everyone else, he figured the Julian team would come out here, show what they could do, and that would be that. He was proud when George got his homer over the short fence, but when Larry and Jerome came gunning for right, it seemed almost unfair, like the tricks those barnstormer teams pulled off. Moose shouted, "Let's go, boys," not sure who it was meant for.

At the plate, Ernie was thinking about the Russians. They had the A-bomb too. How they stole it didn't matter a whole lot now. They had it. Any sane person would think that had to be the end of war.

"Bear down, Ernie, bear down!"

Sorry, can't bear down. Need to go home. Shouldn't have stayed this long.

"Strike one!"

Yeah I hear ya, Four Eyes. That was a sucker pitch. Black fellow's making fun of me, knows I can't hit. But who's that girl up in the back corner of the stands?

"Steee-rike!"

No need to jump up like that, Hank. Ain't it humiliating enough, can't we just let this go quietly?

"Foul ball!"

I do that? It found my bat. Ought to try to put it in play. Owe 'em that much anyway.

"Foul ball!"

Yeow, right over the dugout. Hope nobody hurt. Can't get around on it. Back in high school, this very field, bat so light. Beadle back then trying to grow a mustache, looking like twelve years old. Ken Mills on that team too. Dated his sister once in high school. But who's that woman up in the stands. Know her from somewhere.

Ernie's bat blooped the next one down the third base line, just over Sam's mis-timed leap. Ernie thought it was foul, and didn't run. Sillman Jones, in left field, thought it was foul, and didn't run either. Everyone else saw it land six inches inside the line and bounce into foul territory. By the time Sillman sprinted over, grabbed the ball and air-mailed it six feet over Jerome's head, the first two Scarboroughs had scored and the Ernie was standing on second.

The collective sigh could be heard all the way to Kansas. The gandies were just gandies after all, and Ernie was Ernie. The Hornets had cut the lead in half. Things were going to work out. But that colored pitcher was getting his velocity back. PD Klyber struck out, and Ken Mills hit a bullet straight at Ice.

43

NICE CHATTING WITH YOU

WELCOME TO JULIAN!	1	2	3	4	5	6	7	8	9
VISITORS	4								
HORNETS	2								

Chick's arm had tightened up from sitting. His warm-up pitches were all over the place. Jack delayed as long as he could, but when Hank made them start, Chick walked the nine-hole hitter on four pitches. Sam came up again. He'd gotten some instruction on the bench, because this time he never looked back, and the best Jack could get was a little grin by making up nonsense rhymes. "You're no dandy, handy gandy, you're too small to hit that ball." Still, the kid managed to beat out PD's throw on a grounder to third. Then scarface came up again. He too had been schooled to ignore Jack, and hit the first pitch hard up the middle. Frank Abernathy, sinner that he was, might have turned a double play on that ball, but the good minister booted it. For the second time in as many at bats, Ice survived on an error.

Jack went out to the mound again, and was joined by the rest of the infield.

The minister apologized, but Jack saw the hitch in his step. "Evan, are you limping?"

"Turned my ankle. Just have to walk it off."

Everyone watched him try. The limp got worse, not better. Jack took a step toward the dugout and yelled, "Grab your glove, Ronnie."

Ron Littman was regretting that he let Dave talk him into this foolishness. He'd hardly played at all in the last ten years, just a pick-up game here and there. Dave said he wouldn't have to play. Evan could take Frank's place. He was just there as an emergency fielder, and was not happy the emergency came in the second inning. Ron marched grimly onto the field.

George was a numbers guy before there were numbers guys. He was proud of the gandies' .625 batting average so far, which he had calculated in his head. Giving Ice a hit was generous; probably should be two errors, but never mind. As he strolled up to the plate his satisfied gaze took in Bones at third, Sam on second, Ice on first. Who did these cowboys think they were messing with, anyway? The gandies had gotten in their heads, and now that farmer faced the meat of the order up with the bases juiced, no outs, and one of their starters hobbled in the dugout.

That farmer did seem to have turned it up a notch, though. He was throwing fire. George studied Chick's style, looking for tells. Methodically, he worked the count full. The next pitch would be a heater that he could turn on. No doubt. It looked like the heater off the hand, but the ball dove out of the strike zone, and he couldn't hold up. On his way to the dugout George added "nasty sinker" to his mental list of the pitcher's arsenal.

Big Larry had no such complexity of thought. Back in Arkansas they liked to say, "Dance with the one that brung you." In this case, it was a left-handed dance and his partner was that right field fence. The pitcher tried to stay away from him, but the pitcher made a mistake. He got a hold of one that cracked his bat and still had enough to clear the short porch.

A sick silence descended on the home bleachers. Nick Reilly muttered that Chick hadn't given up a slam all season. Moose's glance swept across the crowd. Most everyone in the home stands was kin to someone on the field. The faces showed confusion and disbelief. It was as if the bedrock beneath the town had cracked, and a chasm opened. That they could lose, and lose badly, to a pick-up team from a railroad gang—it wasn't in the constellation of possibilities. Moose felt sorry for them.

Charly T had no such sympathy. "Now they got Jerome to deal with," he said gleefully.

The first pitch came in high and tight. Chin music, message pitch. Jerome fought it off and dinked an impossible single into short right—a hit that sent a message right back.

"How the heck'd you get that one?" Dave said, as Jerome joined him at first.

"Just trying to get out of the way." Jerome watched Delran stalk to the plate, looking like he meant business. The boy had taken a teasing the way he struck out before. Between pitches, Jerome and Dave had a nice chat.

"So which one's your wife over there?" Dave asked.

"One on the right, with Jerome Junior on her lap. We call him JJ around home."

"Fine looking boy."

"Getting him his first mitt this summer."

A genial conversation and a six run lead can make a man careless. While Jerome was thinking what to say next, Delran hit a hump-back up the line. Dave retreated a step, and used all of his reach to snag it, and casually stepped on the bag. Double play, unassisted, side retired.

"Nice chatting with you, Mr. Wallace."

"Yeah," said Jerome, heading off the field.

44

FOUR EYES AS GOOD AS HIS WORD

WELCOME TO JULIAN!	1	2	3	4	5	6	7	8	9
VISITORS	4	4							
HORNETS	2								

In the dugout, Jack was a whirlwind of encouragement. "Only the bottom of the second," he shouted, tossing his shin guards in the corner. "We'll get it back!" He clapped Chick on the back. "One at a time," he hollered.

Ron Littman was first up, with Chick on deck. The other guys told him to be patient, but that was not one of Ron's virtues. He swung at the first pitch, and connected. Jack, on the dugout step, might have thought, "Seeing-eye single." Moose Burdock might have turned to Charly and said, "Bleeder." But to Millie and Carlin and the rest of the fans roaring to their feet, it was a hit. A clean bright single for the man once known as Speedo.

And then Speedo stole second. On a two-two pitch, he just took off. Chick Beadle, shocked to see it happening, let strike three go by, and Jerome came up throwing to the bag. Ron, the ball, the second baseman, and the shortstop all arrived at the same instant. The collision left Ice and George sprawled on the base paths, the ball trickling into center, and Ron sitting on second. Ooohs and Ahhhs all around.

Roy Hurst, batting ninth because he'd been having back pains, popped meekly to the pitcher, although Delran made a juggling act out of catching it. Now it was Jack's turn again, his first AB since getting plunked. Bat cocked, man on second, Jack felt electricity coursing through him, and he cranked a mile high foul that Sam ran out of room chasing, luckily. It plunked loud off the dugout in front of the nuns. He scolded himself to be patient. Get the count in your favor, and look for something middle in. He did just that, swung hard, and found the gap between center and left. Jack slid into second, beating Bones' throw, and bringing Ronnie home.

Randle Bazin dribbled one to shortstop. Should have been an easy play to end the inning, but Ice wasted time chasing Jack back to second, and his hurried throw pulled Big Larry off the bag. Bazin was a fast little guy.

Dave came up. Jerome had some idea of teasing him, trying to return the distraction. But with two on and two out, his instincts took over. He'd seen Dave and Ernie bat, and he knew which one he'd take his chances with, regardless of past reputations. He went to the mound, and threatened Delran's life if he threw anything anywhere near the plate. The postmaster walked on five pitches. Dave gave the bat a frustrated flip, and shot Jerome a hard look. The home fans went wild to see Ernie coming up with the bases loaded, but Jerome knew that Dave knew what they both saw in Ernie's first at bat, the lucky double notwithstanding. The pick-on-someone-your-own size glare of the big brother almost made Jerome squirm.

Almost. As he worked the corners with Delran, Jerome mentally debated his friend the postmaster. It's not about you or your brother. It's about respect for the game. While he was thinking such thoughts, the count went full and Delran was in danger of walking in a run. Jack was giving him heckle hell from third base, distracting him. Jerome shrugged and dialed up the heater down the middle. It sailed in at the knees, maybe a touch below, and Jerome readied himself for a needling as Jack trotted home on the walk.

"Strike THREE!" Hank hollered.

Ernie made no protest, but the crowd went rabid. Boos rained down on Hank Benkleman, along with jeers, of which "Four Eyes" was the mildest.

A happily surprised Jerome sprinted to his dugout without a backward glance, and told his hooting and hollering team to button their lips.

45

THE PITCHERS SETTLE IN

WELCOME TO JULIAN!	1	2	3	4	5	6	7	8	9
VISITORS	4	4							
HORNETS	2	2							

Jack was so furious he could spit. He yanked on his shin guards, grabbed his mask, and went out to give Hank several pieces of his mind. The crowd was on him too, releasing new salvos of outrage every time he called a ball. The whole team was off kilter, and it affected the pitcher. Chick Beadle was wild, sandwiching a strike-out around two walks to the bottom of the order. After the second walk, Jack called time out and went to the mound. The infielders joined him there, all except Ron, who waited it out at second base. They told each other to stop worrying about the calls and start playing ball.

Meanwhile, Jerome was asking Sam if he'd ever bunted before, or even knew what one was. It's not something that ever came up back on the hayfield. He decided against the bunt, chiding himself for getting too managerial. He told the kid to swing away. Instead, Sam gave a one-handed slap more like someone with a fly swatter than a bat. It somehow nicked the ball, which dribbled slowly back to the mound. Chick had no play but to first. Sacrifice completed.

Ice came up and clocked a single—his third time on base, but first time not by error—and brought the two runs home. Then Ice made an error of his own, taking too big of a lead, and failing to anticipate a snap throw from Scarborough to Scarborough. Dave started the run-down by flipping the ball to Ron, who was in too much of a hurry to get rid of it, and threw it back to Dave too soon. It took a great play by Randle Bazin, taking the return throw and blocking second, to complete the rundown. 2-3-4-3-6 for those keeping score.

The Hornets got a run back in the bottom of the frame, but it wasn't pretty. The Gandies made a couple quick outs. Ken Mills hit a double off the wall, and went to third when Sillman Jones overthrew second. With Chick Beadle at the plate, Delran had one get away from him. It hit the dirt in front of home plate and skittered past the catcher's glove. Jerome scrambled after it, and would have had a play if Delran had thought to cover the plate. Ken scored, but Chick went on to strike out.

A sense of doom was settling onto the home stands. They were down 10-5 in the fourth. But worse than that, it was looking like one of those rare off-days for the Hornets. Maybe Roy Hurst's back was tenderer than he let on. Maybe Ernie was in shell shock again. Maybe Randle Bazin was thinking about getting the wheat in. Worst of all, Chick didn't have his best stuff. Happens to every pitcher from time to time. Nick Reilly said to no one in particular that maybe it was time to let PD take over and put Chick at third.

The postmortems were premature. Charles Montgomery "Chick" Beadle did not get to be a four-time Country League All Star by being stupid, or by folding under pressure. In the top of the fourth, he went to the mound straight from the batter's box after striking out, and had an extra scoop of dander for that. More importantly, he'd been through the gandy line-up twice. He knew who would chase upstairs, and who to pitch on the corners. Facing the heart of the order, he put down George, Big Larry and Jerome in order, pop-fly, ground out, strike-out, getting Jerome to lunge for the same nasty sinker that had fooled George in the second.

The home crowd buzzed, primed for a rally. But Delran, too, was hitting his stride. Roy Hurst popped out to center. Jack hit it hard, but right at George. Randle hit a two hopper to deep third that looked like a single, but Sam gobbled it up and threw a frozen rope to beat the speedy shortstop by a step.

46

AN ACCIDENTALLY EPIC AT-BAT

WELCOME TO JULIAN!	1	2	3	4	5	6	7	8	9
VISITORS	4	4	2	0					
HORNETS	2	2	1	0					

In the fifth Chick went out and did it again. He wanted very badly to strike out Delran, and gave up a double instead. That put kerosene on his fire, and he went on to strike out the side almost exclusively with fast balls. Jack's glove hand was hurting by the time he sat down on the bench.

Dave came out to start the home half. "Going to pitch to me this time?"

Jerome figured it best to say nothing. He didn't want to give the lanky first baseman anything to hit, but he didn't want it to look so obvious. He signaled for Delran to throw the ball outside. The pitch was at least a foot off the plate, maybe two feet. It didn't matter. Dave stepped across and golfed it over Big Larry's head for a double down the line.

Jerome gave a mental tip of the hat to that one, and settled in for Ernie.

The Delran-Ernie duel of the fifth inning, Julian Field, Fourth of July, 1950, did not start out as one of the epic at-bats of the century. The catcher was being careful; the batter was distracted by too many thoughts. Ernie was thinking about the conversation he'd just had with Dave in the dugout. Dave had said, "Remember that time I swam the river?"

Ernie remembered all right. It was his first taste of terror, a feeling that had become too much a part of his life.

"You were so mad at me," Dave went on. "You were only ten or twelve, and you cussed me right in front of everyone in Watson, Missouri." Dave chuckled, shaking his head. "You really let me have it."

That was strange. Ernie did not remember that part of the story, not even a little bit. After the next pitch, Ernie had to concentrate on Hank to get the count. One and two. He hadn't swung yet. Or didn't think he'd had.

Dave had gotten to his point with sudden intensity. "And I promised you on that day I'd never do that again, and I'd always look after you. Well, I couldn't always keep to that promise. But I've tried my best, and you know that's true." He had sat forward then, his face close to Ernie's. "I organized this game, and what started out a joke is turning into a catastrophe. If we don't pull it together we're liable to get mercy-ruled right off our own field. We'll never live that down. We need you, Ernie."

Ernie wished he could help. He really did. He just didn't have it in him. Not now, not with boots on the ground in Korea. The count had gone full, and he expected to strike out on the next pitch, but he fouled it off. Then he reached out and spoiled the next one. Then he sliced one into the stands, breaking the bat.

Ernie settled in with a new bat, and fouled off two more pitches.

In the stands Moose sputtered, "What in the Sam Hill is going on?" It wasn't just that Ernie was fouling off every pitch, it was the way he looked doing it, with a casual, half-hearted swing. The tension in the stands was rising with each foul ball. Ernie had come to the plate looking so pitiful that people were turning their heads away. Now it seemed as if the tables had turned, as if Ernie was toying with the colored boy, spoiling pitches in a manner so offhand it seemed like mockery.

In the actual case, Ernie was just distracted. He had finally identified the mystery woman in the stands as Maureen Fallon, assistant to Max Moore. Dave had told him she'd called to apologize after the terrible telegram cancelling the exhibition with LTF. Ernie remembered her compassion, right on this field, they day they came down from Lincoln. He remembered she was pretty, a tall drink of water in a tight skirt. He looked up at her between pitches, and she gave him a little wave. Whoa. That pitch was inside. Just got a piece of it. Bring your best stuff, Satchel Paige.

The next one was further inside, neck high. A gasp went up. A crack. The pitch sawed the bat out of Ernie's hands, a clean break right at the handle. The ball trickled up the first base line. Ernie took off, with Jerome right behind him chasing down the ball. It was going to be a close play. Ernie running like a man afire, Jerome hurling his mask aside, and . . .

"Foul ball!"

Well. Hank got that one right. The ball definitely rolled clear of the line before Jerome scooped it up. Moose saw it. Carlin saw it. The nuns saw it. Foul ball.

The buzz in the crowd was electric. Ernie went to the dugout for a new bat.

"Sorry, mistake," Jerome said, apologizing for the pitch. He waited for Ernie's nod, then went out to the mound.

"That one got away," Delran said. He was agitated, eager.

"We're going to put him on."

"What you say?"

"I said we're going to walk him."

"What you say?"

"What *you* say, you backwoods hick? If you hit him, they'll be coming after us with pitch forks."

"I can take him out."

"You know what that is?" Jerome whispered hotly, gesturing to the plate. "That's a big-league hitter. He's playing with you. We've got a base open and a lead to protect."

"I can take him," Delran pleaded.

Jerome took a breath. The boy was all of, what, twenty-three years old? Barely knew the game. They had two more innings to get through, and nobody else to put on the mound. He lifted his mask and spat. "Okay. Pitch to him."

Delran looked up, his face eager again.

Jerome shrugged. "Just pitch. If he tags one, don't worry about it. But for God's sake, don't hit him."

The foul parade began again, this time on a whole new level. Delran brought the gas, and Ernie shook off his demons. No one knew exactly how many more pitches Ernie fouled off, some said a dozen, some said more. Delran rose to the challenge. Each pitch was better than the than the last. Jerome was amazed. The kid was learning, on the job, how to pitch. Jerome hadn't seen the like since Ace Hill. And Ernie just kept spoiling them. His concentration was back. He stopped looking up to the corner of the stands, but he was more than aware of her. There was someone special rooting for him. He knew it. Finally, when nobody could take the pressure any longer, Ernie spotted the one he would nail. Saw it out of Delran's hand. The kid who'd made Richie Ashburn the second-best high school player in Nebraska history clubbed a monster home run over the deepest part of the fence. Whether it actually broke the school window on the fly, or broke it on one hop, or didn't break it at all—just the fact that people remember it that way says all you need to know about that hit.

Two runs in and still no outs. PD Klyber came up and hit a long loud out to left. Ken Mills hit a single. Ron Littman hit a single. Chick Beadle, who'd struck out twice, hit a gapper to left. Mills scored easily. Ron came flying down the line next, and it looked like there was going to be a big collision, with Jerome guarding the plate, awaiting the throw. But Sillman Jones once again threw it a mile over his head, so Jerome played matador, stepping aside as Speedo flashed across to score.

One more time, Jerome called time out and went to the mound. This time it was to keep Delran from marching into left field and killing Sillman Jones. "That's the third one!" Delran fumed. Ice came in from short to complain that George was playing out of position, letting those singles through. George told Ice to cram it. Sam and Big Larry wandered in to see what the fuss was about.

Jerome told them all to shut their yaps. "Delran," he said sternly. "Do not look over there, but that pitcher standing on third base, he's smiling right now."

Delran looked anyway, glaring at Chick. Chick smiled back.

"Delran! All of you. Listen up. This is where we show what we're made of. Are we going to fold, or are we going to win this thing? Here's an idea."

Hank Benkleman was coming out to break up the conference, so Jerome had to rush his instructions in a whisper. He hoped to heck Sam was listening.

Jerome took his crouch once again. His legs were aching, but he had to ignore that and find some spring. After two pitches to Roy Hurst were called high and outside, Delran slammed down his glove, and stalked around the mound in a fit of temper. Meanwhile, Sam snuck in behind Chick's lead off third. The diversion worked. Jerome snapped the throw to the bag, and Chick was out before he knew what happened. Delran tried to suppress his grin as Chick muttered curses on the long lonely walk to the dugout. A rejuvenated Delran struck out a very frustrated Jack on three pitches.

47

MOOSE ON A MISSION

WELCOME TO JULIAN!	1	2	3	4	5	6	7	8	9
VISITORS	4	4	2	0	0				
HORNETS	2	2	1	0	4				

In the stands, Charly T was chortling over the trick play. "It worked!" he kept saying. "It worked!"

"Yeah," said Moose, "but I wouldn't want to face Beadle right now. Who's up?"

"I think it's Sam."

"Oh no," said Moose. "Sam put the tag on him."

"He surely did," said Charly T.

Perhaps Hank Four Eyes had a similar worry for Sam's safety. In any case, the umpire stood up and waved his arms, calling time out. He walked out on the field, motioning Sam back to the dugout. "A seven-inning game," Hank announced, "gets a Fifth Inning Stretch. We'll have a ten-minute break here."

Nick Reilly stood up, stretched, and blew the air out of his lungs. He felt like he'd been holding his breath for an hour. "I swear this beats last year's finals over Plattsmouth, and that was a lulu."

"Better even than the 2-1 Talmage game in '48," said Ken Mills' dad.

Old Jacques Bazin pronounced it better than the Auburn game in '28, the one where Ron Littman, aka Speedo, had an unassisted triple play.

Ernie came out of the dugout to look up to the corner of the stands, but it was empty.

"Hello, Mr. Scarborough."

She was right there in front of him. "Call me Ernie," he said shyly.

Across the way, Denton Henry said to Malcolm, "Lincoln Thomas Ford be damned! This is the best damn game I've ever seen!" Catching himself, he added, "Excuse my French."

"That's not French," said Sister Mary Michael, who now had JJ on her lap. "Oh, look who's here!"

"Mary Michael, you're with child!" Carlin said, sending a ripple of giggles down the line of nuns.

"So I am," said Mary Michael. "Aren't I, JJ?"

The boy looked up, smiling. He'd overcome his initial fear of nuns, and was having a great time.

"Carlin," said the sister, "this is Lucy Wallace. Her husband is the catcher. And these are the Freemans. You know Mr. Henry, I think."

Greetings were made all around, and Carlin sat down to chat.

Moose Burdock stood and shook his left leg, which had the tingles. He felt like he hadn't moved a muscle. Put through a wringer, that's how it felt. What a game. He had come there thinking he didn't care a red bean who won it, and found himself, along with everyone else, hanging on every pitch. 10-9. The gandies clung to the lead, but the Hornets had come charging back. After that trick play, it was impossible to know who had momentum.

Hank stepped out with another announcement. "I'm asked to tell you that after the game there will be a picnic lunch at the school yard. Everybody is invited, and we hope you'll come."

Shading his eyes, Moose Burdock could see figures way out past center field. Five or six people, scurrying around, carrying things. Millie Littman was no longer sitting behind him. And even from this far, he could tell that another one was Cook.

"A picnic for everybody." Charly T gave him a mischievous grin. "That's where you pay off your bet."

"Oh, no," said Moose. "I said I'd do it with white people and Black people around. I didn't say a whole picnic of 'em."

"You're not welching on me, are you, boss?"

"No, it's just . . ."

"Moose! Hey Moose!" came an urgent whisper. Dave Scarborough, leaning around the corner of the dugout, was motioning him to come over. When he got there, Dave said, "I need you to do me a favor. We're about out of bats. They broke both of theirs. We broke a couple, then Ernie used up two more. Never seen anything like it. We're down to our last bat."

"I don't have any," Moose said, confused.

Dave held out a ring of keys. "What I need is for you to run down to the store, go inside, and get those bats in the trophy window."

"Why me?"

"Because you're here," Dave said impatiently. "I don't have time to hunt down anybody else."

"But I'll miss the end of the game."

"If we break another bat, it'll be the end, and a sorry one at that. It's the square one, says Yale on it."

Moose took off. He wanted to take his truck, but it was way over by the school, and chances were some fool had parked him in. Two and half blocks to Marchon's. He half-walked half-ran down a deserted Main Street. He was breathing hard when he got there; his fingers were shaking. The bats were right there in the window, pretty as you please. He just had to get the right key.

As he fumbled with the lock, Moose Burdock heard a sound, perhaps the only sound on earth that could have detoured him from his mission. It was a planging sound of metal on metal, irregular, harsh. It was not a sound that anybody else would have paid any mind to. But Moose Burdock was not anybody else. He had been on the railroad thirty-five years. Some folks knew bird calls. Some knew sonnets. The planging noise, innocent to everyone else, rang out to Moose as the unmistakable sound of sabotage.

And it was coming from Littman Grain. Wishing he had brought his truck, Moose hauled his considerable stomach at a run, and was bent over panting, holding his chest, by the time he got to the door of the elevator. Sure enough, Frank Abernathy was banging with a crowbar on the main leg, making dents in the metal sheeting. Moose had had a pretty good idea what was up as soon as he saw the black pick-up parked across the road.

Frank was panting too, and paused from his business when Moose came in.

"This ain't no concern of yours, old man," Frank said. "Go away and you won't get hurt."

It had not occurred to Moose Burdock that him getting hurt was in the realm of possibility, and he said as much to the boy. He added, trying to catch his breath, that Frank did not seem to have accomplished very much. "You consider a sledge hammer? Or a spike maul? Spike maul would go right through that tin."

Frank frowned at his crow bar. "Sledge hammer wasn't in the shed where we keep it. This is all that was laying around."

Moose nodded his chin. "That cigar box by your feet there, was that laying around too? I heard Ron keeps cash in a cigar box."

Frank didn't answer. He turned the crowbar around and started using it the way crowbars were meant to be used, prying metal from metal along a seam in the leg.

"I'm going to ask you once to stop that."

Frank laughed. "I'm not stopping, and you're not stopping me. And by the time you tell anybody, I'll be in Kansas. Now get out of here, you old bastard." Frank brandished the crowbar and took a step forward, as one would do to scare off a dog.

Moose was not a dog, and Moose had never been scared off in his life. For the second time in three days, Frank Abernathy had a potentially lethal crowbar taken out of his hands by a much older and unarmed opponent. Moose was more brutal about it, and more methodical. Moose put Frank face-down on the grate where the trucks dump, knelt on his back, and hit him on both sides of the head. Moose picked up the kid by his shirt and threw him against a wall. "Keys."

"You going to theal my thruck?" said Frank, through a rapidly swelling lip.

"Borrowing it. You ain't gonna be needing it today."

FIELD NOTES

Site: A red brick residence on a tree-lined Nebraska City street, three stories with a cupola, once home to a Missouri River steamboat captain. At some point wheelchair ramps were installed, rusting now, and a low, lengthy extension was added to the rear, giving the appearance of a shabby motel. A dim basement room, something between a supply closet and a chapel. Cleaning supplies and mop buckets line two walls. Between the window wells, a card table altar holds two-foot-tall Mary with a chipped face.
Subject: The one I call "Frank Abernathy."

As my eyes adjust, I discern the bulk of a heavy slumped figure on a discarded section of church pew. He clutches a rosary, and barely turns in my direction when I say his name.

I had worried that the expulsion of Frank Abernathy from Julian too conveniently served the exceptionalist proposition. Especially after the only other antagonists, the faintly clownish Buchalter boys, have been sent packing. How nice it would be if the rascals and racists could be separated out and dispatched from every good-hearted community, leaving only sunny days on fields of dreams.

But he is still here. He is always still here. If you had known the cocky red-haired boy with the shiny black truck, you would never recognize him in this husk of a man, wrinkled, bald, and enormous. When I say his name again, he looks up briefly, and returns his gaze to the floor, his fingers working the beads. A while passes, and I try again. "They tell me you spend all your time down here, day after day, hour after hour."

He looks me up and down. When he speaks, his voice is shallow and rusty, an unused instrument. "If you know about me, you know I was not a good man. I hurt a lot of people, especially the ones closest to me." Long pause. "Two wives, one dead, one left town. Two kids who hate me. Cousins, neighbors. I was prideful. I stole, I adultered, I bore false witness. In jail I was a snitch. I brought sorrow to everyone I knew."

"And now? Here?"

"I ain't worthy for a church. I take confession every time the priest comes . . ." he pauses for a deep, rattling cough, "but nothing helps. I can't get past how disgusted I am for who I was."

The room feels heavy with impotent contrition against the bleak disarray of mops, the chip-faced unconsoling Mary. I just want to leave, but I ask if he remembers Julian, the time the gandy dancers came to town.

"Them guys." He looks up briefly, makes a noise that might be a chuckle. "I was wild back then. They wanted liquor and I took 'em to town at five bucks a head. Let 'em find their own way back. Or go to jail."

"And you feel bad about that?"

"Naw, not them. I had a truck. I had a service they wanted."

"They played baseball—or fast-pitch?"

A phlegmy noise. "Not hardly. They wanted to play us, and we told them to go to hell. They couldn't be on the same field with us."

"Because they were Black?"

"That, and they weren't any good. They had a couple hay bales down by the crick. We were Country League champions five years running."

"Mmm."

"One thing I did do. I kept our girls away from them. Girls are foolish, you know. Attracted to Blacks, somehow. And gullible. Lord, they fall for any kind of flowery talk. I kept our girls safe. I credit myself that much." He raises his eyes to the Virgin Mary, who has no comment.

The glimmer of gloating fades, and he is quiet. I ask about the team, but he's lapsed back into his sullen posture of penitence. I have an urge to cross over to him, shake him by the fat neck, tell him what he really is.

The emotion passes, and I just want to be gone from this shrine to misplaced despair. And anyway, it's not about him. Not really. The roots of America's original sin run more than four hundred years deep. Expiation is going to take more than thoughts and prayers.

48

A TABLE OF BROTHERHOOD

Another familiar sound greeted Moose as he got out of Frank's truck by the school yard. It was also the plink of metal-on-metal, but the furthest thing from sabotage: a game of horseshoes. It was coming from behind the line of trees, along with the voices of people laughing, talking, and carrying on.

The game was over. The bleachers were ghost ships flanking an empty green sea. Out beyond left field, the schoolyard picnic tables were heaped high with serving dishes. The sound of laughter filled the air. The foreman caught a whiff of fried chicken.

"Moose, come over here. You got to try this." Charly T was motioning from a large steel pot, a pot that looked suspiciously like the property of Mr. Mopac.

"The pork and beans?" he said.

"Something like that." Charly T scooped some out on a paper plate, took the bats from Moose, and thrust the plate in his hands in one smooth motion.

Moose saw the ring of expectant faces. They included Charly, both Larrys, PD Klyber, Mrs. Littman, and—a few paces away and giving him a wink—Cook. The taste was dark and meaty, heavier than regular. Then he felt the heat. It blossomed across his tongue like live charcoal. Sweat sprang to his forehead. He needed water, fast. The faces erupted in merriment, saying "How is it?" and "You like that?"

Moose swallowed, licked his burning lips, looked around, and said, "It might could use a little more spice."

Over by the school were tin washtubs full of Storz Triumph on ice. Dave Scarborough plucked one, pierced it with a church key, and handed it to Moose.

"You tried the A-bomb beans? Your crew eat that every day? No wonder they hit the willy out of the ball. I'll take those." Dave took the bats from Charly T and leaned them against the side of the school. "Turns out our last bat held up, but thanks for getting them."

Moose started to ask about the game, but got side-tracked by the sight of Dave handing a beer to Charly T. His men could not be drinking with civilians, and Charly knew that plain well. Absolutely against regulations. Then he saw Big Larry and Little Larry had beers. Jerome had a beer, and the other couple with his wife had a beer. Farmers had beers. Nuns had beers.

Millie Littman approached, her face flushed with a smile, and encouraged him to eat. Get some chicken, and there was potato salad and coleslaw. Moose shrugged his shoulders and took a long cold drink from the can. It was mighty good. Why should men or women be deprived of the taste of a cold beer on the Fourth of July? Regulations be damned. He heaped a plate up with food, and went to an open spot at a picnic table where George and Sillman Jones sat across from Ken Mills and Randle Bazin. They were still laughing about the beans.

Moose ate happily. George talked baseball with the hardware man, Klyber, who was a Cubs fan, and could match George stat for stat. Moose wondered who won the game. Looking at the faces, it was impossible to know. He was about to ask when Bones rushed up to George and said he had to come see the horseshoes, quick. The nuns were terrorizing everybody. Two farmers had already lost, and at this moment Ice and Big Larry were getting shellacked.

The boys hurried off, and Moose was left alone at the table with his fried chicken, potato salad and slaw, dinner roll and beer. He'd never had a better feast. He finished, and returned to the serving table for a second helping. On the other side were the grain man and his sullen-looking son. That reminded him. "Say, Ronnie, I ran into Frank Abernathy down at the elevator today."

Ron stared at him. "I ran him out of town."

"That may be, but I found him beating the hell out of your equipment."

"My equipment?"

"The main leg took a few good wallops. He also had a cigar box, one that might've come from your office."

Ron threw down his plate. "Timmy, stay here. I have to . . ."

"Hold up, Ron," Moose said. "It's Fourth of July, and you were in the big game. Have three goldarn beers for once in your life. Your cigar box is in the second drawer. As for Frank, it seems he managed to get himself locked into that empty corn bin south side of your office, the one with the crowbar shoved into the latch. Maybe you'll want the sheriff to let him out."

Timmy's eyes were wide. "Frank locked himself in a corn bin?"

"Mystery to me, son."

A boy Timmy's age was in the arms of the big man, who was walking towards the playground. He'd seen the boy at the game. He followed shyly.

Jerome waited for Timmy to catch up, then pointed down at him, just like he'd done that first time at the store. His boy pointed down too. Timmy pointed back up, and they all laughed.

"I'll bet you know how to swing real high."

"Yeah, I do," Timmy said, hopping on.

"And there's one for this little man." Jerome swooped his son into the companion swing. "I'll be right over there, where mommy is. If you finish with the swing, you come straight over there."

The two boys began to swing, pumping legs and leaning back, going higher and higher.

Jerome went to the picnic table where Lucy, Malcolm and Vera sat across from the two older Scarboroughs and two women. The conversation paused politely as Jerome joined them, giving his wife a squeeze around the shoulders as he sat down.

"I had heard," said Jerome graciously, "that you boys had a big leaguer." He tipped his beer to Ernie. "And now I've seen it. That was some at bat. My guy was throwing fire."

Ernie smiled shyly. "You didn't have a bad day yourself. That first shot of yours went damn near to the state highway."

Jerome said he was happy to meet the missus Scarboroughs. There was an awkward moment as the younger woman blushed and looked away.

"You got it half right," said Dave. "This is my wife, Sandy."

"This here's Maureen," Ernie said. "She works for Lincoln Thomas Ford."

"So they sent someone?"

"No," Maureen said. "I'm AWOL." She pointed to Dave. "Mr. Scarborough called me this morning and said the game was on, so I decided to drive down."

"Sorry for the mistake," said Jerome. "It seemed like you two know each other."

"We kind of do now," said Maureen.

"This is wonderful chicken," said Lucy. "Is JJ all right?"

"He's right there on the swing," Jerome answered.

Denton Henry came by. After general greetings, he zeroed in on Malcolm. "There's the man of the hour, the real union rep." He said it in a grand voice, so everyone nearby turned to listen. "He knew that a crew not able to be home for a national holiday, they're entitled to hardship pay. Next payday, each gandy gets a ten-dollar bonus. Of course, it couldn't happen without the timekeeper signing off on it."

All eyes turned to Ivan Tarp, who tipped his beer in the direction of the gandies.

Moose, two tables over, turned to Charly T. "Ivan Tarp being social? And treated social? This is some special day."

Delran was hovering nearby, looking hopeful. At a break in the conversation, he said nervously to Ernie, "Can I talk to you?"

"Sure can," said Ernie.

"Uh. In private?"

Ernie excused himself and walked down the tree-line with Delran.

"I just need to know. I mean . . ." Delran looked away, collected himself, and turned back to Ernie. "When you fouled off all those pitches and broke those bats . . . uh . . . You didn't even look to be trying. Some of the boys said . . . I just gotta know. Was you poking fun at me?"

"Good lord, no!" Ernie exclaimed. He took a breath and continued. "Truth be told, I was just trying not to embarrass myself. Listen, your arm is as good I've seen, ever."

"Really? You just saying that?" Delran broke into a grin. "Like maybe I could play professional? I got overhand too."

"Easy way to find out. Omaha Cardinals. Single A. Open try-outs every year." Ernie pointed at Jerome. "You want to play ball for real, you ought to be asking the pro on your side."

"That's great!" said Delran. He motioned with the beer. "All this is so nice. All this food, and they got buckets and buckets of beer."

Ernie froze. His sea-legs wobbled beneath him, and an image of bulkheads seized him. The hand on Delran's arm turned to a vice-grip, digging deep.

Delran did not flinch. He didn't know what caused it, but he knew panic when he saw it, and knew instinctively what to do. He stood real still, whispering, "It's okay. It's gonna be fine. You just hold on to Delran."

Delran's arm, hard as steel cable, gave Ernie the stability to ride out the wave.

"It's gonna be fine," said Delran. "Your wife is right over there for you."

Ernie started to correct him, but when he turned, Maureen was just a few yards away, watching. He knew she had seen his bad moment, and was not scared off. He went to her.

At the horseshoe pits, Ice examined the shoe closely, as if looking for a flaw in its construction. Then he demanded a rematch. Sister Stephen Mark and

Sister Paul Peter looked at each other, and up at the sky, considering his worthiness. "You must have had help from up there," Ice said, pointing heavenward. "Because Big Larry and me, we don't lose at this par-tic-u-lar game."

"You just did lose." Paul Peter swigged her beer.

"I was taking it easy on you. Out of con-sid-er-a-tion. But you're in for it now."

"If you could throw as well as you talk," said Stephen Mark, "we might have some competition."

"I like y'all's style," Ice said suavely. "We be next in Nebraska City, ain't that where y'all live? You sisters ever go out to the cin-e-ma?"

The swings had been going non-stop, two boys pumping their legs and sailing upward and back. Finally, they paused for breath. Timmy asked the boy his name. The boy said Jerry, and asked his name. "Timmy," he said. "Let's see who can go higher!" And they started again, going up in the air so blue.

"Sam, hello!" Carlin walked up to him right in the middle of everything, as if daring people to stare or say something. "You remember Sister Mary Michael."

Sam was more bashful, feeling conspicuous and a little frightened. He nodded to the nun with a tight smile.

"Oh, I've been meaning to ask you," Carlin said, normal as asking if he heard the weather report, "what happened to your poetry book? It wasn't in my pocket when I got home. You think it's in the headhouse?"

"No, I got it," Sam said. "It was on the ground."

"Did I bleed on it?"

"It got torn. Jerome helped me fix it."

"The Housman?" asked Mary Michael.

"No," Sam said. "Langston Hughes." He still liked saying it. It was a musical sound. And the poems were taking root inside him, one after another, a great and tremulous feeling.

"Housman." Carlin laughed. "Those poems. We had a heck of a time figuring them out, didn't we, Sam?"

She said it louder than necessary, and there was an edge to her voice, like she wanted other people to hear. But before Sam could figure a way to say something back, Carlin gave a sigh, her mood softened. "You're moving tomorrow? That's what I hear."

"Yes, ma'am."

"You're still calling me that? Well, I guess this time it really is good-bye. I'm just full of rue about that." She grinned, this time he smiled back. "You keep reading that poetry, Sam."

"I will."

"It's going to be awful boring around here." Carlin turned to the nun. "I have half a mind to plant a big sloppy kiss on him, just to rile things up." She held it a beat, and laughed at their frozen faces. "But seriously. Don't ever forget me, Sam Washington, because I won't ever forget you. Deal?"

"Deal."

"Never ever."

"I won't," said Sam. "I promise."

49

SOAP BUBBLES

Jack stumbled as he went down the half stairs to the boys-room in the lower level of the school. He'd had three beers, but it felt like ten to his bladder. Someone else had the same need; he heard the steady splash of urine as he entered. One of the gandies was in the stall, the back of his head visible above door. Jack went to the steel trough, laughed, and said amiably, "I ain't been in here in a while. I forgot how low to the ground this was. Nothing ever changes, I suppose."

"Suppose not," came the reply.

Jack was right, the voice matched up. He had wanted to talk to him, and this was a fine, manly place to do it. His stream made a high-pitched whine peppering the metal, so he spoke loud. "Jerome? Uh, Mr. Wallace?"

"Mr. Scarborough."

"That's Dave. I'm just plain old Jack. I wanted to say it was terrible what happened down at the elevator. Those Buchalters, they always were bad seeds, I'm glad we managed to run them off with nobody getting hurt." He waited, but the only sounds were concussive splashing and wet metallic ringing.

"What I want to say is . . ." But Jack didn't know what he wanted to say. Part of him wanted to confess, to say he should've stopped them when they first grabbed Sam. He wanted Jerome to know his hesitation wasn't racial, it was because he was in love with her. He'd be the same about Ross Tedrow. Too complicated. Start over. "What I want to say is, you should know about Dave." This was clear and true, and something that needed saying. "If not for Dave, none of this would've happened today. The game, the food, everybody happy together."

Jerome had come out of the stall, and was washing his hands at the basin. Jack, who wasn't finished, nodded to him, wanting acknowledgment of Dave's righteousness.

But the face Jerome turned to him was harder, colder, than Jack had ever seen it. And when he spoke, his voice had an edge. "You do know," Jerome demanded, "this is a soap bubble. You know that, don't you?"

Jack grinned weakly. "Beg pardon?"

"It may look pretty now, floating up in the air. Then it's going to pop, and be gone, and leave no trace."

Jack frowned, not following. "I don't think you heard me right. I was trying to say about Dave. If someone says something about Blacks, even joking, he's all over them. Dave says everyone should get a fair shake . . ." He trailed off, an awkward silence hanging in the fetid air.

When Jerome spoke, he was back from the brink, forcing a lighter tone. "We got our equipment all packed up. Every spike maul and lining bar. When the freight engine comes tomorrow, all the gandies go poof and disappear." Jerome held up his hands, and his fingers popped open like bursting bubbles. "This town will settle back to what it was." A pause. "You do understand that except that we're leaving, and never coming back, none of this could have happened? Not the game, not the picnic, nothing?"

"I don't see as how the things are connected," Jack declared, zipping up with some force. "This ain't Kansas. Like the pastor said, Julian is different from other places. Dave is different. Ron and Millie, they're different. I'm different."

"We all like to think that," Jerome said, and was gone.

Jack stared at himself in the mirror, finding his pink cheeks unsatisfactory. And the conversation was unsatisfactory. It wasn't the Jerome that he'd expected. Didn't the man see what was going on out there? Everyone together, with no hard feelings over the best damn game anyone would ever want to see? He lifted his shirt and touched the hot spot on his ribs where Delran's pitch had nailed him, now blooming as a perfectly circular bruise of lurid colors. It seemed symbolic, a badge of honor. He had a notion to march out there and show it to Jerome.

He rinsed his fingers under the tap, and stepped into the stall where Jerome had been for some toilet paper to dry his fingers. There were words and symbols scratched into the paint up and down the stall. The vandalism amused him, a gentle reminder of his school days. Then a single word leapt out at him, gouged savagely in the paint. The gleam of bare metal showed it to be a fresh wound. The N was giant and jagged. Beside the word, in the same savage hand, was a crudely carved noose.

50

UP IN THE AIR SO BLUE

A two-fingered whistle pierced the air. Dave Scarborough had turned a wash-tub upside down and was standing on it, asking for attention. People looked up from the picnic tables. Cook and Millie paused from carrying dishes. The gang at the horse shoe pit drifted over.

"Well," said Dave. "I asked Ronnie to talk, and he said we should get back to the wheat harvest." Laughter. "And the minister asked if he could talk, but I said one sermon was enough. How's that ankle, Evan?"

Evan waved, a good sport with one foot up on a chair.

"So I guess I'm your speech-maker, and I don't know the trade. But before I say anything, I've got a request to have Mr. H.H. Burdock of the Mopac have a word."

Moose got up, reluctantly. "This ain't no speech," said Moose. "But I have to say it on account of a bet." He cleared his throat. "I, H.H. Burdock, affirm that there is no such company as Gandy Manufacturing of Chicago. The term 'gandy dancer' comes from how the crew moves together to the song of the caller, like the mating dance of geese."

"And the lie . . ." Charly prompted.

"And the notion that there's a Gandy company, that lie is put out by rail-road bosses to demean the art of the gandy dance. That enough, Charly?"

Charly gave him a thumbs up.

"Woo yeah, you tell it, boss!" cried Ice.

What Jack noticed was how the gandies cheered, while the townsfolk looked at each other, confused. And when Dave made his jokes, the gandies were silent. Everything was different now. When Dave climbed back on the washtub, and said it was about as perfect as a Fourth of July could be, Jack felt vaguely embarrassed. He didn't like feeling that way, and wanted to blame Jerome. Those people should be grateful. That they were leaving tomorrow had nothing to do with anything. Jack tried to concentrate on his brother, thanking folks.

". . . who put this spread together, and that would be Ron and Millie Littman. Millie spent all morning on this feast, with the special help of Mopac chef Armond Levolver."

"Le-val-YAY!"

"Thanks, Skipper."

Carlin. Jack marveled at her fierceness, standing there next to Sam after everything that happened. Even so, he couldn't entirely suppress a small flair of envy. But he would never scrawl something like that. His gaze went to his teammates, his townsmen. Someone did. It took some time. He imagined lookouts, sniggering at the doorway. Jack wanted to climb on the washtub and shame his neighbors. He wanted to scream, "We're better than that!"

Dave thanked Hank Benkleman for an honest game, for making the tough calls. Jack recalled that if it had been up to Hank, there never would have been a game. He thought back to that awful scene, just two days ago. Bobby Buchalter, the shotgun, Frank's lies. Where his mind settled was on those Cass County farmers, going along with Bobby and Frank, ready to back up some made-up version of what never happened. Were Otoe County folks really any better?

"You eat something bad?"

"Oh, hey, Carlin."

"No, seriously. Are you all right?"

"I'm fine."

"Don't lie to me, Jack Scarborough. We're best friends. What happened?"

Jack told her. The rest room in the school. Jerome's coldness. The carvings in the stall. He winced to hear himself say the word out loud. "And it's like everything's ruined. Evan Carpenter got it directly wrong. What the gandy crew coming here showed us is we're not any better, we're just like everybody else."

"Can't it be some of both?" She looked at him a long moment. Something like pity shown in her eyes. "Did you really think Frank and the Buchalters are the only ones? You should take a walk in my shoes, Jacky boy, get a load of what I've had to deal with. The looks. The insults—straight to my face, playing them off like they're just kidding around."

"But all this . . ." Jack said, sweeping his arm at the crowd.

". . . is a good thing," she broke in. "Maybe Julian's a little better place for them being here. And maybe the crew will say this was one of their best stops. Heck, maybe they'll all quit railroading and be a barnstorming team, The Dandy Gandies."

"I can vouch for their pitching." Jack pulled up his shirt.

"Oh, my lord!" Carlin gasped. Slowly she lowered her hands and reached out a finger to touch the circular bruise. "I forgot about that. He hit you so hard I thought you were dead. And then, the way you jumped right up, smiling, joshing the guy. You saved the day right there!"

"Aw . . ."

"You did! People yelling. Players running on the field. It could have been awful. And you stopped it. I swear it, Jack Scarborough, I had tears in my eyes. Wait here, I'm going to get you some ice for that."

"It's okay," Jack laughed. "Really."

"No, I am," she insisted. "Don't run away."

As Jack watched her hurry off, he declared, "I'm gonna marry that girl."

She disappeared into the crowd, and he felt dumb just standing there, so he wandered a little ways to where Timmy and Jerome's son were swinging their hearts out, side by side, a picture of the American dream.

Timmy's face was flushed with exertion. "Jack! Push us higher!"

Jack did so, giving each boy gigantic shoves, eliciting squeals of terror and delight. He watched them go way up, come back, and go up again, up in the air so blue. He saw how they lifted off their seats at the apex, and he envied that moment of weightlessness, that instant of disconnection from the earth. He would marry that girl. And if she wanted to go to college in Chicago—or New York, or Timbuktu—he'd be right alongside cheering her the whole way. He suddenly saw his life unfold before him. He knew he could do it.

Jack did not know, and it is better that he could not imagine, that in a matter of days he would get his draft notice. Six months later, with Chinese troops flooding North Korea, earthly disconnection would be visited upon him. Not on a swing, but on a frozen road in the Chosin Valley, where he would hover in the air for a brief moment, and be dead from the shrapnel before he hit the ground. He was part of the rearguard action that let tens of thousands of U.S. soldiers break out and fight their way to the coast. He was one of those that saved the day, or such of it that could be saved.

For his part, Tim likewise did not know his future, but his present was no longer right. Sam had not been murdered by a mob; he had outsmarted the bad guy and been vindicated. Carlin's honor, or some racist notion of it, was unbesmirched. But the incident at the elevator had not been without collateral damage. Timmy's sister had called him a liar in front of a ring of onlookers, and his father had not disagreed. In the hustle of the harvest, the thrill of the game, the elation of the picnic, no one noticed his distress.

When the catastrophes arrived, they came, for Tim, as an acceleration of the same downward spiral. Jack's death left a part of Carlin broken. She had drifted further from him, and she had gone off to college a smaller, less bold version of herself. The next winter, his parents went off to church one day, and never came back. From then onward, Tim's life was a dishwater-gray wash of events that carried him along in its currents—to Uncle Nick's lonely farm, to boarding school, to college, and beyond. In that land of lost content, he could no longer evoke his mom's soothing voice, his dad's quick gait, or the grain bins, or the boxcars or the ballgames.

Some day, far in the future, when he resolved to excavate layers of this darkened past, he would begin in Marchon's store, looking up with wonder into the face of the first Black man he had ever seen. He would end here, on the tall swings, careening wildly beside that same man's son. He would try to go back to and rediscover all that came in between, and he would mostly fail. But for now, for one little part of a second at the top of each swing, he existed purely in the moment of flight. He soared above hurt, above regret, over river and trees and cattle and all.

FIELD NOTES

Site: Otoe County, NE. County Road 64A outside of Julian, between Rock Creek
bridge and the railroad crossing. February 3. The fields are brown; the rail is backed
by stands of bare trees. Above the trees rises the damaged tower of the abandoned
grain elevator. On the passenger seat, four cans of Pabst Blue Ribbon lie sideways in
their plastic ring. The can in the driver's hand is down to suds.
Subject: Tim, despondent and slightly inebriated.

It's been almost forty minutes. I thought they came by more often. This is a stupid
idea. As if something's going to happen out here, something to confront the old
trauma.

A knock at the passenger window. A man's face peers in, shading his eyes from
the winter glare. I toss the beers in the back, and roll down the window. He's in his
sixties, maybe seventies, with a coffee-with-cream complexion and lively, penetrating
eyes.

"Just checking if you're okay," he says. "Car trouble?"

"Train-watching."

"Colorado plates." The man pats the car roof. "You're not from around here."

"Not anymore. I'm staying in Nebraska City."

"That right? If you're headed that way, I could use a ride."

"Yeah, sure," I say, not bothering to inquire further. "If you're not in a hurry." I
wag both index fingers above the steering wheel to indicate the crossing.

He opens the door, hesitates. He mimics my motion with his finger. "You're not
thinking of . . ."

"No."

"Well, that's good." He settles into the seat. He is well dressed in a dark navy pea
coat and gray scarf.

"Train suicides," I offer, "are almost always pedestrians. That's the sure way to
finish the job."

Some time passes. We stare out at the tracks. He says, "You want to talk about
it?"

"Sure," I say. "Anniversary. Right here." I do the finger thing again. "My parents.
A freight train. The road wasn't paved back then. I guess there was ice—or maybe
mud. Maybe bad judgment. My dad, he was the impatient type."

"Mmm hmm."

"The feast of Saint Blaise. They were going to get their throats blessed. Funny I remember that." I finish the suds, stare at the empty can. "I was supposed to be with them. But I was a brat by then. I threw a fit, and they left me home alone."

"So you had some guilt to work through."

"Or run away from. For years I forced myself never to think about it. My mind got the message, and erased them."

"Erased?"

"I mean, I can look at pictures, and I recognize them, but it's mostly all gone." I look over, and he raises his eyebrows, bidding me to go on.

"Then I got this idea. You see, before they died, there was this exciting time when a railroad repair crew came to town. They were all Black. There was a baseball game. I thought if I could document that story, bring it back to life, it would be something worth doing. And it might help me connect back to my life."

"Did it work?"

"I was too late. I talked to people—here in Julian, Nebraska City, Omaha. I researched. I even went to Arkansas looking for the crew. Everybody dead. Or most everybody."

"You must have gotten something."

"Anecdotes. Contradictions. The gandies were definitely here. Parked on the side rail." I tap the windshield three times with my fingernail. "Right. Over. There."

"But?"

"But nothing adds up. No storyline."

There is a pause, into which he says, mildly, "Isn't that your job?"

I glance over at him. "You don't understand. I wanted it to be real, like historical. But I also wanted it to be bigger than real, better than real. I wanted it to be *Heroic*."

"Can't it be some of both?"

"I'm not sure it can." I start to reach over the seat for another beer.

"Hold up on that," he says, touching my arm. "How does the saying go? *Two beers is social, three beers is a drunk?* Remember that?"

"Oh no," I say, as his features morph into a more familiar arrangement. "Oh no, no, no, no."

Morgan Freeman raises his eyebrows at me at me across the seat.

"No, no, no. I'm hallucinating," I say with bitter comedy. "And all I can do is conjure the iconic Hollywood actor of every role of the Wise Black Man?"

"But I'm not wrong," says Morgan Freeman. "Listen to me. All those old folks you talked to? Those stories they told? They were gifts, and you owe them. You know the plot. Weave them around it and into it. And maybe you'll find your mommy and daddy inside there too." He bathes me in a warm-hearted, charismatic smile.

A sudden mechanical clinking. Red lights flashing. The freight train thunders across the intersection with noise and violence. Engine, engine, tank car, tank car, flat car, grain car, grain car, grain car, grain car. It goes on and on, until it doesn't. A caboose flashes by.

In the silence, I stare across at the empty seat.

A crackle on the car speakers. "And don't forget the Epilogue. People like to know what became of folks, down the line a ways."

EPILOGUE

NEW YORK, 1970

Car worked her way through the dim crowded hallway behind the stage. Everyone was talking excitedly. Tie-dye and day-glow flashed around her, with shouting voices and the clunk of big jewelry. The air was redolent of pot and patchouli.

"Excuse me," she said. "Excuse me." Car felt over-dressed, over-the-hill, and way too square, but she pressed on through the college crowd, which got denser as she neared the stage door, the reek of bodies adding to other smells. At the door, her way was blocked by a large Black man with an even larger Afro, and gold chains.

"I have to go in there. I know him."

"Everybody knows him."

"I really do. I know Sam."

The Black man didn't move. "He doesn't answer to the slave name. He's Ali Alfred Mohamed."

"Oh please," she said. "I knew him when he . . ." The door opened halfway, and she saw him inside. She waved and shouted, "Sam!" Angry looks and hissing. She did it again anyway, "Sam Washington!"

The door was closing, but the poet called out to her, and pushed past the doorman to join her in the crush of the hallway. "Carlin Littman. Oh my word." They came together in a long hug, then pulled apart still holding each other's elbows and looking into each other's eyes.

"Look at you!" said Carlin. "Still as beautiful as ever. And look at all that hair!" She patted his 'fro. "Did you get my note I was coming to the reading?"

"No. You sent it to Sam, didn't you?"

"Of course."

He grinned. "Most of the notes I get talk about killing me for changing my name. I'm running neck and neck with Kareem Abdul Jabbar."

"That basketball player? Lew Alcindor?"

More hisses, and Car glared around her. "Well, that was his name, wasn't it?"

Ali Alfred laughed. "Same old Carlin. Tell me everything. You live in New York?"

"It's just Car now," she said, "and yeah, Upper West Side." She had to raise her voice, with all the people pressing in, trying to get his attention, calling out to him and holding up books to sign. He focused on her, despite the distractions. Car shouted a rushed resume. DePaul, and then NYU for a masters in French, the job with the charter airline, now a vice president. "I'm off to Rome tomorrow. Oh, and I'm married. To a German, of all things! No kids."

"Mr. Mohamed," said the door guard, "the car's outside."

"Two minutes," he said.

"What about you," she said quickly. "Married?"

Ali Alfred grinned at her, leaned in and said, "Turns out I'm queer."

"Queer?"

He laughed. "Bet you didn't know A.E. Housman was queer. And Langston, too, though you won't hear him say it. Folks tell me I'm too open, I should be more scared of what could happen. I tell them, 'Listen, sisters and brothers, I spiked rails alongside Ice Cantrell. I survived that crazy jive brother, I can survive anything.'"

Car took a second to absorb all that. "Did you know? Back then?"

He smiled. "It's easy to say, I've always known. But where I grew up, we didn't even have words for it. I was different from other boys, I knew that much."

"What about—what was his name, the older man?"

"Jerome. Jerome and Lucy. I got them to thank for getting me off the rails. Lived with them before I went to Howard. They gave me James Baldwin. Gave me Malcolm. Jerome's in politics, been on Omaha City Council for years."

More commotion. Sam waved to the door guard with the afro and chains.

The big young man swam through the crowd to them. "You ready? Car's outside."

"Abdul, this is Carlin. From the old days. That baseball game at the farm town?"

Abdul took her hand warmly. "I remember a party with a lot of white folks, and a big old swing. And a boy."

"You were there? In Julian?" Car added brightly, "Tim, the boy. He's in Denver now."

Some yelling from outside. Abdul turned back to Ali Alfred. "We got to go. We're blocking traffic. Peace to you, sister." He bowed and left.

Ali Alfred gave her a shrug. "Can't keep the mayor waiting. We'll get together soon."

"Take my card," she said, handing it.

"You want a book? Someone grab me a book."

One materialized, and a pen. Ali Alfred leaned it on his thigh, scrawling hastily. He gave her the book, a hug, and was gone.

The fresh air was bracing after the stuffy hallway. Car walked up Broadway in a swirl of traffic, noise, and emotions. She'd seen Sam! He wasn't Sam anymore. But he was! In the eyes, in the grin, in the way he moved his hands. She sighed in frustration. There was so much more to tell him. About Jack. Poor Jack. Her parents' tragedy. And Tim—she felt a shiver of guilt. After the funeral, everyone had told her to go back to college. She had to get on with her life, they said. There was nothing for her in Nebraska. Nothing but the terror in Timmy's eyes as she boarded the train for Chicago.

Tim adrift in Denver. The sporadic grad student, would-be historian, cab driver, bartender. She was terrified the draft would take him and kill him, like it had Jack. She forced the thoughts away, forcing a happier vision. She imagined Sam on a book tour, in Denver. She would arrange a meeting, and Tim would be inspired to get his act together.

She stopped short on the sidewalk, struck by a sad certainty that she and Sam would never get together. Their lives had drifted into different orbits. It was a miracle they'd had those few frantic moments. The book was now closed on the boy who had once stirred her heart. The book! She pulled it out of her bag. *Blue Remembered Hills.* She opened to the flyleaf and read the scrawl.

For Carlin,
Who may find her face too clear in some of these,
love
Ali Alfred (Sam)

AUTHOR'S NOTE

Sometime in the 1940s or 1950s, a crew of African American railroad track workers was stationed at my home town, the tiny farm village of Julian, Nebraska. Growing up in the 1960s in nearby Nebraska City, I heard family lore of a pick-up game between the gandy dancers and the Julian team. In some accounts, the game was epic. In some, there was also a picnic. As the decades passed, and my life took me far away from Nebraska, this ragged bit of story teased me from the fringe of my consciousness. As my awareness of racism and its consequences enlarged, the glow from this story grew brighter in my mind, a flickering candle of hope and good will.

Between 2008 and 2012 I made regular trips to southeastern Nebraska, reaching out to anyone old enough to remember, and to anyone with a connection to Julian or to the railroad. More than sixty interviews later, I had a jumble of anecdotes, contradictions, and fragments. It seemed the truth of the game itself was always hovering just beyond my reach.

Thus, what started as a quest for historical truth became the blend of myth and memory called *Brave in Season*. It is a work of fiction. The characters and actions have been created by me. However, certain scenes, moments, and character traits are inspired by the interviews—the novel would not have been possible without them. The "Field Notes," with the obvious exception of the final one, are reconstructed from my interview notes (I made no recordings). The accounts are true to my memory of them, with minor alterations for continuity and fit. All names have been changed, with the exception of Clarence "Ace" Hill, who appears both as live interview subject, and, off-screen in the story, as the super-star of 1950s Nebraska fast-pitch that he was.

The antagonisms and violence depicted in this book are entirely made up, with the exception of the lynching of Will Brown in Omaha in 1919. That happened. The indomitable Carlin is based on my sister, who was a headstrong teenager ten years after the time of this novel. Young Timmy is proxy for my brother Michael, who would have been about Timmy's age, and whose wisps of boyhood memory inspired this work. My parents did not die at a railroad crossing, but there is sufficient tragedy in my life to account for the implied trauma of the writer, grown-up Tim.

The settings are presented with as much historical accuracy as I can manage. In Julian, Marchon's store was Epler's store. A modest monument commemorates the location of the Julian school; the playing field and playground are still there. St. Joseph's is a gem of a country church. Among Nebraska City locations, John Brown's Cave merits special mention. As a child, I visited the historical attraction many times, and it always gave me a sense that my town was on the right side of history—a stop on the underground railroad, a somewhat sensationalized testament to the common-sense ideal of equality among citizens. My recollected pride gives rise to the "Otoe County Exceptionalism" proposed in the novel by Reverend Carpenter. (And yes, I am aware Julian sits just across the line in Nemaha County.)

I hope this story will inspire readers to cling tighter to the hope and the wish for our better selves to prevail, as they mostly do in this book.

For their immense help and generosity, I extend heartfelt thanks to the following persons and organizations for supporting my work, and I wish peace to those individuals who are no longer with us.

Maryanne Allee, Dorothy Aufenkamp, Jerry Bell, Rodney Bernard, Wade Birnbaum, Denise Brady, Margie Connor, Loraine Cooper, John Davis, Malcolm Davison, Charles Duckworth, Joe Epler, Bob Ferguson, Gary Fischer, Pat Friedkin, Luther Givehand, Mary Givehand, Janice Grimes, Barbara Hegr, Dave Heng, Clarence "Ace" Hill, Joan Lovelady Hodges, Rev. John Hodges, Michael Jensen, Beth Johnson, Mary Beth Kernes, Gary Kinney, Douglas Kreifels, Fran Kreifels, Janet Lipsi, Charles Lock, Patricia Lock, Gary Lockwood, Diane Meyer, Wayne Naro, Jackie Oelke, Orville Oelke, Thomas Palmerton, William Pollard, Steve Powers, Rev. Charles Rice, Oliver Richardson, Dorothy Rieke, Ken Rieke, William Rosenthal, Dick Ryker, Patricia Schroeder, Jim Shell, Lucine Shrewsbury, A.J. Smith, Jane Smith, Marilyn Snodgrass, George Stukenholtz, Keitha Thompson, Gerard Timothy, Marylea van Daalen, Christopher Volkmer, Gary Volkmer, Keith Volkmer, Marlene Volkmer, Rev. Michael Volkmer, Ronald R. Volkmer, Roselyn Volkmer, Shirley Wilberger, Sumpter Wilkes, Nancy Woodhams, Arthur Zech, Carl Zech.

Arbor Lodge State Park
The Brotherhood of the Maintenance of Way Employees
The Kimmel Harding Nelson Center for the Arts
The Nebraska City News-Press
The Morton-James Public Library
The Union Pacific Railroad Museum
Ursinus College

ABOUT THE AUTHOR

Jon Volkmer's books include a travel memoir, a collection of poems about grain elevators, and a YA biography of Roberto Clemente. His work has appeared in *Commonweal, Parnassus, Cimarron Review, Maine Review, Prairie Schooner*, and many other venues. He teaches Creative Writing at Ursinus College.

www.ingramcontent.com/pod-product-compliance
Lightning Source LLC
Chambersburg PA
CBHW011405010726
47495CB00009B/2781